"I'm Willing To Settle This Here and Now."

Camry dug into her reticule and pulled the greenbacks from the lining. She extended them to him and he took them.

"Your dowry, I assume?" he said.

"I should say not," she replied tersely. "I'm worth far more than that! No, it's a peace offering."

Nicholas spread his legs slightly and rested his elbows on his knees. He clasped his fingers together. "A bribe," he said bluntly.

She fidgeted with the strings on her bag. "You could call it that. Oh Lord, I don't want to marry you any more than you want to marry me."

"But I do want to marry you, very much." He walked to the bureau and after placing his Stetson over his silky locks, he faced her. "I'll hold onto this for you. I don't know what sort of man you think I am, but tomorrow I'm getting married and so are you."

"I won't marry you!" Camry snapped. "I won't! You'll never make me happy."

"Darlin', I don't think you know what happiness is."

D1408014

STEF ANN HOLM

SILVER DESIRES

LEISURE BOOKS ❧ NEW YORK CITY

To my parents,
Frank and Gloria Wysocki,
who have always encouraged me to be creative.

A LEISURE BOOK

Published by

Dorchester Publishing Co., Inc.
6 East 39th Street
New York, NY 10016

Copyright©1987 by Stef Ann Holm

Printed in the United States of America

1

May 20, 1875

Steel wheels of the Central Pacific clacked over iron rails stretching across the arid Nevada desert. Sagebrush and dull-gray vegetation blurred before Camry Dae Parker's greeen eyes, and her reflection appeared in the train's window. A sable-colored felt hat tilted pertly over her upsweep of copper curls. She lifted a gloved hand to adjust the wide brown satin ribbon tied saucily under her chin. She frowned, brushing a smudge of dust from her nose. Her reflection faded as she concentrated on the scenery once again.

What did her father see in the God-forsaken land? Why had he left her behind in Philadephia? So manv questions plagued her since she'd left Pennsylvania almost a month ago.

She had been boarding at the exclusive Hoaks Academy for young women when Miss Hoaks herself called Camry into her office to inform her that her father was a month behind with tuition. Camry was humiliated to be singled out for an oversight on finances. Appalled when Miss Hoaks suggested she sell some of her gowns for payment, she stormed out the office.

Camry sighed. She hoped nothing was wrong with her father. Why hadn't he sent the money? She hadn't received his monthly letter in April and it was May. Who knows what could have happened since she left Philadelphia.

Her father had had enough time to set up his brokerage business in Nevada. His promise of a few months turned into a year. If he was having financial difficulties, he needed her. All his warnings that Virginia City was no place for a proper young lady of twenty went unheeded and she did sell some of her gowns, but for train fare, not tuition.

The train slowed into the Carson City depot, wheels squeaking as pressure was applied to the brakes. Camry stood, the muscles in her legs adjusting to her weight once again. Thank goodness she was almost through riding trains, she thought, brushing the traveling dust from her brown plaid skirt.

Disembarking, she meshed with adventurers, mountaineers, miners and passengers that crowded the depot platform. Feeling closer to her destination renewed Camry's spirits. She fought her way to the ticket booth where, behind the counter stood a bald-headed man with a pencil resting above his ear. His cheeks were full and round, and he spoke with a slur.

"Can I he'p you, ma'am?"

"I want to purchase a ticket on the V & T Railroad to Virginia City." Although she felt ruffled and slightly wilted, Camry's voice was smooth and collected.

"All trains full-up 'til six tonight," he replied, moving his wad of chewing tobacco below his lower lip making his mouth appear swollen.

"You don't have any seats now?" Her confidence momentarily faltered.

"Six o'clock," the man repeated adjusting his jowls. He spit a stream of brown juice into a nearby brass cuspidor.

Seven black engines hissed and smoked like angry dragons, waiting to be connected to tails of yellow and green passenger cars in the roundhouse. "I fail to see how *all* trains can be full. There seem to be ample cars," Camry said pointing to the roundhouse.

"Full up, ma'am. Best I kin do is take yore luggage fer the freight car and direct you to the stage. The Overland Express and Pioneer Stage leave from Ormsby House. Wells-Fargo from the St. Charles Hotel. They don't take more 'an twenty-five pounds a luggage, so like I said, I kin put yore trunks in a freight car."

Camry tapped her gloved fingernails on the counter. She wanted to reach Virginia City before nightfall and saw no other choice than to take the ticket man's advice. "Fine," she finally agreed. "I have four trunks on the Central Pacific No. 11 just arrived from Reno. They're labeled: Camry Parker."

"That'll be two dollars." He spat again. Missing the spittoon, his spittle splattered on the wooden floor.

Outraged by his manners and the fare, she flashed her eyes indignantly. "That's the price of a seat!"

He scratched his bald head and shrugged. "I don't make the fares, ma'am." Pointing to the depot window, he continued. "Go up the block an' turn left. Walk 'bout three quarter a mile and the Ormsby's on the right. Cain't miss it. Three story brick building." He handed her a claim check.

Camry raised her head high and squared her shoulders. Turning, she made her way through the crowd, holding tightly to her skirts. The early afternoon sun was warm on her cheeks as she stepped onto the loose boardwalk in front of the passenger depot; then, reaching Carson Street, she turned left.

Stage lines, freight wagons, buckboards and carts rumbled down the dusty street. Clouds of dirt coated everything from coaches, horses and mules to mailbags and pedestrians, giving them all the same monotonous taupe color. Sparse, dull-green pine trees dotted several of the blocks. One and two story wooden buildings, some with balconies, smelled of fresh cedar and pine. Brick buildings towered higher, their sides painted with colorful advertisements.

Crossing the road, Camry dodged a fast-paced buckboard, the snapping reins and clicking harnesses ringing through the street. The noon train's whistle screamed behind her from blocks away. Her lips pulled into a mild smile. Her luggage would probably reach Virginia City before she did! Of all the luck. She moved more determinedly through the pedestrians. Jingling spurs and heavy boots pounded over the rickety planks on the boardwalk. Bawdy piano tunes sang from the many saloons. The smell of sweet rum and sour whiskey merged with the talc scent of dry earth.

Men stood in front of the saloons, their faces lighting as Camry passed by. Her eastern clothes were cause for attention. Most tipped their hats and smiled; some mouthed innuendos. She held her head high and ignored them, gently bred as she was.

Several dance hall girls filled a saloon doorway, a rainbow of bright spangles on their dresses. Camry tried to hide her interest, sneaking a peek at them from the corner of her eye. The sun shone off their sequins in bright reds and golds, and for a moment she pondered what it would be like to wear such gowns. They appeared to be made of liquid gold. Never had she seen such elaborate costumes. Even the feathers and face paint, heeled shoes and fishnet stockings that decorated the women, were intriguing.

Finally reaching the three-story brick Ormsby House, she entered the lobby, her skirt swishing. Behind the front desk was a rather handsome man with flaxen hair and friendly brown eyes.

''Is this where I purchase a ticket for the Pioneer Stage to Virginia City?'' she inquired in a brisk, businesslike manner.

He smiled courteously. ''It certainly is, ma'am. Stage boards just out front.'' He then told her the fare.

''Good.'' Reaching into her reticule, she counted out the correct amount.

Handing her a ticket, the desk clerk gestured to the upper floors. ''May I make you a reservation?''

She blinked in puzzlement. ''Whatever for?''

''The stage is booked until tomorrow at five-thirty a.m.,'' he replied.

''Oh brother! What *does* a person have to do to get to Virginia City?''

''I'm sorry, but—''

Her patience had been tested long enough. "Never mind!" Twirling on her heels, she headed out the lobby.

The heat was almost unbearable, the dust even worse. Camry wished she could unfasten several of the top buttons of her traveling suit. Shading her eyes from the scorching sun she decided she wasn't going to stay in Carson City one minute longer than necessary. It was that simple.

A dull-black coach with yellow wheels and red leather interior waited at the curb across the street, while one of the drivers checked the harnesses on a team of six chestnut horses. The other driver sat on the seat above the cab checking over his shotgun. She saw the bold letters Pioneer Stage Co. above the door. That was all she needed to know.

Walking with a deliberate sway of her skirt and an easy smile dancing on her lips, she made her way to the stage. Deep in thought over her strategy, she never saw the towering horse and rider coming toward her until she walked into the massive beast. Jumping back, she barely looked up when the horse reared and whinnied.

"Sir! You've nearly run me down. Please control your horse and allow me to pass!" she ordered, brushing her sleeves.

The rider calmed his horse with a reassuring hand. He spoke in low tones, silky and soothing. Camry tilted her head to view him, but all she could make out was his set jaw, strawberry blond mustache and tight mouth. The wide brim of his hat shaded the rest of his face. There was a definite ruggedness to him. For a fleeting moment, Camry wondered what it would be like to flirt with such a man. Certainly he would not be as easily won as the men in Philadelphia. She dismissed the thought, scolding herself for thinking so ludicrously!

"Just what in the Sam Hill—" the rider began, but she went around him before hearing him out.

Upon reaching the coach, she had returned her thoughts to the problem at hand and gave the passengers a quick perusal. A young couple. A tattered miner. A merchant. She singled out the latter who was impeccably dressed in a navy pin-striped suit.

"Pardon me," she purred coyly, pointing to the Ormsby House. "The desk clerk said you left your wallet on the counter."

The man fumbled through his vest pocket and produced a calfskin billfold. "As you can see, there must be a mistake."

The miner leaned forward to stare at her. Camry paid no attention to him and moved closer to the open stage window. She was five feet, four inches tall and the large wheel almost reached her chin. She deliberately pouted her coral-tinted lower lip, her eyes shimmering as she looked up through thickly fringed lashes. When she was sure her perfume wafted to his nostrils, she continued. "But I'm sure he said it belonged to the handsomely dressed man in the Pioneer Stage. Goodness! What now? There was five hundred dollars in it."

The merchant tugged his hat over his brow to conceal a glimmer in his eyes, then cleared his throat. Standing, he unlatched the door. "Miss, you are most right. My other wallet is missing."

Camry smiled sweetly as he stepped down. Tipping his hat, he mumbled, "Obliged."

"You're quite welcome." Her words dripped like honey. "Take your time. I'll tell the driver to wait for you."

He turned and practically ran through the street, nearly colliding with a rig. Camry's smile left with him. She gripped the sides of the door and pulled herself up. All eyes rested on her, but she ignored them. Settling into the worn, red cushioned seat, she removed her moist, soiled gloves.

The driver came around to collect the tickets. He looked questioningly at Camry. "Wasn't there a man here before?"

"Oh!" she exclaimed. "That was my brother. He'll be staying over tonight. I'm taking his place." With a warning glare, she dared the others to dispute her.

She'd come too close to her father to be set back another day.

The coachman adjusted his bandana and heavily laden holster. Pulling on thick, leather gloves, he mounted the seat and called down. "Whatever you say, lady." He released the brake and flicked the reins. The stage lurched sharply forward and rolled over potholes in the street, finally gaining speed as it left town. Only then did Camry settle back into the lumpy cushion and fluff her skirt around her.

Even though he told himself he wouldn't, Nicholas Trelstad continued to watch the woman in plaid board the coach. His horse shook its head as if warning him not to, and he patted the velvety softness of the roan's neck. He rested his arms over the pommel of his saddle, his long legs lightly hugging the horse's girth. There was something in the way she carried herself; the jaunty walk and easy toss of her head. Why, she never blinked twice after running into an animal four times her size! He could tell right off, she was a proud one. He had caught a slight glimpse of her hair as she turned in his direction. The only time he'd seen hair that color it had come from a bottle, but she didn't look the bottle type. And what was she up to now? Hiram Wyatt never ran that fast in his life.

Tilting his Stetson over his forehead, Nicholas brushed a strand of sun blond hair from his midnight blue eyes. Well, he'd know who she was soon enough. There was only one destination for the Pioneer Stage and that was Virginia City. If he took the grade, he'd be there an hour before it arrived.

He'd be seeing her again; of that, he was sure.

The young couple stared openly at Camry and the miner gave her a curious glare. The lad spoke up. "What 'bout that man's bags?" His English accent was so thick, she could barely decipher his words.

"What about them?" she returned, challenging him.

He recoiled like a frightened animal, not anxious for a tongue-lashing. The tattered miner laughed to himself and shook his head.

"Well?" Camry asked crisply. "What are you laughing at?" She turned to look out the window as the miner pushed the brim of his hat over his eyes.

Endless brown hills rolled past. Gray sagebrush and greasewood trees dotted the dry desert earth. Camry pushed back a loose red curl, feeling a droplet of perspiration roll between her breasts with her movement. She hated the landscape. It was ugly. No greenery like that of Philadelphia. Even the brick buildings of the west bore garish marks, unlike those of Independence Hall whose stately white trim gleamed majestically, unmarred by desert dust!

There was nothing soft about this savage land. Everything was coarse . . . even the men. Her thoughts drifted to the horse and rider. What had made her think about him? She put a hand to her temples and gently rubbed. Possibly too much sun? That was it. She'd been out in the sun too much. She wasn't used to it—all that walking in Carson City. Oh, to have a nice bath in a comfortable hotel!

Focusing on the countryside once again, she caught a fleeting glimpse of a jackrabbit scampering into his den, the fluffy tail a gray blur. Small patches of shimmering white rocks appeared through the desert terrain as the stage veered to the left and began climbing a trail to what she had been told was Mount Davidson. The slopes housed three mining towns. Though the scenery didn't please her, Camry felt a surge of excitement. This was a new place—a place she'd never been before. She scanned her fellow traveling companions as if their appearances could unlock the mystery why anyone would *want* to live here.

The young English girl across from her slept on her husband's arm. Though Camry wasn't sure, it appeared she was in the early stages of pregnancy. What kind of man would take his wife on such a journey in her condition? Camry had no intentions of marrying and giving herself to a man's keep.

"What's in Virginia for you?" The miner's pleasant voice broke into her thoughts. Camry looked at him. She had thought him to be sleeping. He was dressed in light cotton trousers and a loose-fitting work shirt. A worn for the worse felt hat perched on his salt and pepper hair. The face, though roughly worn and tan, was interesting to look at.

She didn't readily divulge her personal status to strangers, but something about the man seemed harmless and she felt in the mood for conversation. "I'm meeting my father."

"That's nice. Can always use another woman in the mountain."

Camry wasn't sure what he was implying. "My father and I won't be residing in Virginia City."

"What line of business your father in?"

She hesitantly answered. "He's a stockbroker."

The man nodded. "Well and fine. We'll miss a good broker. I know a few of them, but now there's so many people in town I can't keep track of everyone. Back in '64 I could ride my mule down C Street and know every-one by name. Nowadays, you're lucky if somebody speaks English."

"You've lived there for *eleven years*?" No wonder he looked so worn out, Camry thought.

He nodded again. "I had me a small bakery on Gold Hill. Made a fortune. Those miners would rather have a homemade pie than a night with a hurdy-gurdy gal."

She was surprised. "You bake? I thought you were a miner—y-you wear the boots I've seen so many wear—" she stammered. "Baking is women's work. Men don't cook."

Laughing heartily, he slapped his leg. "Honey, I'm no man. My name's Martha Zmed. The gang at the Ophir Mine call me Ma Zmed."

Camry's lower lip dropped, dumbfounded. "I thought—"

Martha Zmed chuckled, lifting her worn felt hat. A fat braid was coiled into a bun at the back of her head. "That was a pretty dirty trick you pulled in Carson," she commented dropping her hat back on.

Camry's defenses arose. "I had no choice. I'm finding out a woman has to use her head in order to get anywhere in this territory."

"I'm not condemning you for it. I learned long ago women are smarter than men."

The lad across from them frowned. "If I'm supposed to be a bleedin' sod, 'ow come I left a seventy-five cent a day job in England for a four dollar a day job in Nevada? Cripes," he shook his head, "it took everythin' I 'ad for passage over 'ere. The missus and little 'um will 'ave plenty 'ere."

"Don't ruffle your feathers, boy. Sure you'll make money, just like everybody else," Martha said.

The Pioneer Stage twisted and turned through the many switchbacks up the hill. Soon the horses slowed their pace as they entered Silver City. Camry stared out the open window. The town was not large; a couple of hotels, stores, smithy and plain houses lined the traveled Wells-Fargo road. Two mills were located at the edge of town, grayish smoke billing from their stacks. The rocks became monstrous, taking over what vegetation there was. Twin, towering boulders at least fifty feet high were on either side of the road as they exited Silver City.

Ma Zmed pointed out the window. "Well folks, you've just passed through Devil's Gate. Too late to turn back now," she teased.

The Englishman's wife woke up. Her straight yellow hair hung limply and her blue eyes were pale. Camry hoped the girl wouldn't be sick.

Martha turned to Camry. "What's your name, honey?"

"Camry Parker, daughter of Michael Angus Parker," she proudly informed.

Ma Zmed extended her hand for Camry to grasp. Camry had never shook hands with anyone before. She found Martha's grip strong and assured. "Pleased to meet you. We've got quite a few of your Irish neighbors in Virginia City. Mackay and Fair run the place."

"Who are they?"

"They own this hunk of rock we're on, honey," Martha said. "But never you mind about them seeing you won't be staying."

Small wooden houses were scattered upon the hillside. Sagebrush began to thin, inviting the sun to reflect off bare patches of earth. A flume curved between the granite boulders, large logs riding the swift currents. Below the flumes, what appeared to be rock pieces, rolled quickly down the chutes from the mills and into waiting freight wagons. Once again, the mills rumbled noisily and a whistle sounded. Camry wondered what was inside. The streets were congested with dusty miners and various wagons. Women were few and it put a fear in her that this might be . . .

Reluctantly, Camry faced Martha. "Is *this* Virginia City?"

"Dear, Virginia makes this look like a speck o' gold dust," she replied matter-of-factly.

The young couple looked out the windows in awe. The stage climbed higher, rounding hairpin curves and ledges with steep drop offs. Camry held her breath at each turn, certain they would fall of the mountain. She gripped the leather hand straps with determination and shut her eyes tightly. I'm not afraid, she repeated over and over in her mind.

Finally the road uncurled and the rough swaying stopped. She lifted her lids slowly, focusing clearly. The sight before her caused her to gasp reflectively. Never had she seen so many people in one spot. It seemed as if the world lived here.

This was Virginia City!

2

The Pioneer stagecoach rolled down the main section of town called C Street. It seemed odd to Camry that such a grand town would exist on such a dry, steep slope. In the distance to her right, mills churned black smoke from tall stacks. The mills ran down to the base of the mountain and farther than she could see. The town itself consisted of many of the same businesses Philadelphia did. There was a newspaper office, school, restaurants, smithy, boarding houses and saloons. Of course there weren't nearly as many saloons in Pennsylvania—and they called them taprooms. And there were assay offices too. She wondered what they were—they certainly appeared to be busy.

But the citizens of Virginia City! They were unlike any of her acquaintances back east. Here, there were about five men to one woman. The men were rugged and colorful—adorned in silver and turquoise. Even the cowboys wore polished silver spurs. Women sauntered by in silks, satins, taffetas and . . . oh! their hats! Every species of feather stuck from the crowns. Parasols and ruffles, lace and bows—Camry didn't miss a thing.

The stage passed the International Hotel and went one more block, turning left up the hill on Sutton Street, then rolled to a stop at the two story brick and wood Wells-Fargo and Company offices.

After the drivers stepped down, one entered the office, and the other kicked a small crate below the stage door. The English couple wasted no time disembarking. After positioning the crate, the driver climbed on top of the cab and proceeded to toss

16

luggage to a freight boy. Camry and Martha alighted and the driver called to Camry.

"What do you want done with your brother's bags?" His leather-gloved hands gripped a satchel and carpetbag, heaving them overboard to the boy.

"I'm sure he'll be by tomorrow to collect them," Camry ventured.

Ma Zmed gathered her rawhide case and suggested Camry walk down to the center of town with her.

They headed for the street from which they'd just come. Echoes of tapping nails and hammers filtered between several buildings. A pungency of charred piñon pine wafted through the air and Camry noticed one of the shops had recently burned.

Reaching C Street, they could see white clouds of steam from the V & T Railroad rising behind the Bonanza Saloon and Silver Dollar Hotel. Wagons and freight lines rambled down the street making crossing a game of man against animal. Piano and banjo music twanged from the many saloons. The squeaking dry hinges of the bar's batwing doors were a constant rhythm.

"I'm going on down to the Ophir Mine to drop off a few things for the boys," Martha declared, shifting her case from one hand to the other. "Where are you meeting your father?"

"I . . . well, he doesn't know I'm meeting him."

"I see. I reckon you might try the Territorial Enterprise. Dan's a right nice man who'll be glad to help you find him. He knows what's what around here." She pointed down the road. "It's about two blocks on the left."

"Thank you for your help."

"Nothing at all. It's been nice meeting you, honey." She shook Camry's hand in departure. Camry watched her go and smiled, then started for the newspaper office.

The sour smell of beer assaulted her nose as she passed a brewery. Most of the buildings were two stories. Her father had said in one of his letters that he

had rented the top floor of a shop. Possbily his advertisements on the building side would make him easier to
track.

A gathering of miners and a handful of painted women
hurried down the street. Some held fists of paper money
bellowing the name: "Trelstad!" Others laughed heartily
shaking their heads and responded with the name:
"Reddick!" The group trampled the boardwalk with such
enthusiasm, Camry found herself blending in and
moving back toward the street she'd just come from.
She tried to break free from the assemblage, but found
it impossible as they headed for the mine buildings
below the main street. The hills were so steep, she
couldn't avoid practically running down them with the
others.

When they'd reached the bottom, Camry was out of
breath. She got a close look at the mills she'd seen from
the stage. There were mounds of dirt and timber
corralling them, the lumber obviously used to generate
the steam. Blasts of different pitched whistles sounded
and the earth rumbled as a dynamite charge blew.
Camry jumped at the unexpected movement of earth.

Her eyes widened as she scanned a group of miners
gathered at the entrance of a mine called the Consolidated-Virginia. The men were naked from the waist up
and they sat on old crates and boxes; some were
perched on the mill rooftops swinging their soiled shirts.
She blushed profusely.

The center of attraction was a roughly constructed
wooden arena squared with ropes. Inside the ring were
more crates, a large rum barrel and two teams of half-
naked miners. One man held a sledge hammer and the
other gripped a long steel bit that chipped away on what
had to be at least fifty pounds of solid rock—a granite
boulder. After each powerful strike, the second man
would twist the drill a quick quarter turn causing small
rock fragments to fly.

Fearful one of the spectators would knock her hat
from her head, Camry held onto it as the crowd pushed

and shoved, trying to get a better look at the double-jackers. Her eyes rested on the two teams and she singled out the man called Trelstad. Towering over six feet, his bare, tightly worked muscles rippled and danced at every swing of his hammer. He wore only light-blue cotton pants, cinched at the waist with the hems rolled up. His bare feet spread apart for leverage as he raised a corded arm again for the blow. Blond hair lightly covered his chest which glistened with perspiration. A perfectly chiseled nose and firm chin were separated by a full, blond mustache. His eyes squinted and teeth gritted as the hammer pounded again and again. Small rivulets of sweat dripped from his sun-bleached hair, spraying a fine moisture into the air.

He tilted his head slightly, and at that moment, Camry realized he was the man she ran into in Carson City! Even now, as his mouth was set determinedly, she felt her heart beat faster. She had never seen a man . . . well, never seen one stripped before! It was quite unnerving. She didn't like the feelings it evoked . . . she . . . oh! She needed to find some shade to rest in!

As the contest came to an end, the crowd chanted the name of its favorite. They hooted and hollered, some threw up their hats as Trelstad released his final blow, winning the race. His partner peeled yellow, pigskin-gloved hands from the drill-bit, then grinned triumphantly.

A referee mounted the ring and shouted, "The winners and still unbeaten champions of Storey County! Nicholas Trelstad and Rigdon Gregory!"

The defeated Reddick and his partner shook hands with the victors. The announcer waved his arms to silence the crowd. "For the champions, a goddamn fifty gallon barrel o' rum worth two hundred dollars!"

Rigdon made a fist and held it high, a smile on his flushed face. Nicholas bent above a water bucket and poured the contents of the dipper over his head. As the liquid dripped down his face, a sharp slap cracked the air, followed by a torrent of accusations.

Camry glanced at the drunk next to her and demanded he apologize for his conduct. He mumbled he was sorry, then backed off as she straightened her spine haughtily. Brushing her skirt, she looked up to meet the deepest midnight blue eyes she'd ever seen. Then taking in his whole countenance, she found he was laughing wholeheartedly. Laughing at her! Their stare was broken by a voluptuous tawny-skinned woman who congratulated Nicholas with an affectionate hug. She was sultry; her long, wavy black hair hung loosely to her hips and her lips were a soft scarlet.

Angrily, Camry turned and pushed her way through the spectators. She wasn't sure where she was going, but the fact she'd come down from the hill, made going back up it seem logical. Laughing indeed! How could she ever have thought of flirting with such a skunk?

The street was at such a steep angle, she had a hard time climbing it in her heeled city shoes. The altitude was taking its toll on her and she stopped to rest. Wiping her brow with a lace handkerchief, she leaned against a gas-lamp post.

Few buggies and horses could travel these side roads with steadiness, so little traffic passed her. Rested, she continued, then hearing hootbeats behind her, she turned to see a jet black buggy surprisingly unmarred by the gray alkali dust clouding around it. Large red wheels glowed in the afternoon sun and two dark brown stocking bays strained up the hill.

"May I offer you a ride, ma'am?" the driver asked.

He sported stern, handsome features and dark brown hair slickly combed back. Riding at his hips were two very large silver-barreled revolvers with pearl handles.

"No thank you," she refused politely.

He paced his horses to walk next to her. "I can assure you you'd be safe with me."

She glanced at him askance from under the small brim of her hat. Her feet hurt terribly. . . . "No thank you," she repeated.

He kept the brim of his hat low to shade his face. "See

the top of this hill?"

She put a hand over her brow and squinted. "Yes. Way up there?" She hadn't realized she'd ended up so far down.

"If you're headed for C Street, and I assume you are, you've got a long way left. Now, ma'am, will you change your mind?"

Sighing resignedly, she dabbed the back of her neck with her handkerchief. "Very well—" Then she hesitated, resting her eyes on his guns again. "Are you the law?"

Chuckling deeply, he conceded, "Of sorts. My bailiwick is the card room." He gripped the reins in one hand and offered her the other, gloved in tan kid. Camry climbed in and settled back as he released the brake and flicked the reins over the horses' rumps.

He tipped a fancy gray felt hat. "Frank Marbury at your service."

"Camry Parker."

"Where may I take you?"

Camry smoothed her gloves. "I'd like to go to the Territorial Enterprise."

"Do you know Dan Wright?"

"Not directly, but I'm told he runs the paper smoothly." She was not in the mood for idle chitchat. He seemed to respect her need for silence and clicked his tongue, urging the team upward.

Taking the opportunity to examine Frank, she did so from the corner of her eye. A waxed brown handlebar mustache complimented a clean-shaven chin with a small cleft. His physique was lean and lithe, not burdened with heavy muscles. He wore an expensively tailored suit with an ornate red and gold silk vest. His unique blend of silver-gray eyes never left the road as he turned onto C Street and headed west toward the International Hotel and newspaper office.

Just before Taylor Street, on the left, stood a wooden building: No. 87, H.S. Beck—Dealer in Furniture. On the second story was a small white sign with bold black print reading: *Michael Angus Parker — Stockbroker*. Camry couldn't conceal a small cry of joy.

"Oh! Please let me off here!" She was halfway off the seat when Frank halted his team. She slipped down without waiting for his assistance. Calling over her shoulder, she bid him a hasty thank you and good day.

"Say!" Frank shouted over the street traffic. "May I buy you dinner tonight?"

Camry didn't take the time to reply, but instead, raced for the narrow passage of steps leading to the second floor. She felt giddy. She wondered if he'd changed much in the last year . . .

The stairs were rickety and creaked as she climbed them. On the top landing, to the left, was a full-length window shade drawn over a glass door. Her father's name was painted on the pane. Drawing a deep breath, she turned the doorknob and entered.

The furnishings were sparse. A heavy grandfather clock, several file cabinets, two chairs and a long desk. A man bent over stacks of papers on the cluttered desk, only the top of his unruly red-orange hair showed. "I be with you inna moment," he said without looking up, his Scottish brogue lovingly familiar. A gray cat scampered from under the desk and jumped onto the windowsill.

"Da?" Camry asked softly.

The man looked up. His face was covered with a full, red beard six inches long and a coarse mustache. His soft green eyes opened wide, unprepared for the woman before him.

"Da?" Camry repeated, almost uncertain. "Is that you?"

"Camry!" Michael's voice cracked. "I been worret sick!" He rose as she flew into his arms.

"Oh, Da!" she cried. "It *is* you! I have you back."

3

Sitting at a corner table in the Bonanza Hotel's dining room, Camry lovingly held her father's hand. They relaxed over steaming cups of coffee as she glanced at her surroundings. The room was filled with round tables covered by white clothes and small candles in each center. Patterns in crimson paper decorated the walls along with brass framed oil paintings. The carpet was richly designed in black and gold. Camry had not expected such elegance in a mining town.

Michael squeezed her hand. "I still canna believe you came all this way. When I got word from Laura Hoaks, I was worret sick."

Camry's eyes held a sparkle of purpose and she smiled prettily. "I had to come. I couldn't bear another day away from you."

Concern filled Michael's face. "It's nay because of the money, Camry? I sent it, but it mustta got lost in the Express."

"That was partly the reason," she confessed. "I was angry and humiliated when Miss Hoaks singled *me* out."

"I dinna mean for your embarrassment, Missy. I never expected—"

"Oh, Da!" Camry broke in to reassure him. "I didn't mean it like that. You could never humiliate me."

"I did send the money," he repeated.

Her face glowed with adoration, a healthy peach blush tinged her creamy, petal-soft cheeks. "Of course you did," she smiled. She playfully tugged his long beard. "I almost didn't recognize you. The last time I saw you there wasn't any hair on your face, nor was the red mop on your head so unruly. You have crow's-feet at the corners of your eyes," she pouted. "Have you been wearing your glasses?"

He sighed joyously and continued for her. "And I've gained twenty pounds and have taken up the notion o' tobacco chewin' anna good swig a Irish whiskey now and then."

"Don't be smart." Camry frowned. "I just didn't expect you to look so . . . so—" She couldn't put her finger on it.

"So frontier-like," he finished.

"Yes, that's it," she giggled.

A loud blast shook the earth, the rumble vibrating up the mountain. The crystal chandeliers and lamps in the lobby tinkled like musical instruments.

Camry gripped the edge of the table in fear. "Saints have mercy! What was that?"

Michael laughed with jolly amusement. "It's Sutro's boys diggin' a tunnel."

"Good Lord, Da!" She put a hand to her breast where her heart felt as if it would leap from its confines. "*Whatever* possessed you to come to this—this hill of gopher holes?"

His round, rosy cheeks puffed and his mouth straightened seriously. "I'm gonna be a rich man, Missy. The money's here for the takin'. Just four months ago, Consolidated-Virginia was sellin' at seven hundred a share. California at seven hundred eighty. With one share o' Con-VA I made seventy dollars. The market's wide open, Camry."

"But don't you have enough saved to go back to Philadelphia now?" She pouted softly. "You've been here a year."

"A man canna ever have too much, Missy." Michael pulled a plug of tobacco from his vest. "I've got shares too. I canna pull out now. That would mean sellin' everythin'."

Camry wrinkled her delicate nose with disgust as her father bit off the end of the brown roll. "Do you have to do that?'' she asked, creasing her forehead. ''The man in Carson City missed the spittoon and I was nearly ill.''

He ignored her request and rolled the wad under his tongue. ''You're in the west now, sweetheart. You canna put a moth onna lantern and expect it to fly away.''

She failed to see the connection between tobacco and moths, so she dropped the subject. ''That reminds me, my luggage is on the V & T. I couldn't take the train; it was full. Did you know it costs the same to ride the train as it does to take the stage?''

''Thanks to Monk,'' he stated.

''A monk!'' Camry laughed.

''Not a monk. Hank Monk. Works for the Wells Fargo. Hates the V & T. Would race the bleedin' train up the hill. There's been a war goin' on betwixt the two for years.'' He stood and patted his small paunched waistline. ''Let's get you a room, then see about your bags.''

Camry was disappointed. ''But can't I stay with you?''

''There's not enough space. All I've got issa office anna small room in the back. You'll be more comfortable here.''

It puzzled her that her father didn't have an expensive suite in a lavish hotel. He'd always showered her with luxury. Yet, what he lacked in environment, he made up for in attire. His stylish dark blue suit, starched shirt and black silk bow tie partially hidden by his beard were very fashionable. She didn't question his judgment this time; she was still too happy just to be near him.

The sun was beginning to slide behind the mountain and a shadow crept over Virgina City. Gas lamps were lit, the yellow flames flickering in the mauve dusk. Instead of thinning out, street activity seemed to grow. The aroma of broiled steaks, gravy-smothered poultry and tangy fish scented the night air.

Michael hugged Camry in the hotel lobby before his departure. ''Sleep well, daughter. We can talk more on the morrow. I'll send somebody over with your trunks.''

She kissed his cheek affectionately. ''I love you, Da. Everything will be just fine.''

"We'll talk on the morrow," he repeated. He paused for a moment to look at her beauty. "So much like your mother . . . I love you too. I must attend to me office—" His voice cracked slightly and his expression seemed worried before he turned to leave.

Camry climbed the carpeted stairs of the lobby, her hand brushing the balustrade. She couldn't help noticing how tired Da looked. Well, things would change now that she was here to take care of him. She veered to the left and made her way to room nine. The suite was cozy and comfortable. A rose and olive patterned carpet covered the floor, the same colors repeated in the light wallpaper. A carved cedar headboard framed the bed with a powder blue dust ruffle and white quilt spread. A corner washstand held a blue and white flowered washbowl and basin. Resting in front of one of the two windows was a carved rocking chair. All in all, it was just as nice as her room at the Hoaks Academy.

Unfastening the jacket of her traveling suit, she tossed it on the bed. Her thin chemise was much cooler. She pulled the ribbon of her hat and dropped it next to her jacket. The heat was dreadful in the room, so she slid one of the windows up. A faint, warm breeze stirred the lace curtains.

Darkness had settled over Sun Peak. Loud saloon noise strayed into her room. The pianos and reed organs belted tunes one after the other. And the mills which her father had told her were called stamps, continued to pound in the distance. She looked out the window toward C Street. The men were dressed in finery —lavish suits and polished boots. The women wore gaudy, low-cut gowns with jewels dripping from their necks.

A low whistle pierced the night and Camry looked up to see an intoxicated cowboy hanging out the window of the Silver Queen Saloon across the street. She shot him a scornful look. "Put your eyes back in their sockets, you skunk!" She pulled the shade down with such force, it nearly rolled off the brackets.

A light tapping sounded on her door. Camry slipped into her jacket, hastily fastening the buttons. "Who's there?"

The voice was masculine and deep. "Mike Parker sent me with your trunks."

Relieved to hear he was from her father, she unlocked the door. Opening it, she stared into familiar deep blue eyes with astonishment.

"Well, well." Nicholas Trelstad grinned. "We meet again."

"I wasn't aware we had met. What are you doing here?" she snapped wishing the man outside her door was anyone but *him*.

"I'm an acquaintance of your father. I believe you know my name. That was *you* I saw today at the contest, wasn't it?" He seemed to relish in her discomfort. "And didn't I run into you in Carson, or I suppose I should say, wasn't that you who ran into *me*?"

"I haven't the faintest idea what you're talking about."

"When Michael asked me if I could do him a favor by fetching his Camry's bags from the station, I never realized what a pleasant job it would be." His lips turned softly into a smile.

His gesture didn't go unnoticed with Camry. She nearly melted at the irresistible grin. "Well then, where are my trunks?" she asked tersely.

"In the lobby." Nicholas rested against the door frame crossing strong arms over his broad chest. An ivory Dakota Stetson capped his golden hair. Muscular legs were wrapped with softly worn denim pants and mule-ear cowboy boots that fit snuggly over his lean calves.

"Are you going to bring them up?" she asked impatiently.

"I could," he drawled.

She tapped her foot with annoyance. "Well?"

"Whatever you say, darlin'." He turned down the hall, the jinglebobs on his spurs clinking merrily.

Pacing nervously over the floor during his absence, she stopped abruptly in front of the cedar washstand

and stared at the mirror. She patted the soft roll of copper waves dipping over her forehead.

Nicholas returned, and to her amazement, had all four trunks piled on a dolly. They were extremely heavy and it surprised her he handled them all at once. Wheeling the luggage into the room with ease, he removed them from the cart.

"Do you need any assistance with your unpacking, Miss Parker?" His eyes shone bright in the kerosene light of the room.

"I'm perfectly capable." She avoided his stare.

"Is that right." The bridge of his nose was slightly pink from the sun.

Camry hastily dug into her reticule and withdrew a coin. "Thank you for your time, Mr. Trelstad. Good evening."

Nicholas didn't take the money. "Didn't you ever hear it's not polite to insult a favor by offering a tip?"

"Well, I most—"

"Good night, Miss Parker," he cut in, then tipped his hat. "Sweet dreams."

Aghast, Camry slammed the door in frustration. Walking to the washbowl, she splashed cool water on her burning cheeks. Of all the people her father could have sent!

Nicholas took the stairs two at a time, whistling as he left the lobby. Camry Parker was a beauty, all right. And, her hair was real. He'd seen for himself all the different shades of copper and bronze. And a temper! He smiled, remembering the way she had slammed the door on him. Well, Mike Parker certainly had his hands full now! He didn't envy the man the task.

Rounding the corner, Nicholas headed for D Street and Sporting Row. He'd pay Garnet a visit. At least *she* didn't slam doors on him.

Camry luxuriated in unlacing the ties on her boots and rolling down her silk stockings. The traveling suit was tossed carelessly to the floor. Peeling off her white chemise and petticoats, she stood naked. Refreshed, she went to the cedar stand, cleansed her body, then pulled the pins from her hair. Red tresses fell free to her waist, the natural curls glowing under the candlelight. She tilted her head and flirted with her reflection. Emerald eyes glittered with approval. Her skin was pale and soft, and high cheekbones a peach color. Her breasts were shapely, but not large, waist small and hips narrow. She was well-proportioned for her height.

Sighing, she decided to order a bath tomorrow; she was too tired to bother with it tonight. Lifting one of the trunk lids, she slipped on the first nightdress that came into view. It was pink satin with a snug-fitting lace bodice. She pulled back the quilt and turned down the lamp. Sliding onto the mattress she kicked off the covers. She left the window open, deciding the noise from C Street was more tolerable than the stuffy heat.

Camry stared at the ceiling. The saloon patrons yelled and laughed. Dice clicked, roulette balls rattled and cards slapped. The stamp mills constantly pounded ore. Each thrust of machinery shook the earth. Miners' boots scraped over loose boardwalks as the shifts changed. After what seemed like hours, she finally dozed. Fitful visions of mocking blue eyes and sun-kissed blond hair clouded her dreams.

At midnight, she woke to the high-pitched whistle of the Hale & Norcross. At two, gunshots rang down the street from the Delta Saloon. She tossed and turned the rest of the night. At five-thirty, the bell from the No. 27 Virginia & Truckee Railroad clanged and Camry sat up, disgusted. Sleepily, she pushed her tousled curls back. She would never get used to Virginia City and the sooner she talked Da into leaving, the better.

4

A waitress placed hot cups of aromatic coffee in front of Camry and her father. The Bonanza Hotel dining room was full of morning patrons, the air thick with the tangy smells of breakfast.

Michael Parker dropped two lumps of sugar into his cup and stirred vigorously. He dreaded his task, and to make things worse, Camry had done nothing but dote on him since he had met her in the lobby for breakfast. Sipping his brew loudly, he asked, "How did you sleep?"

She smoothed her linen napkin over her lap. "Horrible. Whistles, bells and gun shots argued all night."

He smiled, his soft green eyes distant as if remembering his first night in Virginia City.

"Really, Da, this hotel isn't even decent. They wouldn't bring a tub into my room this morning. I had to use the common privy down the hall. I don't see what attraction this town holds on you."

His smile faded and he became solemn. She had brought the subject up.

"Father?" Camry's brows furrowed with concern. "What's the matter?"

He stood. "I think we'd better be goin' to me office."

She followed him into the lobby. "You're frightening me. Is there something wrong?"

"We have some things to discuss." Michael couldn't tell her here.

They walked over the rickety boardwalk toward Taylor Street. Though the heat was not too bad yet, Camry had dressed in cooler attire than the previous day. She had chosen a white cotton dress with tiny pleats in the skirt and bodice. Puffed leg-of-mutton sleeves were accented around the wrists with yellow satin ribbons and lace. Small pearls dangled from her earlobes.

Street traffic was lighter at nine o'clock in the morning. Reaching H.S. Beck's furniture shop, they climbed the narrow stairs. Michael took a small key ring from his pocket and unlocked the door. The gray cat looked up and padded lazily across the room.

"Well?" Camry could stand the silence no longer. "What is wrong?" She bent down and picked up the cat.

"Inna moment," he stalled. How could he . . . "Ah, Single-Jack likes you." He shuffled papers on his desk and smiled at his daughter and the cat.

"That's a funny name," she said, scratching the cat's soft head. She took a seat across from her father's desk.

"Nick Trelstad brung him to me."

Her green eyes drew dark and stormy at the mention of the name. How could the man affect her so? Just the very idea of him . . . She shooed the cat from her lap.

"He found him in one a the shafts at Con-VA. Brung him to me knowin' I was alone." Michael walked to the tall grandfather clock and opened the glass door covering the time face. He wound the key and shut the case. He was stalling. How could he tell her? He'd never denied her a thing before. But now that she was here it would be harder for him to . . .

"Do you know him?" Camry asked coolly.

Pulled from his thoughts, Michael took a seat behind his heavy desk. "I do some broker work for him. He issa good man. A real hard worker. Respected too."

Camry stuck up her nose. "He's conceited."

"I wouldna condemn a man you donna know, Missy. He issa fine gentleman."

She ignored her father's stare and looked around the room. It seemed so bare, lacking warmth. "Why don't you have a fancy hotel room?" She changed the subject.

"I need an office too. This suits me fine." He was quiet

for a moment. He scanned the lovely daughter before him, a hidden pain in his eyes.

She met his gaze. "Well?" Camry sighed. "You've got me on pins and needles. Scold me if you will for my crossing half the country to get here."

"I willna scold you, Missy. You're twenty. Far beyond the age offa switch; not that I ever raised a hand to you."

She pressed closer to the desk and took his hands in her own small ones. "It *is* money, isn't it? Are we poor?"

He shook his head negatively, then came right out with it. "I'm sendin' you to your Auntie Maeve."

Her eyes widened in horror. "To Scotland!"

"I've thought about it all night. You canna stay in this town without proper supervision and I canna give it. You need the care of a woman. It's nay right for a well-bred young lady here."

"But, Da," Camry protested. "I've seen plenty of women in town."

"Widows, strumpets . . . or *married*," Michael emphasized the last word.

She froze. "Well, I won't get married!"

A timid knock sounded on the glass door and a boyish face appeared in the doorway. "Sorry, Mr. Parker. I didn't know you had a client."

"It's all right, Matt." Michael waved the young man in. He needed to collect himself. It wouldn't be easy being firm with her. "Come and meet me daughter."

Matt's face lit up. "I've heard a lot about you, Miss Parker."

"Matthew Price," Michael introduced. "He used to be me assistant."

"Charmed," Camry said mechanically, but her thoughts were on her father's previous words.

"Sweetheart," Michael said, pulling a coin from his pocket. "Wouldya run downstairs to Mr. Beck's and buy me a big red apple?"

She took the coin, realizing he wanted to speak privately with Matthew.

"Nice to have met you, Miss Parker." Matt tipped a tan hat that covered his sandy locks.

"Charmed," she repeated again and left. She descended the stairway and turned into the shop, her thoughts jumbled.

A small bell tinkled above her head when she opened the door. H.S. Beck stood behind the counter stacking shelves with tins of Snow Flake baking soda. He wore a fresh white shirt, black ribbon tie and, around his waist, a clean apron. He turned to greet Camry, his face friendly. He had slightly receding black hair and smiling azure eyes.

"May I help you, ma'am?"

Camry looked about before answering. "I thought this was a furniture store."

H.S. delighted in telling her of his good fortune. "Well, it was when I started, now I've expanded. As a matter of fact, my new sign should be here this week. The painters could hardly fit all the words on it. They had to sort of twist the wording fancy-like." His hands gestured in the air. "It reads: H.S. Beck—Dealer in Furniture, Carpets, Bedding, Stoves, Tin-Ware and Crockery. Of course, I dabble in general merchandise as well."

She was almost sorry she had asked. "I'm Michael Parker's daughter," she finally stated bluntly. "He wants an apple."

Mr. Beck's lips turned into a smile. "I should have guessed! The same red hair and green eyes. I know exactly what your father wants. I keep my Rome Beauties in the cellar. Excuse me a moment."

The way Virginia City was constructed, most buildings had two entrances—a front and rear. The mountain was such a steep slant, you could enter an establishment on A Street and exit on B Street without realizing you'd gone down hill. Camry had made that mistake earlier this morning, by exiting from the wrong door of the Bonanza Hotel, and ended up in the alley behind a fish store!

Beck's had a rear door that worked on that principle. The front door opened on C Street and the back door opened on D Street. The downstairs door opened and Camry heard Mr. Beck's muffled voice from the cellar.

"I'll be right up." The customer's heeled shoes tapped up the stairs.

Looking around the store, Camry fingered a bolt of French cloth that was priced a staggering $32.00 per yard. A woman appeared at the top of the steps and turned to the glass case that housed tobacco.

Camry kept back, partially hidden by a cold potbellied stove in the corner. The woman was the same one she had seen with Nicholas Trelstad at the drilling contest. Her long black hair was braided neatly down her back, a piece of suede tied at the end. Wispy bangs rested on shapely dark brows arching above brown eyes. Her tawny skin was flawless, accented with a deep rose blush on her cheeks. She picked up a pouch of tobacco and put it to her nose. Nostrils delicately flared as she inhaled the sharp aroma. Red lips parted in a faint smile to reveal even white teeth with an ever-so-slight space between the front two.

Without making her presence known, Camry eyed the woman coldly. Her figure was very curvaceous; full breasts pressed against the bodice of her earth-toned calico dress that complimented her skin beautifully.

Beck returned with a small gunny sack in his hands. "Miss Parker?" he called, not seeing her hidden in the corner.

She stepped forward with an air of dignity. The woman turned abruptly, unaware there had been anyone else in the store. "I'm still looking," Camry answered.

"Very well," he replied, then faced his other customer. "Will that be all, Miss Silk?"

Silk? Camry strained her eyes. . . .

"For today," she spoke with a sweet Spanish accent.

H.S. wrote up the order and Miss Silk paid. She looked at Camry for a moment, then left. Mr. Beck wiped his hands on his apron. "Can I help you find anything, Miss Parker?"

"No," she said, choosing her next words carefully. "Actually, I was wondering who that woman was."

Beck shook his head and clicked his tongue. "It's a

shame. I knew her when she lived above Hanbridge's with her husband and son. She was Garnetta Silquerro Evans then. She calls herself Garnet Silk now. Her kind always change their name."

"What kind?" Camry pressed with ignorance.

"Miss Parker, I don't want to come right out and say it." He rubbed his face nervously.

"For heaven's sake, I'm an adult."

"I don't like to say the word, Miss Parker, but there's no other way I can say it." He lowered his voice to a whisper. "She's a soiled dove."

Camry met his azure eyes for a moment, then straightened. "How much do I owe you for the apple?"

"Five cents."

She dropped the coin on the counter and picked up the apple. Without saying good-bye, she exited and climbed the flight of stairs to her father's office. Wouldn't you know it! Nicholas Trelstad kept company with that sort of woman!

Michael was alone, sitting behind his desk. Camry handed him the apple. "Are you angry with me?" he asked remorsefully.

"No," she answered, watching Single-Jack in the windowsill clawing the tassel on the shade-pull. "I just don't understand. Don't you love me?"

"That's nay fair. I love you with all me heart. I canna watch over you."

"I'm not asking you to. You haven't watched over me for fifteen years," Camry reasoned. "I don't want to go back to Scotland. I haven't been there since I was five. I can't go back without you . . . or mother."

She remembered the day they left Scotland for America. Though she was only five years old, she faintly recalled boarding a large ship. The voyage was long and hard and when they finally reached New York, her mother, Heather, took sick. Several months later, she died of influenza. Michael had enrolled Camry into the finest boarding schools available, visiting every weekend.

Tears clouded Michael's eyes and he quickly rubbed them away. He too was remembering. He had been in the banking business then . . . but things didn't work as they should. Because of that, he had moved to Virginia City. He could not let Camry find out . . . He had to be firm. He stood and massaged his temples. "I'll give you a choice. It's either marriage or your Auntie Maeve's."

"You can't mean that!" she exclaimed in disbelief.

"I can and I do. It's high time you settled down. There are some fine men here. Take Trelstad for example," he spoke authoritatively.

"I won't!" she shot back.

Pain etched his face. She was making this very difficult. But he had no choice. "If you donna, I'll not be payin' your bills and then where will you be? You wouldna last a day."

Camry bit her lower lip with contemplation. He had her over a barrel. How could he be so cruel? This mining town had hardened his heart! "Very well. If I *have* to marry, I shall. But," she raised her finger toward him, "it might take me a while to find the right man."

"You have two weeks."

"Two weeks!" she repeated aghast.

"In me day a match was made. Shall I be choosin' the husband?" he threatened.

Her breasts heaved in indignation. "I can't believe you're doing this to me! I knew you'd be angry when you found out I left the Academy, but I never dreamed you'd react this way."

He spoke softly. "You did it to yourself, Missy. You never shouldda come."

Camry composed herself; she wouldn't cry. Crying was for babies and weak-minded women. "Very well. I guess I'd better start looking. As much as I hate the idea of marriage, I hate the thought of another separation from you even more. Goodday, Da. I still love you." She opened the door and departed.

Single-Jack jumped onto the desk and stared at the misery engraved on his owner's face. Michael Parker wrung his hands together. How could he have explained his situation? How could he have confessed . . . Unable to contain himself, he rested his head in his arms and wept.

Roughly, Camry pushed her way through the crowd on C Street. Deep in thought, she paid no attention to her steps and soon found herself staring at the lapel of a man's jacket.

"Watch where you're going!" she bade testily.

"Miss Parker, if my memory serves me right." She looked up into Frank Marbury's handsomely chiseled face. "Did you find your father?" he questioned, although he appeared more interested in why her cheeks were so flushed.

She studied him with more than casual interest. His suit was expensive. The eggshell-white, silk shirt smelled freshly laundered and his blue vest housed a gold fob chain. Ungloved, his hands revealed a large diamond ring on the small finger of his left hand.

"Yes." Her attitude changed sweetly. "Yes, I did find him. I never would have managed without your charming assistance."

Frank held back a chuckle at the abrupt change in her manner. "I'm glad I could be of service."

"So am I," she laughed coyly. "I've decided to accept your dinner offer, Mr. Marbury."

"Indeed?" He raised his brows, amused. He hadn't thought she'd even heard him over the traffic noise, much less remember his name.

"Would you be so kind as to escort me back to my room?" Before he could answer, she linked her arm in his and steered them in the direction of the Bonanza Hotel. "Tell me, Mr. Marbury, do you own any of these silver mines?"

"A few," he laughed at her sudden, but obvious interest.

"Big ones?" she asked, innocence lacing her query.

5

Camry had taken a refreshing bath in the brass tub down the hall from her room, and now sat in the cedar rocking chair wearing a white chemise and full petticoats. The frilly straps rested off her creamy shoulders while she brushed her hair until it gleamed.

A knuckled rap sounded on the door. "Housemaid, mum."

"Come in." She stood and pulled a pink satin wrapper around her waist.

The maid carried an apricot taffeta gown over her arm. "I have yer dress. Nice and pressed."

After securely fastening the stays on her corset, they fit the dress down over her head. The neckline was scalloped and the bodice fit snugly over her breasts. The skirt fanned out glossily, free of any decorations. The maid assisted Camry with her hair, pinning it in a fashionable style by leaving a few wispy curls to frame her face.

"Will that be all, mum?"

"No," Camry stated. She went to the washstand and hastily scribbled a note excusing herself from dinner. Folding the paper in half, she handed it to the young girl. "Please see that Mr. Michael Parker gets this. He lives above Beck's Furniture Shop."

"Yes, mum." The maid took the note, curtsied and left.

Looking in the mirror, Camry checked her final appearance. She decided to wear the earrings her father had given to her on her eighteenth birthday. They were retangular cut topaz, clasped in a curling gold leaf. To complete the toilette, she dabbed perfume between her breasts and on her wrists. After all, if she had to marry, why not catch a rich man? Satisfied that Frank Marbury would find her irresistible, she left her room.

As she descended the black and gold patterned carpet, she saw Frank was already waiting in the lobby. He wore a gray broadcloth suit. The fabric intensified the silver-gray color of his eyes. His handlebar mustache was waxed and his chin clean-shaven.

"My dear Miss Parker." He took her hand and led her to the street where his carriage was tied. After helping her up, he settled into the black leather seat. "You look exquisite."

"Thank you, Mr. Marbury." She folded her hands in her lap and sat straight.

Frank released the brake and flicked the reins. His profile was silhouetted against the Sierra-Nevada mountaintops which had taken on a purplish hue in the early dusk. His white shirt contrasted with the natural tan on his face. He was indeed very masculine. Camry was slightly nervous at the proximity of their bodies. She'd never been with an older man—unescorted. Maybe she shouldn't have been so hasty. She hadn't even asked him where they were going . . . "Might I inquire about our dining arrangements, Mr. Marbury?"

"Certainly, my dear. I've reserved a table for us at Duprey's in Gold Hill. It's rather comfortable and there's quite a selection on the menu. I thought it might make you feel like you were dining on the east coast."

She smiled. Why, he really was a gentleman!

The road to Gold Hill was busy with horse traffic and brightly painted omnibuses that made regular runs between the three towns on the mountain. Within fifteen minutes, Frank was halting the team in front of the Main Street livery stables. He paid a strapping youth two bits to take good care of the bays.

Duprey's looked much like the other buildings in town; wooden and painted in a whitewash. But upon entering, Camry couldn't believe the opulence. Velvet wallpaper, in cream colors, was accented by gilded picture frames.

Crystal chandeliers hung low over small tables. The maitre d' led them to a table in the corner.

The host held a plush chair out for Camry, and after she sat, politely pushed her toward the table. Frank sat, and was immediately handed a parchment menu. He studied it for both of them.

"Might you allow me to order for you, Miss Parker?"

"I'd be delighted," she accepted.

Their waiter was attired in immaculate black with a stiff, starched white shirt under his jacket. "Mr. Marbury. Always a pleasure to see you."

Frank nodded his head faintly in acknowledgment.

"A bottle of your usual?" the steward asked.

"Yes, and we are ready to order now." He spoke in a stream of indecipherable French words. Camry looked at Frank with admiration. A gentleman indeed, she repeated for the second time that evening.

Frank Marbury interested her. Men rarely did. But this one seemed to be wealthy as well as refined. She decided the best way to see his true colors was to have him talk about himself. "Tell me, Mr. Marbury," she said coyly. "What do you do for a living?"

He rested an elbow on the table and supported his chin in his palm. Absently, he rubbed his lower lip with his index finger. "I invest."

"In what?"

"What else? Silver." He seemed uninterested with talk of his business and to Camry's chagrin, he changed the subject. "Is your father glad to have you here?"

"Oh, he was surprised to see me—I mean, we met just fine—" she said, remembering she had told Frank she was meeting her father, not surprising him. She mustn't give him the impression she was one to tell fibs.

"Might I ask where you traveled from?"

"Philadelphia."

Their conversation was disrupted by the arrival of their wine. The waiter poured sparkling rosé into silver goblets. Camry hadn't had many samples of wine in her years at school, but she liked this one—it was light, not heavy.

Determined to find out more about Frank, she pressed on. "You said you owned several stocks?"

Frank smiled, his white teeth flashing handsomely in the low light of the room. "My dear, if you want to know how much I'm worth, why don't you ask?"

Flustered, Camry took a long sip of wine. "I never meant—"

"Yes, you did, but don't worry, I'm not upset with your interest." He looked her directly in the eyes.

"I was only making conversation." She composed herself, taking a deep breath.

"Let me say that I have enough money to buy you earrings that would make those on your lobes look like cut glass." His facial expression remained the same— cool and aloof.

She angrily put her hands to her ears. "My father gave me these, and he's certainly no miser!"

Frank chuckled. "Hold your temper, my dear. I'm only stating a fact."

She was saved from further scrutiny as the steward served steaming scallops, vegetables in cream sauce and veal on ivory china plates. They ate in silence. Camry forced her thoughts to remain on her father's threat—it was either marriage or her Auntie Maeve's in Scotland.

After dinner, they rode back to Virginia City. The sky had blended to a deep blue-black and the air hung low with warmth. The moon shone brightly amid a blanket of twinkling silver stars.

"Would you care to see one of our saloons, Miss Parker?" Frank asked as he guided the bays down C Street.

"I beg your pardon?" A *Saloon*?

He laughed softly. "It is I who should beg *your* pardon. Of course you wouldn't know that we call our gaming establishments 'saloons' when in fact, they are quite grand."

She hesitated. What time was it? Surely it was still early . . .

"I would have you home within a respectable hour,

and women *do* visit the saloons."

"All right, Mr. Marbury. I'd be delighted."

He turned the team toward B Street where Pat Lynch's Saloon was located. The town was alive with activity. The fancy gaming houses and hotels on B Street blared piano and banjo tunes. Gambling was in full swing. Cards changed hands quickly—as well as the money.

Camry hadn't realized how tense Frank had been, for once they were in sight of Pat Lynch's, his facial expression seemed to relax. He looked years younger than she had originally thought him to be. He even reached up to his neck and slightly loosened his tie.

Frank helped Camry down with a strong arm, his hand lingering on her tiny waist as they entered the establishment. Camry was not prepared for the grandeur of it all. Watercolors set in silver frames rested on gold walls. Couches, lounges and divans of rose satin were scattered around the side of the room. Heaped on them were cushions of crimson, gold, green and azure of every shape. Marble tabletops held Bohemian vases filled with wild flowers. The light from veiled lamps bathed the room gracefully. Fine chandeliers were reflected in the many floor-to-ceiling mirrors. At the back of the saloon, behind the gaming tables, was a portrait of an amply endowed nude woman. A flowing piece of gauze rested on her shoulders, then trailed behind her. In her hand was an overflowing goblet, elevated in a toast.

"Welcome to Virginia City, Miss Parker," Frank whispered in her ear.

She shivered as his moist breath caressed her skin.

Frank pulled several double eagles from his pocket. "Would you care to play?"

"Oh, I've never played these games. I don't know how."

"Watch me." He guided them to the faro tables. She took in all the equipment on the felt table, but still failed to understand how the game was played. What she did understand was that after half an hour, Frank had more than tripled his money.

"Nice game, Frank," a sweet voice called out.

Camry looked up to see a stunning black-haired woman staring at Frank.

"Martinique," he acknowledged, without introducing her to Camry.

"Would you care to try a game now, Miss Parker?" he asked, smiling at his winnings.

She shook her head. "Oh no, I'd only lose your money."

For the next hour, Frank circulated to the roulette, rondo, *rouge et noir* and blackjack tables, nearly making two thousand dollars. Stimulated by his good luck, Frank was talkative on the ride back to her hotel. He explained some of the different games which actually boiled down to the knowledge of simple addition and subtraction principles.

Camry was undecided whether she wanted him to kiss her good-night or not. She certainly didn't want to discourage him from calling again. The hotel lobby was quiet; only the desk clerk was visible and he was dozing in a chair behind the counter.

Frank took her hand and pressed it to his lips. He had decided against kissing her. The way she tilted her head was too obvious. He knew she was toying with him and that's exactly why he refused to play. "Until tomorrow," he said.

"I had a divine time, Frank," Camry purred. They had dropped formalities.

"And I," he smiled handsomely, "had a delightful evening." He turned on polished boot heels and left.

She was slightly disappointed that he *didn't* try to kiss her. Though she had no romantic interest in him, it made her wonder if he had any in her. He certainly was a man who took what he wanted—that was proof in the gaming room. *Until tomorrow*, he had said . . .

She climbed the stairs with confidence.

6

Camry didn't see her father the rest of the week. It wasn't her idea, rather his. He sent her a message saying he would be busy going over books. The days passed quickly as she absorbed the routine of Virginia City. At midnight, the shifts changed and at five-thirty, the first train departed. Between two in the afternoon and two in the morning, the Washoe zephyrs set in. Sometimes they were powerful, capable of blowing roofs from buildings; other times, they provided refreshment from the heat.

Frank Marbury called twice. He took her to Barnam's Restaurant for brandy and oysters; then the next night, they strolled to the taproom of Jacob Wimmer's Virginia Hotel for five-dollar cognac and gambling. After all the glamor of the evening, Frank continued to play the gentleman. He never made an advance more than a kiss on her hand. Camry wondered if there was another woman, yet he continued to call, so she ruled that out.

Sunday, she rose early and dressed in a cool gown of cream muslin. Hastily pinning her hair, she grabbed a Bible off the washstand and hurried down the stairs to meet her father in the lobby for chuch. He waited at one of the tables, nervously de-petaling a daisy he had plucked from the vase. He stood as she approached, then planted a featherly kiss on her cheek.

"Good morning, Camry," he greeted.

"Good monring, Da," she returned. "How are the books coming?"

"Books?" he hesitated for a moment, then cleared his throat. Running a hand through his beard, his fingers trembled slightly. "Fine. They're fine. Are you ready?"

Michael hired a hackney and they drove down the steep slope to E and Taylor Streets where St. Mary's in the Mountains graced the hillside. He fidgeted with his beard habitually. Things hadn't gone as well as he'd hoped during the past days. He'd skimmed more than he had intended in order to pay back several debts. "So, how have you been? I havena seen you for three days. You donna think I'm a bad father for not chaperoning you, do you, sweetheart?" He rolled his r's in the familiar brogue.

She lowered her lashes. "Of course not."

"Are you ready to give up this notion a marriage and go live with your Auntie Maeve?"

"Never!" she exclaimed. "I want to be with you. I've spent the last ten years of my life in Hoaks Academy. I'm tired of it. If I can't live with you, I want to at least be in the same town."

"But Missy—" Michael pleaded.

"It was your rule, you know. You can change it." Camry looked at him with bright eyes.

"Nay, I canna. I canna watch over you and I told you as much. Virginia is no place for a lady a breedin' to be alone."

"I hate to point it out, but you haven't watched over me for three days and I'm unscathed."

He was flustered by her observation, his voice harsh. "Donna be smart with me, Missy. Since you so choose matrimony, you have eight days left." His face softened in regret for his sharp tongue.

"Well, don't worry yourself about it," Camry snapped. "I'm practically engaged."

Knitting his bushy red brows, he asked. "Who is the man?"

"Frank Marbury. He helped me find you."

Michael's face reddened. "The bloody hell! Frank Marbury! He's got the reputation of a no-good gambler. I donna think you'll be marryin' him. I shouldda been lookin' afore, but by God, I'll start now. I'll meet you up with some proper gentleman if it's the last thing I do!"

"Stop being fatherly, Da," Camry said patting his hand affectionately. "What would the difference be if I met him in Philadelphia? You'd never be the wiser, so what's the fuss now? He's rich and that's all I need to know. And, he is a gentleman," she reasoned.

"I invited Nick Trelstad to sup with us after church," Michael announced as the hackney slowed in front of the chapel. "He issa good man and you'd do well to marry him."

"Ha!" Camry gruffed. "I wouldn't marry him if he were the only man in Virginia City."

Michael helped her down. "We'll discuss this after worship."

Outside the church, a small group of men clustered in deep conversation with a handsome man in his early forties. His dark eyes and hair blended well with a full, neatly trimmed mustache. His clothes were regal, without an air of conceited wealth.

"Who is that man?" Camry whispered.

"John Mackay," her father replied shortly.

The name sounded familiar and she bit her lower lip in thought. Martha Zmed had mentioned Mackay and Fair owned the town. "Who's Fair?"

"They're Micks who, along with their damned San Francisco banks, control this mountain."

"Oh?" Camry turned her head to get a better look at the silver king of Virginia City. "Is he married?" she asked lightly.

"Aye, and with two children."

"Where are they?" She searched the crowd of congregation. Surely Mrs. Mackay would be exquisite.

"I've nay seen her nor the offspring since I've been here. They live in Europe."

"He's separated?" she inquired with curious hope. John Mackay would make *Frank Marbury* look like cut glass!

"They have an arrangement. Queer if you ask me. He pays her bills and visits her once or twice a year. She's quite notorious as the hostess in Paris."

Her eyes narrowed with envy as they entered the church. If only she could be so lucky.

St. Mary's was a beautifully constructed church with a multitude of cross topped spires. Its red brick was accented with white limestone. High in the central gable was a carved window which housed a silver bell that tolled the hour. Inside, Gothic carved redwood trusses and arches peaked fifty-three feet high. Intricately patterned stained glass windows were vivid blues, greens, reds and golds. A large opened Bible rested between three gold candlesticks on both sides of a marble altar.

Camry watched John Mackay bow, make the sign of the cross, then kneel in prayer in his family pew. Michael guided her to a pew in the back. She genuflected, then looked at Father Patrick Manogue with studied interest. He had curling brown hair receding from a high fore-head. His eyebrows were thick, and seesawed with emphasis as he spoke. His soft, gentle voice seemed like it should belong to someone else. He towered well over six feet and was of stocky build. His white alb was crisp under a flowing green vest and purple stole. She liked what she saw, until the thought crossed her mind that he would probably be the one to officiate her nuptial vows. She frowned and her eyes wandered.

Behind them was a carved redwood balcony where the organist and more pews were located. She scanned the parishioners casually. Her eyes flashed like green ice when she saw the familiar Spanish girl. Garnet Silk was dressed in black organdy, her long hair pinned loosely to her head. Michael nudged Camry irritably, and she turned around to face the altar once again. Her mind strayed while Father Manogue spoke. All she could think of was the audacity of the Silk woman.

After the final prayer was said, the congregation milled into the Nevada sun. Father Manogue greeted each member with a hearty handshake. Camry mechanically introduced herself, not bothering to stop long enough for conversation.

Michael tugged a black hat over his red hair. "Shall we supper at MacDougal's? I'm in the mood for some fine Scottish cooking."

"Not if that miner Nicholas Trelstad will be there. The man is rude." Camry slipped her fingers into netted gloves.

"I canna understand your hate for the man. You donna even know him."

"I know him. He's a vermin that runs around with trollops. A trollop who has the gall to show up in the house of the Lord. Heavens, she'll probably be in the confessional for weeks. Look there." Camry pointed at Garnet as she walked up Taylor Street. "It's a known fact that she's a harlot. I find it contemptible that her sort is allowed in church."

"You should bite your tongue, Missy," Michael scolded. He hitched his fingers in his suspenders. "Garnet issa fair woman."

"Dear Lord, Da!" Camry burst. "Don't tell me you know her!"

"I've done business with her—"

She clasped her hands over her ears. "I can't believe you're saying this!"

His face turned red with anger. "How can you think I would tell me own daughter of me indiscretions? I've done broker work for her." He flushed. "And how can you think I'd—"

"I'm sorry, Da," Camry broke in and touched his arm. "I suppose the heat gets me a little hotheated. Forgive me?"

"Aye."

She kissed his cheek affectionately. "I'd rather you dropped me back at the hotel and go on to supper without me." She climbed into the hackney. "Aren't you going to ride back with me?"

"Nay." He shook his head. "You go on. I'd like to walk a bit."

She waved fondly at him as the carriage moved up the hill.

Michael turned to walk up the street. He ran a trembling hand through his beard. He wished he had more control over his daughter. If only he had remarried. She would have had the love of a woman, instead of the firm hand of Miss Laura Hoaks. There was a grand difference, and it seemed to take its toll on Camry. She was a good girl, but she could be unfeeling at times.

"Parker!" It was Jessee Drury, owner of the feed store. "You look in need of a drink."

Raising tired green eyes, the crow's-feet etched deep into the corners of Michael's countenance. "I believe I do." His beloved Heather's face hovered over him. Maybe in drink his worries would vanish.

7

The week was promising for Camry. Frank Marbury
treated her regally to glasses of champagne and
antelope steaks smothered in burgundy sauce at
Chuvel's Restaurant. Later, they visited the Gentry and
the Crittenden roulette parlors. There she was awed by
the many entertainers singing and dancing. The money
seemed to pour out of Frank's pocket; a never ending
vein of gold. He enjoyed flaunting it for Camry and she
enjoyed it equally! Once while they were gaming at
Johnny Newman's Saloon on Sutton Street, John Mackay
entered. He played several games of faro, finally settling
for a recreational hand of blackjack. After thirty minutes
of play, he stormed out cursing angrily. No one could
equal his wager. He had argued what was the point in
playing, when his winnings didn't amount to a drop in
the hat.

Johnny Newman's Saloon was first choice for Camry.
Second was Pat Lynch's Place. Newman's was full of
vitality and aristocrats. Men wore elegant broadcloth
suits and women fine silk gowns. Magnificent coaches
with liveried footmen pulled up adjacent to the three-
story structure. Inside, the soft light from gas
chandeliers reflected on starched shirt fronts and
gleaming evening studs. Silver collars on crystal
decanters proclaimed the names of different whiskies.
Double eagles, the brilliant twenty-dollar gold coins,
clinked on green velvet gaming tables.

Camry loved the excitement. Frank was a master at the
craft and soon she understood some of the simpler
games. He insisted she spend at least one-hundred

dollars at the gambling tables and when she asked him if
he could afford it, he had laughed heartily.

Everything was going well. Her father breakfasted with
her most mornings. His mood veered cheerfully when
Exchequer stock rose to four hundred twenty-five
dollars per share, and his disapproval of her involve-
ment with Frank Marbury seemed to fade as his mind
became occupied with business matters. Sunday came
quickly, but much to Camry's dismay, Frank had not
proposed. She had two days left before her father
would insist on sending her to her relatives in Scotland.

This night, Frank was taking her to Piper's Opera
House for the opening performance of the Oates Opera
Troupe. Surely on the eve of such a gala event, he
would ask for her hand. She thought of Frank as a
husband—he was pleasant to look upon, his features
were striking, his eyes unique and observing. His
gambling expertise intrigued her. She rarely saw him
lose a hand of cards or a turn of the wheel. And though
she hadn't really associated Frank with the dreams that
had plagued her on her first nights in Virginia City, she
felt as if his company protected her from visions of
Nicholas Trelstad's mocking blue eyes.

The morning-shift whistle blew in the distance as
Camry moved about her room readying for church. It
didn't surprise her a bit the town didn't rest on Sundays.
The stamp mills never stopped. She laughed out loud.
Why, once she'd made up her mind to stay in Nevada,
the rumbling noises were almost a comfort to her at
night and helped her to sleep rather than hindered it.
She wondered if Frank would buy them a house further
up the hill where the noise wasn't so loud, or if they
would continue to live at the International Hotel where
he resided.

Camry dressed in a sea-foam green gown with a full
ruffled skirt. The sleeves and neck were also layered in
ruffles the same color. She liked the way it shimmered
like ocean waves when the breeze caught the material.

Michael wasn't in the lobby as usual, so she stepped onto the boardwalk to wait for him.

"Good morning, sunshine," a resonant voice greeted from her right. She turned to see Nicholas Trelstad reclining in a rocking chair facing the hotel. Moccasin-covered feet and calves stretched out, elevated before him, on the brick wall. Only the back rim of the chair touched the boardwalk. In his hands was the morning copy of the Territorial Enterprise. Maintaining his position, he tipped his ivory Stetson. "Your father sends his regrets."

Her heart suddenly fluttered. She hadn't seen him since that night he brought her trunks to her room.

"W-what?" she stammered. "Where is he?"

Nicholas brought down his legs in one swift move, then stood. He towered over her, his body large with powerful muscles. White denim trousers covered his lean legs and a light-blue work shirt clung to his hard shoulders and chest. He tossed the newspaper on the swaying rocking chair. "He's with a client. It seems you're stuck with me."

"That's impossible," Camry quickly returned. He smelled clean and fresh like castile soap and his sunny blond hair was damp at the ends—probably just out from a bath. *Did men take baths on Sunday mornings?* Two blue eyes filled her vision and she backed away, suddenly embarrassed at being caught giving him such a close perusal.

"What are you looking at?" he asked, the ever-present grin on his tanned visage.

"What are *you* looking at!" she shot back.

"I asked you first." He gave her a smile that sent her pulses racing.

Camry inhaled angrily. "This is getting us nowhere. Good day, Mr. Trelstad." She turned to leave, but his vise-like grip caught her arm.

"Please, remember yourself!" she insisted.

Nicholas laughed, his voice booming under the awning. "How could I have forgotten?"

"Oh!" Camry admonished. "You have no manners."

"Of course I do. I've come to escort you to church."

"I don't want to go to church," she hissed under her breath.

"Good," he whispered. "I'm not Catholic."

"You vile, contemptible, rodent—" She filled her lungs to continue.

His voice was humorous. "There's more?"

"—arrogant, conceited—"

"Hold on there, mister." The proprietor of Boone's Drug Store stomped onto the boardwalk. "Ma'am, is this man bothering you?"

"Yes—" Camry said, but was suddenly crushed to Nicholas' chest. His arms gripped her strongly, her face nestled in the soft material of his shirt and for a split second, she thought she smelled peanuts.

"She's my wife," he declared, patting her back. "I'm trying to get her to see Doc Hall. She's just a little upset. In the family way and all."

Camry kicked his shin and struggled in his arms. "I am n—"

Nicholas pulled her tighter to him and without another means of silencing her protests, his lips came down on hers. His mouth was warm and forbidden, snatching her breath and poise as well. The battle had turned to something she was unequipped to fight. Her wits and retorts left. Instead of finding him repulsive, he swept the very energy from her. And after he lifted his lips from hers, she could barely stand, so she rested against his hard muscled chest, the warmth of him seeping through the cloth. Or was that her burning cheeks?

The proprietor shook his head and gave Nicholas a hearty slap on the back. "Sorry, old boy. I thought she was a jade. We don't take kindly to roughing up our whores. But if she's your wife, well, that's different." He winked. "I hope it's a boy. Can always use another Comstock miner." He disappeared into his shop again.

Keeping an arm around her, Nicholas walked them down the boardwalk. "Come on, darlin'. You look like you could use some fresh air."

Camry was in a daze. She made no resistance. Never had she been kissed like that. She had trifled with men in Philadelphia, but they had only given her sisterly pecks on the cheeks, or a quick, dry brush of her lips with their own.

She finally found her voice and asked waveringly, "Where are we going?"

He smiled at her upturned face. "For a ride. J.B. hasn't been out of town for a week."

"Your horse?"

He ran a finger over her high cheek. "Nope, J.B.'s my hat." He doffed it gallantly. "John B. Stetson, creator of this magnificent eighteen-dollar Dakota felt and fur."

They descended upon Light and Allman's Livery Stable on B Street. They stable boy saw Nicholas coming and ran into the wooden barn. A few minutes later, he returned with a splendid gray roan, dappled with darker shades on the hindquarters. Saddled in shining black leather, the sun reflected off the horse beautifully. Camry backed away, her common sense returning. The animal was so large, she barely came to its shoulders. "I'm not going anywhere with you!"

"I promised your father I'd take his place today." He placed a moccasined foot in the stirrup and pulled his weight up with ease. "And I'm a man of my word." His strong arm reached down and circled her waist. In a smooth motion, he lifted her to the roan and planted her behind him so that she sat sideways. Camry frantically dug her fingernails into his back for fear she'd slide off.

Nicholas flinched. "Don't draw blood." He pulled her arms around his flat abdomen. "Hold on this way." He kicked the flanks of his horse and they clip-clopped down Sutton Street.

Oh! If Frank saw her now, all would be ruined! "People are staring at us," she cried. "Can't we please rent a hackney?"

"And leave S.D. in Virginia? I don't care if people look." He waved at a dowager across the street. She stuck up her nose and turned away. Nicholas clicked his tongue and the horse gained speed to a canter.

Camry gripped his waist tighter, her breasts pressing closer to his back. "For heaven's sake, you act as if that hat of yours is a person!"

"S.D. isn't my hat," he laughed. "J.B.'s my hat. S.D.'s my horse." They turned down the road of Six Mile Canyon where the dwellings thinned to vast prairie.

"Why do you initial things? I won't even ask what S.D. stands for," she sniffed.

"S.D. actually stands for two things. I couldn't make up my mind between Silver Dollar and South Dakota. The latter is where I hail from and the first is the color of my steed. The two initials overlapped, so I think of him as my silver dollar from South Dakota." He patted the roan's neck affectionately. The horse shook his head, flicking the dark gray mane.

The countryside was dry and scattered with clusters of sagebrush, the earth pale and dusty apricot. They rode down the switchback trail quietly, even Camry was absorbed in the wonder of the desert. Sugarloaf jetted from the landscape. Named by the Washoe Indians, it was a towering rock shaped like a loaf of bread. At the bottom of the canyon, terrain leveled and small groups of green pinon pines climbed to the sun. Trees, twisted and turned from the desert winds, were rooted in the hard white granite. A narrow stream appeared and Nicholas followed it east. Indigo-blue water widened, tumbling over chips of sparkling rocks. Green desert grass sprouted in silky blankets on the sandy shore.

Nicholas halted S.D. and dismounted. He tethered the roan to a glittering manzanita bush, then moved to help Camry down.

"I can do it myself," she declared, not trusting herself in his arms again.

"As you wish, Miss Parker." He crossed his arms over his chest and waited.

Camry wished he weren't staring at her. It made her nervous. Though Miss Hoaks had horses at the academy, she'd never ridden one as she saw no purpose to it. Horses were for getting from one place to another—so why not ride in the carriage? Comfort was better than a horse's rump. She rolled onto her stomach and lay across the saddle. Her feet dangled four feet from the ground as she slowly began to slide down. S.D. dug his hoof into the earth nervously. Camry struggled, grasping onto the pommel, but slipped too fast and landed with a thud. Nicholas was by her side in an instant.

"Give me your hand," he ordered.

She sat up and brushed the pebbles from her bruised elbows. Pushing back a loose tendril of copper curl, she narrowed her eyes vexatiously, angry with herself for appearing inexperienced. "I wouldn't take your hand if it held the last piece of silver in Virginia City." She turned onto her knees and stood, slapping the blades of grass from her full, ruffled skirt. "Step aside." She pushed past him and went to the stream to wash her hands.

The water was cool and clear. It refreshed her burning cheeks and soothed her parched throat. Nicholas joined her and rested one leg on a large sandstone boulder; the other was planted firmly on the ground. He watched her soft lips take the water from her cupped hands and cast his eyes down. What was she thinking, he wondered. Her dress fluttered and it reminded him of a glittering manzanita bush. He reached down and snapped a blue flower from a strong green stalk.

"Mike tells me you're getting married. Who's the gent?" He tossed the flower into the river, and the star of petals floated downstream with the current.

Camry patted her temples, replying tersely, "What concern is it of yours?"

"I only asked." He walked up the bank and sat under a pine tree burdened with heavy cones; then stretched his moccasin-covered calves in front of him. "Come, sit in the shade."

Shaking the water from her hands, she sat next to him, leaning against the base of the trunk. "Did he also tell you he's forcing me?"

"No," Nicholas said, lowering the ivory Stetson over his forehead. He leaned back and clasped his large hands over his broad chest. "He said you had a choice."

"Some choice! Marriage or Scotland."

Nicholas sighed. "So you're willing to sacrifice yourself." He plucked a dry blade of grass and brought it to his lips and clamped down. His strawberry blond mustache rippled when he rolled the blade to the corner of his mouth. "Since you're in the market for a husband, shall I tell you about myself?"

She gave him a bland smile. "It doesn't matter in the slightest to me."

He grinned at her rude remark. He was thoroughly enjoying himself. She was awfully pretty when her lower lip pouted slightly. He was tempted to kiss her again; he had meant the first kiss in jest, but in truth, it affected him more than he cared to admit. Undaunted, he continued. "I was born in Rapid City, South Dakota. I'm in the middle of four brothers and one sister. My pa runs a cattle ranch."

"That's fine and well," Camry shrugged, "but it doesn't impress me in the least."

"I wasn't trying to impress you." Nicholas was silent for a moment, then decided to be point blank. "What do you have against me?"

She looked up at him through thickly fringed lashes. Her peach-hued cheeks were smudged with dirt as she smiled with sarcastic sweetness. "You're poor," she stated simply, fluffing her skirt.

"You sure don't mince words. I didn't know you could tell the size of my bank account by looking at me." He lifted the brim of his hat to view her directly. His midnight blue eyes were sharp and assessing.

"Quite simply, you are a miner, Mr. Trelstad. I've envisioned my husband to be chairman of the board."

"Frank Marbury isn't the chairman of any board—and if he were, it would most likely be the gallows."

She shot him a furious glare. "What do you know of it!"

"Your father mentioned him. He doesn't approve."

"It's none of your affair. I'll marry whom I wish."

"You don't know anything about him," Nicholas

cautioned. "It's rumored he killed a man in Frisco."

Camry defied his words. "That's not true. He's been a perfect gentleman."

Nicholas stood and brushed off his pants. "Come on, I think you've had enough sun for one day."

She scrambled to her feet, then placed her arms akimbo. "I'm not ready to go yet. I haven't finished looking at the scenery."

"When *will* you be ready?" he queried, his patience dwindling.

"When I'm ready, so you may as well go on without me because I don't want to ride on that horse with you anymore."

"Is that right?"

"Yes!" she shot back.

Nicholas heaved a heavy sigh, and shaded his eyes to scan the small cloud of dust in the distance. Must be Old Tinnerty the mule-trainer. Then an idea struck him. So, she wanted to stay . . . He spoke in a gruff voice, hoping he sounded convincing. "Very well, Miss Parker. You want to stay, I won't stop you. You're not worthy of my horse."

"*Your* horse isn't worthy of me!"

The mule-skinner was fast approaching, the beasts braying and hawing. Camry caught sight of them and on an impulse, said, "I'd rather ride those mules than your horse."

Nicholas laughed inside. She'd played right into his hands. "Then by all means, do!" He swung his weight over his saddle and sat proudly. He kicked S.D.'s flanks and steered the horse from the stream.

Camry didn't think he'd really take her up on it! Heavens! Mules! Oh, what had she done in her haste?

"You there!" she called to the skinner.

He stopped the train and grinned a full wide toothless mouth. "Yes, lil girly?"

She gathered her skirt with determination and headed for the train. If it was the last thing she did, she would get even with Nicholas Trelstad!

8

The three-thirty V & T was pulling into the station when Camry entered Virginia City on one of the long-eared mules. They were slow and smelly; the rickety harnesses chafing her hands as she held on to them. She had torn her dress on the splintered yokes and was nipped at by the braying beasts. By the time they reached town, she was a shambles. Her hair had fallen free from the pins and hung in her dirt-smudged face. She was desperate for a glass of water to ease the dryness in her throat.

When old man Tinnerty refused to take her to the Bonanza Hotel, she was forced to walk down C Street looking disheveled. Once in the hotel lobby, she quickly fled up the stairs and summoned the maid to draw a cool bath. Sitting in the brass tub, she scrubbed her long hair twice with lavender-scented soap, making sure all traces of the smelly mules were off her hair and skin.

Once back in her room, she prepared for the evening with Frank and finally let her thoughts trail to Nicholas Trelstad. How could one man make her so angry? She'd always had a trigger temper, but *he* set it off continuously. And why? He was nothing but a miner . . . but a handsome one, she had to admit. Oh! Now more than ever she was determined to stay in Virginia City. She would parade the streets as Mrs. Frank Marbury and show that miner a thing or two.

Camry took special care in dressing so Frank would definitely propose. A few minutes earlier, he had sent her a box of red roses and they were now in a glass vase on her washstand. She wondered where on earth he found roses in the middle of the desert. How considerate of him. She stood in her petticoats and looked in the mirror. Her nose and cheeks were pink from the sun. Angrily, she powdered her face to dull the color. With diligence, she brushed her curly hair into controlled ringlets. Piling some of the tresses in an arrangement at the top of her head, she left the rest to hang silkily on her creamy shoulders. She placed two silver combs in the coiffure to complete it.

Opening the cedar armoire, she shuffled through her gowns, choosing a pale lavender satin. The bodice was embroidered with silk tulips the same shade as the dress. The balloon sleeves rested off her soft shoulders, a large bow on each top edge. The skirt was full with a wide sash around her small waist. She fastened amethysts around her neck as well as in her lobes. Completely satisfied with the effect, she grabbed white gloves and a lace fan from the top drawer, then left for the lobby.

Frank waited at the bottom of the stairs. He was dashing and elegant in a black suit, gray tie and a silk vest in shades of brown. His trousers fit well with shining black boots over the cuffs. His mustache was well-manicured and he smiled, flashing perfect white teeth. Bowing, he kissed her finger tips, the waxed mustache tickling her delicate hand. "I've never seen you look more beautiful, Camry," he whispered deeply.

It pleased her the way he said her name and she coyly replied, "This shall be an evening to remember."

His silver-gray eyes met hers. "Indeed it will."

Piper's Opera House was at the corners of D and Union Streets. The two-story wooden structure was white with a picket fence balcony on the second level. Paned windows were covered with thick, olive-green velvet curtains. The first floor housed four double doors in which to enter the theater.

Frank took Camry's arm and guided her to a private box. The seats were diamond-tufted gold brocade. Several slowly rotating fans twirled softly overhead. The walls were decorated with many playbills from previous performances. Six private boxes were actually on stage. As the patrons trickled in and took their seats, Camry noticed John Mackay had taken a green and gold curtained box across from them. Again, she thought of what an advantage marriage to him would be.

The orchestra tuned and the lamps dimmed, followed by a light applause from the audience. In the low light, women's jewels sparkled brightly as well as the men's cuff links. A Grecian scene was painted on the drop curtain which, with a crash of cymbals, was raised slowly. The troupe performed an English burlesque opera, "Princess of the Trebizonde".

Camry sat stiffly, watching Frank out of the corner of her eyes. He sat with a slightly bored expression on his face. The lines around his mouth were tight and he absentmindedly twirled the end of his moustache. She tried to concentrate on the lively opera, but could not, for her destiny relied on *her* performance. She glanced at the many playbills on the wall until her eyes rested on an ad for a French opera. The man in the picture bore a startling resemblance to Nicholas. She shook her head; no, she was being ridiculous. She had him on her mind, that was all. . . . She recalled his kiss in front of the hotel and her cheeks burned. She should have slapped him on the spot.

Shifting his weight, Frank stretched his booted feet in front of him. Camry found herself wondering what it would be like to be kissed by him. Once she became his wife, he would have liberties and that scared her. The girls at Hoaks Academy discussed bedroom rumors and the horrors men inflicted. She shivered at the thought. He looked at her quizzically. "You can't be cold?" he inquired.

She shook her head and fanned herself vigorously; continuing to gaze at the stage. No matter how frightening the thought, she *had* to marry Frank Marbury.

After a brief intermission, the opera ended shortly before eleven and afterward Frank escorted Camry back to the hotel. Once in the lobby, he took her hand.

"I think there's something we should discuss." His slate eyes held her.

She read the expression on his face and inhaled deeply, knowing his proposal would follow. "Let's sit in the dining room."

He put a hand on her satined waist. "I'd rather we go to your room where it's quiet."

She arched a pale brow. "But that's not proper."

Lowering his head just above hers, he murmured, "Under the circumstances, I think it is."

"Very well, just for a moment." She swallowed hard, knowing she must humor him a while longer. Just until he proposed . . .

They mounted the stairs and turned down the hall to her room. A small kerosene lamp had been lit and the shades drawn. With only the bed or rocking chair to sit on, Camry stood.

"You look ravishing tonight," Frank spoke huskily. "Indeed dressed to win a man's heart."

"Oh?" She fanned herself innocently.

"Is that what you want, my dear?" he asked deeply. "My heart? If it is, you have it."

She lowered her lashes coquettishly. "Are you trying to tell me you love me?"

He stifled a laugh. It frightened her. "My heart does not contain love, sweet, it contains want."

Camry's mouth dropped open.

He moved forward, trapping her in the corner of the room. "What are you after, Camry?"

"I don't know what you mean," she lied coolly.

"Come now. All of your light questions probing my financial holdings. Do you need money?"

"Certainly not!" she retorted, trying to free herself.

"Did your father put you up to this? I did a little checking. He's short of funds. Is that why all the lace and finery? The sweet-scented perfumes?"

"No!" she denied, twisting to no avail.

"You're a very desirable woman, Camry. As you well

know." His handsome face was shadowed in the low light. "We're alike, the two of us. We'd both go to extremes to get what we want. I know what I want. . . . Do you know what you want?"

She thought for a moment to deny his accusations, but for the most part, they were true. So why go on any longer? She gathered her courage and held her head high. "I want you to marry me."

Frank stared at her, momentarily speechless in surprise, then threw his head back in laughter. "I would have guessed anything but that! Marry you! You don't strike me as the wifely kind. You can't be serious."

"Well, I am! Why did you send me the roses? Take me to dinners and fancy gaming houses? The opera? Certainly I mean something to you."

"You bet," he stated matter-of-factly. "I enjoy your company and I was investing in you. I want you as my mistress."

The words stunned her. "M-mistress! How dare you insult me so!" Camry choked. She brought back her arm and released a stinging slap on his arrogant cheek. "You cad!"

His silver-gray eyes flashed daggers and he clasped her wrists, pinning her to a wall, his lips crushing hers. He kissed her long and hard, artfully parting her lips, he thrust his tongue inside her mouth possessively. She struggled to be free from his hold and finally he raised his head.

"I hate you," she hissed between clenched teeth. How could she have been so blind to him? "Get out."

Frank released her and straightened his lapel. "I'm willing to give you another chance, Camry. This town can drain a person to a dry stream bed. You'll need me one day. You're lucky I won't hold a grudge." He turned and departed. Closing the door behind him, he leaned against it for a moment. He'd meant everything he'd said. He knew she'd come back. She was like a royal flush; it wasn't dealt often, but when it showed up, the value was extremely great.

The crash of ceramic hitting wood vibrated behind him. A small trickle of water seeped under the door and onto the hall carpet. He drew his watch and checked the time. Still early enough for Pat Lynch's. He descended the stairs to the lobby. He'd put up with all the trivialities of a proper escort and now it was time to play the way *he* wanted to. It was his turn to deal the cards. He'd wait. All cardsharps had patience when the pot was worth winning.

Camry collapsed onto the bed, her emotions in a turmoil She was more frightened than she'd ever been in her life. She stared at the crushed roses and fragmented vase on the patterned carpet. To think, she had actually defended him as a gentleman! What had made him change so abruptly, or had he been that way all along and she just hadn't seen it? What would she do now? It was Sunday night and her father expected her to marry on Tuesday. How she loathed Frank Marbury! And what had he said about Da? Certainly her father wasn't short of funds. He never was . . . why, he'd spoiled her all her life . . .

The Washoe zephyrs blew into the room, ruffling the half-drawn shade. The wind extinguished the kerosene flame and she sat in darkness. N*ot the wifely type*. The insult hurt her far more than she cared to admit.

The Hale & Norcross whistle let off steam in the distance and a few minutes later, the miners' boots scraped over the boardwalk. Two voices drifted up from the street, their speech slurred with liquor. One yelled an obscenity and the other retorted with an even cruder remark. Camry lifted the shade and looked at the pair. Her green eyes narrowed hotly. She had taken enough abuse for one night, even if this wasn't directed at her, she still had to listen to it. She went to the washstand and picked up a bottle of perfume and stood in front of the window. Hurling the glass atomizer into the street, she just missed one of them. In the darkness, the drunks couldn't tell where the bombardment came from.

She pulled the shade down roughly and sat in the rocker. The sun wouldn't rise soon enough. She must ask her father for an extension. She needed more than two days to find a husband.

9

The fiery orange ball of sun peeked over Sugarloaf announcing a new day. Heat rained through the sky dropping on the inhabitants below. Chinatown stirred. Already, large cast-iron vats of lye soap bubbled. Steam rose from the black tubs, filling the air with pungent alkali. Chickens clucked and pecked at the dusty earth. The roosters regally watched the hens, then jiggled their combs and crowed. Dogs yelped and nipped at the feet of the men in camp. The Chinamen wore loose-fitting tunics of gray. Their long black braids fell down their backs like kite tails and stiff satin caps crowned their heads. Shanties lined the narrow streets with flimsy wooden signs hanging above the doorways. Though the names etched in the boards sounded different, the services they offered were the same—See Yup: Washer; Hong Wo: Washer; Sam Sing and Ah Hop: Washing.

Further up D Street, was the infamous red-light district nicknamed Sporting Row. Small cribs cluttered the lane, single story dwellings void of paint, their raw wood exposed to the elements. One of the finest Virginia City bordellos was the Brick House, operated and owned by Caroline ''Cad'' Thompson. The girls were expensive—ten dollars, sometimes twenty. The two-story brick building was quiet. Thin curtains hung outside the sills of open windows. The doors had shut an hour ago, and only Sluice, Cad's bloodhound, slept on the porch.

Nicholas walked down the deserted street, the rumble of stamp mills stirring the earth. His steps were long and brisk. Little dust clouds puffed each time he set his boots back on the thirsty ground. His tin lunch pail rattled and he shifted it from one hand to the other. The heat made his forehead bead with perspiration and he wiped it with a red bandana that was tied around his neck. Stopping at No. 14, he climbed four rickety steps and looked in the front window. Dust covered the pane and he rubbed it with his shirt sleeve. The front room was quiet; a few chairs, bureau, table and mirror were neatly in place. A crucifix hung above the doorway to the back room.

He knocked on the door. "Garnet?" There was no answer. "Netta, open up. It's Nick." He peered through the window again. The door to the back room slowly opened and Garnet Silk appeared. She tied a saffron cotton wrapper around her waist and squinted brown eyes sleepily. Recognizing Nicholas' face through the window, she frowned and yawned.

"You *loco hombre*." She opened the door and blinked in the bright sunlight. "Do you know what time it is?"

Nicholas patted her derriere and grinned. "Five-thirty. Say, do you have a spare cup of mud?"

Garnet ran a hand through her tousled mane, the rich jet tresses resting on her hips. "I'll give you mud, Nicky. Right in your *loco* blue eyes."

"Don't be sour. I've got twenty minutes before the Con-VA blows." He smiled, his dimples impish. "Come on, darlin'. Be a sport and put on some coffee."

She scowled and went into the back room. The furniture consisted of a small bed and black potbellied stove. She piled wood chips into the center and struck a match. "You know, I only went to bed one hour ago." Her voice was muffled and Nicholas heard the rattling of iron pots.

"You have a busy night?" he asked from the front room.

"Everybody went to a wedding." The back door opened and the squeak of a pump handle vibrated the ground. The dry hinges on the door creaked and groaned shut. Garnet joined Nicholas and sat at the table with him. "Annie got married."

"Is that right?" He stretched his feet in front of him

and rolled up the sleeves of his brown work shirt.

Lifting the lid of a cigar box resting on the table, Garnet pulled out a pouch of tobacco and rolling papers. "Last month she gets a johnny who cannot pay. So he say he give her the deed to his mine." She layered the onion skin with the dark weed, then brought the cigarette to her lips and sealed it. 'He do not think it worth nothing. Annie, she think different. She starts to work the claim and no kidding if she do not find rich silver ore!"

Nicholas chuckled and struck a match for her. "So the gent married her to get the claim back."

Garnet shrugged. "You *hombres* are all alike. You think we dames do not know nothing."

"On the contrary, I think you're quite resourceful."

She smiled at him. "You're pretty when you smile, Garnet," Nicholas remarked softly. "You rarely do."

The expression immediately left and she frowned. "What do I have to be happy about?"

"You got out of Cad's, didn't you? You're on your own," he pointed out.

"On my own and busy. There were *mucho* of the groom's *amigos* to amuse." The coffee pot sputtered and she went to the stove to retrieve it. Setting the chipped blue pot on the table, she poured two cups. "What's biting you, Nicky? You have a problem? You need *amiga?*"

She could always tell whether he came as a friend or as a lover. And she was right this time. He needed to talk to a friend. His escapade with Camry Parker left him with more guilt than it had satisfaction. He had watched her enter town on Tinnerty's mule pack and had actually felt a pang of regret for his harshness. And then when he saw Mike . . . Nicholas looked up to meet Garnet's velvety orbs. "I saw Mike Parker yesterday. He asked me if I'd marry his daughter."

Garnet's face remained calm and unsurprised. "It would not surprise me if you did."

He wrinkled his forehead. "Why not? I've been a

bachelor for a long time. That's a hard habit to break."

"Nicky, I have seen her. She probably be the only true *rojo* head in Virginia. She be quite *bonita*."

Ignoring her statement, he sipped his coffee and continued, trying to sort out his feelings as he explained. "Mike's having money trouble. I don't know what he did with his money. He can't cheat any of the mines, they keep tabs on stock shares. His daughter came into town and he can barely support himself, much less a girl who wants the world."

She listened attentively, taking drags on her cigarette.

"At first, he gave her the choice of marriage or living in Scotland with a relative. She chose marriage, but Mike's not confident about the man she's set her sights on. Now, he can't afford to ship her across sea even if she wanted to go. Yesterday, he went to Will Sharon at the Bank of California."

Garnet's eyes narrowed. "Ha! *Bastardos*! All those high and mighty *hombres* who fight to control this mountain."

"Bastard or not, Sharon gave him a loan at three percent interest to hold him over." Nicholas drew a breath for his next words. "I'm thinking about Mike's proposition seriously."

"You be *bueno el esposo*, Nicky."

He grinned. "Yeah, I would. I sort of feel I owe Mike. Hell, last year when I broke my wrist, he fronted me a loan."

"Do not marry her for a favor, Nicky," Garnet admonished. "You give me money, but it do not mean I marry you."

"Why not?" Nicholas asked, his blue eyes flashing. "You could divorce Scott if you really wanted to. You'd make a damn good wife, Garnetta."

"Do not call me that!" Her Spanish temper fired. "Garnetta Silquerro Evans is dead. Only Garnet Silk lives now. You do not love me as I be. Not the way it should be . . . not the way it could be."

He slammed his cup on the table noisily. "Damn it! You buried her, Netta! You buried yourself here." He felt a sharp pang of regret. He knew why she was a prostitute and it was for all the right reasons to right the wrong things. He was mad as hell he'd mentioned it.

"No, *amigo*," her voice was bitter. "Scott Evans and Cyprianna Banning did. And after they were through piling earth over her, they spit on the grave by taking her *hijo*." She stared across the room blankly. *Oh Caleb, my son,* her heart cried. *Will you remember me?*

Nicholas' face was solemn. He knew what she was thinking. "We'll get your boy back. If you'd let me give you—"

"No!" she broke in. "I do not give my *dinero* to Cad anymore, I have enough to do this myself. This may not be as fancy as her velvet room, but it is my place."

Rubbing his temples, he shook his head. "Damn it, Netta, I wish you'd come back up the hill. This is no place for you. You don't have to live at Hanbridge's. People are changing, darlin'. They don't remember you were Mrs. Scott Evans. You could start all over."

"You do not understand, Nicky. You cannot change the way things be. I cannot go back on the hill." She relaxed in her wooden chair and sighed. "When I be a *nina*, I walk barefoot on a red ant hill. They bit me." She paused for a moment and took a deep drag on her cigarette, the grayish smoke mingling with her words. "When I took my foot away, they forget I be there, but I know. I *know*, Nicky, I am not going up there to get stung again. I am what I am now. I am not thirteen-year-old *nina* from San Antonio anymore. I had dream, Scott Evans be my fantasy. He take me away, we live happy. He sing opera in the theater and I love him. But he is gone. So is our son. I do not know . . . When I find Caleb, well," she shrugged, "we will see. It be different."

"The boy will be three, Garnet," Nicholas stated. "This is no life for him."

"I do not want to talk about it," she said firmly. "You come to talk about you—not me. Marry the Parker girl, Nicky, only if you will love her more than life itself. You are a *bueno hombre*. It do not change nothing between us. I

be here if you need me. Do not pity her like you do me.
It be written all over your face and I cannot stand it."
She stood and replaced the pot on the stove.

"I don't pity you, Garnet," Nicholas said and stood
also. "I respect you more than anyone I know. You live
for your son and the life you're trying to build for the
future. I admire you. Someday, maybe I'll have someone
who I can cherish just as much."

The Consolidated-Virginia whistle hollered from Mill
Street. "You better go, *mi amigo*, if you want to see Mike
Parker before work. I think you maybe tell me a small lie.
You be in love already but say you do it for Mike when I
think you will marry her for you. I see it in your eyes.
They never can cover a lie. You know what they say
about *rojo* heads, heh? You will have lots of *niños*.
Besides, you love a challenge."

He wished he could love Garnet the way she deserved
to be loved, but she had too many scars that put a
barrier in front of anyone who tried to hold her. "You're
right," he winked. "I keep coming back to see you!"

Garnet smiled faintly, then frowned. "Hey, you pick up
those peanut shells." She pointed to the tabletop.

"They're not mine," he defended, following her eyes.

"Pick them up anyway. They are usually yours." She
patted the lumps in his shirt pocket and gave him an "I
told you so" stare. "You owe *me* a favor after waking me.
Now get out of here. I need sleep."

Nicholas took her in his arms, kissing her softly on the
lips and rubbing his palms on her back. "I love you,
Netta." He did love her the only way she would permit
it.

"*Sí*, sure you do," she said teasingly. "Now go. Do not
forget the shells." She shut the back room door and
Nicholas grinned. Scooping up the nut debris, he
grabbed his tin pail and left.

Garnet slipped out of her wrapper and relaxed on her
bed. She wished Nicholas didn't remind her so much of
Scott Evans. Their features were alike in so many ways,
but their mannerisms were totally different. She sighed

and closed her eyes, resting a hand over her forehead. She would not think about Scott. Only Caleb. *Oh, Caleb . . . what are you doing at this very moment?*

Camry climbed the narrow passage next to H.S. Beck's furniture shop. Her cheeks were flushed with determination. The bold lettering of her father's name on the glass door seemed to jump out at her. The yellowing shade was up and she could see Single-Jack bathing in the morning sun. She opened the door and entered. Michael Parker was no where in sight. The desk was cluttered with papers and ledgers and she wondered how her father could keep track of things. The grandfather clock chimed nine times.

The private quarters door opened and Da appeared. "Good morning! This issa surprise," he said fingering his tie. He kissed her cheek.

"I would have thought you were expecting me," she spoke in a gloomy tone.

"Are you ready for the morrow? Who shall I tell Father Manogue the groom is to be?" He took a seat behind his massive desk. Large hands clasped over his full middle. His red beard was unruly; his moustache needed trimming.

"That's what I want to talk to you about, Da." Camry sat in the patron's chair, her blue skirt fanning crisply around her. "I need more time."

Michael scowled, his red-orange brows ruffled. "I dinna think Mr. Marbury would consent to wedlock."

"He would," she lied smoothly, "only he's thinking about relocating to Europe and I didn't want to be separated from you."

"Is that so?" he inquired skeptically.

"Very well!" she gritted. "You were right. He had no intentions of marriage. That's why I need more time."

"I canna give it." Michael stood and hitched his suspenders. Walking to the window, he turned and looked firmly at his daughter. He tried to ignore the pleading in her eyes. It had to be this way and no other. "You'll marry Nicholas Trelstad."

"What!" Camry burst in disbelief.

"He consented to making you his wife and I approve."

"Well I don't approve!" she rebuked. "Do you know what he did to me yesterday?" She gave Michael no time to answer. "While you did not come to take me to church, he did. He kidnapped me on his giant horse and then he had the nerve to leave me in the desert! I could have died! No thank you. I wouldn't marry him for all the crown jewels in Europe! I wouldn't marry him if he were the last man on this mountain!"

"If he were the last man on this mountain, you would have to wait for priority. He told me you dared him to do it and I canna say I blame him. You can be a sharp-tongued lassie when you take the notion." He bent to scratch the gray cat's head.

"I won't marry him," Camry pouted. "I'd rather go to Auntie Maeve's."

"Well you can forget about that now, Missy. It's too late. You'll marry on the morrow."

"I can't believe you're being so cruel, Da." Tears artfully rolled down her cheeks. "Don't you love me? Want to see me happy?"

"I do," he stated, running a hand through his beard. He had to be firm. He couldn't back down this time. "Nick Trelstad issa good man and given the chance will make a fine husband."

"I doubt it," she said sullenly. "He's got the manners of a rogue. He's rattled with some sort of urge to see me miserable. He's been out to get me from the moment I set eyes on him."

"I donna think that." Michael straigthened. "You've nay seen the man but two occasions."

"That's just what I'm talking about. Twice he has been rude and arrogant. So it's no coincidence he's out for my blood."

Michael disregarded her assumption. "I'll talk to Father Manogue this very afternoon. I donna hope there will be any problem—Trelstad not bein' Catholic and all."

Camry raised delicate brows. "He did mention he

wasn't Catholic. Maybe the Father won't perform the ceremony," she said hopefully.

"I think I'll go to St. Mary's and have a visit," Da stated. Moving toward the door, he grabbed his hat from the rack. "Are you coming?"

"No." She folded her arms in indignation, staring out the window.

"Well then, turn the lock when you leave." He perched the felt Frontier on his fiery tangle of hair. "I'll see you on the morrow for coffee."

She refused to answer and he shut the door. It was for her own good, he told himself as he made his way to Taylor Street. The money William Sharon had loaned him was dwindling faster than he liked. He had to get back on top of things. There had to be a way to do it. There just had to or else . . .

Camry tapped her fingernails on the windowpane in frustration. There had to be a solution. She couldn't marry Nicholas Trelstad. Marriage for her meant she would call the shots. If doomed to the miner, she would be at his mercy. She knew it by the way he had kissed her. Heaven forbid she become his wife and have to allow him rights the law would say she had to succumb to. He would certainly cause her pain. She knew it. And besides, he was poor. He was a simple miner with nothing to offer her.

Single-Jack ran from the window sill and pounced on the desk, scattering papers. Camry waved her hands. "Get down from there. Shoo!" The cat saw her coming and darted from the desk top. His back legs slid, causing several documents to sail to the floor. She retrieved the ledgers and was plopping them on the table, when her eyes spied the name: Trelstad. She picked up the paper and examined it. It was a receipt for two shares of Gould & Curry stock bought at seventy-five dollars per share. Her father's bold writing filled in the necessary information. Name, date, address . . . address . . .

She repeated the words, a thoughtful smile creasing

her lips. No. 20 Carson Street. She could hire a thug to hide in his room and slit his throat when he was off guard. As relieved as she would feel to be rid of Nicholas Trelstad, even she was above murder. Violence was out of the question.

Placing the receipt back on the desk, Camry sat in her father's chair. Her green eyes clouded in deep thought. What did every person want? The answer was simple. Money. She ran a manicured fingernail over her full lips. She could buy the miner out of the ridiculous idea of marriage. Anybody could be bought if the price was right. She fingered the sapphire and diamond necklace hanging around her neck. She caught her reflection in the windowpane. Sparkling blue stones dangled from her earlobes. With a devilish smile, she stood abruptly causing Single-Jack to jump into the sill again.

She eyed the cat thoughtfully. "Ha! Trelstad has *you* to thank for this. You worked against your own rescuer. All I needed to know was where to find him." Camry turned excitedly, her heels clicking and satin skirts softly rustling through the doorway. She paused once to turn the lock, then dashed down the stairs.

10

B Street was decorated with a wealth and finery unlike the dull gray buildings further down Sun Peak. One of the Virginia City kings, James G. Fair, lived in a square, two-story dwelling with chaste white pillars supporting an ornate balcony trimmed with all the glitter of Comstock silver and gold. Though most of the town disliked him for his ruthlessness and greed, Camry had admired him all the more for it. North of Fair, resided John Mackay. It puzzled her why such a powerful man lived so simply. Granted he lived comfortably, but he gave away money as if it were a thorn in his side. She frowned at the latter thought. John Mackay wasn't the type of man she would marry after all. It was just as well he already had a wife.

Continuing down B Street, she stepped carefully on the sidewalk planks, so she wouldn't get her heels caught in the cracks between them. She had remembered an establishment called Werldorf's which was next to Pat Lynch's Place. She had noticed it when Frank took her to the saloons. Though Frank Marbury was vile and unforgivably rude, he did show her an interesting time. Images of the gaming tables and the excitement of slapping cards filled her head.

Ignoring the catcalls from men standing in front of Lynch's, Camry turned into Werldorf's Pawn Shop with dignity. Her aristocratic nose and chin were firm and proud, even in a dwelling serving those in financial need. She didn't want to seem desperate.

Gaudy dresses and dust-covered suits hung on racks next to a pile of chartreuse feather boas. China dishes and silver services collected a thin film of dust in the corner. A Persian rug was tacked to the wall next to a painting of the San Francisco harbor. The counter was cluttered with odds and ends. Broken watches, combs, mirrors, old tin pans and other worthless items left by crusty miners in a last chance for a few bits.

Helmut Werldorf greeted her enthusiastically. "Vat kin ve do for you, *fraulein*?" His accent was thick German, and he called himelf "we" instead of "I." His pale yellow hair was thin and greased into a part on the side. The thick goatee on his chin was like a shaving brush.

Camry set her reticule on the counter and dug into the velvet lining. She produced a leather pouch and emptied the contents. "I'd like to sell these, please." A tangle of rubies, emeralds and sapphires sparkled on gold chains and rings. It killed her to have to stoop so low. She had collected the jewelry for most of her twenty years, but she had no choice.

Helmut's face lit. "Vat do ve have here?" he questioned. "Dis is yours?"

She tapped her foot impatiently. "Of course they're mine. Who else would they belong to?"

"Ve kin never be too sure. Der are slews of thieves in Virginia." He produed a thick, glass monocle and stuck it against the muscles around his eye, squinting in order to hold the lens in place. Gritting his teeth, he examined each piece thoroughly. "Vell now. Dis is goot. Very goot."

Restlessly, Camry scanned the shop. She hated parting with the gems and transferred that hate onto Nicholas Trelstad, for it was because of him she had to sell them. All except the gold leaf, topaz earrings that Da had given her for her birthday. Those were safely tucked away between the ruffles of her petticoats in the armoire at the Bonanza Hotel. "How much will you give me?"

"Ve kin give you five hundred dollars," he finally stated, removing the monocle.

"Five hundred dollars!" she croaked peevishly. "You're out of your mind. These are worth ten times that!"

"You've come to sa vrong town to sell sa jewelry, *fraulein*," Helmut said knowingly. "Mrs. Mackay has a string of pearls vorth over ten sowsand dollars. So how kin ve buy dis for somethink so common. It is like trying to sell silver to sa miners or eggs to sa chickens. Vhy do sey need it?"

She glared at him, irritation flashing in her green eyes. "Mackay! I'm sick to death of hearing *that* name. I'll take my business elsewhere." She was about to put the gems back into the leather pouch, when the shop door opened, turning her attention to it.

Frank Marbury leaned against the frame looking extremely dashing in the early sun. His brown hair was neatly combed and slicked, and his expression was amused. He admired Camry's beauty lazily, while he flicked a piece of lint from his lapel.

"Good day, Miss Parker," he drawled with all the formalities of a well-bred gentleman. "And how are you on this fine morning?"

She seethed with anger at his mockery. His silver eyes darted to the counter and it was quite obvious why she was visiting Helmut Werldorf's Pawn Shop. "I said this town could drain a person dry. I didn't think you'd parch overnight." He moved forward with deliberate slowness. He stood behind her and examined the jewelry lightly with a glance.

Camry composed herself. "As a matter of fact, this is only costume jewelry and rather than have it collect dust, I thought the cash would be more useful."

"Is that so?" Frank queried with a sardonic smile. He called her bluff. As an expert of the gaming tables, he'd won wagers of all sorts and knew how to detect falsities without ever picking up the items. He'd seen more watches and rings lost to cardsharps than the average jeweler would sell in his lifetime.

"Yes! That's so!" Camry shot back. "I don't believe it's any of your business." She turned to Helmut who had been watching the two with interest. "I'll take the money, Mr. Werldorf."

He was glad for the interruption of the suave dandy, for it had gained him the sale. Quickly, he reached into his black cash box. "Zat will be five hundred dollars."

Frank's deep laugh filled the shop. "Five hundred dollars is a lot of money for costume jewelry. Werldorf, you had better have your eyes examined. I wouldn't give her more than two double eagles for the lot."

Camry fought the urge to scratch Frank's eyes out. She wished to scar him on that handsome face of his the way he had wounded her pride. Haughtily, she grabbed the greenbacks from Helmut's hand and pushed her way past Frank.

He followed her outside and held her shoulders, harshly turning her to face him. "Why are you doing this, Camry? I can buy you anything you desire. Those trinkets you turned over to Werldorf were the best pastes I ever saw," he said, applying pressure on her arm. He felt like shaking the stubbornness out of her and make her succumb to him.

"Take your hands off me," she demanded in a low, even voice.

The veiled plea in her eyes caused him to loosen his grip and realize the transaction that had just taken place confirmed his first belief about her motives. She needed money to help Mike Parker out of ruination. If that's what it wouldd take to sway her . . . he spoke in a calmer tone. "Do you need money that badly?"

She would never admit to him what the money was for. It would be like admitting she had no backbone. His sudden concern brought a glimmer of rationalization to her and she wondered if he had a change of heart and wanted to marry her now. As if he read her thoughts, Frank cupped her chin. "You don't have to pawn baubles, my dear Camry. Become my mistress and have anything you want."

Her temper soared. How could she have thought . . . "You loathsome rogue! Do you think I'd ever stoop to becoming your harlot? How could I have considered marriage with you! Now take your hands off me," she repeated in an even, murderous tone.

Frank stared at her for a moment. God she was beautiful when her eyes were full of fire. Her lips were moist
and parted, with her breath coming rapidly. Fists
clenched at her sides, her molded breasts heaved in
indignation. He was almost tempted to agree with her
scheme of marriage, but knew he could have her
without the ties of a legal bond. "You are one of the
beauties on the Comstock, and someday, you *will* come
to me, sweet. We're alike, we two. Neither of us has ever
been denied what we want, and I want you. When you
find you can't have your way, you'll be back." He
released his hold.

Frightened at the powerful confidence in his words,
Camry dashed down the street, his deep laugh haunting
her until she reached the other side of town.

The mining houses on Carson Street were plain cabins
and cottages, a handful, whitewashed. There were no
boardwalks, only dirt sidewalks fenced by hitching posts.
Camry clutched her blue skirt to keep it from dragging in
the dust. She forced Frank from her mind as she
stopped at No. 20. It was a pleasant building three
stories in height. The front door was painted bright red
and a flower box rested on the window ledge. Although
no flowers grew in it, assorted succulent cactuses
basked under the burning sun.

She entered the house with an air of confidence. A
small sitting room was visible with a narrow hallway
leading to stairs. Climbing the steps, she reached the
second landing, hesitating, wondering which way to go.
The hall ran in both directions, lined with numerous
doors, the transoms above them open.

"Can I help you?"

Camry turned to see a woman behind her. She was
short and slightly pudgy.

"I'm looking for Nicholas Trelstad."

The woman's eyes narrowed protectively. "What do
you want with him?"

She brushed a spot of dust from her skirt. "It's

personal. Who are you?''

''Mattie Petroski,'' she stated. ''I'm his landlady.''

''Is he here?'' Camry asked firmly.

Carefully examining the woman in blue, Mattie finally replied. ''He's not here. He's at work.''

Her patience was faltering. ''When will he be home?''

''In thirty minutes, usually, but he might not come right home. He's very popular.'' Mattie delighted in Camry's apparent irritation. Nick had never brought a woman to his room in the two years he'd been there and she doubted he was expecting this one. Especially now that he was engaged to a sweet Scottish girl.

''May I wait in his room?'' Camry questioned, her voice teetering on the border of propriety.

''I don't know if that is possible. He's getting married tomorrow.''

Unable to conceal her identity any longer, she snapped, ''I am aware of that.'' She lowered her voice so it wouldn't carry down the hall. ''I'm his fiancé.''

Mattie's lips pursed and she knit her brows. Oh dear! This is the sweet Scottish girl? She was more like a spicy bowl of chili with her flaming hair and hot temper. ''Well, in that case, follow me.''

She led Camry to the right and stopped at the end of the hall. ''In there. He shares a room, so don't touch anything.'' She hoped she was doing the right thing.

Camry slammed the door noisily and looked around. Damn the old busybody. Two beds with printed spreads, one on each side of a large window, were neatly made. A black furnace was in the corner next to a coat rack with work pants hanging on the pegs. She knew immediately which side of the room was Nicholas'. His chaps lay carelessly on top of a footlocker at the base of his bed. The ivory Dakota Stetson perched on a dresser next to a photo album. A shaving cup and brush were damp and smelled of soap. She fingered the hat. It was soft felt and fur combined. She placed it on her copper tresses and smiled at her reflection in a small oval mirror on the wall. Picking up the picture book, she sat on his bed and began turning the pages.

Faded photographs and captions filled the paper. Nicholas at age sixteen sitting on a dark horse. A group picture of what appeared to be a mother, father, daughter and four sons in front of a plain ranch house was simply titled: Home. Camry scanned the photo and was sure one of the boys was Nicholas, although they all bore a resemblance to him, even the girl. Hadn't he told her he was in the middle of four boys and one girl? She turned the page to view pictures not so faded and dull. A beautiful woman with light hair fashioned in corkscrew curls sat poised on a rawhide couch. She held a rose with both hands. The caption read: My Rose.

"Mattie said I had a visitor."

Camry slammed the book, startled, and looked up to see Nicholas towering over her. Behind him was Ridgon Gregory. They were both dirt-smudged and soaked with perspiration. Caught off guard, she was at a loss for words.

Nicholas moved toward the bureau and set his tin lunch pail down. "I see you made yourself at home."

She suddenly felt guilty, as if she'd invaded his privacy. Following his mocking midnight blue eyes to the crown of her tresses, she realized she still had his hat on. With embarrassment, she promptly set the Stetson on the chintz bedspread.

Rigdon eyed her curiously. He was about the same height as Nicholas, with warm hazel eyes. Jet black hair curled around his face in a disarray after a long day in the mines. He offered a calloused hand to Camry.

"Rigdon Gregory, ma'am."

"Sorry," Nicholas mumbled, having forgot his manners.

She hesitated when hearing Nicholas' voice, then accepted Rigdon's offer. His grip was firm and he gave her hand a squeeze before releasing it.

"I've seen you before," she remarked casually, ignoring Nicholas' presence.

Rigdon scratched his stubbled chin. "If I had seen you,

I'm sure I would have remembered. Say Nick, you weren't fibbing when you said she was pretty."

Against her will, Camry blushed. "I saw you in a drilling contest last week."

"Oh yeah?" he smiled. "And you'd choose this Norwegian Viking over me?" He pretended to be hurt. "I'd make a better husband than him."

Nicholas untied the damp, red bandana from his neck. "You old bear, Rig. You wouldn't get married if the mountain caved in."

"If I could marry up with this little gem . . . I might consider it."

Camry stood angrily. She had remained silent during their barrage of words long enough. "I'm nobody's fiance!"

Rigdon caught the glint of fury in Camry's eyes and bowed gracefully from the room, not wanting to be in the line of fire.

Ignoring her outburst, Nicholas shut the door. The transom was open, along with the window, allowing a warm breeze to billow through the room.

She sat on the bed again. "Your old bird of a landlady almost didn't let me in. I had to degrade myself by telling her you *are* my fiancé. As farfetched as *that* is!"

He hadn't looked at her since Rigdon left, and now he was moving about in the room as if she weren't there. He'd been asking himself just what the hell he was getting into. "Mattie is protective. You're not the first woman to visit."

"Am I supposed to be impressed?"

He turned around to meet her gaze. "Am I? By your visit?" He strode to the washstand in the corner and began unbuttoning his brown work shirt. She looked away as the material fell free from his broad back.

Taking a deep breath, Camry began. "Let's get to the problems at hand." Unconsciously, her eyes moved like magnets to his powerful body. Tightly corded muscles danced with each movement as he splashed water on his dirt-smeared face. Powerful biceps flexed with each dip into the bowl.

"I didn't know there was a problem," Nicholas pretended, rubbing his face dry with a thick cotton towel. He sat on Rigdon's bed, across from her, and began removing his boots. They fell to the floor with a thud.

"Do you have to do this *now*?" Camry snapped, annoyed.

"Darlin', I'm hungry and the Sundowner has a two inch thick steak with my name on it." He pulled off his socks and wiggled his toes.

She frowned. "My heaven's, are you going to remove your trousers also?"

He winked and the familiar grin etched his lips. "I was getting to that." Standing, he began to unbutton the waistband of his lightweight work pants.

Camry bolted to the window and concentrated on the activities below. The dusty street was crowded with miners—the clean men, leaving for the deep shafts; the dirty and perspiring men, coming out of the black bowels.

"This is ridiculous!" she said, her nerves on edge. "I've come here to discuss our situation and you're making it quite difficult."

"Darlin'," Nicholas's voice was muffled as he searched the footlocker for a clean pair of denim Levi's. "Like I said, I didn't know there was a problem."

She continued to stare out the window. "This whole idea of our marriage is ludicrous."

"That's a matter of opinion." He'd been thinking quite a bit about it. He felt he owed Mike a favor—but that wasn't the real reason. He wanted to break her, tame her as he would a wild mare—but that wasn't really the truth either. He thought he was capable of protecting her, something which she needed, whether she knew it or not. And he thought he could truly love her and she could love him. He would be good for her. It might take time, but they would be good together. "Yes," he repeated, his words clearing and the deepness of his voice flowing free of the trunk lid, "that is a matter of opinion. You can look now."

"I fail to see why—" Turning, she clipped her words. "You, you! You are the rudest man I have *ever* met!"

Nicholas's mouth turned into a grin and he crossed his arms over a bare, golden-haired chest. Lean legs were slightly spread apart and he was dressed in a pair of red long johns cut off at the knees. "You're blushing," he teased.

"You tricked me!" she cried. "You are a rodent and vermin of the lowest grade and I hate you!"

His strong laugh filled the room as he slipped his sinewy legs into a pair of Levi's. All doubts were washed away. "And I adore you."

She balled her fingers into fists at her side. "Why do you want this marriage to take place?"

"Because I want to get married," he said matter-of-factly.

"Well, why pick on me? I've done nothing to you."

"I don't want to marry anyone else." He buttoned a blue plaid shirt which illuminated the deep color of his eyes. His cheeks wore a healthy glow and sun-blond hair rested around his neck and wide shoulders. The strawberry-blond moustache was neatly trimmed. Hitching his suspenders, he sat on Rigdon's bed and put on clean socks. Picking up his discarded boots, he turned each one upside down and shook it out before stepping in.

Camry looked at him quizzically.

He caught the stare and explained. "It's a habit I picked up in Arizona. You never can tell if a fuzzy terantula is sleeping in the bottom of your boot."

Involuntarily, she curled her toes in the black kid slippers on her feet. She had wasted enough time and came right to the point. "I'm willing to settle this here and now." She dug into her reticule and pulled the greenbacks from the lining. She extended them to him and he took them.

"Your dowry, I assume?" he asked.

"I should say not," she replied tersely. "I'm worth far more than that! No, it's a peace offering."

Nicholas spread his legs slightly and rested his elbows

on his knees. He clasped his fingers together. "A bribe," he said bluntly.

She fidgeted with the strings on her bag. "You could call it that. Oh Lord, I don't want to marry you any more than you want to marry me."

"But I do want to marry you, very much." He walked to the bureau and after placing his Stetson over his silky locks, he faced her. "I'll hold onto this for you. Maybe I'll have your father invest it in Con-VA. I don't know what sort of man you think I am, lady, but tomorrow I'm getting married and so are you. So to hell with all this."

"I won't marry you!" Camry snapped. "I won't! You'll never make me happy."

"I make everybody happy." He placed a hand on the door knob. "But, darlin', I don't think *you* know what happiness is." He disappeared down the hallway.

Angry and flushed, Camry stood in the center of the room. "I know how to be happy!" she declared loudly. She had come with the intention of dominating him, instead, he had turned the tables. There must be a way to get the best of him. And she wasn't going to stop trying!

She left the boardinghouse and hailed a hackney. Sitting on the worn, leather seat, she contemplated all the vile things she wanted to do to him. Nicholas Trelstad was a conceited bore and the way to get to him would be to damage his male ego. She pondered several deeds, finally settling on humiliation. Who liked to be humiliated? She would figure out something so horrible, he would never want to show his face again.

The driver stopped in front of the Bonanza Hotel and asked for the fare. She reached into her bag and halted in mid-motion. Nicholas had all her money! She was filled with fresh anger.

Even out of her sight, he caused her nothing but trouble.

11

Camry irritably slammed the hotel door and moved about her room noisily, tipping over a crystal vial of perfume. She had had to run upstairs and snatch a few coins from the bottom of her empty jewelry box in order to pay the driver. Now alone, boiling mad, she could barely keep from hurling the blue and white washbowl out the window. She rang for a glass of sherry. It didn't matter if it was only three in the afternoon—she needed something to calm her frazzled nerves.

Removing her net gloves and blue satin hat, she dropped them on the carpet. As she sat on the bed, she crushed a rectangular box that she hadn't noticed before. Pulling it out from her her skirts, she lifted the lid. Yards of white silk and Venetian lace tumbled onto the bedspread. An envelope floated into her lap and she revealed the card. The gown was from Nicholas.

Camry raised the dress to her chin, examining it critically in the full-length mirror. The bodice was shimmering satin. Sheer, long, puffed sleeves were embroidered with satin roses around the cuffs. Seed pearls buttoned down the back, flowing into a train that was at least ten feet long. The dress was beautiful . . .

She dropped the gown in the box, angry at herself for even taking the time to look at it. The nerve of the man! He was impossible. No lady would accept such a gift from a man.

A timid knock sounded, one Camry was getting used to. Dora, the housemaid, entered with a silver tray and crystal glass of sparkling sherry.

"I 'ave yer wine, mum."

"Bring me the bottle," Camry ordered. She had the sudden urge to see if being drunk could solve her problems.

Sitting in the rocking chair, she sipped the liquid, pondering her dilemma. She could sell some of her gowns and leave Virginia City. But without any other money, where could she go? She had no more jewelry, except the topaz earrings, and she wouldn't part with them. She rocked vigorously; her hands dangled over the arms of the chair, her left hand gripping the wineglass tightly. She would have to stay in Virginia City. Besides, her father was here and that was her whole reason for coming. She wouldn't leave without him. If only he would leave with her . . . Dora returned with the sherry bottle and quickly left.

Nicholas Trelstad. Nick Trelstad. Trelstad. Mrs. Nicholas Trelstad. Mrs. Nick Trelstad. Mrs. Camry Parker Trelstad. She repeated the names over and over. She couldn't marry him. Not in a hundred years. She finally had to admit his masculinity intimidated her. It wasn't only his social standing, it was him. He wasn't a man to be trifled with. She didn't think he could be as easily manipulated as Frank Marbury. And now she even had her doubts about Frank. Maybe she just wasn't using her head. She never had any trouble with her beaux in Philadelphia, but then they weren't as experienced as Nicholas . . .

The afternoon wore on and the fiery globe of sun slid behind the Sun Peak. Street lamps were lit, tiny insects attracted to the halos of yellow brightness. Pianos tinkled and banjos twanged. Screams and loud excited voices belted through the hot night. Camry continued to rock, slowly, the familiar noises of pumps and stamps soothing her emotions. She had drunk half the bottle, and her problems became distant and unimportant. Before long, the glass slipped from her fingers and fell to the padded carpet. With no solution to her quandary, Camry Dae Parker closed tawny lids to a dreamless sleep.

* * *

There was a knocking, continuous and annoying. Camry tried to roll over and blot out the disturbing tapping, but her back ached too much to move. The pounding continued.

"Mum? Are ye abed?"

She fluttered her lids open, the emerald eyes dull, focusing sleepily. To her surprise, she was still clothed in yesterday's blue gown, now a withered and wrinkled mess. Even the soft kid shoes still covered her small feet. The infernal knock rapped again.

"What? What!" she snapped. She stood slowly, rubbing the small of her back while opening the door to see Dora's concerned face.

"I've been 'ere for nigh ten minutes, mum. I was just 'bout to fetch the 'ouse key."

"Well?" Camry pulled a pin from her copper waves where it dug into her scalp. "What is it?"

"Yer father, mum," Dora spoke softly. " 'e's down in the lobby waitin' fer ye."

All too soon the doom of the day flooded through her. She massaged her temples. "Tell him—" She needed time to think. "Tell him I'll meet him at the church."

"Yes, mum." Dora departed eagerly, before Camry's grumpy mood worsened.

Splashing water on her face, she stared at her reflection in the mirror. What was she going to do? As if to add to her dreary mood, sorrowful music drifted through her open window. She peered down C Street to see an assemblage of mourners. Two black stallions pulled a white coach encased with glass. She could see the dark, shiny casket with bright gold handles. A pile of wild flowers topped the coffin in vivid blues and reds. The mourners trailed slowly behind. Men with sober expressions walked automatically, while women cried, veiled in black, hands covered with dark gloves. A band marched in the rear, the trumpets blaring remorsefully.

She smoothed back a dark brow. Heat made a fine mist on her forehead. The hearse passed under her

window, making its way to the edge of town and finally
Boot Hill. If she were only so lucky to be going to a
funeral instead of a wedding—preferably Nicholas'
funeral. She watched the procession disappear into a
cloud of dust left behind by the horses' hooves. With a
sigh, she dropped the lace curtains back into place.

Sun streaked through the stained glass windows of St.
Mary's in the Mountains, causing a kaleidoscope of
blue, green, red and gold to splash on the redwood
pews. The marble altar was covered with a scarlet shawl
and two silver candle holders. Several people sat in the
pews, but for the most part, the grand church was
empty. Father Patrick Manogue, Michael Parker and
Nicholas Trelstad stood in front of the altar, whispering.

Michael fumbled with his watch chain, periodically
drawing out the timepiece. His unruly red hair was
combed into a mass of flaming curls; the beard and
moustache still jagged. Father Manogue held a small
Bible, his large hand almost hiding the black book from
view. A beaded rosary swung from his hips, rubbing
against the long, black cassock that enveloped his giant
form.

"She's nay comin'," Michael said, patting his
perspiring brow with a handkerchief.

"I hope she does, Parker," Father Manogue replied. "I
normally don't perform marriage ceremonies unless
they're Catholic, but I've been in enough mining towns
to know that a parson for each denomination isn't
always possible."

Michael pulled a plug of tobacco from his vest pocket
and was about to bite the tip, when he caught a glare
from Mattie Petroski who was sitting in the front row.
She shook her head, the silk violets on her straw hat
bobbing warningly. Feeling guilty, he replaced the plug,
realizing there were no cuspidors in the house of the
Lord and he certainly couldn't spit on the floor! He
checked his watch again. "She's too stubborn for her
own good. Damnation, I shoulda sent her back to

Scotland when I had the chance."

Nicholas, who had remained silent during their exchange, spoke. "She'll come," he said confidently.

"I donna know how you can be so sure, Nick. She's got a Scot's temperament."

"And I have a Norwegian temperament, but I'm here." He paced slowly in front of the altar, his hands clasped behind him. He was dressed in brown trousers and a waistcoat with two shades of gray. The jinglebobs on his best leather boots rang with each step. A blue silk bandana was knotted around his neck—he refused to wear a tie—and a crisp, white shirt was buttoned so tightly, he often stuck a finger in the collar as if to loosen the binding material. His facade was calmer than his internal feelings. What if she didn't come? What if she had talked Marbury into marriage? He told himself he would almost be relieved, but he wasn't as convincing as he'd hoped. A faint smile etched his lips. He wondered if she had the courage to wear the dress he'd bought for her. He knew no gently bred lady would accept the gift . . . but if he was going to be her husband— what did it matter? He thought the dress was rather beautiful.

He hadn't slept much during the night, wondering about a life with her. He finally admitted she was the only woman he would want to marry. Even if her edges were ruffled, she just needed time to adjust to things. He felt a pang of melancholy. Garnet had adjusted. He wished she had come to the ceremony. She had been by his side for quite some time. She knew him better than he knew himself at times. Yet, she would not come.

One of the two heavy foyer doors opened and shut, the loud noise echoing through the quiet church. A figure moved under the back balcony of pews, where sunlight bathed her dark form.

Father Manogue's full brows arched. "Excuse me a moment. She must be one of the mourners from St. Paul's." He started toward the petite woman clad in black. Her hands were gloved and face veiled.

Michael put a hand on the priest's broad back. "Never mind." He addressed the woman in a tone louder than decorum permitted in a church. "Missy!" his voice boomed. "What is the meanin' a this?!"

Camry took a step forward. The sun filtered through the black veil, revealing the face beneath it. The chin was set defiantly, the eyes flashing daringly. Several guests murmured softly, each staring at the dark figure who was supposed to be the bride.

Patrick Manogue frowned. "I don't understand. This was to be a wedding, not a requiem mass."

Nicholas ran a hand through his thick hair. "I'll handle this." He took long stride and reached Camry, forcefully taking her elbow, and leading her back to the foyer. Releasing her abruptly, his eyes clouded with anger. "What the hell sort of joke are you playing?"

She smiled smartly beneath the sheer veil. "Maybe now you can see, I'd rather go to a funeral than marry you!"

"How could you do this to your father? And where is the wedding dress I bought you? It cost a damn week's pay."

"*That* wedding gown is in the rag bag where it belongs. You're angry? Maybe embarrassed I'm dressed in widow's weeds?"

He studied her a moment. Blond hair curled around his shoulders in a handsome disarray. Camry backed away as his eyes caressed her lightly, then he laughed deeply. "I'm not embarrassed at all. You've only succeeded in making yourself look like an ass—not me." He pulled her roughly to him, sinewy arms wrapping about her small waist. His face was inches from hers and she could feel his warm breath through the thin veil. He spoke evenly, "We're getting married. I'm not Catholic, but by God—and I do believe in him—when the Father asks you anything you don't think you can answer truthfully, don't look me or him in the eyes when you lie." His voice was strong and she wished he wouldn't hold her so tight.

"Come on." Nicholas guided her down the aisle, the guests gasping at her scandalous wedding garb.

Father Manogue rubbed his temple lightly. "Do you still want to go through with this?"

Nicholas looked sharply at Camry, his face tight and stern. She meekly replied, yes.

Michael's countenance relaxed and he sighed, then took a seat in the front pew. He mopped his forehead with his damp handkerchief before kneeling.

The priest gestured for Camry and Nicholas to kneel at the altar. His cassock rippled as he took a white stole from the marble mantel. He kissed the gold lettering at the hem before placing it around his neck.

"Wait a minute." Nicholas turned to Camry and lifted the dark veil, adding softly, "In case you decide to look at me."

The Father opened his Bible and began. "I shall go unto the altar of God—"

Camry blocked the rest from her mind. This couldn't be happening. She was certain his anger at seeing her in widow's weeds would convince him to drop the whole thing. But where had she gone wrong? All he had to do was hold her and gaze at her with those magnificent midnight-blue eyes. This wasn't supposed to be happening.

The ceremony proceeded quickly and soon Camry felt the weight of a gold band around her finger . . . for better or worse. She felt as if she were suffocating. Once they were pronounced man and wife, she turned to run down the aisle, but Nicholas circled her waist with a protective arm. "I believe this is when I get to kiss the bride." His mouth was surprisingly gentle on hers. He lingered over her, his body pressed close, melting with hers. All the sensations of the other day in front of her hotel came back. A spark in her stirred and she was relieved when he released her. Or was she? "You don't want to miss the party, do you?" he asked huskily.

"What party?" her voice was hoarse.

"Our wedding feast." He gripped her hand tightly and

led her to the exit. She was his forever.

Camry saw her father beaming proudly, Rigdon Gregory next to him . . . and Mattie Petroski . . . and others she didn't know.

A carriage waited for them in front of the church and Nicholas helped her up. They took a short drive up the hill, and stopped a block from Nicholas' boarding-house. She moved in a daze as he took her hand and they entered a large hall. It was their first appearance as Mr. and Mrs. Nicholas Trelstad . . . .

12

The meeting hall was decorated with colorful paper lanterns and streamers in glittering ribbons of silver and gold. Tantalizing aromas wafted from tables laden with juicy meats: curried lamb, peppered rib-eye roasts and broiled Cornish hens. Various salads chilled on ice-filled bowls. An assortment of confections, shortbread cookies, apricot foldovers and lemon pecan danties were trimmed with pastel-colored icings and sugars. And of course, there was a snow white, two-tier wedding cake graced with cherubic pink angels and candies. Unlit kerosene lamps hung from the rafters, the sunlight spilling through the open windows and gleaming off their brass handles and bases. In the corner, a small group of musicians played western tunes. The fiddler tapped his foot heartily to a reel.

An immediate buzz filled the room as the newlyweds entered hand in hand. Several women covered their faces behind lace fans to conceal gossiping chatter. Men only admired the fair beauty whose creamy white skin complimented her dark unusual wedding gown.

Camry instantly broke from Nicholas' hold and made her way to the refreshment table, her head held high. Her delicate hand passed over fruity punch glasses and grabbed a goblet of red wine instead. She brought it to her lips and drank it in one gulp.

Michael was suddenly behind her. "Donna go drinkin' yourself under, Missy," he warned.

She turned around, startled by his unexpected presence. "I've not nearly had enough to get through the rest of this day."

"I wish to bestow my congratulations, Missy. I know you wouldda rather have—"

"Save your explanations," Camry cut in. "You're happy now, but I'm not."

"Give the man a chance." His red-orange brows ruffled into a frown. "He's more than twice the man you think he is."

"Oh, bother about him!" She said seizing another glass of wine. Her father stormed away, not wanting to argue further. The deed was done. Until death do they part. He had a feeling Camry would do her best at carrying out the latter. It was out of his hands now. There was nothing he could do.

Couples danced merrily around the room, taking advantage of an event to celebrate, even though the bride was disinterested in the party. She had been introduced to the majority, but their names left her memory quickly. She didn't want to know any of Nicholas' friends. She sat dismally in the corner, watching him on the other side of the room in conversation with Rigdon Gregory. Mattie Petroski gave Nick a hug. The gesture made Camry feel more like an outsider. In fact, the whole affair was making her ill.

The band stopped and Nicholas walked deliberately toward her. She turned away, pretending she didn't see him. All too soon, he reached her. "I'd like to propose a toast to my wife." He spoke loud enough for everyone to hear. Gripping her under the arm, he lifted with gentle firmness. "To the sweetest gal on the Comstock. May she give me many sons!" He grinned easily at her exasperation.

Drawing a hand back to slap him, Camry checked herself in mid-action. Too many faces stared. Trapped in a hopeless situation, she was unable to thwart his advances as he took her to the dance floor. The music started, humming a soft waltz. Her mind whirled . . . *many sons* . . . how could she fight off such a brute of a man? His arms were like iron, his hands like steel, his lips like . . . fire. She shivered.

"Do I make you tremble?" he murmured against her hair.

Camry met his stare and smiled frostily. "You could never make me tremble, Mr. Trelstad."

Nicholas tightened his jaw as well as his hands on her waist. She was painfully aware of the heat he conducted to her body. He growled. "Your display of widow's weeds has certainly brought you attention."

"Isn't the bride always the center of attention at a wedding?" She was glad he was irritated. "I think this whole affair is amusing."

"Then I'm sure you'll find me just as amusing tonight, darlin'," he whispered softly in her ear.

Her blood raced quickly, making her skin tingle. He had hit her where it hurt, and she tried to control her look of fear.

Rigdon Gregory cut in and Nicholas graciously bowed away. His lazy grin made her want to scream.

Rig's face was above her, the hazel eyes warm and uninformed over the lover's strife. He smelled like sweet rum. "Interesting gown, Mrs. Trelstad."

Lost in thoughts, she was brought back to the present. "What did you say?"

"I guess it takes a woman a while to get used to her married name."

Camry didn't answer. She would never get used to *his* name being associated with hers. Her gaze drifted to Nicholas' broad back. He was engaged in a conversation with her father. Once, he looked up at her, the midnight blue eyes full of desire. It was too much to bear.

Rigdon's arm was like a firebrand around her and he continued to muster polite talk. "So, how are the lovebirds?"

She glared at him, her eyes stormy. "One of them is flying the coop." She twisted free and dashed for the exit, snatching another glass of wine as she passed the refreshment table. She would be damned if she would take any more of Nicholas' scrutiny.

She was about to leave when Nicholas clutched her arm causing some of the red liquid to splash on the floor.

"You can run away, but I'll see you later tonight." He was taunting her, making her panic. How she loathed him! She pushed off his hand and darted down the street like a scared rabbit. Stopping only once, she drank what was left in the wineglass and tossed it carelessly in the dusty road. The hot sun had set; magenta streaked a sapphire sky as the first silver stars were lit.

Camry entered the lobby of the Bonanza Hotel and bolted up the stairs to her room. She slammed the door and turned the key. Her heart raced rapidly, pumping the alcohol faster through her veins. She stared at the door thinking Nicholas would appear at any time. All was silent. She realized, if he really wanted to enter, he could easily break the lock. She moved quickly to the washstand and pushed it in front of the door. Temporarily satisfied, she collapsed into the cedar rocking chair.

A small gold box rested on the white quilted bed-spread. Probably a wedding present from Nicholas, she thought. After staring at it for several minutes, curiosity got the best of her and she pulled the red bow. A pale pink, silk voile nightgown floated in her hands. The material was so light, it seemed as if she held nothing at all. Delicate lace and ribbon accented the low neckline. A card fell on Camry's lap and she picked it up. A scribbled message in black ink jetted from the paper:

> Thoughts of you and our future. Save this for me.
> The miner won't last long. All you have to do is say
> the word and the world is yours.
>
>   Frank

Camry wadded the gown into a ball and hurled it out the open window, along with the box. A roar of hoots rose from a group of passing miners. "Where's the body that goes in this, Sugar?"

She was so appalled at Frank's gesture, she grabbed the washbowl and pitched it as well, the ceramic pieces shattering on the boardwalk. She slammed the window shut. The wine made her head spin and ache. One thing was certain, she wouldn't wait like a sitting duck for Nicholas to come. She slid the washstand from the entrance and opened the door. The dry hinges echoed in the hallway so loudly, Camry was sure all of Virginia City could hear her. Quickly, she padded on th carpet, her hands and body close to the wall.

An arm blocked her path suddenly, the attack sending her heart racing with a start and she silently thanked God for adrenaline or surely she would have been dead.

"I think this is yours." Nicholas held up the diaphanous pink gown.

"You skunk! Unhand me!" Camry demanded.

"That's no way to talk to your husband," he warned in a smooth, silky voice. A lock of golden hair rested on his forehead and in a single motion, he lifted her easily into his sinewy arms and hoisted her over his shoulder as he would carry a sack of flour.

She kicked and fought the distance back to her room, even clutched onto door frames—anything to slow down the assault and certain raping.

He pushed the door open with a thud, sending it crashing against the wall. Depositing her on the bed unceremoniously, he stood over her, legs apart, hands on hips. Camry rolled onto her elbows and bared her claws. If he wanted a fight, she would give him one, because under no circumstances would she give in to him. Never!

He stared a moment, those deep blue eyes silently undressing her, then he turned and left, slamming the door loudly. Camry darted to the door and put her ear against it. She couldn't hear anything. Where had he gone in such a hurry? She slid the washstand into place again and leaned on it, her breasts heaving from the effort.

Throwing herself on the bed, she grew tired and dizzy

from the wine. She wouldn't sleep. She wanted to be
ready for his return. Searching the room for a weapon,
the best she could find was a silver-handled comb. She
wondered if he would tear down the barricade . . . he
had every legal right. Miserably, she admitted he *was* her
husband. What anguish. To be the object for a man's
lust. It was more than she could bear. She couldn't—
wouldn't give in to him. She had heard too many tales of
the pain a man caused. Her head swam and she wished
she had eaten at the party. She fought the urge to close
her lids and sleep . . . she was so tired. She wouldn't
think about Nicholas. He didn't exist . . . her lids fluttered . . .

The five-thirty whistle from the V & T woke Camry with
a start. Her eyes focused sharply and she braced herself
to ward off an impending intruder. She scanned the
room. The washstand was still in place and the door still
locked. Hadn't Nicholas come back like he threatened?
She pushed back a tousled curl and rubbed her forehead where a dull ache had settled. A lump formed in
her throat and she dismissed a pang of desertion she
suddenly felt. She was confused. He had been so force-
ful, had made a point of telling her he would seek her . . .
she narrowed her eyes as his words came back to haunt
her . . . "I'*m sure you'll be just as amused tonight.*"

"Oh! The snake!" she said out loud. He had duped her
again! Had he seen the fright in her eyes? What was
worse? The actual act, or the anticipation of unknown
things to come? He intentionally scared her and knew
he wouldn't come back after finding her in the hallway.
He wanted her to suffer!

How she loathed the man! He was probably with the
harlot Garnet this very moment, laughing at her! Camry's
angry eyes fell to the card on the floor . . . "All you have
to do is say the word." How easy it would be!

13

Camry sipped the remains of strong coffee from her cup, trying to clear her foggy head. She never should have drunk so much yesterday. Oh, Nicholas Trelstad! He had bested her! Well, she wasn't going to stand for it. The dining room's waiter scurried by, stopping quickly to give her a refill and set a plate of toast in front of her. She hadn't eaten in twenty-four hours, yet her appetite was not ravenous.

A small woman made her way to Camry's table and paused uncertainly. Though clothed in loose-fitting smock, her condition was well revealed.

"Mrs. Trelstad?"

"Who? I mean, yes," Camry answered slowly.

"I'm Molly Sinclair. Your husband asked me to help get you settled at the boardinghouse."

"Oh he did! What boardinghouse?" Camry snapped, staring at Molly's rounded belly. Lord! Was that the condition of all the Comstock wives? "Where is my husband—er—Mr. Trelstad?"

"I'm sure he's at work with Hank. That's my husband." Molly looked like a wilting flower, her mousy brown hair drooping in a messy bun at the back of her neck.

"Well," Camry bit her lower lip in contemplation. "Where is this boardinghouse?" At least she could go and have it out with Nicholas once and for all. She had no intentions of moving into a common house.

The waiter stopped at her table again. "Is there anything else, ma'am?"

"No," she said sharply, waving him off. His constant hovering was becoming tedious.

He didn't budge. "Very good, ma'am. Where then shall I have your trunks sent?"

"What?" Camry narrowed her eyes suspiciously.

He backed away slightly, seeing her impending outburst. "Mr. Trelstad paid your bill in full this morning and checked you out. Dora took the liberty of packing your trunks. They're in the lobby now waiting for your instructions."

"Isn't it a little late for my instructions?" she cried. "How dare you take such liberties!"

Molly intervened, "Maybe you should come with me, Mrs. Trelstad."

"Oh, I'll go with you all right," she declared, grabbing her bag. "Long enough to see Nicholas and demand a divorce!"

The Bonanza manager hired a buckboard to tote Camry's luggage. Taking Union Street to A Street, the driver guided his team past a string of whitewash lodging quarters, finally stopping at No. 25. The building was plain, but appeared to be cozy and inviting from the outside as yellow and white checkered curtains covered the windows. A painted sign hung above the front door: Martha's Place.

Molly led Camry to the sitting room and untied the calico bonnet from her neck. Dropping it into a rawhide chair, she looked at Camry for approval. The house was simple, but neat. Several chairs and a table for the boarders' meals were to the left. A worn damask divan, with assorted throw pillows was at the far end next to a fireplace. And to the right were a chessboard table and two slat-backed chairs.

"Molly?" a female voice within the house called. "Is that you?"

"Yes, Martha," she called back. "I've brought Mrs. Trelstad."

A woman in baggy pants appeared. Her head was down and all Camry could see was gray hair and hands being wiped on a cherry print apron around her waist.

Her task complete, she lifted her head and greeted in a surprised tone. "Well! Hello! This is a surprise!"

"Ma Zmed?" Camry questioned.

"Mrs. Trelstad, huh? Say, you didn't waste any time. Almost every woman on Sun Peak has been after Nick. I was sorry I had to miss his wedding yesterday. Just look at you! You look lovely, honey. A nice glow to your cheeks."

A glow was right, Camry thought. A glow of burning rage. She managed a sour mutter, "Isn't there anyone that doesn't know him?"

"There isn't a miner on the Comstock that hasn't worked with Nick. He used to single-jack down in the Ophir."

The hired driver entered the front room with hat in hands. "Ma'am, where do you want them trunks?"

"Molly, show her their room. I've got a stew on the stove." She turned to Camry. "I'll see you in a bit. Welcome to the family."

"Thank you." Though the reply was sincere, she had no intentions of staying.

Camry followed Molly down the hall and to the right. The room she showed her was warm and spacious. All the furnishings were made of white pine. A cozy bedstead was adorned by a tan spread with Indian designs in rust and gold. A washstand, brass bowl and towel were in the corner. A three-paneled dressing screen graced French windows that were framed with tan linen and opened to the hills behind A Street.

The driver deposited her trunks and left. Molly patted her forehead with a lemon-scented handkerchief.

"I'll leave you to unpack," she said. "I'm rather tired. The heat has been bothering me and the baby's been kicking all morning."

"Fine," Camry acknowledged, not paying attention to the young woman and her ailments. Her eyes rested on the pair of fancy boots in the corner. So, Nicholas had been here already and moved his things. She opened the clothes cabinet to find his shirts and trousers neatly in place. Even in his absence, the items freshly scented the air with his presence. She shut the door quickly.

Camry unpacked several dresses so they wouldn't wrinkle, but kept her mental commitment not to stay. She ventured down the hall and found Martha Zmed in the kitchen.

A roasting pot sat on the stove, a bubbling aroma of carrots, celery, onions and beef wafting through the room. A small table and two chairs were in front of a cheery window, and next to that, was a large, black wood-burning heating stove. The heat was more intense in the kitchen and Camry tugged at her blouse to circulate the warm air over her skin.

Martha looked up and smiled. "Honey, for a new bride, you look dismal. Nick will be home soon, don't you worry."

She took a seat at the table. "I don't care when he comes home. This marriage was arranged."

Ma stopped stirring and pointed the spoon at Camry. "Now don't you fret. Nick is a patient man. Lots of women would trade places with you."

"They can have him. There's no love between us."

"There, you're wrong." Martha insisted. "I've known Nick for several years and he wouldn't have married you unless he loved you."

"You don't know him as well as you thought," she replied bitterly. "He's had it in for me from the moment we met." She wouldn't take the time to ponder Ma Zmed's comment. Nicholas Trelstad *did not* love her.

"I wouldn't be so quick to deny it. Sometimes anger, and even hate, are a thin line away from love." Her tanned face beamed knowingly. "Anyway, enough women-chatter for now. Let me tell you about our routine here. Sundays, everyone usually dines together. The rest of the time, you ladies decide amongst your-selves who'll do the cooking, unless I take a notion to do it."

"But I don't know how to cook," Camry broke in. "Besides, I won't be—"

"You'll learn," Martha assured, ignoring her protests.

That afternoon Camry learned there were only four rooms in the house. Hank and Molly Sinclair occupied the room across from hers and at the other end, lived Martha and an elderly couple named Ty and Emeline Gillespie. The four rooms were divided by the front room, kitchen and the small attached bath in the back.

Martha explained she used to be the cook for the gangs at the Ophir Mine until two years ago when she retired. Nicholas had been a single-jacker up to the spring of 1874, when he got a job offer at the Consolidated-Virginia mill as shift boss. Martha said she had her fill of the early Comstock days and was now ready to settle down and live off her small bank account from her bakery days and her lodging money.

The three o'clock shift whistles sounded in different keys and, not too much later, the kitchen door swung open. Nicholas was smeared with dust and red clay; his silky blond hair tousled and damp.

"Hello, Ma," he greeted with an impish smile, then looked at Camry. He strode to her and kissed her cheek. "Hello, darlin'."

His casualness infuriated her, his kiss even more. He acted as if they had been married for twenty-five years.

"I'd like a word with you," she hissed between clenched teeth. He made no move. "Privately, in your room."

Nicholas winked at Ma Zmed. "She's affectionate. Damn, I haven't been home for more than five minutes and she wants me for herself."

Camry walked away, hearing his heavy footsteps behind her. She entered their room and slammed the door shut.

"Just what in heaven did you think you were doing? Paying my hotel bill and leaving me stranded," she yelled decisively.

"I didn't leave you stranded," he pointed out. "Molly got you."

"A fine husband you are!" Her words were shakier

than she would have liked. "Ordering me about. Well, I won't take it. Last night was bad enough. I don't even want to know where you were!"

Nicholas raised a golden brow. "Jealous? You act disappointed."

"Never!" she challenged.

"I thought I'd let you stew in your own pot. Speaking of which, that's what I smell. Let's eat." Removing the soaking bandanna from his neck, he washed his face and hands.

"I'm not hungry." Camry rudely turned her back on him, arms crossing over her breasts. How could he be so casual?

"Suit yourself." He brushed the dust from his pants and made his way around her.

Alone, Camry slammed her fist into one of the bed pillows. She asked herself what she was going to do; then paced the floor until she was sure she had worn right through the carpet.

After what seemed like an eternity, she stalked out of the room. The kitchen was deserted. Her stomach rumbled with hunger when she saw several leftover biscuits on the counter. Buttering one, she popped it in her mouth. The kitchen was hot and stuffy so she decided to get some air. She opened the back door, but to her surpise, it wasn't a back door at all! It was the bath!

Nicholas reclined in a brass bathtub, a cheroot resting on his lips. He looked up to meet her stare. "Have you come to join me, darlin'?"

"I thought this was—" Her voice trailed and she looked away. Embarrassed, she turned to leave.

"You don't have to go on my account," he spoke deeply.

"Oh yes I do!" she insisted, quickly shutting the door. Camry then ran to their room.

Falling onto the bed, she brought her hands to her burning cheeks and tried to convince herself she hadn't noticed anything in the room but the decor. The

porcelain, pull-handle commode, washbowl, brass tub
with lion's paw feet . . . but she noticed *him*. The way his
bare chest softly rose and fell as he breathed. The water
glistening on blond hair and broad shoulders, and chest
tapering to a flat abdomen . . . she feared to look
further. She had some inkling of the male private parts
having seen male animals, but wasn't sure it would be
the same on a man . . .

Camry didn't dare undress for bed. Suddenly, she
panicked. She would run to Da. He would take her in. He
had to. Before she could escape, Nicholas towered
under the door frame. He strolled leisurely to the
bureau with only the protection of a towel draped
across his hips. His barefeet left small water spots on the
floor.

"Aren't you going to ready for bed?" he queried
lightly.

"No," she stated flatly.

A muscle quivered at his jaw. "I'm in no mood for this,
Camry. I have a big day tomorrow, so you can rest
assured I won't rape you tonight." His tone was sarcastic
with the latter remark. Sensing her misgivings, he added,
"I've never been called a liar. You're safe with me
tonight."

Camry moved behind the dressing screen and sulked.
She was tired. Maybe he was sincere . . . She undressed
and selected a long-sleeved, high-neck nightgown and
pulled it over her head. She let down her hair, the
tresses curling softly to her waist.

"You can put out the light now," she ordered in a tone
that was more steady then her nerves. No man had ever
seen her in her night garments.

Nicholas moved quietly to the table and put a hand
half over the lamp's chimney and blew out the flame.
She saw him in the shadows. He was removing the
towel. In the dimness, she thanked God she couldn't see
him clearly. He crawled onto the mattress and sighed,
pulling the sheet carelessly over his waist.

Walking from the screen, Camry went to the bed and

looked down on his face. "I'm not getting into this bed unless you put on some underclothes." She held her voice down so no one in the house could hear her.

"For Christ's sake, Camry," he whispered. "If I wanted to make love to you, clothes wouldn't prevent me from doing so. I've always slept bare and I'm not going to stop now. It's too damn hot. If you had any sense, you'd get rid of that winter flannel you're wearing." He rolled over with finality.

Hesitantly, she pulled back her side of the covers and laid down. Nicholas' back was to her, but just the same, she stayed so close to the edge of the bed she nearly fell out. She was stiff and tense, anticipating his attack. Only when his breathing slowed rhythmically did she relax. She felt her body growing lighter and soon she slept as well.

Camry dreamed of Nicholas. His shining golden hair in a disarray around his handsome face. Midnight blue eyes framed with light brown lashes. A strong nose and firm chin separated by sensual lips. Lips that she could succumb to only in her dream. She could wrap her arms around his broad back, the muscles fluid under her touch. A warmth spread through her and she stirred. A delicious tingling coursed through her veins. A strange, unfamiliar, but delightful sensation caused her to wake.

Nicholas's face was above hers, the sensitive eyes passionate and questioning. His lips claimed hers again, softly and expertly he played his tongue across her full lower lip, then delved into her sweet mouth and tangled with her tongue. Too startled to resist, she allowed his kiss to deepen, her body turning traitorous. Before long, she tightened her arms around his neck, wanting him closer to her, drinking in all he had to offer.

Nicholas wrapped his fingers in her silky mane of copper hair, his thumbs stroking the softness of her flushed cheeks. His hands left her hair, tracing a path down her neck and shoulders still encased by the winter flannel. He ran his fingertips down her slender side and waist, then back over her flat stomach and finally the firm mound of her breasts. Camry blinked her lids in surprise as his fingers expertly massaged her breasts. The pink nipple had grown taut under his skillful teasing. She frantically fought to push him away. His lips captured hers once again, lightly, pleasingly sweet.

The realization that she had not been dreaming before, but physically responding to Nicholas caused her to shiver with a mixture of arousal and fright. An ache filled her loins, the pain crying to be quenched . . . but by what? Her dreams had never come this far before . . . .

As if Nicholas could read her mind, he whispered softly in her ear. "Don't be afraid, my love, I won't hurt you." Beyond all reason, Camry pulled him closer, her fingers deliciously caressing his soft hair. She lost all fears . . . Just this once I'll succumb to him . . . just this once . . . then I'll leave him.

Swiftly, her gown was discarded and their bodies met; warm flesh mingling together. Nicholas teased her earlobes, then burned a fiery trail of kisses from her throat to the hollow of her neck, and then her shoulder. Camry didn't protest when he ventured further to her breasts, rising and falling with her jagged breaths. The pink nipple needed no coaxing from him and his tongue artfully circled the sweet prize he sought.

A sigh escaped Camry's lips and she clasped him tighter, her inhibitions dissolved, waiting for something more. The something she knew had to happen with a man and woman.

Nicholas slowly parted her legs with his knee and for a fleeting moment, Camry trembled with fright. Everything had been leading to that secret part of her body that tingled with anticipation . . . of what? Moving over her, Nicholas continued to kiss her moist lips then a sharp pain invaded her body, causing her to cry out. He stopped. She was confused . . . . It had felt so wonderful before. Why did he hurt her? He said he wouldn't. She remained still, her breathing coming in short gasps.

Slowly, he began to move again, and the sensations returned in a burst of fervor. The fears quickly vanished as a tide of pleasure washed over her and she wished to be drowned in the glory of it.

Her body had a will of its own and she arched to meet his masculinity with a passion she never knew she possessed. As one, they soared to a plateau she could never have dreamed about. A warmth spread through her as Nicholas shuddered and whispered her name, kissing her deeply. She returned his kiss passionately. How could she have been afraid of something so unbearably wonderful?

He cradled her in his arms, gently stroking the damp waves of hair that clung to her head. A silent tear rolled down her cheek and he brushed it away. She cried for something lost forever and something found for eternity. The dizzy aftermath lingered, a blazing flame flickering to ash. Camry's breathing slowed and her senses returned. No matter how glorious the experience had been, he had betrayed her in her vulnerable sleeping state.

She bolted upright, clutching the sheets to her bare breasts. "You lied to me!"

He ran his fingers down her back, sending shivers down her spine. "No, I didn't," his voice broke with huskiness. "I said you could keep your virtue for one more day. It's after midnight, so now it's tomorrow."

His idiotic logic infuriated her. "I hate you for this."

"Don't be a hypocrite. Hate me for what? Making you accept you're a woman? Who are you trying to kid, Camry?" he smiled sardonically. "It wasn't that bad."

Her eyes flashed emerald daggers. She had no intention of letting him dominate her feelings and her body.

Nicholas got up and stepped into a pair of worn Levi's. He pulled a cream-colored shirt over his muscled chest. His weight dipped the mattress as he sat to put on socks.

She eyed him suspiciously. "Where are you going? It's dark outside."

"Not for long. It's time for work, darlin'." He over-turned each boot and shook it before stepping in. "I've got to make a living."

"I hope you never come back," she declared.

The insult hurt him more than he cared to admit. He had been patient with her. It had nearly sapped all his strength to keep his promise to her and yet here she looked up at him with doe-like eyes, challenging him to leave her forever. No, he couldn't do that. Swiftly, he cupped her chin in his hands and kissed her hard, his grip not letting her twist away. The tingling sensation returned and Camry thought he would make love to her again. Lifting his mouth, he winked. "There are many ways of making love and kissing. I intend to explore them all with you in our years to come."

She opened her mouth, aghast. He meant every word.

"You are lovely, my Scottish wife. It's a pleasure being married to you. I can't imagine any man in his right mind not wanting to come back to you."

Nicholas filled the door frame and turned to bid her good-bye. The moment he faced her, he ducked his head in a quick reflex as a china figurine whizzed past his shoulder and shattered on the wall behind him. "Tsk, tsk. Remind me never to buy you anything breakable. Good morning, Mrs. Trelstad. I wish to have steak—rare—for dinner."

"Then wish hard!" she shouted at his disappearing figure. "Oh bother!" Her words rang down the empty hall and she didn't care who she woke up.

Camry buried her head in the pillows and sobbed for the first time in years. Not for her lost virginity, but for the newly planted ache in her body to be nurtured. Her fear was that Nicholas Trelstad would be the only one to quench it.

14

Nicholas had made a special point of stopping at Michael Parker's that morning. He had to ease Mike's conscience. Though the hour was early, the window shade on his door was up and Nicholas saw a thin shaft of light coming from the back room.

"Mike?" Nicholas entered and quietly closed the door behind him.

"Nick? Is that you?" Michael appeared, looking as if he hadn't slept all night.

"It's me." He set his tin lunch pail on the desk and picked up Single-Jack. "How are you boy?" He scratched the furry softness under the cat's chin.

"Is everything all right?" Michael asked hesitantly. He had been feeling guilty all night and wondered if his haste in seeing Camry married would bring more harm on her than good.

"Everything is fine," Nicholas assured. "That's why I came by. I wanted to let you know, Camry is fine. She's at Martha's."

"Oh . . . I'm glad—"

Nicholas decided not to play with small talk. "Mike, I know the wedding wasn't ordinary, but I wanted you to know, Camry is my wife now and I intend to see her safe and happy."

Michael ran a hand through his beard. "You donna know how glad I am to hear that. I have been worret—"

"Well, don't. I'll be good to her."

The shift whistle pierced the early morning air and Nicholas set Single-Jack in the windowsill.

"How about lunch today?" Nick asked.

The older man felt much better. "Aye! That would be grand. I canna tell you how happy you have made me. You've always been like a son to me in many ways—"

"I know. You've sort of been a pa to me here too. Let's meet at Beck's say eleven. I want to see Garnet for a minute and thank her for making the wedding cake."

"Fine. I'll be there." He smoothed his tie and hitched his pants. "And, Nick. Thanks."

Nicholas gave his his saucy grin. "Sure." If Michael only knew the favor he did him in pushing him toward Camry. After lying with her that morning, he felt a stronger bond than he thought possible. In his own way, he already loved her.

Camry walked swiftly down C Street. She must speak to Da immediately. Surely he would help her out of the marriage once she told him what a brute Nicholas was.

As she reached the Crystal Palace, Frank Marbury was stepping outside. Bright sun caught the diamond on his finger, the gem flashing. His suit was regal; the shades of gray and ebony enhancing his brilliant eyes. He blocked her path and doffed his hat.

"Good afternoon, Mrs. Trelstad." He mockingly emphasized her married name.

"Don't you have anything better to do than bother me?"

Frank's eyes lightly examined her gown of deep green muslin and the pert feathered hat that tilted on her head. "You look radiant. Marriage agrees with you."

Angrily, she read through his hidden meaning. She continued to walk, but he put a hand on her shoulder.

"Where shall we have dinner tonight? Duprey's?"

"You're vulgar." She brushed off his restraining grasp.

"Why, Camry," he said sarcastically, "does this mean I don't hold a candle to . . . Nicholas?"

"Really, Frank, you're making a scene."

His voice grew angry. "Then why did you blush when I mentioned his name?"

She quickly covered her hot cheeks with her gloved

hands. "I most certainly did not!"

"So fickle, my dear. He must be a master behind closed doors—"

"How dare you!" She cut him off. She pushed by him and ran across the street. *How dare he*! His deep laughter mingled with the jangling harnesses and rattling buckboards that rumbled down the dusty road.

She vowed never to see Nicholas Trelstad again. She was terribly humiliated that Frank could sense her lost virginity. As she neared H.S. Beck's, the oath vanished as swiftly as it had been made. Nicholas was conversing with her father in front of the furniture shop.

Camry darted behind a wooden Indian in the entrance of Nowell's Tobacco Works. She was too far away to make out their words. Her father placed an affectionate arm over Nicholas's broad shoulders and gave him a hearty pat. Soon after, Garnet Silk stepped out of Beck's and joined them. She smiled, then spoke, Nicholas and her father laughing.

With an angry turn, Camry stalked away, her green skirt swaying briskly. How could her father do this to her? He would be no help now. Why was he associating with that harlot? Or even worse, allowing his daughter's husband to. She fought back stinging tears. An uncontrollable twinge of jealousy seared her heart, but she refused to acknowledge it.

Slamming the door to Martha's boardinghouse, Camry haughtily made her way to her room.

"There you are," Ma Zmed called. "I wanted to introduce you to the Gillespies."

"I don't have time," she rushed, throwing as many of her belongings as would fit into a wicker case.

"Where are you going, honey?" Martha asked, concern etching her tanned, worn face.

"There's no sense in you getting involved. The less you know the better." She wiped small beads of moisture off her forehead with the back of her hand. Fastening two leather straps on the case, she tugged the handle. In her haste, crystal bottles of perfume clinked against mirrors and heeled shoes that were thrown together.

"Maybe I could help," Martha offered. "Did you and Nick have an argument? That's to be expected with marriage."

Camry struggled with the heavy valise. "Tell me—is it always this hot in Virginia City? I feel like a roasting side of beef." She pushed a strand of copper hair from her face and tucked in under her hat. "Don't worry about me. I can take care of myself."

Martha followed her down the hall. "But what should I tell Nick?"

She pondered the question. "Tell him I'd like to wear my widow's weeds for real."

The foyer floors in the International Hotel were grand marble, running to thick wine-colored rugs. Large crystal chandeliers, illuminated by coal oil, hung proudly from gilted ceilings. A heavy, oak front desk was protected by a covering of thick lead crystal.

Camry's suitcase rattled as she dragged it through the lobby. She had chosen the most majestic hotel in Virginia City to sort her thoughts. The desk clerk gave her a curious stare when she dropped the bag with a thud.

"May I help you, ma'am?"

She began filling out the registration. "I want the best suite in the hotel."

He raised his brows. He'd never registered a woman without a chaperon before. And the single women were usually . . . "And will you be paying in advance?"

"Are you implying I won't pay the bill?" Camry said curtly.

"No . . . I just . . . I only—" he stuttered. Oh dear, Mr. Wyatt wasn't going to like this. The International wasn't a hotel for businesswomen.

"Just what did you mean?"

The manager came out of the office with a serious expression on his face. He had neatly combed blond locks and his clothes were immaculate. A black suit, navy vest and brown tie with a dash of red fit neatly over his slim body. As Camry looked at him, a jolt of recognition flashed through her, then quickly disappeared.

"What seems to be the trouble, Eugene?" he asked.

"Nothing, Mr. Wyatt," he stammered. "I was just asking the lady—"

"Insulting the lady is more like it, Eugene," Camry added.

"Is there a problem, madame?" Wyatt addressed her for the first time. His brown eyes narrowed as he studied her.

"Not if you give me my key," she announced.

Hiram Wyatt glanced at the register, then smiled falsely. "Give Miss Parker room thirty-eight."

"But, Mr. Wyatt, that's the Imperial Suite and—"

He cut the clerk off. "See to it Miss Parker is made comfortable. Have Lark assigned as her private maid."

Camry was impressed. "Thank you." She eyed him coolly, the feeling of familiarity coming over her again. "Have we met?"

Wyatt's smile remained false. "I don't think so."

She shrugged and followed the bellboy to her room. It was indeed splendid, with three adjoining rooms in shades of burgundy and blue: a bedroom, sitting room and private bath. An immense walnut bed and marble-topped dresser enhanced Nottingham lace curtains that hung from ornate gilt poles. Tufted blue velvet chairs matched the blue carpet which was covered with gold-patterned diamonds. A rose-stained glass lamp, dripping bronze fringe, brightened the corner.

Camry was ecstatic. She would worry about paying for the room later. Right now, she wanted to cool off. The heat was stifling. A petite girl with straight jet bangs, an oval face and perfectly shaped almond eyes, entered the suite.

"Is there anything you require, miss?"

Camry ran a manicured fingernail over her lips. "As a matter of fact, I'd like a bucket of ice for a bath. "

Lark apologized hesitantly. "Ice is only allowed for beverages."

"Mr. Wyatt informed me I would be treated most graciously. Are you refusing?"

"No, miss." She quickly departed.

The bathroom housed a huge porcelain tub with a pump handle which eliminated the need to carry water. In the corner, stood a full-length mirror trimmed with oak, the back made of silver and gold dust so it would never need cleaning.

Lark returned shortly, emptying ice shavings into the tub then taking her leave. Camry discarded her clothes and sank into the inviting coolness. The ice water quenched her parched flesh and she shivered, soon adjusting to the temperature. She sighed deliciously. When some of the ice melted, she pulled the plug to allow the excess water to drain.

She rested her head against the rim and closed her eyes. She didn't want to think about anything. She'd worry about money later. Nicholas no longer existed. At the same time, she banished her father as well.

The suite door opened slowly, creaking. Camry called to the sitting room. "You may bring the ice in."

The floor groaned under the pressure of human weight. She trickled cool water between her breasts, then dangled a shapely leg over the side of the tub.

"Lark?" she questioned. Looking up, Camry saw Nicholas standing under the door frame. "You!" she screamed, struggling to cover herself.

Drops of moisture covered his damp forehead, and his square jaw tensed visibly. "I ought to wring your neck," he threatened.

"What are you doing here?" Her arms folded to conceal breasts and the leg bounced back into the tub.

"I should be asking you that question." He stood, arms akimbo.

"You have no right!" Camry insisted. "Get out!"

Nicholas' eyes were cold, blue steel. "I have every right." He took a step forward, and until then, Camry never quite realized how big a man he really was.

Flustered, she sank deeper in the tub. "How did you know I as here?"

"You gave yourself away registering as Parker. An old friend of yours named Hiram Wyatt recognized your name and, I presume, bewitching face, and informed the sheriff—who in turn informed me."

"The sheriff? I didn't know anyone named Wyatt until today," she protested.

"It seems you stranded him in Carson a couple of weeks ago. I should let the sheriff lock you up for a few days to teach you a lesson."

Heavens! That's why the man had looked familiar.

Nicholas reached into the tub, his fingers brushing a trim ankle, as he jerked out the plug with a splash. "You've got five minutes to dress and be in the lobby."

Camry shrinked from his touch. "I'm not going anywhere with you!"

"You're my wife!" He tried to control his temper. "I'm responsible for you. You cost me a half a day's pay, not to mention the price of this suite and ice. Damn it, that ice is like gold to miners. It's shipped in from Truckee. I don't know how the hell you managed it. And you're sitting here cooling your ass while men are dehydrating in the hole!"

She had never heard him really swear! She'd pushed him to the limits, but his attack only incensed her enough to provoke him further. "It's okay for you to while away your morning with that harlot, but if your wife—"

He stopped her short, and for a moment, Camry thought she had pushed him too far and that he would surely kill her. "She's a better woman that you'll ever be." The minute he said it, he regretted it. It was an unfair comparison, but he wouldn't renege.

"You're got four minutes left," he reminded, "or I'll carry you out naked!" He stormed from the room and slammed the door.

Breathless, Camry didn't move. She was numb, his

words floating around her head. She realized he meant everything he said and would carry her through the lobby—clothes or not. She wrapped herself in a towel and padded quickly to the other side of the suite, leaving small water puddles on the expensive carpet. She pulled a fresh camisole and petticoat over her head. After fastening the last button on a saffron linen dress, she decided she would not go back. He would not humiliate her further.

Leaving the cumbersome wicker case, she walked to the open window. There was no railing or balcony. She cursed having been given a room on the third floor. The second story windows had access to the roof of the Cal Stage Offices. If only there was a way to get to the floor beneath without falling. An old rope line swayed to the left, a remnant of a parade banner. Stretching her hand carefully, her fingertips brushed the coarse fibers. If she leaned a little farther. . . Stepping onto the window ledge, she tried again. Her foot slipped and she felt her weight being pulled. Groping for the frame, she fell, her body tugged inside instead of down.

Nicholas stood over her, his face taut. His hands shook and he backed away. "I don't think I can trust myself to not strangle you. Are you mad? Are you trying to commit suicide?"

Camry massaged her elbow that had skidded over the carpet, then pushed back the damp hair hiding her face. "Anything is better than you."

He rubbed his temples. He was trying very hard indeed. Smoothing his moustache, he strode to the bed and began removing the leather straps from her valise.

Her eyes opened wide. "Are you going to whip me?" She struggled to get up, fear settling through her limbs.

His strength overpowered her and he toppled her to the floor again. "Do you think I'm that much of a cad?" He pulled her legs from under her yellow skirt and tied them together.

Camry tried to knock away his arms, but he caught her hands and fastened them to her ankles. "You—you—

You're mad! What are you doing to me!"

Some of his humor returned as he looked at her immobile state. The blue eyes held a flicker of conquest. "I should have done this sooner. When I went cattle driving with my Pa in South Dakota, he taught me how to deal with dogies."

"I'm not a cow!" Camry screamed.

Nicholas reached down and easily pulled her into his arms. His breath warmed her cheek while he continued. "My Pa wouldn't let that heifer skedaddle back on her own. No ma'am. He hoisted her over his saddle and brought her back home—where she belonged."

Camry's flesh involuntarily tingled at his closeness. "Put me down. I'll go back with you. I promise. Please untie me."

"Nope." He grabbed her case and pushed the door open with his foot. "You had your chance."

Several guests whispered when the tall miner descended the stairs with a bound woman whose copper hair floated like angel's wings.

Nicholas acknowledged Hiram with a nod as he marched by the registry desk. "Beholden to you, Mr. Wyatt."

The manager smiled, pleased at Camry's state. He had had a hell of a time locating his luggage last week. And when he did find it, someone had ransacked his belongings, stealing his silver belt buckle. "Glad I could be of service."

Camry twisted in Nicholas' vice-like arms. "You snitch! I'll spread it all through town what a busybody you are! Then we'll see how many customers you have!"

The sun burned brightly, causing her to squint as he carried her down the boardwalk. As they passed the drinking establishment, onlookers cheered and applauded. Some vowed that that was the only way to treat a woman. Camry fought back tears of shame, and squirmed in Nicholas' arms, unleasing a trail of unladylike oaths.

Concealed in the shade under the awning of the Battle

Born Saloon, Frank Marbury's silver-gray eyes followed
with interest. He took a deep drag of his cigar, the
smoke curling over his head. Trelstad was a curious
fellow. He had never met the man, but now held a
glimmer of respect for him. He didn't put up with
trivialities either; the only exception between the two of
them was Frank wasn't one to let the trivialities go
beyond his control. Obviously Trelstad did.

Frank tossed his stogie on the wooden planks and
pulverized the tobacco with a silver-tipped boot.

"Ain't that something, Frank?" a fellow gambler asked.
"Who said Frisco's got all the class? Virginia hasn't lost
her spirit yet."

"Yeah," Frank scowled. "I'll buy you a drink."

The man entered the saloon first. Frank watched
Camry disappear up Union Street before he went in as
well.

15

Nicholas dumped Camry unceremoniously onto their bed without removing the bonds around her ankles and wrists.

"You've got some growing up to do. I'm not going to put up with your childish behavior," he warned.

"My—" She couldn't control a sarcastic laugh. "My childish behavior! You're the one being childish. Untie me this minute! Why can't you leave me alone?"

He roughly unfastened the straps. "Because you're my wife."

Camry rubbed her wrists. "Well, I don't want to be."

"You can't change the law." He rested a booted foot on the window ledge and faced her. "Tell me, why did you run to the International? Were you planning some sort of getaway with Marbury?"

In her quest for a luxurious escape, she had forgotten Frank resided there. Instead of denying it, she let Nicholas think she was still interested in the gambler.

Sitting on the sill, Nicholas ran a hand through his hair. "Get one thing straight. You're my wife, so you'd better start acting accordingly."

"Why?" Camry rebuked. "You don't act like a husband: You raped me!"

He threw his head back in laughter, the midnight blue eyes twinkling. "I did no such thing."

Tears suddenly formed in her eyes, her words soft, nearly inaudible. "You took advantage of me."

Nicholas stopped laughing and rubbed his chin. "Hell, is that what all this is about?"

Camry was quiet, she couldn't meet his stare. Why did

he make her cry? She hadn't shed genuine tears in years. "Leave me alone."

He stood and perched J.B. on his golden locks. Realizing she wasn't all spirit and gumption, and was a sensitive female, he suddenly felt like a cad. Her life had changed drastically and he hadn't been attentive to her needs. "Come on," his voice held a truce. "I'll buy you dinner."

She didn't answer.

Nicholas sighed. "I said I'd buy you dinner. You don't have to cook me a steak."

"I wouldn't have anyway," Camry sniffed.

"I'll wait for you in the front room." He quietly left.

She looked at her reflection in the mirror. Her hair was in a fluffy disarray of bronze ringlets, having dried without a proper combing, and her green eyes were pink and puffy.

"Bother," she muttered. She would go to dinner with him. It was better than going hungry. He had won the first round, but she would bide her time. She *would* leave him. Just as soon as she figured out a plan.

The Sundowner was not what Camry expected. Having been shown all the finer places by Frank, she wasn't prepared for the active cantina. Off to the side, the barroom was crowded with dirty miners and traders. In the cramped dining room, everyone seemed to be yelling for the waiter at once.

Camry looked in disgust at the plate before her, left by the previous occupant of her chair. A graveyard of mutilated bones and remnants of bread crusts scattered over a wooden plate and onto the oilcloth table covering.

"The food is really very good here," Nicholas said, seeing her skepticism.

She made no reply, not wanting him to know that the tantalizing smells coming from the kitchen sparked her hunger. The waiter came and asked for their order.

Nicholas took command. "Two porterhouse steaks—

rare, fried potatoes with peppers and a few of those apple tarts Curly makes." He smiled at Camry. "Say, do you think you could rustle up a glass of wine for the lady?"

"Mister, you know all we serve is hard liquor and beer. Wine on the menu would be like serving mother's milk." He rolled his eyes and frowned.

"All right then," Nicholas continued. "Two Carson beers."

The waiter hurried away, scribbling on his pad. Camry smoothed a wrinkled napkin over her skirt. She had dressed in a cool peach-colored blouse and skirt with ivory lace accenting the modest neckline and short puffed sleeves. Having been unable to pin her unruly hair, she let it fall to her waist, pulled back by an ivory ribbon.

Nicholas rested his chin on his hand and examined her. "You look real pretty, Camry."

She didn't speak. Why did he have to be so nice? She'd rather have him be his arrogant self.

"Nick?" an excited masculine voice shouted above the crowd. "Nick!"

A tall Indian pushed a chair out of his path and made his way to their table. Camry judged him to be in his early forties and of stocky build. He stood with a slight hunch to his shoulders, and his calves were well-muscled beneath tight-fitting fringed, buckskin boots. A holster was anchored around his hips and thigh, the revolver swaying against suede trousers. A red calico shirt was partially unbuttoned to reveal a dark brown chest, void of hair.

Nicholas stood and gripped the Indian's hand heartily. "Keg! Keg Carpenter! You ol' sump dog!"

"Hell!" Keg grinned. "I almost didn't recognize ya, boy. Ya shucked your prickles!" He rubbed his bare chin in mime.

"Did that after Wickenburg," Nicholas laughed. "Damn, it's good to see you."

"I was sittin' over t'there, when I see'd this purdy gal."

Keg looked at Camry. "And I was a figgerin' a way t' steal her, when sonofagun, I see'd it was Nick Trelstad."

Proud of his wife's appeal, Nicholas introduced her. "This is my wife, Camry."

Keg whistled from high pitch to low. "Ya done all right. Pleased t'metcha, Miz Trelstad." He doffed his black hat. "Thaddeus Carpenter."

Camry examined his friendly face. She had never met an Indian before. His jet black hair was straight and long, tied back in a six-inch tail with a suede piece. His brown eyes were warm and merry, his smile bright, and his noise slightly flat. He certainly didn't look like the Indians she'd seen in the books at Hoaks Academy.

"Have a seat, Keg," Nicholas said, pulling out an extra chair. "What brings you to Virginia City?"

Keg sat so the back of the chair was in front of him, and rested his hat on the table while rubbing the peach fuzz on his tan face. Camry thought at least that was authentic. Most Indians couldn't grow beards. "Same o' thing. Nitro work. Fella named Grimes says this cigar maker from Frisco is a blastin' a tunnel t'run off water from the mines."

"Sure is," Nicholas confirmed. He pulled a cheroot from his shirt pocket. "Adolf Sutro. Started digging six years ago."

Keg reached into his trouser pocket and drew out a small oil silk cloth containing matches. Striking one for Nicholas, Camry noticed the index finger on his right hand was missing. Keg, seeing her eyes follow his hand as he waved out the match, held his palm out for her inspection.

"Ya want t'knowed how I come about this, Miz Trelstad?"

Camry flushed. "I didn't mean to stare. I—"

"I chopped it off m'self," he stated matter-of-factly.

"You cut off your own finger?" she swallowed.

"Sheit yeah!" he exclaimed. "It was either this or the whole arm. Got m'self in a tangle with some live dynamite wire. Ya see, I was a layin' on the floor of a

Union Pacific tunnel, when I see'd the spark a fizzin' down the fuse. Now that fuse burns one foot per minute and I can see'd I got me about three minutes t'get my finger out of the way."

Camry's eyes widened. "How did you get tangled up in the first place?"

Keg laughed deeply. "Mexican friend of mine named Pedro did it—ya remember Pedro—eh Nick? He bet ten bucks I could untie myself in time."

"You played a game with your life?" Camry declared incredulously.

"Life ain't worth livin' if ya don't take risks. Hell," he chuckled. "I had ten bucks on myself sayin' I couldn't! The damn fuse burned t'fast and I had t'make a decision —but quick-like. I took out m'cuttin' ax and chopped clean through the bone in one slice."

Camry shivered. "You bet against yourself? That's horrible."

"It was either that or the right side of me would a been blowed off. Can't tote a whiskey jug and a glass with only one arm." He winked.

Made speechless by his comment, Camry was glad the waiter came when he did and slid two full plates on the table. Turning to Keg, he snorted, "You want anything, Keg?"

"Yeah," Keg replied. "Bottle a tarantula juice. And tell that pianner twanger t'play somethin' other than them undertaker tunes. Get somethin' livelier, m'be like, 'Oh Susannah'."

The waiter rolled his eyes and grunted.

Camry admitted to herself the steak was one of the best she'd ever tasted. She looked at the yellow, foaming liquid in the glass tankard in front of her. She'd seen a similar substance left behind horse's troughs; needless to say, it left her with little enthusiasm to drink it.

"How's your steak, darlin'?" Nicholas inquired.

"It's tough."

"It is not," he insisted. "You could cut that beef with a

fork." She stuck up her nose and pretended the meat was as tough as shoe leather.

"Ya oughta be happy t'eat this here," Keg declared. "There ain't nothin' worse than bein' on the trail with nothin' but jerk and beans."

Camry shot him an irritated look and without thinking, drank some of the beer. Her lips pursed and eyes watered. Gasping, she set the tankard down sloppily, the yellow liquid sloshing over the rim.

"Don't you like your beer?" Nicholas grinned.

"Want some of this here?" Keg asked, gesturing to his drink. "It's part water, whisky and a dash of corrosive sublimate—tarantual juice. I will admit, it's a heap better with saleratus bread and beans fried in grease, but I've sworn off beans for a while."

"What's saler—sal—," Her eyes were misting terribly. "That bread?"

"It's made with sodium bicarbonate so ya won't belch —like this." He demonstrated.

Outraged, Camry reprimanded sharply, "Mr. Carpenter! That's quite enough!"

Nicholas suppressed a laugh.

Keg leaned over the table and tapped his forehead with his thumb. "Miz Trelstad, if ya pardon me for sayin' it, but if ya loosened some of them fancy corset strings and let go, ya could be a real pistol."

Camry narrowed her emerald eyes angrily. "I'll show you a pistol! Why— I'll show you a shotgun!" She grabbed the glass of Carson beer and drained it. Shoving the empty tankard back on the table, she wiped a crescent shape of foam from her upper lip with the back of her hand.

Pounding the table, Keg hollered, "Sonofagun! Order another round!" He gulped his tarantula juice.

Nicholas stopped laughing, a frown creasing his forehead. "Don't get her drunk, ol' boy."

"Don't worry about me," Camry chided. "I'm—" To her horror, an uncontrolled belch escaped her lips. She brought her hands to her blushing cheeks and gasped.

"Pardon me!" she blurted. Oh! If Miss Hoaks could see her now, she'd die!

Keg slapped her back. "I knew ya had it in ya, Miz Trelstad! I'm an envious man, Nick ol' boy."

She felt like sliding under the table.

Seeing her embarrassment, Nicholas squeezed her hand. "Beer does that, darlin'. It wasn't your fault."

Her mind began to feel light-headed. "Can we go now?"

He nodded, then turned to Keg. "Where you staying, Keg?"

"Crazy Kate Shea's." He stood and hitched his holster.

"I thought the sheriff closed that house."

"Naw," he said, puffing his chest. "She's still a runnin'a boardin' house south end a A Street."

Nicholas helped Camry from her chair, then placed his arm possessively around her shoulder. She didn't mind, for the room tilted ever so slightly. She had no idea beer had the same effect as wine.

"Ben Webster still runnin' a post by the Chollar?" Keg asked.

"Sure is," Nicholas affirmed.

"I'll meet ya t'there t'morrow and gulp some mud afore ya go on shift. Grimes wants t'see me about ten." Placing his hat on his head, he nodded to Camry. "Beholden for your pleasant company, Miz Trelstad. Ya really are a pistol. I'd best skedaddle. Got me an appointment at Cad's House. Be seein' ya."

Camry watched him leave with a swagger to his walk. He was more a westerner than an Indian. She asked Nicholas about him during the walk home.

"Keg grew up on the Kansas plains. His mother was a Pawnee and his father a white man. One night, both parents were murdered and it was never determined who did it—the Indians or the plainsmen. Neither approved of the mixed marriage. Keg became a drifter of sorts and wandered to Colorado and Mexico. I guess that's why he's a daredevil. He didn't care about anything after his folks died. I met him in Wickenburg,

Arizona at the Vulture Gold Mine. He's one good nitro man. He carries the stuff like it was water."

They reached Ma Zmed's after everyone had gone to bed. Camry waited in the front room while Nicholas turned up the lights in the hallway. She paced the floor nervously, not wanting to go to their room.

"You're not planning on running away again, are you?" Nicholas broke in on her thoughts. "I swear, I'll find you if you do."

"I won't," she snapped.

"I'm warning you, Camry." His voice was firm.

"I said I wouldn't!" she repeated. "You go ahead. I'll be in in a minute."

He quirked a suspicious brow.

"I have to visit the necessary," she ground out.

Reluctantly, he left her. Camry thought about leaving, but knew it would be futile. After seeing to her personal needs, she could stall no longer. Not to be outwitted, she grabbed the back of an upholstered rust and black patterned chair and began to drag it down the hall.

Nicholas stepped out from their room. "What the hell?" Then realizing her intentions, he pushed her out of the way. "Give me that." He picked up the chair easily and deposited it in the corner of their bedroom. So, sleeping with him was out of the question and the chair would be her sanctuary.

Camry couldn't believe he had given in to her. "I—"

"Save it," he interrupted, lying on the bed fully clothed. "Good night!"

The score was one to one.

16

Camry attacked the water pump handle behind Martha's vigorously. In her cast-iron skillet were the remains of scorched beef, black and hard, resembling petrified wood; as the water hit the pan, it hissed and steamed.

Ma Zmed opened the back door and shaded her eyes with her hand. Seeing Camry bent over the pump, she frowned. "You burned it again?"

Straightening, Camry dropped the pan and kicked it, sending the blackened steak skidding over the dirt. "Why, why, *why*, does he insist on steak every night? I don't know how to make it! I will never know how to make it!"

"Honey, why don't you visit your father? You haven't seen him since your wedding day."

Camry knit her brows. She had seen him. However hard she tried to forget, the picture of him laughing with Garnet Silk and Nicholas remained fixed in her mind. She sighed. He was her father and she did love him. Maybe it was time to make amends. She took Martha's suggestion, deciding a walk would do her good.

While she leisurely made her way to C Street, Camry thought of the other man in her life. Nicholas had stayed out the night after she had insisted on sleeping in the chair. The next day, she was edgy and quick-tempered, telling herself she didn't care in the least if he ever came home. He didn't force her into their bed and she continued to use the chair. No matter how uncomfortable, she would not give in. If Nicholas was any kind of gentleman, he would offer her the bed and take the chair. But what could she expect from a common man?

The afternoon was warm and pleasant, not the melting heat of the previous week. Royal blue spanned the sky without a single cloud. H.S. Beck was washing the windows of his shop when she reached the building.

He smiled when she turned to climb the stairs. "Good afternoon, Mrs. Trelstad. Congratulations are in order."

"Thank you," she called down the stairs as she climbed them, then entered her father's office.

Without looking up, Michael Parker quickly shuffled the papers on his desk and stuffed them into his top drawer. Camry thought he looked guilty as he stood up and smoothed his vest over his stomach.

"What's the matter?" she asked.

"Nay." He forced the corners of his mouth upward. "Donna I get a kiss, or havena you any left?"

"Da!" she quickly protested. "How can you talk like that?"

"Like what?" He took her hands and kissed them.

Forgetting to be angry, Camry hugged him. She always felt safe in his arms. He could make her feel better. She studied his weary countenance. His green eyes were swollen as though he hadn't slept.

Pulling away, Camry smoothed his fiery red beard. "Are you feeling all right?"

"I feel like a four-leaf clover, so donna go worrin' about me. What brung you here?"

She stared out the window and toyed with the shade pull. "Nothing in particular."

"How's your husband?" Michael questioned, his hands nervously concealing a document until he placed a stack of vouchers over it.

"Who?" she asked, looking up the hill. She could see the front of Martha's house. Molly was sweeping the porch, her large abdomen swaying with the broom.

"Nick Trelstad," her father repeated in a stern, Scottish voice.

"Oh, him," Camry replied, scanning the other direction of town toward Gold Hill. "He's all right, I suppose."

Michael slammed a book loudly, the noise startling

her. "Sorry you haveta go so soon, Missy."

"Hmm?" Camry turned to face him. "I don't have to go." Her eyes captured his. "Are you hiding a woman in the back room?"

"Nay!" he cried. "I have work to do."

"Why are you acting so funny?" she persisted, as he ushered her to the door.

"It was good to see you, Camry. Come again. I love you."

Before she could protest, he pushed her out the door and closed it. Though it was not hot in his office, Michael wiped his perspiring brow.

Beck was still in front of his shop and she was about to ask him if he had seen a woman enter her father's office, when a low roar rumbled down C Street.

Camry's heart leaped. "What's that?"

"A lion," H.S. said. "Montgomery Queen Circus has been unloading at the old depot."

"Circus," she gasped. "I've heard of one of those."

"You mean you've never seen one?" Beck rested his foot on the rim of a pickle barrel. "Well, look over there." He pointed toward Washington Street.

A procession of wagons pulled by magnificent white stallions carried canvas-covered wagons. Growls and snarls sounded from each, making people curious about the animals that occupied the cages. The street filled with pedestrians and a trail of children ran after the horses.

"They get off the train at the old depot near the Gould and Curry, then proceed down C Street to the lot across from the Ophir works. It's quite a show."

Small feet thundered through Beck's shop and onto the boardwalk. Two boys, one with his front teeth missing, were out of breath.

"Mr. Beck! Mr. Beck!" the toothless lad exclaimed. "Can we go on down to the Montgomery Queen?"

"Go ahead—"

"Thanks, Mr. Beck!" They started to run, but H.S. caught them by their collars.

"If I hear any of you boys was nipping under that tent,
I'm going to tan you good."

"No, sir!"

Beck released them and they ran down the street, a
cloud of alkali dust puffing behind. Sighing, he returned
to wiping the windows.

"Those boys are drinking?" Camry asked, astonished.
They appeared to be no older than ten.

He laughed. "Nipping," he explained, "is sneaking
under the canvas without paying."

"Oh." She saw Nicholas down the boardwalk, his
lunch pail in hand. "Good day, Mr. Beck." She
practically ran to her husband and caught him just
before he entered the Delta Saloon.

"What's the matter?" He grabbed her shoulders to
stop her from pushing him into the wall. His work shirt
was opened to the waist, the golden hairs on his chest,
damp.

"Take me to the circus," she demanded.

He released her. "For Christ's sake, what's gotten into
you? You've never shown this enthusiasm to see me
before."

"Why didn't you tell me about the circus?" She
stamped her foot on the rickety boards, no better than
the children Beck had admonished earlier.

Nicholas wiped his forehead with a red bandanna. Dirt
creased the corners of his blue eyes. "I didn't think
you'd want to go. It's not exactly tea with the Queen of
England," he said sarcastically.

"I want to go," she stated, then added, "I would much
rather go to Jacob Wimmer's for dinner, but we're too
poor!"

"Don't start with me," Nicholas growled.

"Let's go," she pressed, her eyes bright and cheeks
flushed.

He ran a hand through his sun streaked hair. "I'm dirty
and hungry. Let's go home first so I can get cleaned up
and have dinner, then I'll take you."

"You look okay," Camry commented indifferently.

"Besides, there is no dinner."

Nicholas rubbed his temples. "Damn it all, Camry. Did you burn it again? That's the third time this week."

"Well, if you'd eat something other than steak!" she snapped.

"Darlin', you're forgetting my pa is a cattle rancher. I was weaned on steak."

"You can eat at the circus. Come on," she insisted, giving him a pretty smile.

It won him over. He swatted her behind. "Let's go."

They followed the flow of traffic down Mill Street to the Ophir works. Two large tents had been constructed. One for the circus, the other for the menagerie. The grounds were mobbed with enthusiastic spectators. Children screamed happily and ran in all directions, their cheeks filled with hard candy.

Nicholas purchased tickets for the circus tent first. Hundreds of benches circled a large arena. Clowns on stilts towered over the seats, pretending to throw buckets of water on the crowd, but the containers held confetti. Elephants were brought in and circled the tent, holding onto each other's tails with their trunks. Greta Bell, dressed in a red satin corset with black fringe and spangles, juggled knives while she rode two stallions. Camry was in awe at the rope dancing, acrobatic acts and flying trapeze. She applauded and gasped along with everyone else. Sometimes, she clutched Nicholas' arm and buried her face in his shoulder; especially when the fire-eaters performed. She never realized she held him—too engrossed in the show, she didn't notice his eyes were on her more than the circus. So much a child still, he thought, yet so much a woman.

Afterward, they saw the menagerie tent. Lions, tigers, elephants, birds and reptiles, were on display, most of which Camry had never seen other than in picture books. Spurs clinked behind them and Keg Carpenter appeared, gnawing on a barbecued chicken leg. He was dressed in the same clothes she had seen him in the week before. A turquoise buckle brightened his holster belt. A silver-handled revolver swayed at his hip.

"Nick. Miz Trelstad." He dipped the rim of his black hat in greeting. "How do ya like them critters? Ain't they a wonderment?"

Nicholas tipped his head toward Camry. "Ask my wife, she insisted we come. She threatened to divorce me if I didn't take her," he teased.

Camry shot him an irritated glare. She never should have asked to go. Now she would never hear the end of it. "I thought it was all right." She turned her back on him and crossed her arms.

Keg shrugged and addressed Nicholas. "I moseyed down t'Gold Hill Friday," he remarked. "They gotta La France pump only four inches, but she throws a good stream."

"Skinner says there's talk of dropping a new shaft south of the Con-VA. They did some testing and it shows a large vein. I suggested you for the dynamite work."

Camry scanned the crowd, bored. She didn't want to listen to a conversation she knew nothing about. She wandered away, staring at the spectators. Mostly the women. How she wished she had money to buy new Parisian dresses. All of hers were last year's designs. The horror of being seen in the same gown twice was depressing. Maybe she could ask her father for some money . . . Nicholas wouldn't like that one bit.

As she strolled, she assessed the Piute Indians who were admirers of the circus. They wore finely tanned leather with bright beads in red and blue and feathers. Camry stopped when she saw Garnet Silk. She stood tall and shapely in a low-cut gown of wine taffeta. Her black hair curled into perfect ringlets, a velvet ribbon tied around her exposed neck. She linked a hand through a handsomely dressed gentleman's arm and they walked toward the menagerie tent.

Seeing Camry, Garnet smiled and excused herself from her escort.

"I would like to wish you well, *Senora* Trelstad." Her voice was honey smooth with a light Spanish accent.

Camry flushed indignantly. "How dare you talk to me."

The red lips parted softly, her coolness did not sway. "Nicky has told me *mucho* about you." A breeze ruffled an ostrich plume on her hat, the feather caressing her flawless, rose-hued cheek. She brushed it away slowly, with a sheer gloved finger. "I hope you make him happy."

"What right do you have to advise me?" Camry demanded. "My marriage is *my* business. And your business—well we know what *business* you're in!"

Garnet looked down and softly laughed. Oh, this one did have a temper like a bowl of chili! She would have to make the *rojo* head worry about Nicky. Raising thick, fringed black lashes, she admonished, "It is a good thing there are *mujeres* like me. We entertain *hombres* like Nicky, who are turned away—unsatisfied."

Camry's jaw dropped. "Why you hussy! How dare you announce Nicholas' whereabouts to me! I don't care in the least how many times he visits you!"

"I do not announce my client's business, nor do I break up marriages. I suggest you behave like a *buena esposa* or next time, I *will not* turn him away." She departed with a swish of skirts, her sweet perfume lingering in the dry, desert air. Maybe that would push her toward Nicky. What he saw in her, she didn't know, but the fact was he loved her, even if he didn't realize it yet.

Camry continued haughtily toward Martha Zmed's. How dare the harlot speak in such a threatening tone! So, Nicholas *had* been to visit Sporting Row! Ha! She was sure his male ego had been damaged at Garnet's rejection. Why the woman would turn away a paying customer . . . and one as good-looking as Nicholas . . . Camry shook her head. Imagine . . . thinking her own husband desirable. She wasn't going to think about him at all. It was absurd. At least the Silk woman was keeping

Nicholas' money from her pocket. Oh bother, what did it matter if he had a mint, she never saw a copper of it . . .

And that was just an excuse to hate him! If he had a mint she wouldn't love him either.

A fine drizzle had been coming down since early evening, the light wetness settling the powdery dust on the streets. Yet, as always, the heat remained, now cast in a humid veil. Damp wood scented the air with a strong hickory and piñon pine aroma. Gas lamps burned fuzzy, yellow halos around the glass encasements.

Camry opened her bedroom window to circulate the moist air. Even the Washoe zephyrs would be a welcome relief to cool her warm flesh. The sky had not yet turned black. A majestic gray streaked between indigo clouds, fringed by the last rays of silver sun, before it fell completely behind Sun Peak.

She sat on the window ledge and let down her bronze hair. She leisurely brushed its richness to gleaming copper, enhanced by fiery highlights of red. A faint breeze cut through the night and she closed her eyes to relax in the freshness. Her pink nightgown billowed around trim ankles and the gossamer lace accenting her petal-soft neck slipped slowly off a creamy shoulder.

Nicholas stopped short in the doorway. He held a bottle of ale and a tin of cookies that nearly fell from his hands as he viewed his wife. His breath quickened, his bare chest rising and falling rhythmically.

Opening her eyes slowly, seductively, Camry was unaware she was being watched; she stiffened when she saw Nicholas.

"What are you doing here?"

The flame in midnight-blue eyes dulled, and the guard was replaced. "I live here," he said dryly, walking to the bed.

Camry ran to her chair and pulled the sheet to her chin. "I thought you were working the night shift."

He propped his pillows against the headboard and sat.

Crossing bare feet in front of him, he set the tin of cookies on his lap. "Aren't I entitled to what you women call—prerogative? Rig is working the late shift."

She stared at him, a tingling rush filling her heart. He wore a loose-fitting pair of miner's trousers, held up by a slim cord at his waist. His golden hair rested carelessly on his forehead and curled around broad shoulders. As he bit into a cookie, his teeth flashed white against his full moustache.

He met her gaze and gestured to the tin. "Want an oatmeal cookie? Mrs. Gillespie made them."

"No," she answered quickly. "I want to go to sleep. I have a headache."

Nicholas drank some of his ale, then laughed without humor. "Darlin', you're supposed to say you have a headache when I'm making advances. Which you and I both know hasn't happened as of late. So, you can refrain from excuses tonight. I'm not a molester." His eyes clouded, no longer clear.

Camry curled in the chair, her position uncomfortable. She watched him over the top of the sheet. He was so damned confident of his masculinity. Did he think she would jump into his powerful arms? He brushed a crumb from his chest and turned down the lamp.

In the pale glow of the room, Nicholas rested his head on the back of his arm and stared at the ceiling. He could hear her breathing. He thought back to their wedding night. It had been wonderful for him . . . and for her too . . . but . . . Garnet had told him to have patience. He felt like an ass talking to her about it, but had no one else to turn to. He certainly couldn't talk to Rig about it. She'll come to you, Garnet had said. Well? She never said it would take weeks. He'd thought about visiting Cad's Brick House, but couldn't find the time . . . hell, he had the time, he just didn't have desire for anyone but his wife.

It was some time before Camry slept. Her flesh burned from the warmth in the room and Nicholas' nearness. She would not, did not, want to think about him. Finally, in a dream, she allowed herself to kiss him. Only once . . .

The tan linen curtains moved slightly with the night air, the windows still open. Clouds had parted, revealing a snowy moon. A slice of silver splashed in the room a sliver of soft light. Above A Street, in the distance, a coyote howled, the cry alerting its mate.

Camry's brush, which she had carelessly tossed on the bureau, moved slightly. The lamp rattled, the chimney rubbing against the glass base containing kerosene. The earth rumbled deeply, then stopped. Camry stirred, her lips parting, but her breathing remained steady and undisturbed.

Nicholas' shaving brush clinked against the porcelain rim of a mug. The lamp rattled; the hair brush moved; the earth woke . . . trembling up the mountain. The ale bottle fell off the nightstand. Camry sat up quickly, her sheet falling to the unsteady floor. She looked out the window as a blast shook the ground, vibrating Virginia City sharply.

A cry escaped her lips and she struggled to her feet. Strong arms pulled her from the chair and onto the floor. Nicholas was on top of her, holding her close. She clutched his bare back in fright as the explosion raged, then died.

"It's okay, darlin'," he whispered in a soothing voice against her hair.

"What is it?" she cried.

"I have a strange feeling it's Keg." He stroked her forehead gently, pressing feather-light kisses on her temple. The earth continued to groan and shift for several minutes. When the creaking and stretching of timbers in the boardinghouse roof subsided, Camry became aware of their intimate position and moved her arms away from Nicholas' skin.

"I'm all right now. Let me up," she whispered, afraid of her own voice. She had a feeling of déjà vu . . . hadn't she just been in his arms in her dream?

He made no move to release her, but continued to

press kisses over her forehead, eyelids, cheeks, then finally, her soft mouth. He drew her closer, his body completely covering hers. Lifting his head, his silky voice was husky. "I'm tired of your game. It's time we played mine." His lips reclaimed hers, his tongue brushed and nipped the fullness of her lower lip. Camry could no longer control her emotions and slid her hands over is back to knead the warm, taut flesh. He cradled her head in his hands, his breath warm on her mouth as he parted her lips with an exploring tongue. Her breasts strained against her gossamer gown, the fire of his chest seeming to singe the material away.

Nicholas kissed her earlobes, her neck and the hollow of her throbbing throat. She closed her eyes, waiting for him to remove her gown. When he did not, she looked up, puzzled.

He teased her lips lightly, speaking in a ragged voice. "Is this to be called rape?" He had to be sure she would not protest his lovemaking in the aftermath.

In a silent manner, she pulled him closer, her fingers caught in his thick tangle of golden hair. He grabbed her wrists from his mane and pinned them to the carpet. "I ask you—is this what you call rape?"

Her cheeks were flushed with consuming desire and she could not speak—she could only shake her head, no.

He released his hold. "Then tell me," Nicholas bade, tracing the outline of her breast through the nightdress. "What do you want?"

A sigh escaped her throat and she gave in to all she had fought for weeks. "You." Her voice was hoarse. "I want you."

Nicholas tore the gown free in one swift tug. Camry pulled him to her, her fingernails digging into his back. He kissed every inch of her face and neck, spreading a trail of fire to her loins. He circled her breasts teasingly, not touching the taut fullness of her nipples. She snatched his hand and wantonly cupped it over her creamy mound, offering herself to him. He traced a fingertip over the buds that had swollen to their fullest, then flicked his tongue over the peach rosette. Camry cried, running her hands down his side and over his hips. The material of his trousers was soft and molding to his sinewy legs. He took in his breath as she caressed the tight muscles of his buttocks. She was dimly aware that he discarded his clothing, then felt his burning flesh melting with hers. His hands ran down her waist and thighs as she moaned and pulled him to her.

Their bodies met and she arched herself toward him as he took her. Instinct unleashed her into the domain of desire and she wanted the moment to last forever. Her eager response matched his; his hardness electrified her. A ball of heat burst in her and she cried out in ecstasy, Nicholas' lips silencing her.

Camry held him tightly, unaware of the tears of fulfillment softly falling down her cheeks.

Nicholas kissed her tears away. "Maybe that would be called rape."

Suddenly embarrassed, she pushed at his chest, but he held her wrists and wrapped them around his neck. He scooped her in his arms and placed her on the bed.

"I'm paying you a compliment," he said, lying next to her. "Surely your body is as illegal as the act of rape."

"I hate you." She pulled him closer and entwined her legs with his.

"A few minutes ago, you said you loved me." Nicholas kissed her gently, then with an intensity that sapped her very strength. The moon bathed the room in a glow of silver desires and she allowed herself to make love to the dream Nicholas. Surely there would be no harm in that . . .

17

Sun streaked brightly through the linen curtains as noon neared and A Street activity accelerated. Camry hugged a down pillow and opened her eyes. The sheets lightly covered her bare body as she sat up. Nicholas was gone. Putting hands to her flushed cheeks, she remembered what had transpired during the night. She had behaved wantonly, caught in the pleasure of Nicholas' lovemaking. Yet, somehow, she felt an inner peace, as if the battle within her had ceased.

Humming, she went to the washstand and poured water into the brass bowl. She looked the same, except for a radiant glow on her face and neck. She ran a finger across her lips and thought of Nicholas' mouth tenderly on hers. Picking one of her best summer dresses, Camry slipped into a light yellow dotted swiss gown. The bodice was snug, and the neckline tapered to a vee, accented with ruffles and ribbon; the full skirt was layered in five tiers. She brushed her hair and pinned it loosely to her head, decorating the tresses with a comb made of saffron ribbons and white silk roses. She looked at her reflection and smiled.

Camry was sure Nicholas would be in the kitchen supervising Ma Zmed in the packing of the picnic lunches, for today was the Great Pioneer Picnic at Bowers Mansion. Posters and banners had advertised the event for two weeks. She was surprised to see Mrs. Gillespie at the table, sipping a cup of tea. She scanned the room, wondering if Nicholas was on the porch.

"Good morning, dear," Mrs. Gillespie greeted. "Nasty jolt we had last night. My, my, but don't you look comely this morning."

Emeline made Camry nervous. Her hair was a bluish tint and her skin always looked like she was suffering from jaundice. The old hands shook most of the time, especially when she held a newspaper. The paper constantly rippled in oceanic waves and gave off a crackling sound.

"Have you seen Nicholas?" Camry asked, averting her eyes from Emeline's false lower teeth, which rested on the edge of her china saucer.

"No," she answered uncertainly. "No, I don't think I have. I just got up. Ty, he's playing billiards—" Her words trailed off.

Martha slammed the back door and crossed the kitchen holding a large wicker basket. Camry met her. "I'm glad to see," she lowered her voice, "a sane face."

Ma smiled. "You'll be old one day, honey."

"I intend to age gracefully," she said firmly. "Martha, has Nicholas gone to hire a rig?"

Martha spread a golden-brown roll with creamy butter and placed a thick slice of roast beef on it. "I don't think so."

"Oh . . . are we taking the train?" she asked casually.

"To where, honey? Hand me the cheese."

Camry obliged. "We're going to the Pioneer Picnic."

Martha wiped her hands on her crisp apron. "You're welcome to come with the Gillespies and myself. Nicholas left hours ago. He went to survey the damage from the blast last night. I doubt if he'll be home before dinner."

Camry bit her lower lip and fought sudden stinging tears.

"We're leaving in thirty minutes. Why don't you come with us?"

"No thank you," she managed. "I don't feel well." She hurried down the hall to her room.

Standing at the end of the wrinkled bed, Camry took deep breaths to keep from crying. How could she have hoped . . .

* * *

The Brass Rail Saloon held a handful of gamblers at an hour before noon. The long mahogany bar gleamed with polish, and in its reflection, a bartender mechanically wiped crystal glasses with a white cloth. Of the twenty round tables, one alone was occupied.

Frank Marbury expertly shuffled cards and dealt to four players. His facial expression remained neutral. He rubbed his chin, his sandpapered fingertips feeling the fine shave. Silver-gray eyes scanned his opponents, a faint glimmer of disinterest behind the facade. He was bored.

"Fold."

"Me too."

"I'm out."

The fourth man eyed the coins in the center of the table. "I call."

Frank laid down a full house.

"Dang burn it," the man cursed and slapped his cards face down on the table.

Allowing his win to give him a glimmer of a smile, Frank slid the pot to his right. "Another hand, gentlemen?"

"Not me. My wife expects me to take her to the blasted Pioneer Picnic."

The men departed and Frank strolled to the bar and poured himself a finger of whiskey. His jacket was stylish and expensively tailored, accented with a two-toned vest in red and gold. A gold fob chain decoyed the .22 caliber Derringer attached to it in his vest pocket. Dark brown trousers covered his long legs as he rested a polished, gold-tipped boot on the brass railing and flicked a piece of dust from the heel.

Looking out the dust covered window, he watched C Street traffic pass. He stared indifferently at the many faces, until Nicholas Trelstad walked by. Frank moved to the glass pane, his eyes following the miner as he turned off to Mill Street and toward the mines. So, he wasn't taking his wife to the picnic. Ah, Camry, what did you get yourself into? Always looking for a challenge, Frank decided to find out. He slapped a silver dollar on the bar and placed a white Columbia Stetson on his smooth, brown hair, then headed for A Street.

After making a quick stop in his room at the International Hotel, Frank reached Martha Zmed's boarding-house and took the liberty of entering each room until he found the one he sought.

Camry turned with a start as Frank strolled in.

"How did you get in?" she exclaimed. "What are you doing here?"

He didn't answer immediately, but examined her at his leisure. She was more beautiful than ever. Her face was flushed and he knew that it wasn't because of his staring at her. He'd seen too many women with that same blush to their cheeks. "I saw your loving husband leave for the mud holes."

She turned her back on him, holding back the tears that had threatened all morning. What *was* Frank doing here? "It's none of your business. Please leave."

"I'm making it my business." He took a step closer to her. "The man should be shot for ever leaving your side." And he meant that with half a mind to shoot the miner himself.

"Don't lecture me about propriety, Frank Marbury. You have the scruples of a jackass and the morals of a thief and I won't listen to another word you say."

He laughed easily. "You bet." Then he withdrew the tangle of shimmering jewelry from his pocket that he had retrieved at his suite.

Camry felt his warm hand on her shoulder, then cool gold caressed the decolletage above her bodice. She looked down to see her sapphire and diamond necklace resting on her skin. She turned and grabbed the jewelry from his grasp.

"Where did you get this?" she demanded.

"I thought you'd be interested," he taunted. "I bought your baubles from Werldorf."

"You had no right!"

"Of course I did. You didn't want them. And I knew they would come in handy one day."

Camry was momentarily speechless. She stared at the blue stones in her hand and bit her lower lip. Looking up, she met his gaze. "What do you want Frank?"

He removed his hat and smoothed back his slick hair. "That should be obvious, but for today, I'll settle on your charming company at the picnic."

She toyed with the necklace. "Where are the earrings and the rest of my jewelry?"

"In my hotel suite. Would you care to see them for yourself?"

"No," she tossed back quickly.

"I can give them back to you, my dear, but you'll have to earn them."

She was tempted to throw the sapphires back at him.

Then to tempt her, he added, "I'm running a horse at the picnic. I know of a dealer who would give you several hundred dollars for this necklace . . . you could bet the money on my horse and no doubt make a tidy sum. Does *that* interest you?"

She was silent. If what Frank said was true, *and* the horse *did* win, she would have enough money to leave Virginia City . . . but what about Da? Would she have to leave him behind? Would he come with her? And Nicholas . . . she would finally be able to leave him . . . that was what mattered. "How do I know you're telling me the truth?"

"You don't." He didn't tell her, never take the word of a gambler. That, she would have to find out for herself.

Collecting a matching, ruffled dotted Swiss parasol, Camry drew in a deep breath. "Very well, Frank. I'll go with you."

Nearly all of Virginia City attended the Pioneer Picnics at Bowers Mansion located in the Washoe Valley. Special red and gold locomotives pulled twenty-two cars from Virginia, including three coaches and a commissary car, and eleven cars from Gold Hill, including two coaches. Then they connected with cars from Silver City and Carson City to make the longest train passing through Nevada. Forty-five cars and three thousand passengers along with carriages, caused the picnic grounds to overflow with more than five thousand people.

Frank paid a staggering amount for their private suite on the picnic train. He ushered Camry to a bright green coach with stained glass windows. She closed her parasol and stepped in. An oilcloth ceiling provided a background for swinging gas lamps. Chenille upholstery in shades of rust enhanced rich maple seats and furnishings.

She stared out a pale gold pane in the ornately designed window and studied the crowd. If only Nicholas could see her sitting here with Frank—then he'd know at least one man in Virginia City found her company pleasant. The whistle blew three short times and the red and bronze trumpeted stacks on the engines billowed cloudy, white smoke. The train lurched forward, the bells clanging.

"Can I offer you some port?" Frank queried, serving himself a drink from a mirrored bar.

"Thank you," she replied, as he handed her a glass. "I confess, I don't know anything about horse racing or betting on them ."

"There's nothing much to it. It's no different than betting on a hand of cards. When you know you've got a good hand—you bet high." He took a seat across from her and reclined comfortably, his leather-booted legs stretched in front of him.

"How much money do you think I could win?"

"Depends on the odds." Then he added offhandedly. "Up to a thousand dollars."

"One thousand!" she gasped. "I never realized—" She lost herself in thoughts and Frank didn't continue the conversation.

The train clacked noisily over rails, then soared over

the Crown Point Trestle which loomed ninety feet high and three hundred feet long. Switchbacks were gradual, and mingled with tunnels; the smell of burning pine was stronger in the unventilated tunnels.

They rode in silence, Frank appraising Camry as she gazed at the scenery. The sun through the colored windows cast shades of red, gold and green on her skirt and the interior of the car. If he had been the marrying kind, he would have married her, but marriage was not his destiny. His parents' marriage was proof of that. After his father's murder in San Francisco, his mother had remarried not more than a week later. It seemed as if all women were fickle. He had no desire to be trapped in a woman's web.

After adding the final cars in Carson City, the Virginia & Truckee Railroad headed north for the Washoe Valley. Greasewood and desert dust began to give way to silky green meadows scattered with trees. Prairie flowers in blue and yellow covered the ground thickly, and yellow-green moss glistened on the north side of ponderosa pines.

The train slid into the picnic grounds, steam hissing from the funnels. Frank graciously offered Camry his arm and escorted her to Bowers. The mansion was a white two-story with an elevated, circling veranda. Shiny green ivy clung to the walls, and it was rumored they were cuttings from Windsor Castle. Several sparkling fountains and private gardens enclosed the grounds.

The archery field was crowded with picnickers who laughed gaily, each trying to hit the red bull's-eye in three-ring targets. Men ran around the baseball diamonds, the bases roughly constructed from old flour sacks. Festively dressed dancing partners twirled around on an outdoor dance floor covered by a white canopy. Footraces held the children's interest, their faces rosy under the afternoon sun.

"Where do the horses race?" Camry questioned anxiously.

Frank laughed. "Patience is a gambler's best friend,

my dear. Enjoy yourself. Would you like lunch on the terrace?''

"No," she declined.

"I'll show you the interior of the house," he said, then added on a light note, "Maybe you'll want to buy it after you win the race today."

She shot him an exasperated look. "Where do we place bets?"

"Over there." He pointed. "It isn't time to bet yet."

"Well then, why don't you target shoot or something?"

Frank lowered the brim of his hat over his forehead. "I never point a revolver unless I intend to *use* it."

Camry shivered. Nicholas had warned her Frank shot a man in San Francisco. She dismissed the thought. It was just like him to scare her.

They passed the time mingling in the crowd, watching the various games. Frank tried to explain how betting worked, but it was useless. She had no idea what odds were. Soon, it was time for the racing to begin. The oval track was a quarter mile of fine red earth, enclosed by a white picket fence. Giant eucalyptus trees shaded the spectator area, along with various red canvas pavilions. A crowd had gathered for the event. The horse owners wore fine gray morning coats, their ladies decorated in white and black.

Frank guided Camry to the refreshment canopy. He took an empty pewter mug from a makeshift bar and dipped it into an open wooden barrel of beer. Scooping the foaming liquid, he offered it to her. Recalling what happened the last time she drank beer, she easily declined.

A tall, thin gentleman dressed in dandy clothes and a sugarloaf hat, made his way around the crowd.

"Bets! Bets! Odds five and one; seven and one; nine and two; five and three. Bets!" he shouted.

"What does he mean?" Camry asked Frank.

Frank took a cigar from his vest with his free hand. "Five and one means the horse has one chance in five of winning. Seven and one means one chance out of seven, and so forth.''

''Well, what good is that?'' She knit her brows together, ''I need one and one.''

''Camry, if the odds were one and one, there wouldn't be much of a gamble would there?'' Frank set the tankard down and struck a match, cupping his hand as he lit his Havana. ''Besides, there is no such thing.''

She twirled her parasol. ''Who said?''

''Last chance! Bets!''

Frank produced his billfold. ''Here.'' He placed a wager of one thousand dollars on a horse called Remington Lodi.

''Frank! What are you doing? You said your horse was called Zephyr Gold!'' Camry exclaimed.

''So I did, my dear. This is what we call 'strategy'. Place your bet on Zephyr Gold.''

''But—''

''The lady will place four hundred dollars on Zephyr Gold to win.''

''Thank you, sir. Ma'am.'' The man handed Frank two receipts. Camry took hers and examined the bold print.

''Frank!'' Her voice was high. ''How can this be? Why aren't you betting on your horse? I don't understand any of this.''

''I know Remington Lodi isn't going to win this race. Zephyr Gold will.''

''Then you just threw away one thousand dollars!''

''A drop in the hat, my dear. The odds on your horse are going up with my wager. You'll win more money now. After all, you wouldn't accept money from me—this is my way of giving it to you.''

Camry fidgeted with the strings on her reticule. ''I don't understand any of this,'' she said nervously.

He smiled. ''Trust me.''

''I doubt your own mother does,'' she replied sarcastically.

''Patience. Patience is a virtue of a gambler. Are you sure you don't want any refreshment?''

"That's the only thing I'm sure about." Camry scanned the crowd milling around the racetrack. One immaculately dressed gentleman in particular seemed to be staring at them. She stared back, then turned her back to him. Glancing out of the corner of her eye, she was satisfied he was no longer occupying the chair she'd seen him in. Then facing the track, she was startled that he was standing before them, introducing himself to Frank.

"Hannibal Lucius," he said, tipping a satin hat. "Nice piece of horseflesh you have. I saw him in the holding ground."

Frank grew uneasy with the man's presence. He had deliberately not dressed in the traditional morning coat and garb of an owner. He hadn't wanted any undue attention. "It's a matter of opinion," he returned with measured words.

"I rather think Remington Lodi is a magnificent animal."

Camry eyed Hannibal curiously.

"Like I said," Frank spoke testily, "it's a matter of taste."

Hannibal puckered his face and snorted. "Why are you ignoring your own animal. The register states—"

Frank tilted his mug, the cold beer spilling over the rim and soaking the front of Hannibal's jacket. "I'm sorry, my good man," he apologized. "Clumsy of me."

Indignant, Hannibal Lucius snapped, "I think you've had quite enough spirits. How can you expect—"

"Shouldn't you take care of your suit?" Frank cut in.

Lucius brushed his lapel and left in a huff.

Tapping Frank on his shoulder, Camry demanded, "What was that all about?"

"Nothing to worry about, my dear." He cunningly turned her attention to the track. "Ah, there's Zephyr Gold!"

Camry examined the animal she had invested four hundred precious dollars in. The horse was well-groomed with a creamy mane and tail, and blaze. She didn't see anything special in the horse; as a matter of fact Nicholas' S.D. was much prettier. Frank pointed out Remington Lodi—the horse that would supposedly help her win a big purse by losing. The animal was muscular and jumpy. The black coat seemed to shine silver-gray under the hot sun—just like the color of Frank's eyes . . .

The horses were held behind the starting line, then a shot was fired. The animals took off with a bolt of energy, flinging clods of dirt from their hooves. Camry urged Zephyr Gold on until her voice was hoarse. Her horse remained in the lead until the final turn when the black Remington Lodi seemed to spring ahead. In the end, it was Remington Lodi by a full head.

Camry's jaw dropped and a rush of air left her lungs as if she'd been socked in the stomach.

Frank shrugged sincerely, "I'm sorry, my dear. I thought Zephyr Gold would win."

"But my four hundred dollars!"

"Gone."

"All of it?"

"I'm afraid so."

"And your one thousand? You've made money?"

"I'm afraid so."

"Afraid! Of What? You won!"

"So I did." He crushed his cigar with a boot heel. "If you'll excuse me a moment, I have winnings to collect. Don't look so sad, pet. Why don't we hire a hackney and go into Carson City for the rest of the day. I know of a quaint restaurant."

"Don't bother me with that now Frank. I just lost the only money I had in the world."

"We'll discuss it when I return."

She watched him disappear among the spectators and then took a seat in the shade and fanned her face. A young man ran through the crowd and made his way to the pavilion, stopping suddenly in front of her. Doffing his straw hat, he spoke breathlessly.

"Ma'am, can you tell me where Mr. Marbury went?"

Camry pointed to the end of the track where the betting office was located.

"I wanted to thank him for the tip he gave me last week. I won two thousand dollars on his horse."

She was totally bewildered at the youth's behavior. "I beg your pardon?"

"His horse won the first race," he declared.

"Young man," Camry replied curtly, "I beg to differ with you, but Mr. Marbury's horse is Zephyr Gold."

"I don't know what you're talking about."

"Mr. Marbury had me bet on his horse, Zephyr Gold, while he bet on Remington Lodi to make the odds better."

"I don't know what he told you, ma'am, but Mr. Marbury owns Remington Lodi. He boards him at my daddy's stables. The only reason I can see for him placing your bet on another horse would be to improve *his* odds—"

Camry had tuned him out long ago.

18

She held back a scream. No wonder he was so insistent on placing a bet on Remington Lodi! And he had said it was to help the odds on Zephyr Gold! To think, she had fallen for his trick! And did he hope she'd be so distraught that she'd follow him to a cozy Carson City restaurant? Well, she wouldn't let him get the best of her. If she had a gun in her hands, she could have easily shot Frank between his silver-gray eyes! Silver-gray! She should have known his horse would have *his* coloring.

Camry turned in a rage and headed back toward Bowers Mansion. The train was empty and none of the engineers were about. She spied a conductor on the porch of the house.

"When does the train leave?" she inquired briskly.

"Four-thuty," he replied, biting into a fat pickle, the juice dribbling down his chin.

"Oh, for heaven's sake!" Camry exclaimed. "That's three hours away! I need to leave for Virginia City at once!"

"Might try walking to the main road. Buggy travel tends to be few and far between, but that's the only way I know. At least it'll get you to Carson.

Camry gathered her skirt in one hand and clutched her open parasol in the other. She had no choice but to take the conductor's advice. The heat seemed to burn through the light covering and the top of her nose took on a pinkish hue as well as several freckles. A pebble found its way into her slipper and cut into the ball of her foot. She stopped momentarily to shake it out. Occasionally, the road was covered by the shade of

towering ponderosa and juniper trees. Heather and
shootingstars dotted the rocky meadows with vivid
colors of red, purple and blue.

She would have enjoyed the walk if she hadn't been
alone. Wind whispered in the branches of hundred-foot
pines, an eerie sound that made her alert. A crow cried
from a verdant branch. Maybe she should have waited
for Frank. No! she quickly told herself. He had tricked
her. It was obvious now. Did he think Nicholas would
cast her off once he found out she had spent the day in
the company of a rakish gambler? Suddenly, she felt
very guilty. Well, she shouldn't. If Nicholas cared
anything for her, he would have stayed away from work
and taken her to the picnic himself.

Camry sighed. She had gotten no further away from
Nicholas than a three-hour train ride, and once again,
she was stranded in the middle of nowhere without
money or transportation.

The sun shone hotly on the road. It seemed she'd
been walking for hours when the thunder of hoofbeats
rumbled in the distance behind her. Camry's heart
fluttered. She envisioned Frank Marbury chasing after
her on the giant black and silver horse.

Ducking behind a tree trunk, she peered cautiously at
the trail until a stage pulled by six bay horses appeared
from the cloud of dust. She stepped from her hiding
place and flagged the coach to a stop.

The driver pulled down the triangular, folded
bandanna that protected his nose and mouth from dust.
Several passengers popped their heads out the rawhide
shades that kept the dust from the interior of the stagecoach.

"Ma'am!" the driver questioned incredulously. "What
in tarnation are you doing out here alone?"

"It's rather silly, really," she laughed lightly. "Are you
going to Virginia City?"

"Yup. Gotta make a stop in Carson first. I have
passengers from Washoe Lake." He inspected her
thoughtfully. "You ain't in any trouble with the law, are

you?''

"Certainly not!" she insisted. "I just need a ride to Virginia City."

He scratched the bridge of his nose and sniffed. In all his years as a Concord coach driver, he had never come across a stranded young woman in the middle of nowhere. Pulling off one of his yellow leather gloves, he offered her his hand. "Come on then. I suppose you don't have any money either." Her silence answered his question.

Camry closed her parasol and stepped on a red wheel spoke, then gripped the driver's hand. She had never sat so high on the stage before; it was ten feet from the ground.

"Hank Monk, ma'am." He touched the brim of his hat and shoved his fingers back into the glove. He reached behind her and tugged on a leather strap. Wrapping it around her waist, he fastened it to the base of the luggage rack.

"What are you doing?" Camry asked, wide-eyed.

"Precautions, ma'am," he replied, pulling the bandanna over his nose again. He opened his duster coat and pulled out a heavy, gold chronometer watch and held it on the tips of his fingers. Frowning, he snapped the cover over the time face. "Gotta hurry if I want to keep schedule."

"Are you the Monk that chases trains?" she inquired lightly.

This time, his silence was her answer. Planting his rawhide-booted feet firmly apart, Hank Monk released the brake and cracked a long whip over the horses' rumps.

"Highya!" he hollered, followed by a sharp whistle between his teeth.

Camry was pushed back into the seat by the force of the six bays departure. The small of her back throbbed as she pressed her feet on the floorboard to keep them from flying over her head. Her parasol fell over the side and she craned her neck to watch it tumble into tall prairie grass. She screamed and grabbed the seat, all her concentration turned to staying on the coach.

After a brief stop in Carson City, a little over two hours after she left Washoe, Camry arrived in Virginia City. The town was practically deserted since the train from Bowers wasn't due to arrive for two and a half hours. She would have fallen from the seat if it hadn't been for Hank Monk's strong hands on her waist as he helped her down. Her knees were weak and shaky.

"Thank you, Mr. Monk," she choked in a tired voice.

"You'd best soak in a warm tub for those joints, ma'am."

She smiled feebly and walked down the block to Martha's. She was glad there were few pedestrians on the street to notice her disheveled appearance. Her face was covered with a fine film of gray dirt, only her eyelids remained flesh-toned since they had been squeezed tight for the majority of the ride. Her copper hair was dulled by dust and hung limply to her waist.

Camry reached Ma Zmed's boardinghouse and wearily dropped into a chair. She was glad to be alone. It didn't surprise her Nicholas hadn't returned from work. Would he be angry if he found out she had gone to the picnic with Frank? Oh bother, she didn't care if he were.

She removed her shoes and rolled down her stockings and leaned back to relax for a minute. A scream suddenly echoed through the house.

Jumping up, Camry ran to the back rooms where the cry originated. She opened Molly's door to find the woman standing in the middle of the room.

"What's the matter?" Camry asked in a rush.

Molly moved to the bed. "Go fetch Dr. Hall. I think I'm—" A pain racked her body and she fainted.

Camry screamed, then ran down the hall. She dashed out the front door and headed toward Taylor Street, her bare feet blistering on the hot street.

19

"Gone to the Pioneer Picnic—Back at Sundown." Camry rubbed the back of her neck in disbelief as she stared at the note pinned on Dr. Hall's office door. She turned to go back to Martha's, took two steps, and twirled to face the building again. She rapped on the window a few times before she was convinced he truly wasn't there, then ran a hand through her hair and continued up A Street.

A wooden chair crashed through the windowpanes of Crazy Kate Shea's boardinghouse several feet in front of her, sending tiny slivers of glass onto the boardwalk. Camry ducked as two men followed the chair out the window frame and tumbled into the street. Their fists made bodily impacts, causing a handful of male onlookers to cheer them on. Thaddeus Carpenter filled the doorway, frowned and walked into the street. He raised his pearl-handled revolver and fired into the cloudless sky. He stood over the fighting men, wearing his usual red calico shirt. He attempted to pull them apart, but looked up and saw Camry.

Keg saw Camry before she saw him. He took her hand and pulled her from the path of the scrapping men as they rolled toward her in a dust cloud.

"What in the deuce are ya doin' down here, Miz Trelstad?" he asked.

"I—" she began, then remembered Molly. "You have to come with me. A woman—Mrs. Sinclair—she lives at our boardinghouse. She's dying!"

"Dyin'!" Keg burst.

"Yes!" she insisted. "The doctor isn't in his office and I

158

don't know what to do. She's in the family way and—"

He cut her short. "Doubt if she's a dyin'. Most likely she's goin' t'have a 'lil tumbleweed. Come on, I'll skedaddle with ya."

Keg took long strides to Ma Zmed's, with Camry following swiftly. She directed him to Molly's room, where she was lying on her bed.

"Where's the doctor?" Molly asked, her voice strained.

"Never mind him." Camry's words were calm. "Where is Hank? He knew you were going to have the baby any day."

"I sent him to work," she replied, then tensed with pain.

"Saint Christopher! I never heard of anything so noble."

Looking at Keg, then Camry, Molly queried softly, "Who's he?"

"Thaddeus Carpenter, Miz Sinclair. Don't ya fret none. I knowed what t'do."

"I'll wait in the kitchen," Camry breathed easily. "You can go ahead now Molly."

"You ain't a goin' nowhere, Miz Trelstad. I need help."

"What?" she gasped. "This is doctor's work—man's work."

Keg lowered his voice. "Now I don't see'd no man in that yonder bed and she's a doin' all the work. Ya skedaddle t'the kitchen and put some water t'boilin', then bring me a wooden spoon."

"But—" Camry protested.

"I ain't a takin' no fer an answer. Now go on." Keg turned his attention to Molly and calmed her fears.

Camry stalked to the kitchen and banged the cupboard doors noisily until she found a cast-iron pot. She filled it under the pump in back and set it on the back burner. Striking a match, she lit the kindling. Men! Nicholas used her! Frank tricked her! Da avoided her! And now, an Indian ordered her! She was growing tired of it. Rummaging through a drawer, she snatched a ladle.

Entering Molly's room, Camry handed Keg the spoon. With no other choice, Molly had slipped under the sheet and put her trust in Keg.

"What have you done to her!" Camry exploded, seeing Molly's wrists tied to the brass bedposts.

"I don't need no black eye and this 'lil lady is goin' t'want t'hit someone and I figgered it ain't a goin' t'be me."

"This is barbaric!" Camry said, outraged.

Molly winced and let out a bloodcurdling scream that dwindled to a moan.

Camry shivered and backed toward the door. Keg placed the spoon in Molly's mouth and told her to bite down.

"Go fetch the water and a tub big enough t'wash the 'lil tumbleweed in. And bring a blanket."

She ran from the room, anxious to gulp fresh air. Her heart thundered loudly in her chest as Molly cried out again. She flinched and ransacked the cupboards until she found Martha's stack of linen cloths she used to put over rising bread. Stuffing one into her waistband, she grabbed the pot from the stove, holding the handle with two towels. Water sloshed over the edges as she made her way down the hall.

Setting the kettle in the corner of the room, she stared at Keg. He motioned for her to wipe Molly's forehead. She gingerly patted Molly's moisture beaded face with a damp cloth. The girl had paled, her brown hair wet with perspiration. Camry held Molly's limp hand and squeezed it softly as Keg told her to bear down. Not knowing what else to do, she began to sing a lullaby Da had sung to her when she was a little girl. Her voice was crystal smooth.

After what seemed an eternity, a faint whimper sounded, then grew to a lusty cry. Camry turned to see Keg holding a pink baby.

He held the child up. "Ya got yourself a brave, Miz Sinclair. He even got black hair." He handed Molly her son and winked at Camry. "Ya done okay, Miz Trelstad."

Camry put a hand to her throat. "I think I'm going to faint." She made a dash down the hall, swaying into the walls closing in on her. She swung the front door open and breathed deeply; shutting her eyes, she leaned against the frame.

"Camry?" Nicholas' face was filled with concern when she blinked her lids open. "Darlin', what happened?"

Before she knew it, she clung to him, her body shaking with sobs. He smoothed her long hair with a strong hand.

"Molly almost died. If Keg—" she hiccuped.

"What? What about Keg?" Nicholas soothed.

Camry looked into his blue eyes. "He—" she stopped, the memory of the previous night flooding through her. It was because of a man that Molly screamed in pain. She would *never* let herself get in that vulnerable a condition. She prayed it wasn't too late.

She pushed off his arms and tossed her copper tresses haughtily. "Nicholas Trelstad, if you ever touch me again, I'll . . . You'll wish you hadn't. I never want to see you again!" She entered the house and shut herself in their room. After turning the lock, she flung herself on the bed in a torrent of tears.

A hot gust of air burst from a twelve-inch round hole in the ore wall, the current blowing out Nicholas' candle. No matter how wide a man opened his eyes in the darkness, the black remained. Water trickled and dripped, echoing off the tunnel walls. With practiced skill, he reached into a pouch tied around his hips and pulled out a small piece of oilcloth in which he kept a dozen matches. Mechanically, he struck one against the rough wall and a spark of orange sulphur flickered to yellow as he lit a six-inch candle. Raising the taper, Nicholas secured it in the iron holder he had fastened on a ledge.

"Rig?" Nicholas called, his deep-timbred voice carried in the dips, spurs and angles of the shaft. He eyed the candle; the flame wavered slightly. "How far out are we?"

"We're a mile from the C & C," Rigdon Gregory answered.

"What's the canary doing?" Nicholas craned his head to view the other side of the hole in front of him. He crumbled the mouth with his pick, the loose ore tumbling to the tunnel floor.

"He isn't doing too good. He's flapping his wings like an angel on his way to heaven." The words vibrated to Nicholas and he checked the taper again. If the canary died, they had seconds to get out of the shaft. As a back up, a miner kept close watch on the flame of his candle. If it burned blue, the air was toxic and dangerous.

"Let's get the hell out of here. This bird doesn't look good," Rig shouted.

Nicholas wiped his perspiring hands on the light breechcloth covering his narrow hips and muscular thighs. He picked at the rock a little more.

"Nick? Are you listening to me? This bird just ate his last bite of birdseed. He's gone. Let's get out of here." A small avalanche of pebbles followed his words. "You haven't been worth a damn all day. Why don't you go patch things up with your wife? Nick? Damn it, are you listening to me?"

"I am," he called back. He pulled the candleholder free and grasped his pick. "I'm coming." He had taken several steps, when a bell rang through the drift. Three clangs, pause, then two clangs.

"Shit!" Rig cursed as Nicholas reached him. The light was dim, only the whites of their eyes and the flash of teeth were visible.

An explosion shook the ground, tumbling ore powder falling lightly on their heads. The tunnel began to fill with stifling gray smoke.

"Fire in the hole!" Nicholas yelled. "I thought you said we were a mile from the C & C."

"I did! Come on." Rigdon followed the walls with his calloused hand. Their candles burned low, the flames flickering to a blue halo. "There's a hoist up ahead."

The air became thick and suffocating. Their flames burned out and in darkness, Rigdon and Nicholas operated the hoist, inching their way to the upper tunnel levels. If they came up too fast, their lungs would expand and their skin would break out in a heat rash.

Once on the top section of the C & C shaft, the drift turned in both directions: the left to the California Mine and the right to the Consolidated—Virginia Mine. They took the Con-VA route as miners raced past, carrying buckets of water.

Once they reached the shift house, Rig wiped his forehead with the back of his hand.

Nicholas angrily threw his bandanna to the ground. "Who the hell was blasting in the north winze? McClanahan said they were working on the 1,200 foot level. How the hell do they expect us to look over a new vein while they're throwing a damn barbecue?"

"Hey." Rig grabbed his friend's shoulders. "Take it easy. I'll talk to John Donovan and get it straightened out. You need a drink, Nick, to calm yourself. Your wife has really gotten under your skin. Want to go to the Sundowner for a beer?"

Nicholas stopped at a barrel of ice water and poured a ladle of the cold liquid over his head. The water trickled down his soot-covered face and glistened on his broad chest. "No, I've got things to do."

Rigdon winked, his hazel eyes mischievously twinkling. "I knew you had her on your mind."

Nicholas made no comment and slipped a pair of cotton trousers over his damp loincloth. Gliding sinewy arms into a thin work shirt, he buttoned it deftly. "You think they'll have that mess cleaned up by tomorrow?"

Ignoring the question, Rigdon mimicked, "My darling, will thou forgiveth me for my wicked ways which I know not what I did. I love—"

Nicholas scooped a handful of water from the barrel and splashed it on his partner. He took long strides and left the shift house, Rigdon's laughter following him.

He shaded his eyes against the bright sun and

swaggered up town. Yes, he did have Camry on his mind. Damn it all. Her sudden outburst had left him puzzled, until Keg explained what she had gone through helping him deliver Molly's baby. But what had that to do with him? He had the feeling there was more to it than that, and if he guessed correctly, it had to do with his early departure yesterday morning. He had wanted to take her to the picnic and had all the intentions of doing just that. He had gone to the explosion site with the intention of staying only for a few hours, then going home to get Camry. Only one of the shift bosses didn't show up and Willie Bates was in the hospital with a broken arm. By the time things calmed down, it was too late to go to the picnic, so he'd decided to stay and make a little double-time money. He'd been planning on using the money to buy Camry . . . Oh, what was the use? She had locked him out and he had gone to Mattie's for the night. The old woman didn't ask him for an explanation, she just clucked her tongue and shook her head, mumbling something about the luck of the Scottish.

The weather was clear and warm, a relief from the burning heat of ore in the crooks of the shafts. Nicholas entered H.S. Beck's and snatched a few shelled peanuts from a thick glass jar on the counter. He intended to buy Camry a bottle of perfume, but wasn't quite sure Beck wouldn't needle him about it. That was the last thing he needed.

Beck smiled. "The way you boys dehydrate, you should ingest rock salt. It would keep my supply of pickles and pig's feet from decreasing so fast."

"Hell," Nicholas grinned, "You won't catch me eating pig's feet. You know where they've been walking. I'm a peanut man."

"I know," H.S. feigned a frown. "You leave your shells everywhere." He shifted his weight to sort through various remedy bottles. Blue for indigestion; red for fever; purple for toothaches.

Nicholas dropped a shining bit on the counter for the peanuts. "You didn't happen to see my wife today?" he asked casually.

''She was up to see her pa this morning. Say, I almost forgot.'' He reached under the counter. ''This letter came on the Express for you today.''

Nicholas took the envelope. The green stamp was postmarked: San Francisco. ''Thanks, Beck.'' He decided to get the perfume later. Instead of leaving through the front doors, he walked down the back steps to D Street.

Garnet was behind her small whitewashed crib, hanging clothes to dry. Her wavy black hair was neatly braided and tied with a suede piece. Wispy bangs rested on dark brows, the brown eyes warming as Nicholas approached.

''*Hola*, Nicky,'' she greeted, draping a frilly red petticoat on the line. ''What bring you to Sporting Row, eh?''

Nicholas smiled, then his expression grew serious. ''I got a letter from W. James Quincy. It's posted from Frisco.''

Garnet's tawny skin paled a shade and her nostrils flared delicately. ''Let us go inside.''

She let the screen door slam closed, not waiting for Nicholas to follow. Entering her makeshift living room, she poured a glass of Madeira and took a rolled cigarette from her cigar box. Lighting it, she inhaled deeply. ''Well? What do he have to say?''

He unfolded the letter. ''Quincy has found Scott.'' He waited for her reaction, but when her face remained void of emotion, he continued. ''It seems Scott is performing with a theatrical group on the Barbary Coast.''

''Where is Caleb? My *hijo*, my son?'' her voice wavered.

''Quincy thinks he could be staying with some relatives of Cyprianna Banning, but he's not sure at this time.''

Cyprianna Banning! The name was bitter on her tongue. The woman was the one who had lured her Scott away and taken their child with them. Garnet choked back a sob. ''I cannot believe Scott would let *la familia de mujer* take Caleb. I cannot believe it,'' she whispered. ''Is she still with Scott in the theater?''

''Netta,'' Nicholas soothed. ''Don't get yourself upset. Quincy knows what he's doing. He'll find out for sure where Caleb is."

"Why I play the _gringo, eh_? Why? He no _bueno_."

"I'll wire him some money, Netta. He's the best there is."

"No!" Her hands trembled as she took another drag on her cigarette. "I do this myself. M_io_."

"Christ, you're as stubborn as Camry! Why won't you take my help?"

"No!" Garnet insisted. "I can to for myself. You be glad the _rojo_ head is stubborn as jackass. She be more pigheaded than me, I see that myself. She got temper like bowl of chili. E_l calor_!"

"You're temper isn't far from chili either." Nicholas ran a hand through his damp hair. "So, what are you going to do?"

She shrugged. "What I always do. Work. And more work. M_ucho trabajo_." She ground out her smoke and toyed with a clothspin in her pocket. "What about you, Nicky? What do you do now?"

"What are you talking about?"

"You know. The _rojo_ head."

"Ah, you must mean Camry. Well, according to her, I've got to beg her forgiveness for something and I haven't the faintest idea what for."

Garnet laughed softly. "Oh, Nicky, you do have problem. Why do not you ask her to _el cuatro de julio_ dance next week? All lady like to dance."

"She wouldn't go with me. She said she never wanted to see me again."

"She no mean it. Like me. I say thing I no mean." She sighed. "Time for work. If you stay, it cost you."

"I'm going." Nicholas grumbled. "I don't want to upset your damned _business_." He pushed the door open forcefully and slammed it.

Garnet wiped a tear from her cheek with the back of her hand. She hadn't realized it slipped out. At least she wasn't hardened beyond the walls of tears. She still had her heart. She went to her bureau and slowly opened the top drawer. Pulling a silver-framed picture from underneath her petticoats, she examined the figures in it. Scott Evans held his son while circling her waist with a possessive arm. She could forget Scott. It had been too painful. But Caleb. She ran a finger over his face. Oh, Caleb, if it take all *el dinero* I got, I find you for sure, then it will be us two . . . forever.

20

The moon brightly splashed Virginia City in saffron, adding light to the many glowing lamps and chandeliers from the saloons. Nicholas quietly approached Ma Zmed's boardinghouse, his steps soft so as not to disturb his noisy spurs. Holding a rectangular box in one hand, he removed J.B. and pushed back his hair until it rested around his neck and broad shoulders. Blue eyes framed with light brown lashes searched the empty porch, then he muttered under his breath and unfastened the top button of his shirt, which had been cutting into his neck. No sense in overdoing it, for Christ's sake, he thought.

He plopped his hat back on and smoothed his full strawberry moustache. Making his way to the back of the house, he saw the shades drawn in Hank and Molly Sinclair's window. He continued to the rear, the fancy jinglebobs on his best leather boots clinking on the dusty earth. When he reached the room he and Camry shared, he stopped. The curtains were open and he could see her sitting in the rust and black patterned chair reading Harper's Women's Journal.

The outing at Washoe Valley had slightly colored Camry's face, her green eyes vivid against lightly tanned skin. She wore a simple white cotton dress with small red strawberries embroidered around a modest V neckline. She turned the pages slowly, forcing her attention on each fashion. She imagined herself in frilly watered silks and stiff taffetas. Her concentration continually turned to Nicholas and she scolded herself for thinking about him. She didn't care in the least where

he was. She had heard there was a small fire in one of
the shafts this afternoon and hoped he had perished in
it. Well, she did! she repeated in her mind, telling herself
she would be glad to be rid of him without the complica-
tions of divorce. Then why did her gaze always wander
to the nightstand where the cookie tin was? She
remembered Nicholas sitting casually against the headboard eating the oatmeal cookies with a cocky grin on
his lips.

A tap sounded on the glass window and she turned
with a start. Nicholas easily slid the pane up as she
darted out of the chair to meet him.

"What are you doing here?" she inquired sharply, but
her words were laced with relief at his well-being.

"Is this any way to treat your husband?" he asked,
sticking his head through the frame.

"I thought I said I never wanted to see you again,"
Camry retorted.

"On the contrary," Nicholas declared. "You said if I
ever touched you I'd be sorry for it."

"I said that too."

He held up strong hands. "Observe, these are at least
a foot from your lovely self, so I can remain in your
good graces for the present."

"You're impossible," she chided. "What do you
want?" She brushed a copper curl from her peach-hued
cheeks and stared suspiciously.

Nicholas bent down, then produced the rectangular
box wrapped in brown paper. "A token of my esteem."
He placed it on the sill.

"What is it?" Camry inquired slowly.

"Open it and see."

She picked up the box and it immediately fell from her
hands. She bent to retrieve it. "What's in here? Lead?"
She tore the paper and lifted the lid.

"Ten pounds of the finest chocolate-covered raisins
Hatch Brothers carries," he stated matter-of-factly. He
had changed his mind on the perfume. Lavender
verbena just wasn't Camry.

"How gauche," Camry said dryly. "Only you would stoop to this. You couldn't have bought the one pound box."

Nicholas' good humor teetered. "That box cost me four dollars—what a skilled miner makes in one day. Now don't go spoiling this noble gesture on my part with your damned highfalutin airs. I don't even know what you're so mad about."

Camry folded her arms over her breasts. "What are you bribing me for, Nicholas?"

He removed his hat and held it solemnly in his hands, a grin spread over his lips. "I've come to request your company at the costume ball on July the fourth. It would do me great honor if you would accept."

"Why should I?" She picked up the magazine and began flipping the pages.

He stared at her for a moment before angrily pulling on his hat. "The hell with it. It was a stupid idea."

She looked up and he was gone. She ran to the window, only to see his tall form disappearing toward the front of the house and A Street. She stormed down the hall and opened the front door, just as he reached the boardwalk.

Controlling her breathlessness, she remarked off-handedly, "You can move back to our room."

He stopped in his tracks and turned. His expression was serious, the nose strong and jaw set. "Did I hear you correctly?"

She hesitated and hooked her arm around a wooden post on the porch. "I'll be taking Molly and Hank's room. They're moving tomorrow. He's taken on a nurse for the baby . . . and there's no sense in you moving all your things . . ."

Silently, Nicholas stood bathed by the moonlight. She took in his attire; a green plaid shirt fit snugly over his chest and denim Levis hugged his hips and thighs. She had a sudden urge to run into his arms, but kept herself in check.

"I'll . . . I'll go with you to the ball." She dashed into

the house, her cheeks blushing warmly. Why did he make her feel like one of those silly schoolgirls from Hoaks Academy? Had she really wished he would never touch her again? She was so confused . . .

21

Molly's old room was comfortably decorated in white eyelet. The bedspread and pillow shams were light and airy, trimmed with mauve ribbon. The curtains billowed softly in the morning air as Camry and Martha sat on the floor looking at the contents of a large trunk.

Ma Zmed pulled a faded calico dress from the bottom and held it up to her chest. "I haven't worn this in eleven years. The last time I did, I had just arrived in Gold Hill."

Camry fingered an ivory fan. "I can't picture you in a dress."

Folding the garment, Ma Zmed chuckled softly. "I can't imagine it either."

"What are you wearing to the ball?" Camry examined a gray Confederate jacket with gold braiding and epaulets.

"What I wear every day is costume enough for me. How many women do you know clothed in men's trousers, shirts and boots?"

"None," she replied truthfully. Her eyes lit as she spied yards of teardrop pearls strung on gold wire. "Martha, where did you get these?"

"My mother left them to me when she passed on."

"They must be worth a fortune. I didn't know you were rich. Heavens, why do you keep them in this trunk?"

"Honey, just because a person has pearls doesn't mean they're wealthy, and even if I am, I don't have to show it," she concluded.

"But—"

"Enough on the subject. I'm sure there's something in this trunk to use as a costume. Why not incorporate the

172

pearls? Cleopatra would have worn them." She lifted the strings of creamy luster to the light.

"Cleopatra didn't have red hair, besides, I don't like snakes." Camry brought out a white paper package and placed it on her lap.

"Joan of Arc or Marie Antoinette were lively," Martha suggested.

"No . . . Joan of Arc was saintly." She unfolded the paper. "And Marie Antoinette was French. I don't much like the French. Besides, she was beheaded."

The package contained rich violet brocade, cool and silky from being stored in the trunk. Camry let out a cry of joy. "This is the most exquisite fabric I've ever seen!"

"My cousin in England sent it to me two years ago at Christmas. I have no use for it, but I couldn't bring myself to part with it."

"England!" Camry exclaimed. "That's the answer! Nicholas once said I'd rather have tea with the Queen of England. She was impulsive—just like me," she mused. "And I even have red hair, but my forehead isn't as high as hers." She ran a manicured fingernail over her hairline.

"You can make a royal gown out of this material if you like," Ma Zmed said nonchalantly.

"That's wonderful of you," she exclaimed, then paused. "But I don't know how to sew."

"I'll take care of it." Martha stood and rubbed the small of her back.

Camry gently set the fabric on the bed. "I'll need to buy some things. I wonder if Nicholas will let the moths out of his billfold?"

Martha shut the lid and wiped her hands on her apron. "I heard him in the kitchen earlier."

"I hate to ask him for anything," Camry frowned. "He's such a scrooge." She looked in the mirror and patted her hair. Dabbing rose-scented perfume behind her ears, she smoothed her skirts and headed for the kitchen.

Nicholas sat at the table with a scatter of newspapers

before him: The Territorial Enterprise, Virginia City Union, San Francisco Call and Sacramento Union. He concentrated on the Gold Hill News. He kept his head down and raised his eyes.

Camry took a deep breath and came right to the point. "If I'm going to attend the ball with you, I need to buy several things."

"I'll have Beck open an account for you."

"You will?" She couldn't believe how easily he gave in, then cooled her tone. "That's decent of you."

He put down the paper and took a sip of coffee. "Your costume should be the same theme as mine."

"I wouldn't enjoy playing a she-devil," Camry rebuked peevishly.

"Touche," he smiled brilliantly. "I suppose I'd have to be the Pope then. Or perhaps just a lowly Cardinal?"

"Never mind the smart remarks," she threatened. "I'm to be Queen Elizabeth of England."

Nicholas quirked a brow. "A very good choice seeing you've already had me banished from our bed," he said coarsely. "Good day, Your Highness." He rose and gallantly bowed.

"I should have you guillotined!" she called after him as he left the room.

Camry rummaged through the trunk for thirty minues, taking inventory of what she needed. Hastily grabbing a straw bonnet, she tied the wide scarlet ribbon under her chin and made her way to H.S. Beck's.

The Delta Saloon was in full swing. Bawdy tunes from the piano mingled with the drunken voices of gamblers and the flirtatious giggles of barmaids. The *rouge et noir* ball could be heard from the boardwalk, clicking around the wheel until it jumped into its number, cheers following from those who had the winning red or black. Camry passed quickly, hoping Frank wasn't inside. She was in no mood to speak to him after the trick he pulled at Bowers.

Beck had begun to hang red, white and blue banners from the awning of his shop, and was just fastening a tack as she reached him.

"Hello, Mr. Beck," Camry greeted, setting her reticule on the counter.

H.S. stepped down the rungs of the ladder. "You just missed Nick."

"That's too bad," she said, her words airy.

"He opened an account for you. Said you need some things for the ball."

She produced a list from her purse and handed it to him.

Beck scratched his forehead. "I don't know if I have a farthingale. I might have something that will suffice in the basement, or Bannerman's could have one."

"Could you check? I'll come back later."

"Okay," he mumbled, his face down, reading the list.

Camry bid him good day and turned up the stairs to her father's office. The shade was down, but heated words fired from the glass.

"I'm not above closing you down, Parker! I've shut down mills four times the size of your business."

"I understand, Mr. Sharon. I havena got the money today, but I intend to have it on the morrow."

Camry listened, her father's brogue strong; a sign he was nervous.

"You haven't made one payment. The Bank of California loaned you the money over a month ago. I'm a man that expects payment every thirty days. I'm a man of prompt action," Sharon emphasized.

"I'll have it on the morrow," Michael repeated, "with the three percent interest."

"With accumulated interest," Sharon corrected. He cleared his throat. "I'll give you until noon, then I have no choice but to fold you."

"Possibly, Mr. Stewart could—"

"Stewart! Ha!" Sharon's voice boomed. "He towers above his fellow citizens like the Colossus of Rhodes, and having as much brass in his composition as that famous statue ever had! No, sir! You'll deal with me. Good afternoon, Parker."

Camry hugged the wall as the door swung open and to her surprise, a small, compact man emerged and quietly descended the stairs. She had expected to see a burly thug. She rushed into the office and questioned her father.

"Da, who was that man?"

Michael frantically shuffled through the papers on his desk. "Donna be botherin' yourself with me affairs, Missy," he spoke briskly.

She ignored him and pressed further. "Why was he asking you for money?"

Lifting a ledger book, Michael slammed it on the floor and looked around the room. He ran a hand through his long, red beard and, for a moment, Camry thought he was going to cry.

"Da," she persisted. "You're frightening me. What's wrong?"

"It isna nay I canna handle." He attempted to summon a weak smile. "I haveta send a wire."

"To whom? What's the matter with you? You haven't been yourself in days."

Michael grabbed his hat from the rack. "Nay I canna handle," he assured her again. "I haveta go now." He opened the door and waited for her to exit with him.

"I'll stay and tidy up this mess," Camry offered, heading for the desk.

"You come away from there! Not today, Missy." He ushered her out. "Tell Nick hello." Michael took the stairs easily. At the bottom, he hesitated and looked down the boardwalk. He hitched his trousers and continued at a faster pace. He hoped there wasn't any trouble with the telegraph lines today. He had to send a message to Philadelphia immediately. For the first time since his daughter married, he was greatly relieved she wasn't a part of his daily life. He was in real trouble.

Camry watched her father dart between the traffic of rigs and supply wagons thundering down C Street and wondered what he was hiding from her.

The week passed quickly. Camry busied herself with the Elizabeth costume, gathering odds and ends to add to the gown. Ma Zmed hired a seamstress from

Chinatown to fashion the dress and also fix Camry's hair on the night of the ball.

Camry had called on her father during the week. She had expected to see him sullen and dismal, but on the contrary, he relaxed behind his massive desk wearing a brand-new suit. He assured her, he and Mr. Sharon had had only a minor dispute and everything was fine. The stockbroker business was grand and he was campaigning a new venture with his clientele.

It had been three days since that conversation, and now in her room, Camry wondered why she had bothered to worry about him. Michael Angus Parker was like a cat. He could be dropped upside down and land on his feet.

Martha entered Camry's room with the finished gown over her arm. "My!" she exclaimed. "Ling did a marvelous job on your hair. Have you seen it?"

"No," Camry said, reaching for the full petticoats on her bed. "She wouldn't let me until I was completely dressed."

Ling Star bowed politely, a thin smile creasing her lips.

Martha gestured to the wooden cage-like hoop around Camry's slender waist. "How did you get that thing on?"

She frowned. "It wasn't easy. Ling wanted to 'Fetch Mr. Nick' to do it. I can't imagine Nicholas trying to *clothe* me." She blushed after realizing the implications of her words.

Martha chuckled. "He's been waiting for thirty minutes. He said if you're not ready soon, he's going without you."

Camry's words were garbled as she pulled the fluffy pink petticoats over her head. "What is he dressed as?"

"He doesn't want me to tell you." Martha helped her into the gown and fastened the many tiny hooks in back. She nodded approvingly. "Nick is going to be the envy of every man in Virginia."

Stepping in front of the mirror, Camry sighed in awe. Several strings of the pearls had been taken apart and the tear drop jewels were placed in her sweeping copper curls and anchored in various tucks on the stiff violet brocade of her gown. An ivory lace collar was starched and fanned around her creamy neck. The bodice was square-cut and tight, pushing her breasts upward, the soft curves threatening to spill over. The five remaining pearl strands were fastened on her shoulders and dripped in a U to her waist. The farthingale widened her hips two feet on either side. Subconsciously, she hoped Nicholas *would* find her irresistible.

"You had better come along," Martha chortled. "Nick is sure to be in a foul temper by now."

Camry thanked Ling and started for the door, then stopped. "Wait a minute." She snatched the sapphire necklace from the top drawer of her bureau and quickly clasped it around her neck. She raised a wand butterfly mask, spangled in gold, to her eyes and followed Martha down the hall, her brocade skirts rustling crisply.

Stopping short of the front room, Camry took a deep breath. Her eyes moved over her pacing husband. A black eye patch rested on his forehead, partially covered by a wisp of golden hair. A billowing white shirt wrapped around hard shoulders and opened to his waist, exposing the light blond curls on his chest. Tight fitting fawn breeches hugged his thighs, tucking into knee-length black boots. A scabbard anchored at his hips, the rapier securely housed.

A muscle quivered at Nicholas' jaw upon her entry. He boldly scanned her, breathing in her heady scent, then pressed her hand to his lips. "Your Highness," he spoke deeply. He had never seen her look more desirable and had it not been for the beaming eyes of Martha Zmed, he would have carried her to their bedroom and locked them away for the night. But alas, she was like a frail hummingbird. Ever curious about the nectar, yet not wanting to stop to savor the delicacy or admit she liked it.

Camry wasn't sure he meant the words mockingly, or truthfully. She lightly examined his costume and smiled sarcastically. "I should have known you'd dress like the bluebeard you are. I've often wondered when you'd try and slit my throat."

"Don't be crass, darlin'," Nicholas warned in a low growl. His mouth turned into a slight grin, his dimples faint. "If I am to be beheaded, I want it done the noble way—by my own sword."

Martha intervened. "Now you two have fun. I'll see you there later." She guided them to the porch to put an end to any further arguments. "The carriage is waiting."

Nicholas helped Camry into the liveried coach, his strong hand beneath her elbow. A slight breeze fanned her skirts as he climbed in next to her and he picked up the material so he would not sit on it. The farthingale made her slightly uncomfortable, and he offered the back of his arm as support as the driver reined the horses forward. They rode in silence. Camry's glance strayed to the dashing pirate. Admittedly, he had never been so handsome and she suddenly wished she didn't have to share him tonight.

Music broke the sweet night air as they traveled up the hill to Stewart Street. The Virginia City Dance Hall hummed with the strings of violins and harps. Red, white and blue streamers decorated the long veranda, along with the brightly costumed guests. The town Guard organizations displayed their colors proudly: The Emmets in glorious Irish green, The Nationals in blue, The Washingtons in red, The Montgomerys, The Sarsfields, The Tigers in polished brass artillery metals. Each had taken part in the Independence parade earlier in the day.

Helping her down, Nicholas took Camry's hand in his arm and escorted her inside. Couples twirled gaily over the shining parquet floor. Lavishly set tables exhibited thick cheese sauces, steaming vegetables, various fish— caviar, oysters and pink shrimp, tangy meats—roast beef, pork and lamb, and a multicolored assortment of refreshments—champagne, wine and beer. All the splendor was illuminated by the sparkling crystal prisms of bright chandeliers.

A man with a slight widow's peak, his dark hair combed back and moustache accented by a goatee, greeted Nicholas. He was dressed in a pastel sheet and pillow shams.

"How are you, Trelstad?" he inquired heartily.

"Good," Nicholas replied. "I'd like you to meet my wife. Camry, this is Alf Doten, editor of the Gold Hill News."

"Charmed," she addressed, lowering her butterfly mask.

Alfred bowed. "Delighted, Madame." He scanned the dancers with a twinkle in his eyes, then turned to Nicholas. "Bully time!"

"Where's Mary?" Nicholas asked, lifting a glass of beer off a tray from a circulating waiter. He gestured to Camry, who declined.

"She's home with the baby. I'm going to relieve her soon. Say, did you see the program in yesterday's paper?"

Nicholas kidded, "How could I miss it? It was nearly a column long."

A minuet began, the tune of strings melodic.

"Might I have this dance, Mrs. Trelstad?" Alfred asked courteously.

Camry readily accepted, the custom of the first dance promised to one's spouse easily dismissed.

Alfred Doten, though only several inches taller than Camry, was an agile dancer and guided her gracefully in the intricate curtsies and toe-pointing steps.

"Nick tells me you've been married a month," Alf remarked, "and it only took him two weeks to pop the question. Now, Mrs. Stoddard and myself courted for years before I got enough courage to ask her for her hand. We got married on Lake Tahoe and put our wedding vows to script and stuck them in a bottle and set them to float."

"What a clever idea," she mused, wishing she had had such a romantic ceremony with someone she loved.

"Well, it was more the Missus' idea than mine. That happened two years ago this month—the 24th to be exact. And now we have a baby girl, Bessie. She'll be one in nine days."

Camry's thoughts drifted. Alfred presented an air of contentment with marriage and family life. She silently envied his happiness. There was no similar future for her . . .

"—so I suppose you'll be having children," Alf stated as the minuet ended.

"I really don't know, Mr. Doten. Thank you for the dance." She made her way to the refreshment table and reached for a glass of wine. She put Alfred Doten's assumption from her mind.

"Enjoy your dance?" Nicholas' warm breath tingled her bare neck.

She turned and eyed him indifferently. "Marvelous," then boasted, "He's a divine dancer."

Nicholas threw his head back in laughter, his blue eyes merry. He bent and whispered softly. "When are you going to stop this tomfoolery and act like an adult? You certainly *look* like an adult." He backed away and examined her. "Yes, you certainly *do* look like an adult," he repeated, his glance lingering over her swelling breasts.

"Oh, shut up," Camry growled.

"They're playing our song," he murmured as a waltz began.

"We don't have a song," she informed.

"We do now." Nicholas wrapped his arm around her waist and took her hand, skillfully leading her to the music. Camry was painfully aware of his body close to hers. She seemed to melt at his touch. He stared openly at her, until she was forced to look away, something which annoyed her. She could out-stare anyone . . . anyone but the man she had married.

Several pairs of eyes rested on the handsome couple as they glided in perfect harmony. The orchestra finished and Camry broke free, a sudden urge for fresh air assailing her.

Before she could reach freedom, Keg sauntered toward them, decorated in brilliant finery. His rich black hair was combed into a long braid and accented with speckled prairie feathers. He wore a soft leather shirt and trousers trimmed with turquoise beads. His feet were wrapped in fringed moccasins. For all the glamour his costume emitted, he still carried a large, heavy silver-handled revolver, anchored securely around his waist and thigh.

"How-do, Miz Trelstad. Nick, ya sump dog," Keg remarked playfully. "Ya look purdy, ma'am."

She blushed at his offhand remark.

"Would you look at you! What poor Indian did you kill for those duds? Who the hell do you think you are? A Pawnee Chief?" Nicholas teased.

"Go saber a fly with your sword, boy," Keg jested, "whilst I skedaddle t'dancin' with your wife."

"I'd be delighted," Camry coyly accepted. She was fast coming to respect the salty Indian who had the heart of a Saint and a dash of the lawless west.

The dance was a titillating polka, one which Keg relished greatly. He towered over her, his powerful shoulders slightly hunched. Brown eyes glistened vivaciously, complimenting his smooth, hairless face. The music intensified and Keg whirled her around with such speed, her feet barely touched the ground. She laughed festively, then giggled with abandoned freedom, the strings of pearls bouncing against her waist. The polka ceased on an abrupt high note and Camry joyously hugged him.

Breathless, Keg gripped her slender waist and swung her off the floor, her violet skirts rippling in the shimmering waves.

"I think she'd rather be married to you, than me," Nicholas teasingly broke in. He had been watching from the sidelines, a pang of jealousy tearing at his heart. Why couldn't she have given herself to his arms?

Keg set Camry down gently. She didn't give him a chance to speak, and quickly retorted. "You have to spoil everything. Yes! I'd rather be married to anyone but you and I've told you so on many occasions!"

"Ah, I reckon—" Keg tried to sway their words, but was interrupted.

Nicholas gritted between clenched teeth. "I suppose

you'd like Marbury to—"

Camry refused to listen and angrily stalked away. One minute she had been carefree and gay, the next, her mood darkened and as usual, it was because of the damned miner. She made her way to the terrace. The sweet fragrance of apple blossoms invited her to walk the gardens. The air was warm and night clear, no clouds marked the sky. Twinkling lights of the city below tapered to the silhouette of Sugarloaf, the dark blue-gray billows of smoke from the shift houses lacing the giant rock like a threatening shroud.

Sighing, Camry rested against the path railing. A fluttering shower of the whitish blossoms fell to the ground. She turned to see who had leaned on the tree, when a hand from the dark grabbed her jaw and sturdy arms enveloped her shoulders. She was dragged to a secluded corner of the garden and the hand moved from her jaw to cover her mouth warningly. She twisted and looked into silver-gray eyes. Growling, she tried to kick Frank's shin, then bit his restraining hand.

"You snake, unhand me," Camry sneered, as he pulled away, licking his reddened fingers.

Undaunted, he trapped her between his arms. His face was harsh, his handlebar moustache almost touching her. He spoke huskily. "You left without saying good-bye the other day."

"If I had it my way, I'd never say anything to you again!"

"Lower your voice," he demanded, inspecting her rakishly. "You're looking quite enchanting." He toyed with a strand of her pearls.

"Let me go," Camry ordered evenly. She couldn't help but release her pent-up anger. "Did you expect me to go willingly to some Washoe Inn with you? You are a liar! Your horse was Remington Lodi and you knew I didn't have a chance of winning!"

"You were willing to take the risk," Frank said dryly.

"Risk! When the odds were against me from the start," she cried. "You're taking a risk right now. If my husband finds you with me—"

"So," Frank tensed. "Now he's your husband. Before, you called him Mr. Trelstad. There was a time when you wanted *me* for a husband." He lifted the sapphire necklace from her throat, his fingertips dangerously hot. "I'm sure Mr. Trelstad would be interested to know where you got this."

Camry pushed his hand away, the gems falling on her heaving chest, still warm from his touch. "You're despicable."

"You were anxious enough to get it back," he taunted.

"I want the rest of my jewelry. The thought of you having it sickens me," she snapped.

He smiled ominously. "I told you, you'll have to earn them."

Camry drew her hand back to slap him, but Frank grabbed her wrists in a quick reflex. "As I recall, you cuffed me once before." In a flash, his mouth was on hers. The assault was a cruel ravishment, demanding and masterful. His tongue parted her lips, claiming a sweetness she had given to Nicholas. Frank stroked the sensitive skin behind her earlobes, massaging skillfully.

Twisting away, she hissed, "You're conceited and vain and no gentleman of honor." Her chest rose and fell in quick gasps.

He suppressed a laugh. "I never claimed to be a gentleman, and as for honor, gamblers don't know the meaning of the word. It never stopped you from enjoying my company when you thought it would get you a marriage proposal."

"Well, I'm glad you didn't marry me! It would be sheer agony!"

"Agony?" he questioned sarcastically. "More so than the agony you're in now?" He bent his head and kissed her again. Camry wrapped her arms around his neck to pull at his hair, anything to tug his mouth from hers. She wanted to snap his head off.

A twig snapped and Nicholas' towering form appeared. Frank raised his head, but kept hold of Camry, who was too surprised to move.

Frank measured his opponent with studied casualness.

He had never met the man face to face, only in passing. "So, we finally meet, Trelstad. Camry has told me a lot about you."

Nicholas' eyes were cold and hooded. "Let go of my wife."

Releasing her, Frank brushed a piece of lint from his lapel.

"Get out of my sight," Nicholas warned.

Arching a dark brow, Frank queried, "Who? Your wife or myself?"

Camry's breath was ragged as she glared at Frank. "You, of course!"

Frank remained casual under the scrutinizing stare of the miner. He hadn't been in this type of situation since San Francisco and the whole thing rather bored him. "I was just leaving." Then as an afterthought, he added, looking directly at Camry, "I got what I came for." He disappeared into the apple grove.

Staring at Nicholas, Camry exclaimed, "Are you going to let him go? That man plagues me like a mosquito!"

Nicholas held his temper in check, running his calloused finger over the handle of his rapier. He had seen how plagued she was. Had he not witnessed the way she wrapped her arms around the gambler's neck, he never would have believed it. "It didn't look that way to me."

Camry opened her mouth, aghast. "Your wife was assaulted and you say it was her fault!"

"You're damn right. You provoked him. Did you know he was out here? Is that why you rushed off? Marbury gave you just what you deserved, and from the looks of it, just what you wanted."

"Why, you coward!" Camry sputtered. "You're just too weak to stand up to him."

His cheeks tightened and the fingers on the sword stopped circulating blood, turning to a hard white. A whistle broke the silence and a rainbow of spangles in gold, red, blue and silver painted the black sky, as crackers, bombs and fizzle wheels fired. The light illuminated Nicholas' face and Camry saw how angry he was. He had slid his eye patch from his eye to his forehead, making him look rakish. To Camry, he was a savage, sensual man who could make her weak with one kiss. And that made *her* a coward. Coward enough to fight him with silly retorts and a show of childishness. His intense eyes held her—steel daggers—and she knew she had pushed him too far. The tension of his fury kept the air still as the fireworks died, then his face relaxed, only his nostrils flared slightly and his chin set firmly. It was as if he'd given up.

He rubbed his temples and mumbled. "I came close to wringing your neck, but decided you're not worth the trouble." He sighed wearily. "It is *you* who should be beheaded and put *me* out of my misery." In that revelation he hadn't realized how much he truly cared for her . . . and even loved her. That was why he fought with her. To pound it into her head that he cared—cared enough to fight for her. The sight of her in Marbury's arms was the final blow and framed the truth that their marriage didn't have a chance in hell. He had tried. God, love hurts, he thought as he turned and headed noiselessly back to the hall.

Camry followed him. He took long steps, his tightly breeched legs making sinewy ripples. She held back a sob. Why did everything seem to be falling apart? She was willing to try and love him, but he wasn't willing to love her. And how could he think she had wanted to be with Frank? Had he no trust in her at all?

Another round of explosives brightened the ebony sky, the colors lighting Nicholas' lean figure. A tear silently rolled down her cheek. For the first time, she came to terms with her feelings and found she was terribly in love. How could it have happened? He was everything she *didn't* want. He was not a rich man, but a comfortable man. He was not a poweful man in business, but a powerful man in strength.

Before entering the dance hall, Camry glanced at Sugarloaf again. The jagged mountains were pale and ghostly in the moonlight, ridge after ridge. She shivered and had the feeling Frank was watching her.

* * *

The hired coach stopped in front of Martha's, the horses snorting and shaking their thickly fringed black manes. Music from Stewart Street floated over the mountain on a slight current of the Washoe zephyr.

Camry waited for Nicholas to help her down. When he made no move, she gave him a sideways glance.

He pushed the eye patch off his forehead with a weary gesture and dropped it in his lap. "Well?" he questioned, almost harshly. "What are you waiting for? You've made it quite clear you're capable of taking care of yourself."

Raising her chin defiantly, Camry gathered her crisp brocade skirt and climbed down. The farthingdale hoops tangled and she hit the violet material with annoyance, the entrapment almost causing her tears to spill. She felt foolish and wanted desperately to get away from Nicholas' gaze.

"Don't wait up for me, darlin'." Nicholas drawled. He gave her an enigmatic look as the coach pulled away.

He couldn't be leaving her, but he was! She didn't want him to leave—just stop looking at her as if . . . as if . . . she burst into tears and fled into the house.

Numbly, she made her way to her room and sat on the bed in darkness. The window was open, the eyelet curtains ruffling in the breeze. Everything was wrong. If only . . . if only he hadn't seen her in Frank's arms. She had finally pushed him too far. Nicholas' punishment for her was more painful than she could bear. The contempt she had seen in his eyes . . . She could tolerate beheading, she thought glumly. It was better than the mental anguish she was suffering now knowing where he had gone . . . or more importantly . . . who he was going to . . .

22

Sun spilled warmly into the front room as Camry sat, slowly stirring her morning coffee. She toyed with the saucer, then pushed it away. Sighing, she got up and paced over the floor. Nicholas had not been home all night. Unable to restrain herself, she had quietly peered into his room, only to see the Indian print bedspread still neatly smoothed over the pillows.

Heavy footsteps pounded over the boardwalk and Camry quickly went to the chess table. She furrowed her brows, as if in deep concentration over the game left half-played by Ty Gillespie.

A head covered with curly black hair popped through the threshold and Rigdon Gregory strolled in.

Camry controlled her disappointment. "Nicholas isn't here," she said crisply.

Rig smiled, his hazel eyes twinkling. "I know, I just saw him."

Straightening, she wondered whether Nicholas stayed the night with Rig or . . . she hated to think of him sleeping in the liquid arms of Garnet Silk.

Rigdon helped himself to a fresh marmalade danish on the table. "Nick wants you to pick up something at the Wells Fargo office at noon."

"Oh?" she asked suspiciously. "Why doesn't he get it himself?"

"He's blasting off the C & C shaft." Rig bit into the sweet roll. "I'd do it, but I'm taking Nick's place as shift boss today."

She looked out the window and stared at the passing street traffic. "What do you mean by 'something'?"

188

"I don't know," Rig shrugged. "He said it was important though, and he wanted you to get it."

She was curious as to what the package was. Possibly a present for her, his way of apologizing for last night's behavior. That had to be it. He wanted to surprise her! She tried to conceal a merry smile. "All right. I'll go."

Camry handed another danish to Rig. "Here, have another. I'm glad you came by." She bit her lower lip thoughtfully and raised the dish. "Take the whole plate."

Rigdon chuckled. "Thanks." He grabbed the rolls in both hands and pushed the door open with the heel of his work boot.

A little before noon, Camry entered the Wells Fargo office at the end of the block, and rang the bell for the clerk. A heavyset man appeared, a green visor on his head giving his face an unhealthy pallor. His nose was bulbous, and he scratched it with a stubby finger. His middle protruded from a worn, gold silk vest, with only the top button fastened.

"Yes?" he said briskly, peering at her from beneath the visor, his fatty dewlap shaking.

"I'm here to pick up a package for Trelstad."

He squinted and began flipping through a thick register of papers on the counter, licking his dirty fingertips before turning the page.

The Overland stagecoach rolled to a stop in front of the building, small dust clouds rising. Camry's eyes wandered to the carriage, while waiting for an answer from the clerk. Several passengers emerged from the cab, among them, a tall blonde woman. Golden ringlets tumbled to her shoulders, while the curls around the top of her head were pinned in a loose fashionable arrangement. Deep blue eyes were shaded by the wide brim of a white silk hat. High cheekbones and lips were a soft rose color. Camry felt a slight twinge of recognition, but brushed it off.

"I don't see anything under 'T'." The clerk's words broke her observations.

Camry turned her attention back to the Wells Fargo

office. "There must be. Look again. Trelstad. Nicholas Trelstad."

A melodic voice interrupted. "Did I hear you mention Trelstad?" Camry whirled around. "I'm Rose Creighton. Nick was supposed to meet me."

Camry's green eyes turned cold. Up close, the woman from the Overland Stage was even more beautiful than she had realized. Pale cinnamon freckles covered the bridge of her nose. Dressed in a gown of deep blue that perfectly matched the color of her eyes, she stood several inches taller than Camry.

It suddenly dawned on Camry she *had* seen this woman before. She remembered the picture in Nicholas' photo book and the caption reading: My Rose.

"*Nick*," Camry ground out with pronounced rudeness, "couldn't make it. He sent me."

Rose extended a delicately gloved hand. "You must be—"

"Dense," Camry finished for her. With all the dignity she could muster, she hurried down A Street as fast as possible without running. To think, she had actually fancied herself in love with Nicholas! He was the cruelest man she'd ever met!

Camry heard Nicholas finally come home. She bolted the lock on her bedroom door and slammed the window shut, watching the knob rattle as he tried to enter.

"Open up!" he ordered.

She didn't answer.

Nicholas rapped his fist on the door. "I know you're in there. Open up!"

"Go away," Camry called. He had no right to be angry with her. It was *she* who was angry with *him*. How could she have been so stupid as to believe he had gotten her a gift?

"If you don't open this door, I'm going to break the damn thing down."

Camry patted her hair, unlocked the bolt and stood back as Nicholas filled the entrance. A lock of blond hair brushed his brow and he absentmindedly pushed it back.

"What do *you* want?" she asked coolly.

He placed his arms akimbo. "Why did you leave Rose at the Wells Fargo?"

She was taken aback by his straightforward question. "How dare you have me greeting your paramour!"

The corners of his mouth turned up in a grin. "Rose Creighton is my sister."

"Your *sister!*" Camry exploded. "Why you . . . you . . . why didn't Rigdon tell me!"

"He assumed I did."

"Well?" Camry demanded. "Why didn't *you* tell me?"

"It slipped my mind." He was paying her back for last night.

"Your memory lapse was in poor taste."

"Get dressed," Nicholas commanded. "We're taking Rose to dinner."

Camry picked up a lace handkerchief from the bureau. "I couldn't possibly."

"What does that mean?" He took a step toward her and she backed away.

She fidgeted with the perfumed cloth and placed it under her nose, then sniffed. "I'm not feeling well."

Nicholas narrowed his eyes. "You were okay a minute ago. I'll get Dr. Hall."

Camry flashed him an irritated glare. "Never mind! How can you make me confront her after the way I treated her today? I've never been so embarrassed! Is this part of your punishment for me?"

"You'll manage," he assured dryly. "I'll be back in an hour." He stormed from the room. They were legally bound and he'd be damned if he'd let her make a fool out of him over Marbury. And he'd be damned if he'd give her a divorce so she could make a fool out of herself for Marbury! They were married, and by God, it meant until death do them part! Which would be sooner than God intended if things continued the way they were going.

Reluctantly, Camry sorted through her dresses. Nicholas Trelstad was a puzzle to her. One minute he was angry, the next teasing, the next threatening. As long as she lived, she doubted she would ever figure him out.

23

The dining room of the Silver Hotel was grander than the Bonanza Hotel's, Camry noted as she entered on Nicholas's arm. Burgundy diamond-tuffed chairs circled rich walnut tables inlaid with patterned rosewood and white pine. Gold painted porcelain lamps hung from the ceiling on gilded poles, the soft light reflecting off crystal glasses, indigo china plates and the bejeweled patrons.

The plush Persian rugs were soft under Camry's slippered feet as they followed the maitre d'. She quickly puffed the sleeves on her aquamarine cambric gown with embroidered floral patterns edging the elbow cuffs and bodice. Rose Trelstad Creighton stood elegantly as they approached. Her golden hair curled into perfect ringlets on her shoulders. Dressed in white organdy with a pale blue underskirt, Rose could have emerged from the pages of Harper's Women's Journal, Camry thought. She suddenly felt dowdy next to her fair sister-in-law.

"Hello, Nick." Rose embraced her brother lovingly, then pulling back slightly, she smiled. "You look tired, darling."

Nicholas brushed off his sister's observation. If she only knew that he slept on a lumpy cot in the Consolidated-Virginia's change house! Even though he was dressed in a white shirt and dark brown jacket, and his trousers were pressed neatly, he felt ruffled. He hated the constriction of fancy clothes and wished fervently he was in his worn cowboy chaps and work boots.

He put a hand to the small of Camry's back and introduced her to his sister.

"Well, we've met, of course," Rose smiled. "I'm terribly sorry about this afternoon. I can imagine what you thought."

Camry had been tense, dreading her second meeting with Rose, but now her anxieties were put at ease. She extended her hand, which Rose accepted warmly.

"I'm glad you're not offended," Camry said, then cast a venomous glare at Nicholas. She returned a sweet smile to Rose. "He's such a practical joker." She laughed lightly, concealing her sarcasm. "When he asked me to marry him, I said, you must be joking!"

Nicholas groaned.

Rose nodded. "As well I know, having been his victim more times than I can count."

Clearing his throat, Nicholas gestured to the seats. "Ladies, are we to stand all evening?".

Rose playfully tugged his sleeve. "You don't like being chided do you? You never did. When mother—"

"Shall we sit?" he broke in and held out a chair for each woman, then took a seat himself.

"Camry, you must tell me about yourself. Nick hasn't told me anything, other than he swept you off your feet."

"Oh?" Camry quirked a delicate copper brow at Nicholas, whose only response was a quick wink. He would make the best of the evening. He settled back in his chair and placed his hands behind his head.

"Well, I wouldn't quite put it that way. He—"

Nicholas interrupted. "Darlin', you don't have to be modest. You can tell her how you insisted we have a June wedding." He smiled lazily. "Rose, you should have seen her wedding dress. I guarantee, Virginia City never saw the likes of such a frock before, nor will it ever again."

"Did you have it sent from Paris?"

"No," he interjected. "It was from Drigg's."

Camry fumed. He knew damn well, John Drigg ran the funeral parlor. She shot him a cold stare.

"Do you have family in Virginia City?" Rose inquired

with interest.

Glad for the change of subject, Camry turned her attention to Rose. "My father has a stockbroker business here. My mother died when I was five."

"I'm sorry to hear that. How terrible for you. It's nice that your father is here though. My husband, Kent, is a financier. I suppose that's the same type of work. Figures don't make much sense to me."

The waiter brought a chilled bottle of champagne to the table and poured it into salmon-tinted glass goblets.

"I'd like to propose a toast," Nicholas announced. "To the beautiful women of Nevada. Now there are two."

Rose added, "And to the newlyweds."

"Yes, the newlyweds." Nicholas looked at Camry over the rim of his glass as he drank. Their glances met, then she dropped hers instantly.

The bubbling liquid tickled Camry's throat as she swallowed. She was uncomfortable with Nicholas's eyes on her. Setting his glass down, he let his hand fall on her thigh.

Camry jumped at his unexpected touch, the champagne in her glass sloshing over the edge. "What's the matter with you!" she hissed under her breath.

Rose politely ignored their interplay, thinking of it as lover's folly. "Nick, did mother tell you Ian has taken a fancy to Jenny Lawrence and it wouldn't be a surprise if there were a September wedding. Ren will be the only one of us left not married, and I can't picture him settling down. Do you like children, Camry?"

"I—"

"She loves them." Nicholas's voice was clear. "She insists we have at least six."

Camry's blood boiled. What had gotten into him to make him act like a jackanape? And, in front of his own sister! She'd had enough of his taunting. Flashing him a sugary smile, she dropped her lashes coquettishly. "And we shall name the first one after you, my dearest." She ground the heel of her shoe into his instep, causing him to cry out in pain.

She brought hands to her satiny cheek. "Tsk! Is that bunion of yours bothering you again, beloved?"

Nicholas winced, his blue eyes narrowed in surprise at her unexpected action. So, she would play the evening to the hilt too!

The waiter's voice cut in. "Ready to order, sir?"

Camry basked in her conquest. "I'll have the lobster."

"So will I," Rose agreed.

The waiter addressed Nicholas. "And you, sir?"

"A bucket of ice for my foot," he mumbled inaudibly.

"Your pardon, sir?"

"A steak, rare," he ordered tersely.

"I would have thought you'd be tired of beef by now, Nicky," Rose commented. "Sometimes I feel as if I can't eat another roast for as long as I live."

Camry sipped her champagne. "He loves steak. I make it for him every night, just the way he likes it."

"Since when do I like it petrified?" Nicholas' eyebrows rose inquiringly.

"You don't know how to cook?" Rose asked.

Camry hesitated. "Well, I really haven't—"

"I used to," Rose held back a giggle. "I haven't been in a kitchen in so long, I'd probably set fire to it."

"Me too! Just yesterday, I set fire to my apron!"

"How horrible! My maid does all the cooking. We'd starve to death if it weren't for her."

"I wish I had a maid," Camry sniffed wistfully. "When I lived in Philadelphia, Miss Hoaks had a maid for everything."

"Hoaks? Was that the Hoaks Academy?"

"Yes."

Rose brought a hand to her lips. "I went to Ellsworth Academy."

"You did!" Camry rushed on in amazement. "We had etiquette lessons with Ellsworth. When were you there?"

"In seventy-two."

"Heavens! We might have run into each other."

"Nick," Rose frowned softly. "Why didn't you tell me Camry was from Philadelphia?"

Nicholas threw up his hands in surrender. "I was afraid of this." He was resigned to their camaraderie as the waiter brought their food. He attacked his steak, ignoring their prattle.

The lobsters were cooked to perfection, the shiny shells red, the delicate meat inside slightly pink. Camry savored each bite. She hadn't had a delicacy this sumptuous since she'd been out to dinner with Frank.

Squeezing a lemon slice, Camry said, "Did you attend the Spring Cotillion at Easton?"

"That's where I met my husband. He was on business and staying with John Seldon. Do you know the Seldons of Clifton Heights?"

"Who doesn't," Camry remarked matter-of-factly. She hadn't the faintest idea who John Seldon was, but she enjoyed the conversation and the way it made her look important.

Nicholas rested his elbow on the table, his chin cupped in his hand. The blue eyes moved from left to right, following the flow of female chatter. He informally dropped his silver fork on the china plate, the noise silencing the women abruptly. One corner of his mouth pulled into a half smile. "Dessert anyone?"

Rose sipped her champagne. "None for me."

"I'll ask for the check then."

"Not so fast," Camry interrupted. She lowered her voice for Nicholas' ears only. "You're not getting out of this one. Who knows when I'll have the chance to eat here again. Dig deep into that moth-ridden wallet of yours." She caught the waiter's attention.

"Yes, Madam?"

"I'll have the chocolate mousse, please," Camry turned to Rose. "Are you sure you won't indulge?"

"Well, I really shouldn't."

"Oh, nonsense!" She smiled at the waiter. "She will have one too." Camry turned to Nicholas and flirted coyly. "Beloved, why don't you have the cherries jubilee? I know how you're always after Martha to make it."

"I'll pass," he grumbled.

The waiter hastened to the kitchen and returned shortly carrying a silver tray laden with dessert. The chocolate mousse was rich and fluffy. Vanilla whipping cream capped with chocolate shavings garnished the top.

To further annoy Nicholas, Camry ate with deliberate slowness. He shifted his weight in the chair several times before standing. "Are we ready to go now?"

"Not yet," Rose answered. "There are some things in my room I want to show Camry."

Nicholas ran a hand through his hair. "I'll be at the bar." He stormed off, taking long strides.

Camry dabbed the corners of her mouth with her napkin. "My goodness," she gently rebuked. "Sometimes his manners are nil."

Rose and Camry climbed the hotel stairs to the suites on the second floor. The room was spacious and stately. Camry's emerald eyes scanned the armoire, the doors slightly ajar. It was filled with a variety of pastel-colored dresses. Though her own closet was full, she envied the woman's newer and more expensive creations.

Opening the top drawer of her nightstand, Rose produced a round box. "This is for you."

They sat on the bed, Camry resting the box on her lap. She lifted the lid and caressed the silky softness of a spider web knit shawl made of golden thread. "It's lovely," she admired.

"I'm glad you like it. I don't think wedding presents should be practical. I don't know of any woman who is."

Camry felt a rush if sentimentality. Rose Creighton was everything Miss Hoaks had said a woman should be, and everything she longed to be.

"There's something else," Rose interrupted her thoughts. "It's at the bottom."

She reached under the tissue and found a small velvet jewelry box containing a ring. The band was silver with a brilliant scarlet agate set in the center.

"Nick made it when he was eleven. He swore he'd

never marry and gave it to mother. She thought you'd like to have it. Our parents are terribly sorry they missed the wedding. We didn't even know about it until three weeks ago when Nick wrote.''

Camry looked at her wedding finger. Her simple gold band had been removed long ago and placed in her jewelry box.

''Try it on,'' Rose suggested.

The ring slipped on snugly. A pang of sadness swept over Camry. Being close to Rose gave her a true bond to Nicholas' family. If they only knew their marriage was a mockery, one which she had tried to run away from . . . would the Trelstads open their arms so wide with adoration?

Camry stood abruptly. ''I really must be going. Nicholas is waiting . . .'' Her voice trailed.

Rose escorted her to the door. ''Tell Nick good night for me and I'll call on you tomorrow. It's good to have you in the family.'' She gave Camry a gentle hug.

Feebly, Camry smiled and made her way down the hall. When she heard Rose's door shut, she stopped and looked at the red agate on her finger. Sighing, she hooked the box handle in the crook of her arm. The band was tight and she twisted it in an effort to move it over her knuckle. Her persistent tugging only made her finger swell.

''Oh, for heaven's sake,'' she muttered impatiently. If Nicholas saw the ring on her finger, he'd surely think she was giving in to him completely. Her knuckle grew white, the circulation of blood cut off. She had no choice but to push it back on her finger. Gathering her aquarmarine skirt, she hid her hand in the folds and made her way to the lobby.

Nicholas leaned against her bar railing casually, gripping a glass of amber rum. His golden hair gleamed under the soft lights, his tan face and vivid eyes appraising Camry as she approached. He wished he could get her out from under his skin. He wished . . .

He downed his drink and flipped a silver coin onto the

counter. "What's in the box?"

"A present," Camry replied tersely. "Why didn't you tell me your sister was so charming?"

Nicholas pulled on J.B. "I liked her better, before she married that Creighton fellow and turned into a peacock."

Camry raised her chin with a questioning stare. "Whatever are you talking about?"

"Someone who struts in fancy clothes and acts like they're better than others. Someone you'd like to be, if I let you."

"You don't have to *let* me do anything," Camry retorted. "I can do as I please."

"Sure you can," Nicholas agreed sarcastically. He opened the lobby door and they walked down the boardwalk.

"I'll carry your package for you," he offered, reaching for the box.

"No!" Camry answered swiftly. She would have to free her left hand in order to give it to him. She walked coolly, wondering all the while where Ma Zmed kept the butter.

Tinny sounding piano keys filled the night as they passed the many saloons on C Street. Shattering glass broke the music and a rumble of curses flowed above the batwing doors on the Comstock Bar.

"Get the 'ell out o' 'ere, you drunk Injun."

The crack of wood splintering caused Nicholas to protectively push Camry out of the fighting path. Keg Carpenter flew between the saloon doors and landed unceremoniously on the rough boardwalk planks.

"Ya damned English cur!" Keg struggled to his feet, attempting to return inside. He pushed back his long black hair and brushed a hand on his fringed suede trousers. He threateningly toyed with the handle of his revolver, securely anchored in its holster.

The bouncer blocked the entrance. He was as large as Keg, and any fight between the two would be evenly matched. "I told you, we ain't serving you 'ere anymore tonight. You won the bloody watch, so get the 'ell out.'' Fleshy arms crossed over his massive chest as he dared Keg to pass the threshold.

Keg's stance swayed and he leaned against the awning post for support. Nicholas reached over to stop him from falling.

"Keg!" Nicholas gripped his shoulders and shook him. "You're jagged, friend.''

"Nick, boy. Ya ol' sump dog. I'm as drunk as an owl. See'd this here watch?'' He uncurled his three fingers to reveal a shining pocket timepiece on a gold chain. "This here is worth two hundred and fifty big ones. I won it in the raffle. Howdy, Miz Trelstad,'' he blurted, seeing Camry.

"Hello,'' she acknowledged sharply, disgusted at his stupor.

"This here raffle ticket costed me two dollars.'' His tan face grew mischievous, the brown eyes dancing. "And,'' he slurred, "a damned twenty dollar bar bill!''

"I figured as much,'' Nicholas rebuked tersely. "You're on the three a.m. shift. How do you expect to work with dynamite in this condition?''

"I can nitro in my dreams. Hell, I can nitro in *your* dreams!'' He laughed at his humorous quip. "I can—Ya want t'skedaddle t'Evans Chop House? I got me a hankerin' fer some salted pork.''

Nicholas adjusted his hold. "That's just what you need. Food and coffee.'' He leaned Keg against the post and faced Camry. "Darlin', do you think you can see yourself home? I've got to take care of him.''

Camry nodded and started to walk, when Nicholas' strong arm was on her shoulder, sending a warm shiver through her. His eyes sparked warningly at her upturned face. "You go straight home,'' he said in a hushed command.

"Where do you *think* I'd go?'' Camry snapped. His closeness excited and cautioned her at the same time.

"Stay clear of the Delta,'' he warned again, this time his meaning clear. His lips lowered to hers, searing her mouth with his. She fought the waves of emotion washing over her. She wanted to cling to him, run her hands down his back . . . He broke off the kiss and brushed her lips with his finger. "Take heed, Camry."

She shrugged off his arm and haughtily made her way to Martha's. Her body trembled, traitorous to what she should have felt from his touch—revulsion. But it wasn't . . .

The walk was short and once she was in the kitchen, she turned up the wall lamp. She assumed the butter would be kept someplace cool. Though ice was in demand, Martha managed to keep a block of it in her small varnished wood and cork icebox lodged below the pastry shelf. Camry bent and pulled the knob, then scanned the two wooden racks. Moving a ceramic pitcher of milk, she tipped over the drip-water pan, the cold melted ice splashing on her dress.

Camry stood and angrily brushed her skirt, the water making a stain in the floral print. Her annoyance could only be directed at herself; it was her job to empty the pan. The butter was not there. She examined the counter; the copper flour and sugar canisters gleamed alone. She wished she had paid more attention to Martha's cooking lessons so she'd know where things were. Opening and closing cupboards noisily, her patience thinned; all she found were bowls, pans, and cooking utensils.

"Stop!" a ragged voice ordered. "You vagabond! I'll shoot!"

Camry turned quickly, her heart caught in her throat. Her face paled with fright, but on seeing the intruder, the healthy peach glow returned. Emeline Gillespie held a small pearl-handled derringer in her shaking hands. A white mop cap tilted over her gray curls, and a nightdress wrinkled around her ankles.

"Heaven's." Camry choked, raising a hand to her bosom. "You scared me to death! Mrs. Gillespie, put that firearm down!"

The elderly woman obliged. "I'm sorry, dear. I heard a

noise out here. Martha has gone to Steamboat for the night and Ty never wakes until dawn."

Camry squared her shoulders and straightened her embroidered bodice. "Well, that was very heroic of you but, next time, be a little more sure before you go pointing guns."

Tears welled in the murky gray eyes. "I'm sorry, dear—" she repeated, her voice cracking.

"For heaven's sake, don't cry," Camry gently urged. "You did the right thing."

A smile slightly parted Emeline's lips. "I did?"

"Of course," she insisted. "Now that you're awake, could you show me where Martha keeps the butter?"

"It's over in the pantry." The spindly legs and slippered feet shuffled over the wooden floor to a tall cupboard door in the corner. She opened it and pointed. "On the bottom shelf."

Camry peered into the semi-dark closet. "Thank you, Mrs. Gillespie. You go back to bed now."

"What do you need butter for?" Emeline wrinkled her forehead. "It's after midnight."

Putting a fingernail to her lips, Camry hastily explained, "Well, I'm going to make some oatmeal cookies for Nicholas. He's always praising yours, so I thought I'd surprise him."

Emeline beamed. "How nice! To be young and in love! I was once you know—"

"You run along now." Camry mildly pushed the old woman in the direction of the hall. "Don't forget your pistol, dear."

When Emeline Gillespie finally disappeared and shut her bedroom door, Camry let out a sigh of relief. Faint light from the kitchen barely illuminated the cool darkness of the small pantry, three steps below house level. The shelves were full with jars of preserves and vegetables in a rainbow of colors. A small, chipped blue bowl rested on the lowest shelf. Camry picked it up and lifted it to the light.

"Finally," she spoke aloud.

Bringing the butter dish to the table, Camry grabbed a knife and scooped a generous amount. Smearing it around the silver band, she tried to remove the ring. It loosened slightly and she dabbed it again. The band twisted and in a swift tug, pulled free. The ring slid from her finger and flew across the room, bouncing under the black cast-iron stove.

Camry stamped her foot in frustration. She kneeled down and brought her head close to the floor. Reaching under the oven legs, her hand brushed the powdery surface. The burnt wood left a film of charcoal dust and when she withdrew her arm, it was covered with soot. She stood and pushed back a copper ringlet curling on her forehead, the black dirt smudging her cheek.

Opening the back door, she snatched a broom from the porch. Sticking the wooden pole under the stove, she slowly grazed the floor until she heard the end touch the ring. As soon as she found it, the muffled ping of the soot trap envolved the jewel and it fell in the ash box. Tears of frustration sprang to Camry's eyes. She rubbed the small of her back wearily. It was just a worthless ring, she told herself. It was nothing to worry over . . . but it had been Nicholas' mother's. Why should she care?

"What are you doing?"

Camry was startled. As if her thoughts had conjured him, Nicholas filled the kitchen with his tall form.

"None of your business." Camry returned with measured words. She would have to wait until morning to search the cellar for the ash box. "I'm going to bed." She tried to push her way past him.

His hand caught her arm. "What's happened to you? You're dirty."

"Never mind." Camry suddenly burst into tears. The ring shouldn't matter to her! But why did she feel like the world had stopped? She wouldn't have worn it anyway. Pushing off his hand, she ran down the hall and slammed the door.

24

Thoughts of the silver ring haunted her, until eventually, Camry cried herself to sleep. The following morning, she sleepily strolled into the kitchen. She couldn't understand why such a simple piece of jewelry upset her. If it had been her sapphire necklace, that would have justified her concern. Just the same, she would check the ash trap in the cellar. She would at least have to display the ring for Rose's sake.

Martha was busy at the stove when Camry entered the stifling room. Already, the weather was heavy and hot.

"You're back early this morning," Camry commented, pouring a strong cup of coffee. "Emeline told me you went to Steamboat for the night."

Taking a cast-iron pot filled with oatmeal off the stove, Martha unfastened her apron and joined Camry at the table. "I like to travel before sunup when it's not so hot. Steamboat was very nice. You and Nick should go there sometime."

Camry stirred a teaspoon of sugar into her cup. The wooden floor rumbled and pots and pans in the cupboards started to rattle. The smaller explosion gave way to a larger one and soon a loud blast echoed Sun Peak. Camry had always ignored the charges, but lately, her mind turned to Nicholas with each interval. She wondered if it was him firing the dynamite or someone else taking the risk of being blown up and buried in a cave-in.

"I have a cabin at Lake Tahoe," Martha said, invading Camry's thoughts. "I like to get away as much as I can. Virginia grows monotonous at times." She smoothed a hand over her salt and pepper hair.

"Could you show me where the ash box is?" Camry inquired casually.

"Why, honey?" Martha's tan face took on a puzzled expression.

Camry groped for words. "I dropped one of the spoons and it fell behind the stove. I think it landed in the ash box."

"It's too late now. The Chinaman was here early this morning and emptied it."

"What does *he* want with the ashes?" Camry asked in desperation. Her heart began to hammer.

Martha shrugged. "The Chinese are very industrious. In '64 when most of the trees had been cut for housing and firewood, they dug up the remaining roots, dried them, sold the wood in faggots and made a profit where the white man wouldn't have taken the time with such a difficult task. Pong Sang comes every two days and takes the ashes."

"Well, what does he do with them?" Camry asked urgently.

"I'm not really sure. I think his family makes charcoal writing pencils, or for all I know, they use it in Buddha rituals."

Camry imagined the round-faced Buddhist priest with almond-shaped eyes, offering her agate ring to a stone idol. The image greatly depressed her.

Seeing how disturbed Camry was, Martha patted her hand. "Don't worry about it. I've got plenty of spoons."

"Hello?" Rose Creighton's smooth voice called through the screen door.

Camry went to the front room and ushered her sister-in-law into the house. Rose's satiny pink skirt rustled and the sweet fragrance of her perfume scented the air. Her gown was cut modestly low with short puffed sleeves. Rose adjusted a pearl stickpin in a matching pink hat and veil that perched over her lustrous blonde hair.

"Am I late or early?" Rose asked directly.

"You're neither," Camry corrected. "You're right on

time. I'd like you to meet Martha Zmed. Martha, this is
Nicholas' sister, Rose Creighton."

"I would have known you were related," Martha remarked positively. "You have the Norwegian features of
a Trelstad."

"Would you like a cup of coffee, Rose?" Camry
queried. "Martha, why don't you join us?"

"No, you ladies go ahead. I've got some errands to
run. It was nice meeting you, honey."

Camry led Rose to the kitchen.

"I don't want any coffee," Rose declined. "I'd much
rather get an early start shopping."

"Shopping?" Camry mumbled, putting a fingernail to
her coral lips. How could she go shopping and explain
why Nicholas didn't give her a *cent* to shop with! The only
place she had a charge was at Beck's Furniture Shop and
she couldn't picture herself wearing a davenport! "I
really don't know if I can go today," Camry lied.

"Of course you can," Rose insisted. Her dark blue
eyes suddenly sparkled and she gasped. "Camry! Where
is your ring?"

She quickly covered her fingers with a hand, as if the
gesture would magically conjure the agate. "I . . . I had it
sent to the jewelers this morning. The band was a little
loose and I didn't want to lose it." She couldn't tell Rose
she had *already lost* the family ring. Rose was satisfied
with her explanation.

"Let's go then," Rose declared firmly. "And I won't
take no for an answer."

Camry snatched her straw hat and reticule and rhythmically followed the graceful woman out the door and
onto the boardwalk. The morning was bright and clear,
an endless cobalt blue sky splashed with a single, small
white puffed cloud. Much to Camry's dismay, Rose
headed west toward the more expensive shops.

Howard Street gleamed with all the wealth Comstock
silver stood for. The perfectly sloped timbered roofs on
architecturally   designed   houses   enhanced   the
residential sections. Most yards were lovingly land-

scaped, whether with flora or the more practical rock
and cactus gardens. Grass was a major accomplishment,
but the blades were usually brown. For all the influence
Comstock wealth held, it could not buy the luxury of
twenty-four hour water. The Virginia and Gold Hill Water
Company shut off the main valve at the reservoir at six
o'clock each night and it was not turned on until six
o'clock the next morning. Watering in the heat of the
day was futile; therefore, the lavish white houses were
set on a blanket of golden brown straw.

The steady tap of hammer against nail rang down the
street. Rose and Camry dodged sweat-drenched
carpenters who labored over a new office building
under construction. Their equipment was scattered over
the fresh new boardwalk. The tangy smell of sap and
pine filled the air sharply and the heels of their shoes
stuck to the walk planks as sap oozed from the wood.

Rose touched Camry's arm and giggled softly, ''Look
at that red-haired man dancing a jig!'' She pointed to the
open-framed building. Several carpenters cheered the
dancer on by clapping.

Camry's mouth opened aghast as the man turned.
''That's my Da!'' she exclaimed. She gathered her skirt
and rushed to the open-framed office.

Michael Angus Parker kicked his heels while his fingers
hooked loosely into the belt loops of his trousers. His
round cheeks were rosy from exertion, the color
complementing his full six-inch beard and coarse
moustache. Seeing Camry, he stopped dancing and
smiled, almost foolishly.

''Ah, me girl. What are you doin' here?'' The green
eyes twinkled like jewels, tiny crow's-feet creasing the
outer corners.

''What are *you* doing here?'' Camry reversed the question. ''Why are you making a spectacle in the middle of
the morning?''

He gallantly defended his actions. ''I amna makin' a
spectacle, meerly Christenin' me new office.'' He turned
his attention to the framers and furrowed unruly red-

orange brows. "And what are you ogglin' over me daughter for? She's nay a maiden, but a married woman."

The men backed away and resumed their work. Michael patted the small paunch bulging from his waistline. "Well, what do you think a me new office?"

"It's grand, Da," Camry remarked offhandedly, then lowered her voice seriously. "I thought you were having finance problems? That Mr. Sharon seemed awfully threatening."

"Nay, nay," he assured, straightening his black silk ribbon tie. "Business couldna be better. And here is the proof. Me new clientele issa rich breed." Looking over Camry's shoulder, he craned his neck. "Who's the bonny lassie?"

Camry introduced Rose.

"I'm delighted to make you acquaintance, Mrs. Creighton. Such a jewel betwixt the shimmer o' Comstock gold and silver issa rarity."

Rose faintly blushed and smiled. "Camry, your father is such a charmer; however, Mr. Parker, I fear you're so close to a blarney stone you could touch it! But just the same, I thank you kindly for the most gracious compliment."

"And where are you two lovely ladies off to this fine mornin'?" Michael pulled a plug of tobacco from his vest pocket and bit off the end.

"We're doing a little female shopping," Rose chimed. "A few hats and frills are always fun."

"Well, donna let me keep you then." Michael kissed Camry's cheek. "Stop by soon, Missy. Me new office should be finished by the endda this week. Very nice to meet you, Mrs. Creighton. Have a pleasant stay."

As they walked down the boardwalk, Rose addressed Camry. "Your father is so jolly!"

Camry's lips pressed into a tight smile, her thoughts also on Da. He was as jolly as St. Nick, and with the presents for himself to prove it. She wondered uneasily where he got the money to invest in such a grand office.

She hoped he hadn't taken up gambling but, rather, that good business sense had bought his new office. She would check the Territorial Enterprise for stock prices when she returned to Martha's.

The Crystal Mirror was a dainty shop, its windows filled with enticing plumed hats and stylish shoes. The patron's chairs were made of softly upholstered cowhide. A glass counter stretched the length of the shop, the inside decorated with French silk stockings, corsets, and other lacy undergarments.

The proprietor welcomed them in a business-like, but friendly manner. Rose took a seat and asked to see a taffeta petticoat. While the clerk went in the back, Rose looked gently at Camry.

"Why don't you sit down? You look as if you're suffocating."

Indeed she was. The agony of being dropped into the middle of a candy jar, unable to sample the sweets! How could she explain to Rose she was penniless, thanks to her brother. Instead, she managed a nervous laugh. "I fear I've spent all my household money this week, silly me! If Nicholas knew I bought a new dress yesterday, he'd throw a fit."

"Kent is the same way."

The saleswoman returned with a lavender petticoat, embroidered mauve roses bordering the lacy hem.

"Oh!" Rose exclaimed. "I'll take it. Anything with roses on it . . . I guess I'm superstitious in a sentimental sort of way."

The woman wrapped the slip in a box and tied it with a red ribbon. After strolling to several other shops, they started back to Martha's.

Rose tilted her pink-hatted head curiously. "Tell me the truth, Camry. Are you and my brother happily married?"

Camry was taken by surprise at such a straightforward question. She hesitated, wondering if she should tell the truth, or keep up her facade. "I suppose we are," she answered, deciding vagueness was the best way out.

Turning the tables, she queried, "Are you?"

"Yes, sometimes. Money doesn't buy everything."

The subject was dropped as quickly as it had arisen.

The streets were crowded with afternoon traffic. The miners had switched shifts, their dirt-clad forms jauntily moving down the alkali dust roads and disappearing into the many taprooms and saloons.

As they neared Ma Zmed's, Camry stopped in her tracks. On the porch of the boardinghouse stood Nicholas and Garnet Silk. Her sultry figure was pronounced in a tight-fitting plum calico blouse and skirt. The wavy black hair hung in a loose braid to her curving hips. A tawny-skinned hand moved to rest on Nicholas' shoulder, that was richly outlined by a linen work shirt covering his broad chest.

Rose followed Camry's gaze with her own and also stopped walking. Her pink lips pursed and the dark blue eyes clouded with gray.

Nicholas placed arms akimbo on his narrow, Levi-clad hips. He seemed to be arguing with Garnet. She turned to leave, but he grabbed her wrist and pulled her back. She faced him, her brown eyes flashing tawny fire. Shaking her head, she stormed off in the direction of Sporting Row.

"Well!" Rose cried in disbelief. "Who was that?"

Camry's cheeks burned with an unwelcome blush.

Rose raised a questioning brow at Camry's silence. "If you don't want to know—" She couldn't drop the subject. "I do."

Camry placed a hand on Rose's arm imploringly. "Please, it's nothing really. I think she's an old friend of Nicholas'."

"That was obvious!"

Rubbing her temple, Camry sighed. "I think I'm going to take Martha up on her offer and stay at Lake Tahoe for a few days. The heat here is intolerable."

"Which heat? Nature or . . . actually, all the heat around here has to do with nature," Rose retorted flippantly. She took purposeful steps to Martha's.

Nicholas grinned impishly and winked. "Hello, ladies."

Rose pursed her lips. "Hello yourself."

He gave Camry a quizzical stare. "What were you doing in the kitchen last night, darlin'?"

"Nothing," she mumbled.

Rose glared at her brother. "Better yet, what were you doing—"

Camry interrupted. "I feel a headache coming on. Rose, it's been a lovely day. I'll see you tomorrow." She entered the house and let the screen door slam behind her.

Nicholas shrugged. "What's the matter with her?"

Rose gripped his arm and tugged him to the end of the porch. "As if you didn't know!" she said firmly.

"What are you talking about?" He was baffled by her stern attitude.

"That dark-haired spitfire you were fondling."

Nicholas leaned against the log railing leisurely. "Garnetta Evans is an old acquaintance of mine and she was on the verge of making a terrible mistake."

"If I saw Kent with a *friend* that *friendly*, I wouldn't think the best of things. Just *who* is she?"

Nicholas's eyes clouded. "Who's asking?"

"I am."

"Don't henpeck me, my darlin' Rose. Your thorns tend to draw blood. Who put you up to this inquiry? Camry?"

"No, the poor dear. She got so upset when she saw you, she didn't want to talk about it." Rose pushed up the pink veil from over her eyes to view him more closely.

"I can assure you, or rather Camry," he said dryly, "I've been quite the faithful husband—if thoughts of the mind don't count."

Rose crossed her arms over her full breasts. "And just yesterday I gave Camry the agate ring you made for mother."

"What ring?" Nicholas scowled. "Camry doesn't wear one."

"It's at the jewelers." Rose sighed thoughtfully.

"Camry mentioned getting away. I think it's a good idea. I'm going with her to Lake Tahoe."

Nicholas raised his brow a fraction. "Unescorted?"

" 'Unescorted' is a word for the dark ages. I came here from South Dakota unescorted. Do you think Kent went into a rage?"

"I don't give a damn what he does. This is my wife you're talking about."

"I'm glad to see you realize she *is* your wife," Rose declared hotly. "She's very much in love with you."

Nicholas gave a short sarcastic laugh. "How do you know?"

"Women have ways of knowing about such matters. I'm taking her to the lake tomorrow and that's that." She clutched her package tightly, and before Nicholas could protest, she made her way down the porch with her pink head held high.

25

Camry sat under the shade of a sighing, verdant pine. The dense forest behind her stretched to a brilliant powder blue sky, filling the air with rustic fragrances. The broad lake before her was glassy and clear, indigo waters fanned turquoise fingers to the shallow shores. Camry picked up a pine needle from the deeply carpeted ground she sat on, and toyed with it. The sharp end pricked her finger and she dropped it restlessly.

"I should have known I'd find you here," Rose called, breaking Camry's solitude.

Rose stood with her hands on her slender waist and scanned the scenery.

The giant mountains bordering Lake Tahoe were scattered with landslides and fallen trees, reminding the admirer, nature's serenity was also man's labor. Avalanches and blasting theatened the slopes, as the need for timber increased.

Rose gathered her cotton-skirts and sat next to Camry. "We've been here two days and you look homesick."

"I am not," Camry quickly denied. However, the truth was, she had been thinking about Nicholas. In her absence, he would certainly spend his time with the Silk woman.

"We've come up here to have fun, let's not waste time," she smiled mischievously. Seeing Camry uninspired, she gently nudged her. "Come on, let's go swimming." Rose climed to her feet and began unbuttoning her blouse.

"Rose!" Camry exclaimed in a hushed whisper. "What are you doing? What if somebody sees? Besides, I can't swim!''

''Nonsense! You can paddle. Anyway, the cabins are way down the shore so no one can see us.'' She discarded her skirt and petticoats and stood clad in a white chemise and bloomers.

Camry brought a hand to her mouth and stifled a giggle. ''Bloomers! I thought you were the silk stocking type.''

Rose tossed her golden locks over slim shoulders with a shrug. ''There's still a *little* country left in me!''

Laughing, Camry jumped up and removed her dress also. Clad in undergarments, they ran to the fine pebbled shore and into the icy, but refreshing water.

Camry tentatively sunk into the water, surprised that she wasn't afraid. Gingerly, she paddled behind Rose and then reaching a sun-bleached boulder, they propped themselves on it. Together, they hugged their knees to their breasts.

Rose's teeth chattered. ''It's colder than it looks. This breeze is turning me into a block of ice.''

''Let's go back.''

''No-o,'' Rose stammered. ''I want to feel warmth first.'' She stretched back against the rock and soaked up the radiant sunshine.

Camry hugged her knees closer to her body. Her disheveled copper waves damply encircled her oval face as she pushed back a stray curl from her forehead and stared at the sparkling shore. The glossy leaves of chaparrals twirled in the lake breeze like pinwheels, revealing stunted tawny brown trunks.

Narrowing her eyes sharply, Camry concentrated on the brush until she was sure her mind wasn't playing tricks on her.

''Rose, there's someone watching us!''

Rose propped herself on an elbow and shaded her eyes with a slim hand. ''Where?''

Camry pointed to a cluster of manzanita bushes. ''There was someone there. I'm positive it was a man. I saw his hat.''

"Was he handsome?" Rose teased. "There's no one at this part of the shore."

"I'm telling you, I saw someone!"

"Let's swim in then."

"Right into his arms!" Camry said direly.

"It's either that, or swim across the lake." Rose turned her head and glanced at the expansive water behind them. "I'd say it's about a fifty mile stretch."

Camry found her lack of alarm vaguely disturbing, then her lips broke into a half smile. "I really *think* I saw someone." She tried to convince herself more than Rose. Maybe the sun was playing tricks on her.

Slipping into the water, Rose shivered. "I hope whoever you didn't see, didn't steal our clothes. How would we ever explain to the lodge!" She laughed and swam toward shore.

Camry examined the trees once more, before sliding into the lake as well.

Nicholas tugged on S.D.'s reins coaxingly, trying to disuade the roan from nibbling further at the manzanita bush. The horse nickered and shook his head, the gray mane tangled with small leaves.

"Easy fella," Nicholas soothed, his voice silky. "Hold on another minute and we'll get some nice grain."

He scanned the water again, only to see faint ripples. The two nymphs had disappeared into the dense lushness of pine trees. Pulling the brim of his hat over his brow, Nicholas urged S.D. toward the stables south of the lodge where Camry and Rose were staying.

As he reined his horse, Nicholas' thoughts wandered to Camry. There was no way he would let her roam the shores of Lake Tahoe unescorted. Yet, he couldn't just tell her he was here. He had to let her have some time on her own. In a way, he was responsible. If Garnet hadn't come to the house that day—and yet, he was glad she did. Garnet. She was getting herself in a stir over Caleb, but for the time being, there was nothing she could do even if she did go to San Francisco.

The stables where he'd been bunking for the past two days were uncomfortable—the only salvation, a clean bed of straw every night. Good Lord, what was he doing here? He had left Rigdon in charge of the C & C explorations. What had gotten into him to make him drop everything to be with Camry? And he couldn't even tell her he was here . . .

The July night was filled with bright stars; an alabaster half-moon bathed the tops of spiring pine trees in a heavenly glow. Mosquitoes hovered silently, while crickets chirped in the distance from hollow fallen logs. The shimmering water lapped steadily against soft sandy shores. Giant ponderosas surrounded a rustic stone lodge nestled at the north end of Glenbrook Bay.

Running a hand along the smooth porch railing, Camry stopped at one of the windows and looked inside. The dining room had been cleared of dinner dishes and the tables were now being used for recreational pleasures. Groups of four, in pairs of two, held playing cards, engaged in lively games of whist.

Rose emerged from the lodge and rushed onto the porch. "Camry, you'll never guess. I just ran into the Harkins. They're clients of Kent's."

"That's nice," she sighed listlessly.

"They're here celebrating their anniversary. Why don't you come inside? We're going to play whist. I'm a hopeless addict," she laughed.

Camry brushed a small pine cone from the railing. "You go ahead. I'm rather tired."

"Are you sure?"

"Positive."

"You rest up then. Tomorrow the Harkins are taking the steamer to Lake Tahoe City and then they're going to raft down the Truckee River. They asked us along and I accepted. It should be fun."

"It does sound like fun," Camry agreed, hoping the excursion would break her melancholy mood.

Camry strolled between the trees to Martha's cabin. The

night was alive with unfamiliar sounds. Sounds which Virginia City's stamp mills drowned out. The glowing moon lighted the forest path which connected all cabins. A muffled splash came from the lake and she stopped to stare at a growing ring, rippling the dark waters. A fish, obviously snatching a fly. Continuing at a faster pace, she walked on, the unknown wilderness unnerving her.

Martha's cabin was set further down shore. The log-framed dwelling had only one room, a window on each wall and a single entrance. The crude veranda was rickety and an old porch swing hung from the awning. Inside, a large tester bed, rocking chair, and small table and two chairs furnished the room comfortably. A tall, boulder fireplace stood in a corner, but it was not constructed for cooking. There were twenty cabins scattered around the lodge, all holiday-seekers enjoying the cuisine of a stout Chinaman catering from the main house.

She could see the cabin now, the porch flickering with the beam of a glass lantern anchored to the awning. Tiny moths and winged insects swirled around the warm flame, their shadows lacing the front door.

Camry climbed the steps and turned down the lantern, then sat in the swing and kicked off her shoes. Swaying softly, she sighed, leaned back her head and relaxed. A faint wind rushed through the trees, glossy leaves fluttering. She lifted her head alertly. Had she heard footsteps? The breeze subsided and everything was still. The needled branch of a ponderosa scratched the roof of the awning. Camry sat up, her body stiff, her heart thumping wildly. A pine cone dropped to the porch noisily, rolling to her feet. Two round, brilliant yellow eyes glowed from the darkness, then they were veiled, as if a window shade had been pulled over them slowly. An owl hooted and the shades were lifted, glowing eyes bright again. She screamed and ran into the cabin.

Dropping the bolt on the door, Camry rolled down the canvas window coverings and sat on the soft bed, the dark room surrounding her. She hated to admit it, but this was one time she would have welcomed her arrogant miner.

"Camry, wake up."

She opened her eyes slowly to see Rose's face above her.

"My, you really were tired. I came in at eleven last night and you didn't even wake. Why didn't you put on your nightgown?"

Sitting up, Camry looked at the wrinkled dress clinging limply to her body. "I must have dozed off." The last thing she remembered was wishing Nicholas were with her.

"The Harkins are meeting us at the dock in thirty minutes. I brought some buttermilk biscuits and quince from the lodge. They're on the table if you want them."

Camry went to the washstand and splashed water on her face. Patting it dry with a soft towel, she took off her soiled dress. Standing in petticoats and chemise, she asked, "Just what does one wear rafting?"

Rose bit her lip, bewildered. "I really don't know."

Together, they laughed.

The Governor Stanford was a fine white steamship with funneling, black stacks. A red paddle wheel dug into the current of Lake Tahoe's indigo waters, while the steam whistle tooted three short times. Camry stood on the second level, the fresh breeze caressing her peach-hued cheeks. The Harkins were a well-to-do couple from St. Louis, who were traveling in the company of the Webbs and the Butlers. She enjoyed the sunshine far more than the confines of the parlor, where the patrons played whist.

Camry watched the various boats on the lake. Small skiffs anchored close to shore, men fishing from the bows. McKinney's big boat, the Transit, sailed by with a party of men and women from Crystal Bay, waving hand-kerchiefs and hats.

Removing her straw bonnet, Camry waved back, the bright ruby sash rippling in the wind. She smiled and strolled the deck, her red and white pin-striped skirts swirling around her ankles. She had decided on a simply styled cotton dress, with small round white leather buttons that fastened the square neck at the front.

The whistle hissed steam as the Governor Stanford churned into Tahoe City harbor. Camry joined Rose and the others on the lower level. They disembarked and followed the path to Woodhull's Lodge. Children played on swings hung from tree branches, their laughter ringing through the camp grounds. A small group of boys fed a blue jay puffed white popcorn.

As the party neared Woodhull's Landing, the current of the Truckee sparkled over polished stones and into a calm basin deep enough for swimming.

Rose grabbed Camry's hand and squeezed it, her dark blue eyes merry. "Isn't this exciting! Won't Kent be envious when he finds out about all the fun he missed."

They were welcomed by Conrad Woodhull himself, a rough-hewn man adorned in buckskin breeches and shirt. He led them down a split-wood railed path to the raft dock. Each raft was four feet wide, made from five logs bound together with straps of leather.

Camry whispered to Rose, "Do you think it's safe?"

"I suppose so. The Harkins raft every year."

She began to wonder if riding the Truckee River was such a good idea.

Conrad waded in the water to his knees and strapped down the luggage that would float ahead to Truckee with one of his men. First, the Butlers were helped onto rafts, only one person to a raft; the Webbs followed, then Rose. When it was Camry's turn, Conrad gripped her arm as she stepped on the raft. Her weight caused the logs to bob, her shoes getting wet. He helped her sit, then smiled.

"You'll be a lot wetter before the day's out." He gathered the group's attention and instructed them on the use of oars.

"The current is light enough you won't have to constantly paddle. They're for docking or pushing away from shore brush the river might pull you into. The water rapids slightly at Frazier's Point, nine and a half miles down, but you should be able to ride it out. Watch your time limit. It takes three hours to reach Truckee, you should be there before seven."

Conrad pushed the Butler's raft into the river current. "Have a nice time, folks." The Webbs, the Harkins and Rose floated down the river. He pushed Camry's raft next. "Enjoy yourself, little lady."

Camry smiled enthusiastically. The jade water gave way to a dark navy as it left the sandy bottom and passed over the deeper sections. Green spears of tall river grass blanketed the banks. She began to relax and leaned back on her elbows, not caring if the water dampened her dress. She lifted her face to the sun, the warm rays coloring her skin.

"You-hoo!" Rose's voice sang.

She looked at her sister-in-law, who was several yards ahead of her. Rose's blonde curls shone like gold, her cheeks flushed with excitement. "Isn't this fun!" she called out.

"Marvelous!" Camry agreed.

"We're going to pull along shore in a bit for lunch."

"Fine." Camry dipped her hand in the current and watched the water fan behind her wrist.

After floating four miles, they paddled to shore. Camry dug her oar into the river and guided the raft to a clear landing spot.

Rose helped her up and gave her a hug. "Isn't this the best?"

She nodded. "It's so peaceful."

Rose brushed her wet skirts. "I'm soaked to the bone, but I don't care," she laughed. "Are you hungry? Mrs. Webb brought a picnic lunch."

Camry declined. "I think I'm going to sit on that boulder and enjoy the scenery." She perched on the sun-bleached rock and leaned back. A family of ducks floated by, their rich brown feathers shining. She thought of Da. He would love all this. Someday, just the two of them would come here. An idea struck her. She would bring him a present for his new office.

She called to Rose. "I'm going to look around a while. You go on ahead and I'll meet you in Truckee."

Rose shook her head. "I don't think it's such a good idea. What if you get lost?"

"I won't go far. Besides, how can I get lost on the river?"

"Well . . . I don't know."

"Don't worry," Camry assured.

Exploring the surrounding forest capreted deeply with dry pine needles, she searched for the biggest pine cone she could find. Blue and green dragonflies flew over the tall meadow grass. The terrain grew thick with brush, then a wall of dense piñon pines appeared. She poked around the ground, inspecting the pine cones.

Too small, lopsided, nibbled by squirrels, missing scales—all were discarded for imperfections. She was about to give up, when she spied the grand-daddy of them all. With twinkling green eyes, she picked up a large sugar pine. It was flawless.

Satisifed, Camry made her way back to the Truckee. A horse snorted and the jingling sound of spurs warned her there was a horse and rider close by. But who? Woodhull hadn't mentioned horse travel along this part of the river.

Camry walked faster, her breathing strong. She gripped the pine cone tightly. Visions of savage Indians filled her mind and she began to run. Pushing tree limbs from her path, she hurried to the raft. Her bonnet fell off and the pins in her copper hair loosened, the waves cascading to her waist.

She reached the shore and waded into the water. Pushing the raft into the current, she climbed on, her wet skirts clinging to her legs. Setting the pine cone in her lap, she began to paddle. Only after she had traveled thirty minutes, constantly scanning the empty shore, did she relax.

The sun was starting to meet the towering treetops on

the west side of the river. Camry had dallied longer than she had intended, but shrugged off any worry and leaned back. Worrying wouldn't get her to Truckee City any sooner. She placed her hands behind her head and stared at the cloudless azure sky. She shut her eyelids and sighed.

The rocking current woke her with a start. She sat up, clutching onto the edge of the raft. The water swirled and rolled over large rocks. In some places, boulders jutted from the indigo, obstacles for the thick branches that traveled the rapids swifly.

Camry gripped the paddle and tried to move closer to shore where the water was calmer. The current grew strong, white foam capping the waves. The gnarled branch of a chaparral snared her oar, and she struggled to hold on. She twised onto her stomach, but the rapids were too strong, the paddle was pulled from her hand. Sitting up, she held on to the leather binding, then took a deep breath, forcing herself to be calm. She would just let the raft ride the current freely—and hope it wouldn't run into anything. The raft bobbed sharply, jarring her. She found a large log had rammed her and was pushing the raft at a faster pace.

Wrestling with the log, Camry tried to slide it around her. It was too heavy. She tried again, but lost her balance and fell overboard. The cold water whirled around her, sucking her under. With all her strength, she kicked her legs forcing her body upward. She surfaced, gasping for air.

As the river grew shallow, the rocks increased. Camry attemped to grab onto a submerged boulder, but a thin layer of algae made the stone too slippery. The water pulled her along at a slower pace, giving her a chance to fight against it. She tried to cling to a rock again, this time she was successful. The only problem, she was still in the middle of the river. If she let go, she would be at its mercy.

Camry screamed. She didn't know how far ahead Rose and the others were. When no one answered, she feared they were already in Truckee. She had wandered too long. Her hand began to slip, and she struggled to hold on. The cool water splashed her face, causing her to turn away and squint her eyes.

Something stronger than the river pulled at her wrist and Camry began to fight to stay above water. An arm cradled her chin, then she was pulled from the rock. Powerful legs battled the current, as they left the fury of the rapids. Once in the shallow water of the shore, she was lifted and set down on the sandy bank.

She pushed her wet hair from her eyes. Nicholas' concern-filled face came into view, and she blinked the water from her lashes. He tightened his grip on her waist.

''Are you all right?''

''You!'' Camry was shocked. ''What are *you* doing here?''

26

Drops of water clung to Nicholas's damp forehead, his blond hair dripping on wide shoulders outlined by his soaked shirt. "What do you mean—what am I doing here? I just saved you from a watery grave."

Camry caught her breath. Her dress clung revealingly to her bosom, only two of the round buttons left, leaving the thin chemise amply on display. The pin-striped skirts were torn and muddy. "How did you find me?" she finally managed to ask.

"I've been following you since you left Virginia City."

"Following me!"

"It's a good thing I did. You didn't think I'd just let two women got off unprotected?" He reached out and plucked a wet leaf from her tangled red locks. "I've been camping just outside of Glenbrook. That sister of mine made it harder to keep track of you with this damn rafting venture."

"Does she know you're here?"

"No. I had to find out where the steamer was going, then I took the ferry."

"You! You were the one I heard when I was looking for pine cones. You were the one staring at us while we swam!"

Nicholas grinned. "You can't blame me for looking at such an enticing sight. You are fetching in your undergarments."

Camry grew angry and pushed his hand away. "Get off me, you big oaf." She climbed to her feet, Nicholas following. "Well? What are we supposed to do now? Walk to Truckee? Rose must be worried sick."

Nicholas appraised the sky. "It's too late. The sun will be setting in less than thirty minutes. I left S.D. at the edge of the forest. We can make camp there."

"You mean we have to stay *here*? Among the wild animals?"

His teeth flashed white, contrasting handsomely against his bronze face and damp strawberry-blond moustache. "Darlin', I can assure you, there are no wild animals here," he winked, "but me."

Camry stiffened.

He turned and walked noiselessly. Biting her lower lip, Camry put a hand to her bodice and pulled the material together, then stepped forward and followed him.

S. D. grazed peacefully on silky meadow grass. His gray coat was dappled with darker shades on the hind end. A shining black leather saddle rested on his back, equipped with a bedroll, canteen, Winchester .44-.40 and two saddlebags.

Nicholas unfastened his gear and tossed it to the pineneedle-covered ground.

Swatting a mosquito from her arm, Camry sighed. "I guess we'll have to make the best of it." Her stomach rumbled and she regretted not eating lunch. "What's for dinner?"

He stood over her, his hands on his hips. Tight-fitting blue denim trousers hugged his lean legs, the hems tucked into knee-length, fringed moccasins. "I guess I could shoot a fish."

Camry lifted her chin and aristocratic nose indignantly. "You wretched scoundrel, must you always make a damn mockery of me?"

"I'd better feed you, before you bite my head off." He withdrew his rifle from the scabbard, then tossed her his bedroll. Making his way to the river, he called over his shoulder. "Gather some pine cones for a fire."

She folded her arms across her breasts. "Hmph!" She reached down and wrapped his blanket over her shoulders. In his absence, she collected twenty cones, nineteen for use in the fire, and one for Da. It wasn't as good as the one lost to the Truckee River, but it would have to suffice.

Nicholas returned just as the sun set and the orange sky provided a backdrop for the green black silhouettes of pine treetops. He carried five speckled trout by their gills. Dropping them at her feet, he moved to the saddlebags and produced a knife in a leather holder.

Removing the blade, he handed it to her. "Well? What are you waiting for?"

Her jaw dropped in protest. "Waiting for? What do you expect me to do with them?"

"You will cook and clean them. I've been far too soft with you. I eat at the Sundowner more than I ever did before." He reached into his shirt pocket and drew out a small tin box of matches. Lighting the burrs, he leaned back and watched the red-orange flames grow and lick the night air.

Camry narrowed her eyes and squared her shoulders, yanking off his blanket. She picked up a fish, pinching the tail between her fingers, her hand at arm's length. She placed it on a rock and bent down. Holding onto the body, she squinted and began to slice the head off. The blade was razor-sharp, and she was glad to behead the slimy thing in one stroke.

"I don't know how to do this," she complained.

Nicholas reclined against the trunk of a ponderosa. "Make a slit in the middle and squeeze the guts out." He raised a cheroot casually to his lips and lit it with a glowing tinder. Smoke swirled over his head and into the verdant shadows of fluffy pine needles.

"Are you enjoying yourself?" Camry hissed.

He took a drag and sighed. "Extremely."

"Oh, brother." She cut into the belly and removed the insides, her body shivering with revulsion. Her posterior was hit by a flying sugar pine cone, causing her to look at Nicholas.

His face was painted with innocence, then grew boyish. "You look pretty when you're mad, darlin'."

"You've never really seen me mad," Camry threat-

ened. She finished cleaning the fish and rinsed off her
hands in the river. Nicholas scored the trout on stick
skewers and held them over the fire. In no time, the rainbow skin turned to an ash gray.

Nicholas handed Camry a stick and she sat across
from him, the campfire acting as mediator.

She picked the tender meat from the bone and
popped it into her mouth. "I shouldn't let you have any.
After all, I did most of the work." She gave the fish a
sidelong glance, then smiled proudly at her accomplishment. The light of the fire danced off her hair in a glow
of red and bronze with copper waves swirling to her
waist in a fluffy disarray. Her skin was lightly tanned and
satiny, a rich peach blush colored her high cheekbones.
When she bent to pick up another fish, her chemise fell
loosely from her bosom, partially revealing the soft
curves and pink rosebuds.

Camry looked up and met Nicholas' intense stare. His
firm sensual lips lifted in a smile. The fire crackled,
shooting red ash into the ebony night.

"Why are you staring at me?" She shifted nervously.

"You must have been staring at me to notice."

She threw the fish bones at her feet and stood
haughtily. "Why do you always twist everything I say?"
She watched him as he rose and walked around the fire.

"Why do you always run away from me?" Slowly,
seductively, his eyes traveled her body.

"I do not run away from you."

He took a step toward her and she kept her stance to
prove him wrong. Fear and desire clashed inside her
and she toyed with a tear in her skirt. "Where are we
supposed to sleep? I'm quite tired and I'd like to go to
sleep."

Nicholas' blond brows arched mischievously. "That
sounds like a good idea."

"I don't mean that . . . I—"

Taking slow steps, Nicholas backed Camry to a thickly
barked tree trunk. "Didn't mean what?"

"You know—"

Nicholas' gaze was as smoldering as the burning flames of the fire. "When are you going to stop pretending you don't want me to make love to you?"

Camry responded sharply. "I do not, nor have I ever!"

"You don't? You haven't?" His mouth was inches from hers, his moist breath caressing her lips. Though his body did not touch hers, she could feel the heat cast from his limbs. The air around her seemed magnetic, drawing her to him. She couldn't deny the spark of excitement at the prospect of his touch. Her senses reeled and she shook her head slowly.

"No, I don't want you."

Nicholas whispered against her cheek. "Good."

Camry's breath was snatched from her and she circled his neck with slender arms, molding against him, she gave herself freely to the passion with her kiss. Their lips were like the smoldering heat that joins metals. His tongue traced the moist fullness of her mouth, then explored the sweet recess within. Barely aware she was standing on tiptoes, she blended into his strong embrace, her fingers entwining with his silken locks. Suddenly, he lifted her with ease into his sinewy arms. She nestled her head on his shoulder slipping a hand into his shirt, she caressed the light covering of hair on his solid chest. Beneath her fingertips, she could feel the hammering of his heart.

The night was broken by a flood of burning lanterns and torches. Camry squinted at the brightness and held on to Nicholas tighter. The lights cleared from the forest, as a party of men and Rose Creighton, on horseback, came into view.

Rose dismounted swiftly and ran to the campfire. "Camry!" Her eyes widened with surprise. "Nicholas!"

His mouth pulled into a thin smile. "Now that you've established our names."

"Are you hurt? Why is Nicholas carrying you?"

Camry blushed, her senses returning. She twisted in Nicholas' arms. "Put me down, please," she ordered.

He cursed, then obliged.

She smoothed her torn skirts and made an attempt to hold her bodice together.

"We've been worried! The raft floated to Truckee without you on it. I was frantic. Mark Harkin ordered a search party at once."

Camry flushed with passion and embarrassment. "I fell off in the rapids. Nicholas rescued me."

"I'm not even going to ask what you're doing here!" Rose glared at Nicholas. "Right now, I'm concerned with Camry, you poor dear. We brought a horse for you. You must be worn to the bone." She gently guided Camry to a well-muscled chestnut.

Nicholas angrily covered the fire with dirt, a powdery dust and smoke cloud rising. He cursed again and secured his gear on S.D.'s saddle. He mounted and jerked the reins, his face immediately showing regret at the harshness taken out on his horse. He followed Camry and Rose into the forest, maintaining a small distance behind.

Camry felt Nicholas' midnight blue eyes boring holes in her back. She tightened her hold on the pommel and wished . . . wished what? Wished Nicholas hadn't ignited her passion . . . or wished Rose hadn't come when she did. She turned, pretending to adjust her skirt, and met his smoldering stare. Quickly, she faced forward and swallowed, taking a deep breath.

The Truckee Lodge came into view, a simple one-story house constructed from redwood. The stables were located in back where the party dismounted. Camry slid from her horse feeling numb. Rose put an arm around her waist. "You need a nice warm bath and a good night's sleep." She frowned at her brother. "I'm afraid all the rooms are taken. Had I known you'd follow us, I would have reserved you one. You'll just have to sleep in here. Come along, Camry."

Camry allowed Rose to usher her to the lodge. She looked back and saw Nicholas' form filling the stable door frame. His chest rose and fell strongly, and she remembered how masculine it had been to her touch.

His burning, unspeaking eyes held her, prolonging the moment. She had an urge to break free from Rose and run into his arms, but instead, she turned her attention to the lodge and submissively climbed the wooden steps.

27

Nicholas slammed the red and white stable door with a mixture of anger and frustration. S.D. pawed the ground nervously, making the horses down the line skittish. Nicholas pulled his ivory Stetson off and threw it on the dirt. The scent of hay and horses filled the air and he pushed open a slatted window. Moonlight filtered between trees and streamed faintly into the stable. He paced the damp floor, turned sharply, pounding his fist into his open palm, and cursed. Damn, why had Rose come when she did?

He moved to the stalls and unsaddled S.D. The horse's silky gray coat twitched in response to Nicholas's impatience. Nicholas tossed his bedroll and rifle on the straw, then went to the window and checked the sky. The shining stars of the big dipper were bright against a blanket of ebony. The dipper was to the left of the north star, as the hour signaled midnight. He headed purposefully toward the tall double doors. The night air was soothing on his face, compared to the stifling warmth of the stable. He took the steps of the lodge two at a time, but when he reached the entrance, he stopped.

"What the hell am I doing?"

How could he just waltz into her room? But why not? She was his wife. And he knew she cared for him, and yet . . . As quickly as he had walked to the lodge, he retraced his steps. Damn, he had his pride too. Nicholas stormed to the tack room and scanned the wall of bridles, harnesses and reins, for a brush. He ran is over S.D. in long moves, traveling dust from the horse's coat leaving small puffed clouds with each stroke.

After S.D. was groomed, Nicholas gave him some grain, then moved to the window again. The dipper had slid downward, the hour nearing two. He crossed the stable and patted S.D.'s dappled coat.

He was in love with her. It was that simple. No matter how he tried to deny it, he loved her. From the first day he had seen her, he knew they were destined to be together. And after they were married, he knew it would be forever. Nicholas sighed and stroked S.D.'s nose. The horse shook his head, the gray mane dancing.

"I'm in love with her, boy."

The animal's response was a polished hoof hitting the straw-covered ground. "You think I am? Hell, what do you know? You don't think."

Nicholas ran a hand through his hair while S.D. champed peacefully on his oats. "I know she's not the easiest woman to get along with, but underneath, where the heart is, there's a special sweetness. Did you know she helped deliver a baby? Keg told me about it and I think that's why Camry was upset that day. She was scared. I never told her how I felt about it. I was damned proud—" Nicholas stared out the window.

S.D. snorted and rubbed Nicholas' shoulder.

"You think I should?" He met the horse's soft brown eyes with his own. "She's so damned beautiful."

Camry watched Rose sleeping in the bed next to hers. It was no use, *she* could not sleep. Each time she closed her eyes, Nicholas' face appeared and she longed to be in his arms. After a while, when she was sure her sister-in-law was in deep slumber, Camry quietly moved to the dressing table. Running a brush through her hair, she bit her lower lip thoughtfully, then grabbed a shawl before she could change her mind.

The hallway was silent; dim light from kerosene lamps guided her to the lobby. The registration clerk had long since retired to his room, so she slipped onto the porch without being seen. Camry pulled her wrapper tightly around her fine lawn nightdress and darted barefoot across the damp grass to the stables.

The big door creaked softly as she peered in and quietly entered. Rows of stalls lined the left and she slowly looked in each one. When she saw S.D., she found Nicholas sleeping on a thick pile of hay. His eyes were peacefully shut, his breathing uniform.

Camry choked back bitter resentment and curled her fingers into a fist. Snatching a bucket from the corner, she dumped cold water onto his chest.

Nicholas jumped awake, his hand instinctively reaching for his rifle. Seeing Camry, he snorted, "What the hell!"

"You're asleep!"

He stared at her. He had finally dozed off minutes before. "I'm not asleep anymore."

"You! You make me so angry sometimes . . . I could—"

Nicholas brushed his wet shirt. "What? Douse me?"

In a huff, she turned and stalked out of the stable. How could she have thought he'd be awake, thinking the same things about her as she had been thinking about him?

Camry surveyed the distance between the lodge and the stable, and concluded in daylight, it seemed smaller. She adjusted her netted silk hat, took a deep breath, and made the crossing again. This time, she made no effort to be quiet. Reaching S.D.'s stall, she stopped and stared at Nicholas. He rested on his makeshift bed, an arm over his forehead.

She lifted her skirt slightly and nudged his leg with the toe of her soft kid shoe.

He stirred, pushing back his tousled hair as he sat up. She didn't know he wasn't asleep. He hadn't slept after her visit. Nicholas grumbled and stood, brushing the straw from his shirt. "What were you doing in here last night?"

She ignored him and started for the door.

"Dare I hope you came to sleep with me?"

Stopping, Camry looked at him over her shoulder.

"You must have been dreaming." She continued walking, not waiting for his reply.

He smiled slightly, appreciating the way her skirts barely brushed the dusty floor as she strode from his view. He may not have slept all night, but he didn't feel as tired as he had been before she walked in. She was like a breath of fresh air, even her perfume lingered over the pungent scent of animals. As he saddled S.D. he surmised things would be different once they were back in Virginia City.

Two black and green carriages with bold lettering, Campbells' Stage Company, on the sides waited in front of the lodge. Rose and the others had already taken seats. Camry climbed in without looking back to see if Nicholas was following.

During the ride back to Glenbrook, she was quiet, barely conversing with the other women. She stared out the window and scanned the scenery. Most of the road was in the shade of giant pines, only occasionally sun spilled through the limbs. Thick green ivy clung to the forest floor, several small blue and yellow flowers poking between the heart-shaped leaves. She allowed herself to look back once. Nicholas was a half mile back, S.D.'s coat shining as he kept the pace set by the stage.

By the time they reached Glenbrook, it was eleven-thirty. The Harkins, Webbs and Butlers bid their farewells and each made their way to cabins. Camry didn't wait for Nicholas, but walked steadfastly to Martha's cabin, intent on packing.

Rose caught up with her as she entered the dwelling, concern on her fair face. "Are you sure you want to go back to Virginia City so soon?"

Camry reached for her satchel and began filling it. "I'm sure. There's a noon Wells-Fargo and I plan to be on it. I hope you understand, but I can't stay on with Nicholas here."

Rose sat on the bed, her blue eyes filled with wonder. "What happened between you and Nick in the forest last night? You've been acting strange ever since we found you."

"I'm all right."

"I hate to ask and all, he is my brother, but does he
. . . well, I mean . . . is he having trysts with *that* woman?"

Camry had temporarily forgotten about Garnet Silk.
"He assured me they're only friends." She twisted the
lawn nightdress into a wrinkled heap and tossed it into
her traveling bag.

"That's what he told me," Rose pondered thoughtfully. "Then that must be all there is to it. Nick was never
one to lie."

Camry stifled a sarcastic laugh. No, never one to lie,
but he could sorely twist the truth. She grabbed the
handle of her bag and headed for the door. Nicholas
crossed the porch to meet her and she wondered if he
had been outside listening to them.

Rose put her hands on slim hips. "Well, Nick, Camry is
all yours. She insists on returning to Virginia City. I'm
going to stay on here until the end of the week. Would
you mind telling the hotel to send my things? The
Harkins are taking the stage to Reno next Tuesday and
we're all riding on the train back to South Dakota."

Camry hesitated, unsure she was doing the right thing
by leaving Rose. The fair woman had been someone to
look up to, a friend to confide in even though she could
not confide everything. As if reading her thoughts, Rose
put a hand on Camry's arm.

"I can't tell you how nice it is to have you as a sister-in-
law. Growing up with all boys, I never had another girl to
talk to. You must come visit sometime . . . both of you."

Smiling, Camry's eyes glittered at the woman's
gesture. "I've enjoyed your company equally. I wish
you'd come back to Virginia City with us . . . I've thought
of you as a sister—"

They hugged each other, Rose the first to slightly pull
back. "I really must be getting home soon. Kent will be
in a rage if I don't."

"Then we will write often," Camry sniffled.

"Yes, let's," Rose agreed. She went to her brother and

placed a kiss on his cheek. "Be a good husband to her Nick."

"Aren't I always?"

"That's questionable. Camry, take care."

"You too, Rose." And as a quick afterthought, she added, "Give your parents my love."

Nicholas raised a brow as Camry passed him going down the steps, turning once to wave good-bye to Rose, then heading toward the lodge.

Catching up with her, Nicholas took her satchel from her hand. "I think we should talk. If you didn't come to be with me last night, why were you walking around in your nightgown?"

She ignored his observation. "We have nothing to talk about," she snapped decisively. "Are you staying here? Or returning to Virginia City?"

"I'm leaving too. I belong at home, where you belong."

Snatching the bag from his hand, she lifted her nose. The Wells-Fargo stage was coated with a thin layer of dust, its six matching roans snorting in their harnesses. The driver shut the passenger door and pulled up thick yellow leather gloves.

"I'd like fare," Camry called before he could depart.

He turned to face her, a smile of recognition on his sun-worn face. "Howdy, ma'am."

"Well, hello!" she greeted.

Nicholas looked on with unsettling curiosity, wondering how Camry had come to know the infamous Hank Monk.

"I'm sorry, ma'am, but we're full-up," Hank apologized.

Untethering S.D. from the hitching post, Nicholas said, "I guess this means you'll be riding with me, darlin'."

"Hardly." She turned her attention to the stage. "Mr. Monk, if you'd be so kind."

He understood her meaning and climbed up the cab, securing her satchel with the other luggage. He extended a hand and she placed her foot on the red wheel and pulled herself up.

Lowering his hat over his eyes, Nicholas crossed his arms over his chest. "What are you doing?"

"Don't worry about me. I'm old friends with this seat." She reached back and strapped herself in. "I'll see you in Virginia City, dearest," she dripped with false sweetness.

Hank pulled his bandanna over his nose and cracked his whip over the horse's bobbing heads. The team weaved between the trees and out of Nicholas' view.

His tightened the cinch under S.D.'s belly and mounted, the saddle leather stretching as he sat. He cursed under his breath and kicked his horse's flanks, following the dusty trail left by the stage. Gaining speed until he raced side by side with the coach, he looked up at Camry, who sat as straight as a ramrod, tightly gripping the seat edges. Nodding his head curtly, he clicked his tongue and nudged S.D. with the heels of his boots. The horse galloped ahead and he settled in for the long ride. He'd be damned if he'd ride in their dust all the way to town.

Hank Monk guided the stage through Devil's Gate as they climbed the steep grade to Sun Peak. Road traffic was busier than usual, Camry thought as they passed through Gold Hill. A large number of covered wagons were leaving the city. Activity was booming, men calling to each other over the horse travel noise.

Camry watched logs ride on the current of elevated flumes as the Wells-Fargo coach entered Virginia City. Stamp mills pounded ore rhythmically, rumbling up the mountain. Blasts charged, and smoke from the shaft houses billowed into the hazy sky. Quartz and freight wagons thundered down C Street, the drivers cracking whips in the air. So much for the crystal skies and serenity of Lake Tahoe, she sighed.

"Why is everyone in such a hurry?" Camry inquired, observing the commotion.

Hank relaxed the reins and let the horses trot to the

stage office. "They want to get in and out as fast as possible. Freight prices have gone up from eleven dollars and fifty cents to fifteen dollars a load. The more trips they make, the more money they make. They're in competition with the V & T. Besides, the summer complaint has fired up."

Before Camry could ask what the summer complaint was, Hank Monk had stopped on Sutton Street and climbed down from the cab. She unfastened the leather strap from her waist and let him help her down. She saw Nicholas walk S. D. into Light & Allman's Livery down the street. Just as she received her satchel, he was at her side for it and they silently made their way across the boardwalk to Ma Zmed's.

Martha scurried about the front room, filling a basket with small medicine bottles. "Oh! You're back!"

Camry sank into a chair and fanned her face with her hand. "I think today is the hottest day I've ever lived through, and it's still not over. Martha, what on earth are you doing? Has this heat got everyone in town daft?"

"There's a cholera morbus outbreak." She dropped the lid on the basket and wiped her brow with a handkerchief.

"What?" Camry's voice cracked with fear at a word that sounded deadly. She'd vaguely heard of the disease, and knew that without proper hygiene one could contract it quite easily.

Nicholas put a hand on Camry's shoulder and questioned Martha. "How many have it?"

"Mostly children, as usual. They're dying at a fearful rate."

As Camry stood, Nicholas' arm remained around her shoulder. "Dying! My Lord," she whispered. "What can be done about it?"

Martha grabbed her felt hat and tucked her shirt into her trousers. "Don't eat any uncooked vegetables and boil the water before you drink it. Nick, could you hire a rig and take me to the hospital? I'm relieving Molly Sinclair."

"Sure." He turned to Camry and looked into her eyes with a soul-searching message. "I want you to go back to Glenbrook until Rose leaves. This thing could be dangerous if you don't watch what you're doing."

She resented his treatment of her as if she were a child. She'd never leave without her father. Putting on a courageous front, she said, "I'm not worried. I can handle myself. What's to boiling a little water?"

Trying to lighten the electric air between them, Nicholas managed a slight grin. "If your steak is any indication—" Then more seriously, he brushed her chin with a lean finger. "Please think about it, darlin'. If anything happened to you—" His voice trailed and she thought she heard him say he'd never forgive himself.

She tossed her head jauntily. "I'm going to take a bath and go to bed. First thing tomorrow, I'm going to visit my father and make sure he's all right." She picked up her satchel and gave Nicholas a sidelong stare, then left him in the front room, trying to focus her thoughts on a nice cool bath. She'd never let him know how scared she was.

28

Camry closed the front door of the boardinghouse behind her, then slipped her hands into fishnet gloves. She checked her appearance in the reflection cast on the windowpane. This was her first trip to Da's new office and she had taken special care in dressing. A silky textured white gauze dress with a rich grass-green sash molded elegantly against her slender figure. Flower spot patterns in purple, yellow and green dotted the full skirts and ruffled train in colorful sprigs. She patted the yellow ribbons in her copper ringlets and lifted her train above the gray dust of Howard Street.

Before she could cross the street, Martha pulled to the curb driving a wooden buckboard. "I need your help." There was an urgency in her voice. "Get in."

Surprise drained the color from her cheeks. "What? Where? Has something happened to Nicholas?"

"No, get in. We must hurry."

Camry stepped on the rickety floorboard and barely sat before Martha urged the beige mare forward.

"Where are we going?"

"We're short of help at the hospital. Some of the crew from the Savage Mine were brought in last night. They drank from a contaminated water barrel."

"But what about doctors and nurses?" Camry gasped. "Can't they tend to them? I don't know anything about this sort of thing."

"There are only eight doctors between Virginia City and Gold Hill, and a handful of nurses. For a town with twenty thousand people, that's just not enough." Martha pulled back on the reins to keep the horse from

running down the steep hill. They rode through the
Sporting Row district and then headed north of
Chinatown.

"I'm not qualified for this," Camry protested. "I'm
sure any other woman would be more—"

"Molly Sinclair's baby took sick," Ma Zmed interrupted harshly. "She was tending fourteen men and
women and six children. When her son took sick, she
went into another world and won't eat, drink or sleep
over worrying about the baby. Honey, there is no one
else."

Silently nodding, Camry remembered the joy on
Molly's face when Keg had told her she had a son.

The Storey County Hospital was at the base of Six-Mile
Canyon. The two-story brick building was constructed in
the shape of a cross. The front windows were painted
white, along with a balcony, veranda and eight columns
—four on either side of the entrance.

Following Martha down the hall, they entered a main
corridor. The walls were cut with more halls running in
several directions. Next to the many office doors were
wooden benches occupied by patients. Children cried
on the laps of their parents, while the sick adults
clutched their abdomens in pain. Nurses in white
dresses and mop caps called the names of those who
could have a bed as they became available. Camry
stared straight ahead, as if by looking at the sick, she
would contract the illness as well. Many gaped at her
fine gown. A little girl momentarily stopped crying and
trailed behind Camry in awe, until her mother pulled her
back.

Martha climbed the stairs to the second floor and they
entered a large room located in the east wing where the
sun was veiled by thin shades. The acrid stench of bile
and fecal matter assaulted Camry's nostrils and she put
a hand to her mouth, turning to Martha.

"I can't go in there." She swallowed hard, forcing her
stomach to stay calm. The stuffy heat closed in on her.

Disappearing down the west wing, Ma Zmed left

Camry to one of the nurses.

She was an older lady, with strands of silver hair popping from underneath her mop cap. "We need someone on beds fifty-six to seventy-two. They start by the window and are numbered, your group is at that end. My, but you shouldn't have worn that dress. Pity."

Camry followed the nurse's fingertip with her eyes to the rows of beds. Over a hundred white metal beds, occasionally separated by white cloth screens, filled the room; all were occupied by cholera victims. She fought back tears. "But I don't know what to do."

The nurse handed Camry an apron and mop cap. "Empty the bedpans and waste buckets. Give them the salt tablets on the station counter and make them drink all the water they can keep down. Above all—wash your hands after treating each patient. The newer patients have a bluish-purple skin color, rapid heartbeat and absent peripheral pulses—there isn't much you can do for them now. It will take its course. The others, more stable patients, can have bicarbonate of soda, and if they ask for it, bread."

"What do you mean? I don't know what peripher—" Camry's mind was spinning in utter confusion.

An agonized moan filled the already noisy wing and the nurse quickly fled.

Bewildered, Camry stood still, scanning the crowded room. On closer inspection, she saw dozens of flies swarming over the flushed staleness of bedpans. They buzzed over the flushed faces of the sick. A glossy-winged fly hovered over a small boy's head. It landed, then crawled onto his flushed cheek.

Camry brushed the insect away and felt the boy's forehead for fever. He opened his eyes slowly. She looked into the most beautiful lavender eyes she'd ever seen.

"Where's my ma?" he whispered hoarsely.

Rubbing his warm cheek lightly with the back of her finger, Camry's instincts took over. "I'm sure she's out in the hallway."

"I'm thirsty."

"I'll be right back." She walked quickly to the wing station and fetched a metal pitcher of water. Pouring a small amount into a dented tin cup, she handed it to him.

He brought the water to his parched lips and sipped. "It's too hot."

She remembered what Martha had told her. "Well, they have to boil the water so you won't be sick again."

"I don't like it."

"Well," she soothed softly, "it will make you feel better, so drink as much as you can."

"Ma'am," a man's voice signaled.

Camry looked up to see that she was being called. The man three beds down asked for her again. "Ma'am."

"I'll be right back," she told the little boy.

The man appeared to be in his forties, his face covered with the beginnings of a beard. Sunken, dull eyes were set in a pinched face.

"Yes?" she asked hesitantly.

"I'd be beholden for one of them salt rocks."

"Oh.... yes . . . I'll get them." She pulled the ruffle of her white mop cap over her brow to keep the fine beads of perspiration from running into her eyes, then remembered she was supposed to wash her hands before touching anything. A panic ran through her and all she could think of was the bucket of soapy water at the station.

On the way to it, a hand caught her arm. One of the miners from the Savage Mine curled in pain.

"You gotta give me somethin', lady. I'm loosin' my guts outta both ends. I feel like a goddamn baby."

She shuddered. "I'll see what I can do."

"You gotta get this slop bucket away, the smell is makin' me sicker."

"Ma'am," the man in the third bed called again.

"I'll be right there—" Her voice was nearly inaudible.

"You gotta take this bucket." Her attention was drawn back to the miner.

Without time to ponder, Camry bent and gripped the wire handle of the bucket, only to shiver and set it back down again. She couldn't do it! She had to get out. Seeing the soiled hem of her dress, she held back a sob, remembering how carefully she had dressed for Da. She had to wash her hands.

"Miss, my daughter needs some clean sheets," a woman in the corner summoned.

"You'll have to wait."

"She can't," the woman said firmly.

Camry snatched fresh sheets from the station and tossed them to the woman. "You'll have to do it yourself. I'm sorry, I only have two hands." *And they're dirty!* She felt moisture roll between her breasts, the dampness seeping through her starched white bodice. Moving to the soapy buckets, she scrubbed her hands until they glowed pink, then rinsed them with fresh water. The heat seemed to rise from the floor in waves. "Can't we open a window for air?" she asked a nurse.

The woman shook her white-capped head. "No, don't open one. The flies in here are so thick know, it's unbearable."

"Lady!"

"Ma'am."

"Miss!"

"Where's my ma?" the little boy cried.

The words flooded Camry's mind and she started for the door, not being able to tell if the drops rolling down her cheeks were tears or perspiration. She had to leave . . . but then, her eyes caught sight of a man in the corner bed. He bore a unique resemblance to Da . . . but it wasn't. But could he be here? She didn't know for sure. The man in the bed was somebody else's Da . . .

With forced strength, she squared her shoulders and turned around to face the agonizing pleas swirling in the inferno.

29

Frank Marbury descended the gold carpeted stairs from the Delta Saloon's private floor, with a white broadcloth jacket over his shoulder and a brassy-haired woman on his arm. Handing her a Delta token, he squeezed her curvaceous waist and took a place at the bar. Removing his bleached straw panama hat, he set it on the polished counter next to his jacket.

Casher Tisdale stopped washing beer mugs and tucked his rag into the bar apron around his middle.

"What'll you have, Frank? The old thing?"

"Give me a shot of bourbon." Frank reached into the pocket of his gold-threaded, white vest and produced a rolled cigarette. "Any word on when this heatwave will let up?"

Casher leaned against the bar and lowered his voice. "Even if the heat lets up in town, it's not cooling off for you. A big man, fella named Donnelly Paddock, came looking for you this morning."

Frank struck a match and brought it to his cigarette. "What did he want?"

"Said he was a Federal marshal from San Francisco."

Examining his sandpapered fingertips, Frank rubbed them over the back of his thumb. He felt no imperfection. Smooth as a baby's bottom. "Did he mention where he was staying?"

Casher reached behind the bar. "He gave me this here. Said he's staying at the old Exchange." He handed Frank the card. "Hopefully not for long. I said you was headed for Tombstone last I seen you. Even so, word's around, Frank. Johnny Newman, Pat Lynch and even

Pop over at the Brass Rail, think you oughtta lay low. They don't want any trouble with the law."

"There won't be any trouble." Frank relaxed his silver-tipped boot on the brass rail under the counter. He should have given Donnelly more credit in the intelligence department.

"If you don't mind my asking, what did you do?"

"I mind."

"Sorry, Frank. If I was you, I'd be fixing on leaving town." He pointed to a black-handled derringer resting in a thick glass on the counter. "I ain't never used this on no lawman, and I ain't going to start. Frank, I'm afeared if trouble breaks out, I'd have go agin you."

"Don't bother yourself, Casher." Frank crushed his cigarette and drained the bourbon from his glass. "Thanks for the information."

"Hope you make out okay."

Frank adjusted the panama on his slick brown hair. Swinging the broadcloth jacket over his shoulder, he tossed a coin on the bar. "Goddamn, it's hot. This stinking cholera epidemic makes me leery of touching anything in this town. Even the cards."

Casher slid him a sly smile. "Except Rustine."

"There's always a risk with women, Casher. Soiled doves or not."

Heat rose off the street in waves from mirage pools as Camry stepped out of the Storey County Hospital. Her skin was rosy pink, invigorated from brisk scrubbing, and contrasting with the crisp whiteness of a too-short nurse's dress fitting loosely over her slender form. Under normal circumstances, she would have protested the uniform, but since she hadn't another change of clothes, the clean dress was a welcome offering. She had watched with glittering eyes as the sprigged gown was tossed into the incinerator, flames engulfing the silky gauze. The yellow ribbon she had artfully tied in her curls, now served a more practical purpose by tying back her damp bronze locks.

She wearily shaded her eyes and looked up Union Street. The walk to Martha's was twelve steep blocks. Moisture formed on her upper lip and she ran her tongue over it, tasting salt.

The slow beat of hooves over powdery alkali dust sounded across L Street. Camry turned to see Frank in his black buggy with red wheels, pulled by the two dark brown stocking bays.

"Mrs. Trelstad?" he questioned. "Or is it Nurse Camry?"

She lightly examined him before answering. Though heat consumed the air, he appeared cool. Dressed in white trousers, shirt and vest, the only color to his attire was fancy black garters pushing up his sleeves and the golden threads running through his vest. His jacket rested over the back of the cushioned seat. "Oh, Frank," Camry finally sighed. "I'm too tired and hot to argue with you."

His lean facial features relaxed and he held out a hand. "Come on, I'll drive you home."

Camry accepted, telling herself today just wasn't a day for pride. Climbing onto the seat next to him, she couldn't help remarking, "You have the strangest way of showing up. I'm beginning to wonder if you're following me."

A glint of humor crossed Frank's face before he snapped the reins. "You look worn for the worse."

"Thank you," she replied irritably. "I've been emptying bedpans."

"Ah, Camry, when are you going to stop fooling yourself? Trelstad is not the man for you. You belong with someone who can buy you the finest . . . the best of things."

Her soft mouth twisted into a sour grin. "Hah!"

Frank smoothed his handlebar moustache. "You should be in a cool hotel suite lounging on a satin-covered bed eating chocolates to your heart's content."

"I'll bet I know whose bed, too," she retorted sarcastically.

"Never make a bet unless you can pay the wager."

"Frank, you talk in circles."

Her high cheekbone and dainty nose provided him with a pleasing view of her profile. "Look at you." He scanned her nurse's uniform with disapproval. "You strive for wealth—and don't deny it—and end up looking like a prairie Florence Nightingale."

"If you're going to insult me, let me out this minute."

"Forgive me, my dear. I was rash. But the truth is the truth, or haven't you looked in your silver-trimmed mirror today? The face before you would show a hunger for money. Why, I don't know."

Clenching her teeth, Camry was furious. "Don't talk to *me* about *money*, Frank Marbury! Yes, you have lots if it—gambling and I'm sure you *cheat* at it! You'd chase a dollar to the ends of the earth!"

He laughed richly. There was the Camry he knew. "Bravo!"

She brushed an escaped curl from her forehead and stared at the road as they neared C Street. "You snake, I don't know why I associate with you."

Frank inspected her with silvery eyes, partially shaded by the brim of his panama. God, even in her dowdy clothes, her face scrubbed almost pink, she could affect him. His mood abruptly changed. "Come away with me. We'll go anywhere you want. Reno. The coast. You name it."

"You can't be serious!"

"Damn it, look around you. This place is a rotting hole. Sickness everywhere you turn and you're being caught in it."

Their eyes met and she felt a shock run through her, almost afraid to say the words. "You're mad."

"I've been worse." His eyes never blinked.

"And I suppose you'd marry me if I got a divorce from Nicholas."

He wasn't that mad. His blood raced. At the same time he desired her, he hated her for making him want her.

When he did not answer, Camry shot back, "I thought as much!" She folded her arms over her breasts. "Don't you believe in anything?"

He stopped the horses in front of the boardinghouse and put a calling card in her lap, then placed his hand over hers. "Come away with me."

She pulled away. "Go to the end of the earth and chase your dollar—not me."

"I'll be in Gold Hill if you change your mind. The address is on the card. Go to Captain Billiard's Saloon and ask for Tom Finch. I'll be there for the next couple of weeks."

Camry took the steps of the boardwalk easily and slammed Martha's door behind her.

Emeline Gillespie, Ma Zmed and Molly Sinclair stood in the middle of the room. Molly's eyes were swollen with tears and her face was flushed.

"What's happened?" Camry stammered, almost afraid of the answer.

Emeline put an arm around Molly's waist as Martha answered quietly. "Molly lost her son this afternoon."

Raising a hand to her forehead, Camry squeezed fringed eyelids shut and drew a breath. "Molly, I'm so very sorry." Reaching for the grieving woman, she embraced her.

Molly began to cry again. "It's not fair. He was so little . . . I . . . I only had him for a month—" Her body trembled.

"I think you should rest, dear. Come lie down in my room," Emeline offered.

Molly put a lawn handkerchief to her eyes and Camry backed away, letting the two women guide Molly to the Gillespie quarters.

Walking down the hall, Camry brushed a tear from her cheek and bit her quivering lower lip. She was remembering the look of joy on Molly's face the day Keg told her she had a son. How could God be so cruel? Once in her room, she pulled a plain teal blue dress from the armoire. Discarding the nurse's uniform, she quickly slipped into her own garment and deftly fastened the hooks.

She practically ran out of Martha's and up the hill to Howard Street. Pushing past pedestrians, she reached Da's office quickly. Scalloped kelly green canvas awnings shaded the windows on either side of the stained glass and oak front door. A glittering sign with Michael Angus Parker spelled out in yellow paint hung over the entrance. As she stepped in, her father looked up from a stack of ledgers.

"Missy, whatta nice surprise." He smiled with full rosy cheeks. "I dinna know you were comin'. How was Lake Tahoe. I saw—"

"Da, I have to talk to you." Camry wrung her hands together.

"Inna moment. I haveta check over a stock price and I be right with you."

She sighed resentfully, knowing he wouldn't listen to her until he was ready. Taking a seat, she appraised the decor. Maroon divans and peach chairs framed by carved swags and rosettes lined the walls on either side of Michael's black walnut desk. Files were to his right; and the grandfather clock and small circular stairway to the private suite above, were to his left. Mustard carpets, a marble fireplace and a large oil painting of a fully rigged ship, finished the office.

Camry stood and paced around the regal room.

He shut the assessment and dividend book, and clasped his hands in front of him. "So, how's Nick and yourself? I hope you havena been drinkin' unboiled water. I'm worret sick about the summer complaint. So many are took ill with it."

She moved to his desk and leaned her hands on the surface. "I know. I've been at the hospital all day. It was horrible." Her voice cracked thinking about Molly. "Mrs. Sinclair's body died today."

"I am sorry for her and the lad. I know how you helped brung him into the earth." Michael rubbed her arm. "You're a brave girl. Just as strong as your mother was, God rest her soul."

Camry moved to his side and kneeled next to him,

resting her head in his lap. "But I'm not, Da. I want to go away. Let's go back to Philadelphia—or Scotland. We could go to Auntie Maeve's together." She looked into his soft green eyes imploringly.

He cupped her chin in his large hand. "What's this? Isna Nick bein' a proper husband?"

A tumble of confused feelings caused her mind to whirl. "He's been—" She blushed. "He's been a proper husband, but—"

"But what?" Michael asked with a significant lifting of his red-orange brows.

"I can't live with him."

"And why not? Are you so afraid to love him? I know he's not the man you wanted to wed, but he issa fine man. I canna take part in a plan that would go against him."

Camry hugged his leg and began to cry. "I don't want to love him."

"There, there now." Michael smoothed her satiny waves of hair. "You're a big girl now, Missy. Nick Trelstad is your husband and nothin' can change that in the eyes o' the Catholic church. You go on home now and stop this notion o' Scotland. The sickness has just got you upset." He helped her to her feet, then gave her a hug.

She sniffed and pouted. "I should have known you'd be on his side."

He laughed softly. "Ah, me girl, you break my heart with such blarney. I amna on any side, but what's best for you." He took a large red silk handkerchief from his pants' pocket and wiped her tearstained cheeks. "You go on home now. And mind you be careful on what you be eatin' and drinkin'."

She attempted a feeble smile. "You're too bossy." She sniffed again. "Where's that stupid cat of yours? Is this new office too high-class for him?"

Michael patted his round paunch. "Single-Jack issaround here somewhere. He likes to sit on me window box upstairs."

''If I were him, I'd run away.''

He chortled. ''I doubt that. You're a good girl. Now off with you, Nick is sure to be home.'' Kissing her cheek, he escorted her to the door. ''Good-bye, Missy.''

She sighed and left, feeling no better than she had when she arrived.

30

After a scented bath, Camry dressed in a cool, mint cambric gown. Opening the pantry door, she dazedly stared at the half-stocked shelves and sighed, leaning against the frame. She was still disappointed with Da's reasoning and coming home to an empty house didn't lift her spirits. Even the blue-haired Emeline Gillespie would be a relief to talk to.

"I was hoping you'd be home."

She turned to see Nicholas striding across the kitchen carrying a box labeled Thos. Taylor and Co., Importers of Wines and Liquors.

"Now this takes the hair of the dog. Nicholas Trelstad, what are you doing with a case of Old Jim rum?"

He set the box on the pastry counter. "Stop making dinner," he ordered good-naturedly.

"I never started. There's nothing to eat anyway. I don't know how you expect me to—"

Touching her soft coral lips with one calloused finger, he silenced her. "I saw your father. He told me how you helped Martha at the hospital today." He reached into the box and pulled out two candlesticks. They were silver, engraved with bunches of grapes and fancy leaves running to wide bases.

Camry put a hand to her breast, overwhelmed. "For me?" All the heaviness of the day seemed lighter.

"For us." Reaching in again, he lifted several blue pots with lids. "I stopped by the Sundowner and had Curly pack us a dinner. I wanted it to be special for you today. I'm proud of you, darlin'." There, he had said it. He should have told her that long ago.

She stared, speechless.

Nicholas draped a lace cloth over the kitchen table and set silver cutlery, goblets and a bottle of port wine in the center. "After you." He pulled out a chair and helped her sit.

Camry watched him pour the wine and fill plates with juicy steaks, fluffy mashed potatoes, sweet carrots and buttered rolls. He placed the meal before her and sat, waiting for her to take the first bite. When she did, he smiled and began eating.

Taking small bites, Camry continued to stare at Nicholas, baffled by his strange behavior. "To what do I owe this generosity? Did you find a big vessel of silver?"

"Vein," he corrected. "Nope."

Sipping the wine, Camry batted her long lashes. "I'm shocked that you are spending money. Those candlesticks must have cost a fortune."

Nicholas stopped his fork halfway between his mouth and plate. "I wish you wouldn't always spoil everything. Why do you insist I'm a stingy clod?"

"All miners are poor unless they own the mine. Take John Mackay for example. He owns the mine you work in."

"I don't know why you complain. You have a good solid roof over your head, nice clothes—"

"I don't have a mansion on top of the hill like Mrs. James Flood. And as for clothes, they're outdated and besides, I had them before I married you."

He dropped his fork and threw up his hands. "You don't do your own laundry—it's sent to Chinatown. You rarely cook—thank God. Your idea of poor is completely farfetched. How would you like to live below M Street among the wooden shacks and opium dens? Then you'd really see what poor is!"

Camry stiffened. "Let's drop the subject."

"I've let it drop far too long. What you really can't accept is me and my profession. A miner by trade. Well, I like what I do. I don't want to own the mine. I'm not a damn socialite or mine owner—someone to give you prestige."

She was angry with herself for ever starting the conversation. It really had been a lovely gesture on his part, and now she'd spoiled it with remarks she didn't really mean. "Let's drop the subject," she repeated.

Nicholas' lips broke into a slight grin. "No. Admit it. You want people to say: 'There goes Mrs. Nicholas Trelstad, wife of the Consolidated-Virginia owner and fifty other mines.' Well, it's not going to happen, because it's not me."

Standing abruptly, Camry snapped indignantly, "I'm not going to admit to anything."

He pushed back his chair and moved to her. "I think you object more to the man than the so-called lack of greenbacks. Camry, why can't you want me for me? I want you for you—temper and all."

For lack of a better retort, she answered, "Well, why can't you be a socialite or mine owner?"

He laughed softly. "So, you'd love me if I were notoriously wealthy?"

"I didn't say that," she replied curtly.

Nicholas' laughter died to a flashing smile and he drew her into her arms. He was tired of her flaunting things in his face. "Right now," he whispered, "pretend I'm the richest man in Virginia City."

Conscious of his strong hands moving down her back, Camry relaxed against him, waiting for his lips to meet hers. When they did not, she looked into his midnight blue eyes questioningly.

"You kiss me." It was a soft command, one which she obeyed without further hesitation. Her mouth timidly touched his, her heart dancing with excitement. Blending together, their lips became one. An aching need coursed her veins, and she could not deny the attraction she felt for him. Nicholas intensified her kiss, his tongue entering the sweet recess of her mouth, tasting the wine she had drunk minutes before.

Keg Carpenter stormed into the kitchen from the back porch, causing them to jump apart.

Putting a hand to the brim of his black hat, Keg silently acknowledged Camry, then turned his attention to Nicholas. "We need ya over t' the mines. Couple of men fainted dead away right then and there at the Con-VA on account of cholera. Sutro's got us jackin' in the C & C t'keep production up. Rig's 'bout t'plum lose sight a bullion estimates and there was a car derailed in the 2,500 level. They need ya as shift boss."

Immediate concern filled Nicholas' face, and he momentarily looked away from Camry's flushed face.

"I'll get my hat."

Camry stepped back. "Well, what about dessert?"

"It's cherry pie and you'll have to eat it without me."

She asked impulsively before he left, "Well, when will you be back?"

"Don't know. Say, do me a favor. Go to Beck's first thing tomorrow and bring back the candleholders and silverware. I borrowed them."

Camry put her hands on her hips. "Borrowed! I thought you *bought* them for me!"

His answer was the slam of the front door closing, then heavy footsteps as he and Keg stomped across the boardwalk.

There was no let up in the heat as Camry turned into H.S. Beck's General Merchandise. She glanced at the wall thermometer, seeing the register over 100 degrees.

"I'll make sure Nick gets this." H.S. accepted a small brown envelope from Garnet Silk.

"Gets what?" Camry interrupted, her eyes angrily burrowing into the sultry woman.

Beck's face took on a guilty expression. "Good morning, Mrs. Trelstad."

Pushing back her wispy black bangs, Garnet remained cool and politely greeted, "*Buenos días, Senora Trelstad.*"

"Why can't you leave my husband alone? What's in that envelope? A letter telling him where to meet you for an afternoon tryst?"

Garnet laughed softly, her honey voice smooth. "No."

"Mr. Beck, you should be ashamed of yourself, acting as a messenger for them! Give me that envelope this instant."

H.S. looked at Garnet, his eyes questioning.

"*Por qué no? Sí, Senor Beck,* let her have it."

He handed Camry the envelope and as she opened it, she glared at Garnet. "Such impudence never came my way." Looking inside, she gasped. "Money! What's this? His change for services rendered!"

Garnet covered her full red lips with a hand to hide her smile.

"Why . . . why you tart! I should inform the sheriff of your indiscretions!"

Beck spoke up. "You'd have to arrest half the town on the same charge."

"I be leaving town and don't know when I be back. *El dinero* is for Nicky to pay my house rent with."

"Why don't you just stay where you're going and don't come back?" Camry suggested.

"*Dios mio!*" Garnet controlled her temper and addressed H.S. "*Senor* Beck, see Nicky gets *el dinero, por favor.*" She snatched a floral carpet bag resting at her feet. "*Adios, Senora.*" She departed without giving Camry a fight.

Camry declared derisively. "Well, she certainly has no backbone."

"She'd never say anything against you. She's got too much respect for Nicholas."

"How noble." She set the candlesticks and silverware, wrapped in a damask cloth, on the counter. "I believe these are yours."

"And I believe this is mine." He pointed to the money envelope in her hands.

"You needn't worry yourself about it, Mr. Beck. I'll make sure Nicky gets it!"

Nicholas and Keg sat under the awning of Martha's porch, seeking relief from the heat. A film of ore dirt covered them and sweat beaded their foreheads.

Keg lifted a glass of lemonade to his lips and drank. Pursing his mouth, he frowned. "Ain't that old woman, Miz Gillespie, got anythin' better'n lemon water t'drink? I feel a notion settlin' o'er me t'get lickered up. I ain't worked all night through in a barn door's swing."

"At least there haven't been any more stricken with cholera within the last twelve hours." Nicholas reached into his work shirt pocket and grabbed a fistfull of peanuts. He cracked them mechanically, dropping the shells onto the rough boardwalk. He was glad the sickness had died down. Now he wouldn't have to worry about Camry so much. He wondered where she was. Probably at Beck's talking him into giving her the candlesticks.

"Fuse-man on the 1,500 level said he heard a rumor a buzzin' that the Con-VA's shakin' the money in the Bank of California. James Flood's a tryin' t'cash a voucher for $300,000 and won't accept nothin' but the full currency from Ralston."

"I heard that too. I'll put up a bet William Sharon doesn't like it too much. He keeps watch on the money in that bank like a hawk. Sometimes I think he forgets he's just the agent and Ralston is the President."

"That whiffet! Him and Ralson are 'bout as diff'rent as a skunk and perfume." Keg leaned back in his chair so only the two back legs touched the wooden planks. "I don't much trust Sharon. His eyes are t'close t'gether. I got t'jawin' with some of the miners and there's a good chance the bank is goin' t'fold. I wouldn't put that idea t'pasture, no sir."

Nicholas brushed stray shells off his lap. "I'm withdrawing my money until this thing blows over."

"Gold and silver in this here mountain brings out the deviltry in a man. Mackay, Flood, Fair, O'Brien, Ralston, Sharon, Stewart, Sutro, Hearst—hell, the list goes on forever. All them kings are goin' t'end up in brass-handled caskets afore their times. I can smell it like a bear can smell honey." He rubbed the stub of his index finger over his chin.

"Just like you can smell a gallon of rifle whiskey before you enter the saloons," Nicholas teased.

The Indian licked his chops. "I think I'll mosey on down t'Cad's Brickhouse." As he stood, Camry made her way to the boardwalk and crossed it.

"How-do and good-day, Miz Trelstad. Nick, I'll see'd ya later."

After Keg left, Nicholas gestured to the vacant chair next to him. "Hello, darlin'. Did you give Beck the candlesticks?"

"Don't you 'darlin' ' me." She ignored his inquiry on the silverware and reached into her reticule. "Your Spanish strumpet told me to give you *this*!"

He took the envelope and looked inside. "What's this for?"

"I debated giving it to you, but decided I would like to be the one to tell you rather than you finding out from someone else. She's gone. And good riddance I say."

"Gone? Where?" Nicholas stood quickly.

"I haven't the slightest idea and I don't care. You're supposed to pay her rent while she's away, but after my talk with her today, I doubt she'll be coming back."

"Damn it! If she's done what I think . . . I'll deal with you later!" He ran down the steps, his heavy boot heels scraping the planks.

"Nicholas Trelstad! You come back here! She's gone! Don't you dare try to bring her back or I'll—" Camry watched him disappear in the street traffic, then sank into the chair.

31

Camry stood in the dark hallway staring at a thin shaft of yellow light coming from beneath Nicholas' closed door. It was well past midnight and she had been waiting for him, but now that he had reutrned, she was hesitant to speak with him.

"Are you going to stand there all night? Or come in?" Nicholas' deep voice was clear beyond the closed door.

She drew a breath and entered.

He was sitting in the rust and black patterned chair, holding a glass of rum. Midnight blue eyes held her to the spot. The strong smell of alcohol permeated the room and swirled on a breeze as it floated in softly through the open window.

"You're drunk."

"Am I?" he questioned her assumption.

Turning, Camry put a hand on the doorknob, but froze as Nicholas' words cut the air. "Stay where you are."

She faced him, her emerald eyes challenging. "I'm not afraid of you."

"You're not afraid of anything."

She straightened herself with dignity.

"In case you're wondering, she's gone." He brought his glass to his lips and drank. "She bought a one-way ticket to San Francisco."

"I don't care where she went." Camry tossed her head disdainfully.

"No, you wouldn't." Nicholas stood and poured another drink. "Sometimes I don't understand what goes on in that pretty head of yours, Camry. When you tended the sick at the hospital, did you ask each patient their occupation? You took care of saloonkeepers, miners and seamstresses, and for all you know, Sporting Row girls. Does a wound have to draw blood before you'll have compassion? Garnet's wounds are on the inside."

Camry's temper flared. "What about *my* feelings?"

"You don't have any. Just like your gambler, Marbury."

"Frank Marbury understands me. He's a friend—"

"Well, Garnet is *my friend*!" He slammed his fist on the washstand. "When you hurt her—you hurt me. You could be in her shoes quite easily, so don't tempt me."

"What do you mean by that?"

He moved closer to her, his eyes penetrating. "From the start, you've fought against me. I had hoped . . . When I first saw you in Carson City looking so confident, I saw your beauty, pride, courage . . . the way you could melt a man's heart with one smile. And I wanted you for it. God, I still want you for it, but you push me too far. You condemn things you know nothing about."

Camry's heart pounded. "Then explain things to me." She wanted to understand, wanted desperately to run into his arms, but the dark-haired woman still stood between them. "Why all this concern for *her*? I'm your wife."

He gave a short laugh. "You can't fathom the idea of me loving the both of you, can you? Maybe I'm not even sure what the word means." Nicholas reached out and cupped her chin with strong fingers. "All I know is, if she would have had me, I'd have married her. Maybe we both would have been better off."

Camry brushed off his hand. "You can't be serious. She's nothing but a harlot."

His jaw twitched as he fought to control his anger. "She's more a woman than you'll ever be. The only time I've seen you act like a woman is in bed. The difference between the two of you is, you don't hold out your hand for money, your tactics are less obvious, but the demand for compensation is still the same."

Blinking her eyelids, Camry fought back tears.

"Lady, don't make me feel bad for telling you the truth." He shook his head slowly. "I seem to be able to calculate your moves before you make them. Just once, why don't you do something to surprise me?" He picked up the bottle of rum and left the room.

Camry stood motionless until she heard the front door slam, then her body racked with sobs.

The dry summer's night air seemed to close in on Nicholas as he shuffled down the street. He had drunk far more than he intended. His head was light, his eyes tired. Goddamn things anyway. Kicking a small rock in his path, he looked up the mountain. A half moon glittered hazily. It seemed to be laughing at him. Strolling down A Street, he ended up at Light and Allman's Livery.

Reaching S.D.'s stall, Nicholas sat on a bale of sweet hay, then propped his rum bottle between his legs. The animal nuzzled his shoulder, searching for a tidbit from its owner, unaccustomed to such a late-night visit.

"I don't have anything for you, boy." Hell, I don't have anything for anybody, he thought. He was as mad as he had been in a long time. Not only at Garnet, but Camry as well. Why did women have to be so damned unreasonable?

And Garnet! He had told her not to go to San Francisco alone! That town was filled with nothing but cutthroats. She didn't know her way around. Now he'd have to wire a description of Garnet to W. James Quincy because he'd be damned if he'd let her wander around. The only picture he had of Garnet was the one with her and Caleb . . . He'd have to send that one.

Leaning his head back against the stall, Nicholas felt regret run through his veins as he recalled the argument with Camry. He hadn't meant to say things . . . He didn't wish he'd married Netta. He loved Netta, but not the same way he loved Camry. If only Camry would say she loved him . . . at least give him some reason to hope she'd care for him—if not today, maybe tomorrow.

Taking another drink from the mouth of the bottle, he closed his eyes and before long, fell into a drunken sleep, something he hadn't done since he was in his teens.

The first rays of a desert orange sun crept up the mountain as Camry rolled on her side and stared out her bedroom window at the silhouette of Sun Peak. Soon the townsfolk would be up, refreshed from sleep and ready to meet a new day. Except her; she had not closed her eyes all night.

Nicholas' harsh words had stung terribly. After hours of trying to tell herself she was glad Nicholas would rather be married to someone else, she finally had to admit to herself she didn't want to lose him. Oh, she had tried fighting against him. But it was useless. She was hopelessly in love with him. When had it dawned on her? At the Fourth of July dance? No, it was the moment she had first laid eyes on him in Carson City, just as it had been for him.

Any love that he might have felt for her was now crushed, she was sure. But maybe with Garnet Silk in San Francisco, she would have a chance. She was confused about the Silk woman. Why did she turn down Nicholas' proposal? Why, any woman in her right mind would be proud to have such a fine man as a husband . . . oh, she had been so blind! She was proud of him. Why couldn't she have admitted it sooner? It made no difference what his profession was—it never had. That was just an excuse not to love him, but she did love him. Was it too late?

She sat up and kicked off the sheets that tangled her legs. She must tell him she loved him! Yes, that was it. Why, just last night he'd said she should so something to surprise him! She had to tell him. She had to tell him now before it was too late! But how? How? . . . Thaddeus Carpenter! If anyone woudd be able to help her, it would be Keg.

After throwing on a dress, Camry hurried down the block to Crazy Kate Shea's boardinghouse. The wooden building appeared to be one story, but on closer inspection, it had a lower floor on B Street down the slope of Mount Davidson. She entered and followed a narrow hallway that curved and twisted in maze-like turns.

A miner with thick, white-blond hair and powder blue eyes met her in the hall on his way out.

"Thank goodness! Excuse me, could you tell me which room is Thaddeus Carpenter's?"

"*Vem?*" He spoke in a language foreign to her, a question in his voice.

Camry addressed him in a louder tone, as if his hearing her better would make him understand. "Thaddeus Carpenter! They call him Keg!"

"*Jo! Keg, den Indian! Ned den trappa rum fem.*"

"I beg your pardon?"

"*Fem rum.*" He nodded his head and held up five fingers.

"Room five."

Shrugging broad shoulders, he pointed down the stairs.

"Never mind. Thank you."

"*Tack själv,*" he grinned, still nodding.

Camry hoped he had meant room five and gripped the loose hand railing, descending the steps. A brass number five was nailed to the last door on the left. She knocked softly.

There was no answer and she quietly opened the door. Keg Carpenter was clad in red long-johns, snoring lightly and sprawled on a narrow cot on his back. His head hung over the edge, his full, long black hair dusting the floor. A leather holster and revolver were belted around his middle and thigh.

"Mr. Carpenter," Camry whispered and knocked on the door frame.

His snoring wavered and he licked his lips.

"Mr. Carpenter." She knocked louder.

Keg woke and instantly reached for his gun with lightning speed. "Cut the breeze, stranger!"

Gasping, Camry looked down the barrel of a Peacemaker .45.

Focusing his brown eyes, he relaxed his arm. "Miz Trelstad? What in the deuce are ya doin' here?"

"I've got to talk to you."

He rubbed his face and tied his hair back with a suede piece. "Let me fetch m'skins then." He stepped into a pair of faded trousers that had been draped over a chair in the corner. Resecuring his holster, he sat on the bed again and rested his arms on his knees.

Camry wrung her hands nervously. She had only just recently confessed her feelings to herself, now she had to confess them to a man she hardly knew. "I don't know how to start. I don't—" Tears got the best of her and she began to cry.

Keg reached for a bandanna and gave it to her. "Now what's the salt water fer? Come on, Miz Trelstad, ya'll get your pretty face redder than a mulberry."

"I don't know what's the matter with me. Nicholas and I had words. I said some terrible things. . . . He said some terrible things—" She paused and looked into his dark eyes. "You don't think I'm good enough for Nicholas, do you?"

"Nope. It's yerself that figgered you ain't good enough fer him."

"Maybe at first, but I've changed. I tried to fight it, but I love him. And now he's told me he's sorry he ever married me!" She broke into loud sobs.

Keg went to Camry and patted her back gruffly. "That's plain graveyard talk. He told me hisself, he's plum taken with ya."

"Not anymore. He went after that Garnet Silk woman and when he couldn't catch her, he blamed me."

"Now let me tell ya somethin' 'bout Miz Garnet. She ain't been dealt a fair deck. Her husband done run off with another woman and he took their boy with 'em. She ain't got no friends 'til Nick come along. She's only a tryin' t'get her boy back. It's a wonderment she's beared up this far.''

Camry dabbed the corners of her eyes with Keg's bandanna that smelled like stale whiskey, then sniffed. ''But Nicholas said he wanted to marry her, but she wouldn't have him.''

''He may've thought he wanted t'marry her, but I reckon it were out of duty he done asked.''

''Really? Oh, Mr. Carpenter, if only that were true!''

Keg scratched his ear. ''I sometimes do choose the wrong words for the proper occasions, doncha know'd, but I feel plum confident a tellin' ya—he's done smitten with ya.''

''I must talk to him right away! Could you take me to him?''

''Now? I don't know, Miz Trelstad. They ain't a goin' t'let no female down in them mines.''

Camry pleaded with him. ''I won't be any trouble. I have to tell him how I feel.'' Then suddenly the thought struck her—he might not be at the Consolidated-Virginia! What if he'd just gone ahead and left town and headed for San Francisco to bring Garnet Silk back?! With renewed urgency, Camry insisted. ''You must! It might be too late already!''

''Rattle some sense in your head, Miz Trelstad. They just ain't goin' t'let ya go below.''

She looked at him imploringly and began to cry again. ''But I've got to!''

Massaging his temple, Keg snorted, ''Awright! Sonofagun, ya talked me in t'it! Ya ain't goin' t'be able t' get in like that. There's some ol' clothes out t'the back porch. Get yerself a pair of skins and shirt.''

She wiped away her tears with the back of her hand. ''Oh! Thank you, Mr. Carpenter!'' She hugged him and left.

''I must be witless,'' Keg mumbled to himself after she had gone. ''Witless and drier than a rattler on a hot griddle.'' He poured a stiff drink of rye and lifted it to his mouth. Before the glass touched his lips, Camry's scream echoed through the halls of Crazy Kate's, and he dropped it. Running to the back, his fingers fixed to the trigger of his gun, he reached her, drew, then laughed.

With a hand to her throat, she was backed into the corneer of the porch.

"Sorry, I forgot t'tell ya 'bout Schofield."

A stuffed black and white mongrel dog was poised in mid-leap, with pointed yellow teeth bared. He was perched on an old crate, surrounded by discarded tin oyster cans and beer bottles.

"I got mighty tired of them cats a holdin' caucuses out t'here. Them bottles and cans didn't do no good."

"Does this work?" Camry asked, her breathing returning to normal.

"Better than a horse's tail swats flies!" he boasted. "Come on with ya. Bring in them skins."

She followed his orders and they went back to his room. He slipped into worn mule-ear boots and a light-weight calico shirt. Grabbing his black hat, Keg stepped outside the doorjamb. "Ya put them duds on." He motioned to his head. "And do somethin' with that strawberry hair a yours. There's a hat under the cot and a pair of boots. I'll be waitin' out front." He closed the door and Camry hurriedly unfastened her dress.

The clothes were dirty and smelled and she wrinkled her nose stepping into the trousers. She left her pantalets and chemise on to keep her soft skin from chafing against the rough material. The hems of the pants had to be rolled up and the waist held up by a pair of suspenders. The shirt billowed around her like a boat sail. She repinned her hair close to her head and reached under the bed. The hat was soft suede, frontier style and molded to her forehead. The boots were too large, so she tore strips of her petticoat and stuffed them into the toes.

She shivered with revolt at the odor of mildew coming from the garb, and reached into her reticule. After dapping perfume behind her ears, she stored her dress under Keg's cot and shuffled down the hall.

Keg leaned against the boardwalk railing, taking a drink of rye from his bottle since he had broken the glass. "I don't know'd why I'm a doin' this. Ya still look like a female t'me." He waved his hand in the air between them. "Ya smell, Miz Trelstad!"

"I know—" Her words were cut short as he poured some of his liquor over her shirt. "What are you doing!?"

"Can't have ya goin' down there smellin' like a rose. It'll reflect bad agin me. They'll think I'm a holdin' company with pansies. Never let it be said, Thaddeus Carpenter runs around with jaded miners! Here—take a swig of this here." He passed her the bottle. "Go on, or I ain't a takin' ya."

Camry held her nose and took a short gulp. As the burning liquid coated her throat, she sputtered and coughed.

"Let's be on with this." Keg snatched the bottle, downing the remaining rye whiskey.

Flashing him a sweet smile, she spoke softly. "Thank you . . . Keg." She used his nickname for the first time.

He clutched his stomach in mock pain. "Tarnation, Miz Trelstad! Ya keep smilin' like a flower, I'll surely be strung up afore sundown by the Miners Union! Come on, afore I come t'my senses and change m'mind!"

32

As Keg and Camry neared the Consolidated Virginia Mining Company, a wave of recollection washed over her. It seemed an eternity since she had arrived in Virginia City and seen Nicholas in the very spot she walked over now. The closer they got to the mills, the louder the roars from powerful stamps. Timber piled next to a shaft house with four tall stacks that billowed puffed clouds of black smoke. Buckets of water sat precariously on top of the roofs in case of fires.

Miners scurried in different directions, several staring at her long enough to make Keg nervous. He jerked his head to the left and rolled his eyes, signaling her to duck behind the boiler house.

He rubbed his smooth chin with little enthusiasm. "This ain't a goin' t'work. I can see'd that now."

"But we can't turn back! You promised!" Camry's green eyes glistened, threatening tears.

Keg kicked the dusty earth with the toe of his boot, then a grin spread over his face. "Ya stay right t'here. I'll be back. Keep your head down and don't talk t'nobody."

She nodded and watched him disappear into the main shaft house. Her heart was beating wildly; half from the excitement of her masquerade and half from knowing she would soon be with Nicholas.

Keg returned shortly, carrying a large tin bucket. "Slap some of this here on your arms and face. 'Specially on your chin so'd it looks like ya got prickles." He held out the pail filled with muck.

Hesitating, Camry asked, "What is it?"

"Sump."

Wrinkling her nose, she pinched a little of the mud.

"No! No! Ya got t'get a good handful!" Keg insisted. He dipped his large hand into the fine sump and liberally slapped it on her arm, working it in. "Cover up that yucca flower white skin of yours."

Camry scooped the mud and shivered while rubbing it over her neck and face. After covering her other arm, she took a step back so he could view her.

"I'll be arrow struck if ya don't look like a coati."

"Is that good or bad?"

"Good enough. Come on." They made their way to the shaft house, Keg instructing her. "When they call roll, ya answer t'the name of R.W. McGorham. Once we get down the shaft, I'll call ya Shorty."

"Shorty?"

"Practicality. Look around ya."

Camry did, and found herself to be at least six inches shorter than the men around her. "Why do we have to take roll?"

He looked at her seriously. "This ain't no picnic. They need t'know'd how many bodies go under, so's they can know'd how many t'dig out case of cave-in."

She swallowed a lump in her throat and took a final breath of fresh air before following Keg into the building. She had to do this . . . . She wouldn't be afraid.

The mill, one square room, was as tall as a four story and filled with miners. Some sat on crates and timber piles, some stood in corners smoking cigarettes, others took long drinks from scattered rain barrels. Those who were finished for the day, bare-chested, carried empty lunch tins with their sweat-soaked shirts wrapped around their heads. Those waiting to go down into the endless, black tunnels, clutched square lanterns with fresh white tallows enclosed. Three cages descended and ascended continuously, bells clanging various signals.

A hollow-faced man in a striped shirt began calling names off a pegboard. After Keg's name was read, R.W.

McGorham was called. Camry held her head down and raised her arm, quickly lowering it to her side. Before she knew it, she was caught in a flow of men entering the middle cage. Keg followed and the gate slammed shut. Someone stepped on her toe, and she bit her lower lip to keep from crying out.

The bell clanged twice, paused, then rang three times. With a sharp jolt, the cage slowly began to sink into the ebony pit. Her heart thumped erratically. It was too late to turn back! Bodies pressed against her, most clad in clay-stained coats and blue duck overalls, wrinkled and dirty. They were bathed in the hazy yellow glow of a lantern swinging above them on top of the cage. The man next to her narrowed his eyes, scrutinizing her. She turned away, uneasy. The cage jerked suddenly and she was thrown against him.

"Hold onto the round bar, mister."

Camry adjusted her hat and gripped the railing above her head. She tucked her chin to her chest and mumbled, "Obliged," in the deepest voice she could muster.

"You a Cousin Jack?" his tone held a contemptible connotation.

She hadn't the faintest idea what he meant. Assuming he wanted to know her name, she strained her words to a near-rasp. "Name's Shorty."

"You is then if you cain't answer straight." He turned his back to her.

Not knowing why she had been snubbed, she stood on tiptoe to catch Keg's attention. The men were too tall; all she could see was his calico shirt material between two miners.

A bell clanged once, paused, then once more; on the last stroke, the cage dropped swiftly down the dark shaft as if the cable had snapped. An uncontrolled scream escaped Camry's lips blending with the screech of cords, and she clutched onto the bar until her knuckles were white. Her stomach felt as though she'd left it hundreds of feet above her. Station after station whizzed by, their lights only a flickering blur.

The temperature momentarily cooled, but as they continued to descend, it grew hot once more. Warning bells rang at each level passed, and just when she couldn't hear them anymore, they grew louder and clanged again as the cage came to a new level.

They slowed down suddenly and coasted into their designated level. The men hurtled out of the cage, and Camry was stuck in the flow. She held back, waiting for Keg. The dim, narrow drift was hot and stifling. Already tiny beads of moisture formed on her upper lip. Once by Keg's side, she lowered her voice to a choked whisper. "I can't breath. I need air."

"Ya better not be klaustreefeebic, 'cause there ain't nothin' I can do. Don't get yourself excited or fer certain ya'll faint dead away. Sheit!" he mumbled. "I think we ought t' turn back."

She quickly put a hand on his arm. "No. We can't."

"Awright!" Following the miners, Keg periodically ducked his head from the low dingy rock ceiling. The sway of yellow tapers reflected off the wet walls, slow steady drips echoing down the tunnel.

"I got a mite worried when Eldon was a lookin' at ya."

"He wanted to know if I was his Cousin Jack. My disguise must be pretty good if he couldn't recognize me for sure. At least he thought I was a man."

Keg grunted. "Cousin Jack is a Cornish miner. American miners don't take t'kindly t' them."

"Why not?"

" 'Cause they keep a comin' o'er here from England leavin' three bit a day jobs and takin' our four dollar a day ones."

Had she known that before, she would have ground the heel of her boot into Eldon's instep.

A large gallery came into view where the men instantly began removing their clothing. Camry's eyes widened as she viewed them in light loin-cloths and heavy boots.

Keg nudged her along. "We ain't a stoppin' here."

Further down was a crosscut extending west. As they

passed it, a gust of cold air rippled her shirt. She paused and inhaled.

"How does this air get way down here?"

"Blowers from topside. Ya hear'd all that noise up t'there? That's comin' from the machine house. Don't breathe t'deep least ya pass out. We got t'go down t'the 1,650 and I'm a tellin' ya now, it be o'er a hundred degrees down there. Ya think ya can handle it?"

She meekly nodded and hoped she could. She had to.

They followed the tunnel to the left, the slope going down. Keg's lantern provided a dim guide and Camry kept her eyes on his wide back. Before she knew it, thick mud rose around her stockinged foot. Looking back, one of her oversized boots had stuck in the sump, causing her foot to slide out and into the muck. "Oh! For heaven's sake!"

Keg turned and crossed his arms over his chest. "If ya would've done that on the 1,650 level, your foot would've been sizzled like bacon on a griddle."

She quickly put the boot back on, warm mud oozing around her toes.

Reaching a small station gallery void of miners, Keg stopped and examined the storage room. He snatched several tallows and three sticks of dynamite, stuffing them into his back pocket.

"Do you have to blast!" Camry exclaimed.

"Naw. I'm a nitro man, Miz—ah—Shorty, I'm like the man whose wife made him give up chaw, but he keeps a plug of tobacco in his vest for comfort—knowin' it's there case he needs it. I ain't a blastin' t'day, but it's kind of a habit t'have it here." He patted his pocket. "We're goin' down this hole. Nick is workin' the C & C ledge."

He helped her into a cage and closed the iron gate. After signaling the bell, they descended, cable lines squeaking. Camry leaned to hold onto the edge of the railing, when Keg grabbed the back of her shirt and pulled her away. Even in the dull light, she could see anger written over his face and the white flash of his eyes.

''Don't *never* hold on t'the railing like that! Never!''

Camry blinked back tears, afraid of what she'd done to enrage him.

Keg hit his fist into the palm of his hand. ''I didn't mean t'be so hard on ya, Miz Trelstad, 'cept when I see'd ya, I reacted quick-like. When Nick and me was workin' the Volture Gold Mine out t'Wickenburg, fella was so tuckered, he leaned agin the rail and afore we could hold him back, he fell agin the ledge—iron and timber scrapin' his body, his hands and arms tore off. It weren't no purdy eyeballin'.''

Dimly seeing her petrified stare, he patted her back jovially, quickly changing his attitude to calm her fears. ''You're in the land of gopher holes, Ophir holes ad loafer holes! The latter bein' m'favorite!''

Feebly, she tried to smile. Maybe she should have waited until Nicholas came home . . . No, she couldn't have.

The cage halted and Keg lifted the bar. Some sort of pumps rattled through the timbered drift, along with the steady beat of jackhammers against drills. The heat was unbearable. Perspiration covered Keg, soaking his shirt instantly. Camry felt fine droplets of water trickle between her breasts, and wished she hadn't left her chemise and bloomers on.

As they moved to the main section, Keg hunched his shoulders to clear his head from the six-foot-high ceiling. She knew now why he never quite walked perfectly straight. Streaks of quartz and clay lightened in color with red lines of iron rust. Bodies of soft whitish quartz contained pockets of the ore Da had once shown her a chip of.

Keeping her eyes wide open, Camry watched her footing as she balanced alertly over wet crumbled ore. As water dripped on the scorching rocks, it hissed and steamed in small mist clouds.

Nearing the mining area, the noises grew louder. Ore-cars rumbled over iron rails, the clicking of their wheels steady.

Keg lowered his voice as they entered the drift. "Ya stay close or we're in a good deal of trouble." He narrowed his eyes to get a better view of her.

"What's the matter?" she whispered.

"Ya look like one of them striped horses from the circus."

Camry put a hand to her face and felt the small streams of moisture where it had washed away the mud.

Once in the main workings, she stared at the many half-naked men around her. Their glowing skin dripped with water from their labors. Everyone around her moved—swinging picks, twisting drills, shoveling ore, pushing loaded cars, mounting ladders from level to level, and carrying timbers.

"Keg!" a voice called ahead.

Seeing Rigdon Gregory striding toward them in a brief breech-cloth, Camry kept close to Keg's back and put her head down.

"Keg! What are you doing here? After last night at Cad's, I thought for sure you'd sleep until sundown!"

"Well, ya know'd me. I'm as unpredictable as a gopher. Never quite know'd when I'll pop up!" he laughed nervously.

"Why the hell are you dressed? The liquor must still be in your head. Go on back to the station and leave your clothes if you're working."

"No . . . no. . . I'm fine. I'm a leavin' right soon. Say, have ya see'd Nick?"

"Yeah, he's working the ledge down the north spur." He craned his neck to look behind Keg. "Who's the quiet fellow behind you?"

Camry hunched her shoulders and slouched.

"Him? Oh . . . his name's Shorty. He's a mite shy. He wants t'be a miner, but his ma wants him t'go t'one of them fancy eastern schools t'be a lawyer. I told his ma I'd put him t'work here for a day and he'd change his mind right-quick."

Rig held out his hand and introduced himself "Rigdon Gregory."

She backed away from Keg and kept her eyes down-cast while taking Rig's hand. He squeezed her hand and she gritted her teeth to keep from crying out.

"Shorty, you'd best listen to your ma and become a lawyer. You've got a grip weaker than a girl's."

"Well, we'd best be on our way. Come on, Shorty," Keg ordered. "See'd ya later, Rig."

Ridgon shook his head as if trying to clear it. Amazement shone in his hazel eyes and he chuckled softly. "Lawyer . . . Hell, he could be a seamstress with those hands."

Camry kept so close to Keg's back as they walked down the spur, she nearly tripped him. He stopped abruptly and adjusted the lantern from one hand to the other. "Quit tryin' t'short change m'steps! From now on, don't scratch 'til I itch! Ya walk in front. There ain't anybody down this incline 'cept Nick, so's it's okay."

She took the lead, walking carefully down the slope. Timber moaned and creaked above their heads. Soon, the wood support system ceased and the tunnel fell lower and grew narrower.

"Is it supposed to make this much noise? How come the wood stopped?" Camry asked softly, following the wall.

"It was just put up last week. I reckon it's settlin'. Nick's working on the assumption there's silver ore down here. If there ain't, they don't want t'put the time and money in t'square-settin'."

"But isn't this dangerous?" She grew uneasy with the idea of Nicholas working the ledge, braving the dangers of cave-ins.

"Shore it is. Ever' miner know'd he might not come up and see the light of day."

She became slightly annoyed, her voice reverberating. "Then why do you do it?"

"Money, Miz Trelstad, clean and simple. There ain't no job that pays better on this God-given earth."

A faint glow of light played at the walls ahead of them. Camry's heart fluttered and she drew a short breath.

Hammer and drill echoed sharply, mingled with strenuous grunts. She held back once she saw Nicholas, letting Keg go in front of her. He was here! He hadn't gone to San Francisco after Garnet Silk! Maybe there was hope.

Ridges of sweat stood on Nicholas' broad back, small rivulets sliding over his bronze skin to the loincloth around his waist. He balanced over crushed granite, his muscles swelling like flesh waves with every swing of his rock-hammer. Strong hands were covered with thick tan gloves. He stopped for a minute and removed his hat. Wiping his brow with a dirt-smeared arm, he reached into a leather pouch at his hip. Drawing a handful of large ice chips, he put them in his mouth.

"Nick, ya sump dog." Keg's words were uneasy.

Nicholas looked up. "Keg? What are you doing here? I thought you were working for Sutro tonight."

"Yeah, well—"

"Who's that?" He looked past Keg to Camry's silhoutte on the wall.

Keg yanked his hat off and twirled it in his hands. "Ya see'd it weren't m'idea. She's mule-headed and, well, she sugar-talked me in t'it. I know'd I could be in a good deal of trouble . . ."

Nicholas sat down his hammer and wiped his neck with a bandanna. "What the hell are you talking about? Hey you—come here."

Camry took a step forward, the yellow haze of candles flickering over her. "Hello, Nicholas."

He squeezed his eyes shut and opened them slowly. "I don't believe this! Goddamn it, Keg! What the hell were you thinking? Camry! Why are you here? Haven't you caused enough trouble without getting yourself killed?"

"Don't blame Keg," she said. "I asked him, rather begged him, to take me here. I had to talk to you."

"Why couldn't it wait until I came home?" Nicholas tossed a glare at Keg. "Are you drunk?"

"No, I ain't a lickered up, I—"

"You don't have to apologize, Keg," Camry cut in,

then looked down. "Nicholas, what I have to tell you couldn't wait." Her fringed lashes cast shadows against her dirt-streaked face. "I wanted to tell you—" She paused to take a breath. She'd best say it now before he strangled her. "I wanted to tell you I've been childish and selfish and all those other things you said. And I've been afraid of my feelings. I thought you might never come back and I realized I—" She looked up to see him staring, thrown off guard by her presence. Her eyes glittered as she continued. "What I'm trying to say is . . . I'm in love with you Nicholas Trelstad and I couldn't wait to tell you."

He remained silent, shaking his head. He tossed the hat on the ground then ran a hand through his damp golden hair. Removing his gloves, he threw them next to his hat. "I don't believe you," he finally said.

"But it's true!" Camry insisted. "I do love you. I have for a long time. I just wouldn't admit it."

"And why the hell did you come all the way down here to tell me? Why didn't you wait until later?"

"Because! I thought you might go after—" She cut herself short realizing she had revealed her fears.

"I see. You only came because you thought I'd run to Garnet. Oh, yes. I see quite clearly. Keg, you jackass, how could you do this?" He took a step forward.

Keg raised his hand peacefully. "Now, Nick, ol' boy, ya get a hold a yourself. I wouldn't have brung her, but she's a cagey alley cat. She done trapped me in t'it, but that ain't no excuse t'kill her. It was m'doin' she's here. But Nick, ya got t'know'd, she's done smitten with ya. And that's fer shore!"

Camry watched Nicholas just stand in the middle of the small gallery with a paralyzing look on his face, until she couldn't take it any longer. Her temper boiled, threatening to spill over. "Well? Is that all you have to say? I got my feet trampled and muddy, and my face dirty. I caught the devil from Keg for leaning against the railing and Rig nearly crushed my hand. *You* told me to do something to surprise *you*! Well? What's the matter? I said I loved you! I meant it!"

When he still didn't answer, she turned in a huff to Keg. "What's the use? He's more pigheaded than I am. The cat's got his tongue."

Had she seen Nicholas, she would have realized she was far from the truth. He rubbed his brow and spoke softly. "You're wrong, Camry. My heart has my tongue."

She stopped and faced him. Midnight blue eyes sparkled and a beckoning smile appeared on his handsome face, making her pulse race. "Come here, darlin'." He held out his arms. That was all she needed. She ran into them and buried her face in his neck.

"I was afraid you'd be mad at me . . . or laugh at me! But I had to tell you." Camry cried against his glistening chest. "I do love you, Nicholas. It doesn't matter about . . . about your friend."

He tilted her head and cupped her chin and looked into her eyes. "I know, darlin'. I believe you. Hell, it must be true if you come all the way down here! You're the best thing that's happened my way today. You look more beautiful to me now than you ever have. You couldn't have surprised me more." His last words were smothered on her lips.

Everything was forgotten. Mouths blended as one. Nothing else mattered as their confessions overcame all.

Keg cleared his throat. "Nick, it don't look right ya doin' that. If'n someone comes down here, how would ya explain?"

Nicholas lifted his head and brushed a smudge of dirt from Camry's nose. "How *would* I explain? How did you get her this far Keg without anyone noticing something amiss? Much less wonder why you're both completely dressed."

"Didn't run in t'much trouble 'til Rig see'd us. He was a mite suspicious. Even Eldon called her a Cousin Jack."

"We'd better get her out of here. Darlin', even when you don't try, you give me trouble . . . but this time I'm glad."

Keg plopped his hat back on his head. "We can take the twenty-three cage t' 1,100 level. There ain't nobody around that section. The sooner I get out t'here, the better. I'm a roastin' like a turkey in these duds."

Nicholas gathered his equipment and removed the candleholder from the wall. He wanted to get her out of here as soon as possible before any harm befell her. He had some confessions of his own to make to her and they'd best be said when he wasn't worrying about her disguise. He brushed a kiss on her lips, and whispered, "You are a most extraordinary woman, my love."

She smiled at him, her blush hidden by the thin veil of dirt covering her face.

They followed Keg up the incline, the low light flickering. The rumbling timbers continued to echo. They seemed to be protesting against the pressure of weight above them. A hollow crack snapped the air and a dull groan of stretching lumber ahead bounced off the wall. A mass of crumbling rock suddenly fell through the splinters, forcing air through the spur in a sudden blast, blowing out their candles. A swirl of dust and dirt swallowed the oxygen and pitch darkness settled over the drift.

33

"Don't nobody stir the breezes 'til I spark a light." Keg's gruff voice bounced off the walls which were submerged in total blackness.

Accustomed to candles blowing out, Nicholas quickly found his bearings. "Camry? Are you all right?"

"Nicholas?" She stretched her hands out and searched for him. Her fingertips felt his bare chest and she slid her arms around his waist. "What happened?"

The scratch of sulphur striking ore flickered to a wavering orange flame. In the dim, dust light, Keg reached for a tallow from his back pocket, the low illumination growing slightly on the wick. Timber and rock blocked the exit in front of them.

"Seems t'me the timbermen did a skunk of a job." Keg spat, surveying the splintered rails and crumbled granite.

Nicholas brushed back a strand of Camry's hair and tucked it under her hat. Holding onto her shoulders, he repeated, "Are you sure you're all right, darlin'?"

She shook her head. "Yes. I'm just shaken up a bit. How are we going to get out of here? We're trapped!"

"Doncha go gettin' klaustreefeebic, Miz Trelstad, me and Nick will get ya out. Rig's gang is most likely t'be diggin' on the other side."

After Nicholas was convinced she wasn't hurt, he left her side to assess the damage himself.

Keg rubbed the dirt from his eyes. "I wonder how fur back the cave-in goes. We could be here all night a waitin' t'be dug out. Suppose we could start t'pick it, 'cept ya only got one pick and it ain't t'fast."

Removing his hat, Nicholas wiped his forehead with

the back of his arm. He lowered his voice so Camry wouldn't hear. "The air in here is going stale. We'd better start picking. It's better than just standing here waiting."

With pronounced determination, Keg stated matter-of-factly, "I'm a goin' t'blast." He pulled the sticks of dynamite from his pocket.

"Oh no!" Nicholas disagreed. "You're not blasting with Camry down here. It's too dangerous."

"I can't figgered no other way," Keg growled. "If it weren't for her, I'd not be down t'here in this situation. Not that I'm a bad mouthin' your squaw, ya know'd I'd never do that. It's just she's a cagey piece of fluff. I'd like t'see'd her livin' above the earth, not buried under it like a hibernatin' bear. So what be it friend? Dynamite or dyin'?"

"Keg, you should have been a preacher with the fancy way your tongue twists. Go ahead and blast, you stubborn Pawnee, but I'm warnin' you—"

"Save your breath, boy, this here Injun could blow a hole around a butterfly without makin' it flutter its wings." He lifted a stick of dynamite to his lips and mockingly kissed it. "I knew ya would come in handy."

Nicholas retraced his steps back to Camry's side. She pushed another strand of her hair from her dirt-stained cheeks and secured it under her hat. "What's he going to do, Nicholas?"

"Blast." He tried to say the word in a mellow tone so it didn't sound as dangerous as it was.

"Blast! But we're already trapped. Wouldn't that cave in more rock?"

Calming her fears in a soothing voice, Nicholas said, "I've seen Keg work with explosives for a couple of years. I wouldn't let him do it if it would bring you harm, darlin'." He sighed heavily and looked toward Keg, then back at Camry. "I wish you hadn't come down here. You could have been injured—or something worse than this. I'm glad Keg knows what he's doing. When we get out, you've got some explaining to do."

At his scolding, she momentarily forgot her surroundings. "Well! Of all the ungrateful . . . I told you why I came! If I knew this was the way you'd show your feelings, I never would have!" She squared her shoulders haughtily and wished she could walk away from his arrogant face.

He reached out and grabbed her arm. "I *am* mad, but damned surprised you forged your way down here. And, even more so, damned glad you said what you said." He tilted her head back and pressed a light kiss on her lips. "Damned glad," he murmured against her mouth.

Keg's voice called down to them. "Would ya quit the sugar jawin' o'er there." He cut a piece of fuse and crimped a connector on the end by biting down on it. "Stand back." He stuck the fuse into the dynamite and lodged it in a crevice of the tumbled ore.

Nicholas moved Camry into the far corner of the drift and held her against his wet chest as Keg lit the foot-long fuse.

"One, two, three, four—" Keg mumbled the numbers under his breath as he walked to the drift where Nicholas had been working. When he reached sixty, a flash of exploding powder blazed from the face of the granite, smoke filling the tunnel. A muffled roar echoed down the dark spur, a shower of rock fragments rattling on the floor.

Camry hugged Nicholas tighter as a light sprinkle of dirt fell on the brim of her hat.

Keg slapped the dust off his hat against his leg. "Everybody still got your fingers and toes?" he chuckled, delighted with his display of the talents that had lent him his nickname.

Nicholas's and Camry's eyes locked and he was about to give her a kiss of relief, when he suddenly pushed her away.

"Say! Why did you do that?" she demanded indignantly.

Rig strode across the tunnel to them and then she

understood. They might have been free from the cave-in, but her masquerade must still be played.

Collecting himself, Nicholas growled, "What greenhorn put up that square-set? It nearly killed us."

"I'm looking into it. Everybody okay?" Rig asked.

"Yes, thanks to this powder-crazy Pawnee."

"Don't shower me with thanks all at once. I was obliged t'do it." Keg hesitated a minute, looking at Camry. "Well, boy?" he asked gruffly. "Have ya had enough? Ya'll be wantin' t'go t'that fancy school now?"

She tucked her chin against her chest. "Yes, sir."

Rig laughed. "You better get him out of here before he passes out."

"I agree," Keg said. "Come on, Shorty. Your ma is liable t'tan me good fer ya almost bein' killed."

Picking up his tools, Nicholas added, "I've got a good mind to tan you myself."

"Why you—"

Keg put a hand over her mouth. "Don't talk t'your elders with that tone, boy. I'll have t'wash your mouth with soap. You're as ornery as a polecat."

Nicholas walked ahead of her, without waiting for her to catch up. She stumbled over the crushed ore, almost losing her balance.

Her eyes met Rig's for an instant. He narrowed his gaze and spoke lowly. "You get yourself out of here, Camry Trelstad, or there'll be hell to pay."

She swallowed and kept walking, Keg behind her. "I wonder how he recognized ya?" he whispered.

Camry pondered that question herself, her glance moving over the muddy shirt she wore. She put her hands to her cheeks and gasped. The buttons had somehow come undone and the lacy fabric of her chemise was visible, the soft round curves of her breasts partially exposed. How could she ever face Rigdon Gregory again!

"It's too cold!" Camry cried as Martha emptied another bucket of water over her tangle of copper hair.

"You're not taking all this mud inside." She pumped the handle on the well-pump vigorously, then poured more of the water on Camry who was behind a blanket curtain in the back yard of the boardinghouse. Her chemise clung to her skin as Martha doused her again. Wet curls framed her face, small tendrils resting on her forehead. She wiped the water from her eyes and peered over the top of the blanket.

"Are you finished?" she asked, her teeth chattering.

"Yes. I've got a bubble bath ready for you. I even scented it with your favorite perfume." She picked up the heap of clothes on the porch. "What are you going to do with these?"

"Leave them. They belong to someone else. I suppose I'll have to wash them."

"I figured they belonged to someone else—a man, and certainly not Nick. I wish you'd tell me what you two were up to today. He's as locked tight about this as you are. I probably shouldn't know anyway. If that Thaddeus Carpenter was involved, you can bet it was illegal." She handed Camry a towel through the makeshift screen.

Wrapping it around herself, Camry walked across the porch and into the kitchen, small drops of water dripping off the hem of her chemise. The idea of a bath was extremely appealing and she smiled, expectantly turning the knob of the bathroom door. As it swung open, she gasped upon finding Nicholas in the tub!

His head rested against the rim, a cheroot perched lazily at the corner of his mouth. As he puffed, gray smoke swirled above his damp hair.

Finding her voice, she sputtered, "What are you doing in *my* bath?"

"Your bath?" he replied innocently. "I thought it was my bath."

"Don't play dim-witted with me, Nicholas Trelstad. Since when do you take scented bubble baths?"

"You've got a point."

"Good. Now get out." She held the towel tightly about herself.

"Anything you say." He began to stand.

"Stop!" Camry ordered, staring wide-eyed at his bare chest and the soapy water sliding down to the top of his hips. "Sit back down, for heaven's sake."

"You told me to get out."

She quickly turned away, biting her quivering lower lip. Though they had shared intimacies, she had never viewed him in the boldness of the daylight.

"Am I to stand here all day?" he queried, her back still to him.

"Leave please."

"I don't have a towel."

"Honestly," she huffed, pulling hers off. "It's bad enough you've smelled up the room with that vile cigar. Now you take my towel!" She tossed it over her shoulder and instinctively crossed her arms over her chemise-clad breasts.

"I thought you said you loved me. After all, you went to such great lengths to tell me. Is this the way you treat the man you love?"

"It most certainly is when he doesn't appreciate the trouble I went through to tell him so."

"Ah, so that's why you're mad."

"I am not."

"Well, you can enjoy your bath now."

She heard the sloshing of water and turned around. Nicholas was nowhere in sight.

Bubbles rose from the soapy water in the tub and his head popped through, the cigar limp in his mouth.

"What are *you* doing? I thought you got out!"

"Just putting out my cigar, darlin'. I didn't mean to offend you by it."

"Quit this tomfoolery this instant!" Camry stamped her bare foot on the floor.

"Are you sure you don't want me to stay? I could wash your back?" A grin played on his lips as he tossed the soapy cheroot aside.

"No, no, no! Get out!"

He laughed at her anger, then squinted and winced.

"I've got soap in my eyes."

"I'll bet! You're not fooling me."

"I'm serious, Camry. Get me the pitcher of water."

"I don't believe you."

He raised his voice. "Do you want me to go blind, woman? Get the water!"

She narrowed her bright green eyes.

"Hurry!" he commanded. "I knew a miner once that went blind permanently."

Camry raised her brow. "Are you *really* in pain? The truth."

"The truth—yes!"

Convinced, she quickly fetched the water pitcher and poured the contents slowly over his head. The blue eyes flickered open and focused. He grinned.

"Why you!" she stammered.

He laughed richly and grabbed her wrists, the brass pitcher falling to the floor. He pulled her into the tub, soapy water splashing over the rim.

"What are you doing?"

He took in every curve of her body as the water made the chemise stick to her skin, outlining the fine details. "Forgive me. My ancestors were Vikings. They always took the women they wanted."

"Unhand me!"

Her anger only provoked him to hold her tighter. "Why must we always play this cat and mouse game? I know you want me, so why do you insist on the role of coy maiden?"

"My ancestors were Celtic and I've inherited their temper. So, if you don't let me go, I'll be forced to harm you."

"Do you think you could?" he chuckled skeptically.

She nodded, her teeth clenched.

"Are you mad enough to bite me?"

"Yes I am!"

Nicholas leaned his head back and closed his eyes. "Then I'm prepared for punishment. Choose your spot, but be gentle with me," he bade mockingly.

Camry had to laugh. Her voice was like music to his ears and he smoothed back her damp hair. "Even you have to laugh at how silly you are."

"Silly! That word is for schoolmarms."

Kissing the tip of her nose, he spoke huskily, "Well, we know you aren't."

Her skin tingled with his closeness, and she shifted nervously. "I suppose you should leave now . . . I do have to take my bath . . . and wash my hair." She felt his strong thighs pressing against her buttocks, his desire apparent.

"I'll wash it."

She opened her mouth to protest, but he wouldn't take no for an answer. He snatched the soap from the floor and began massaging it into her long curls. His fingers rubbed gently at her scalp, soothing away the dirt of the afternoon. The room was filled with the fragrance of roses as he poured clean water carefully over her head, so as not to let the soap run in her eyes. After, he squeezed out the excess water and twisted her hair into a loose knot so it wouldn't rest in the tub.

Shyly, she murmured, "Thank you."

"Aren't you going to take off your undergarments to finish your bath?" he asked softly.

"No . . . I don't think so . . . I think I'm clean enough."

His body relaxed and Camry seized the opportunity to get out of the tub. He watched her stand and laughed at her nervousness. "I've heard of your kind. You like to be chased. Shall I wait for you to hide? Tracking a woman is like tracking a bear—both are cagey, so I'll have to move slow—" He began to rise.

She stared at him, from the chest up, then screamed softly and ran out of the bathroom, her heart hammering playfully, giggles threatening to erupt. She reached her room, slammed the door and locked it. Taking a step back, she stared at the knob, then took a step forward and turned the key to unlock it. Walking backwards to the bed, she continued to stare at the doorknob.

Nicholas's deep voice rang through the hallway. "I

must be getting absentminded. I'm having trouble locating my own bedroom."

The door opened and Nicholas shut it behind him, securing the latch. Her towel was wrapped loosely around his tightly muscled waist. They stared at each other for an eternity, Camry taking in every detail of his masculine physique. His damp hair was plastered against his forehead, curling upon his broad shoulders. The fine mat of hair on his chest glistened over bronze flesh pulled taut over his rib cage and abdomen. Slowly he walked toward her. She couldn't restrain herself from putting her arms around his neck, drawing him close.

He drawled lazily, "Is this how it is to be for every time?"

It was an honest question, she knew. One which she should answer honestly, if not to Nicholas, to herself. It seemed as if every time he wanted to share an intimate moment, she had to play a game of cat and mouse. Well, she would change that. She took a deep breath. After all, the man before her was the one she was in love with. Why not play the part of seductress this time? But would she know what to do? As if he read her mind, Nicholas placed a feather-light kiss on her lips.

"Just love me, darlin'," he whispered silkily.

Timidly, she pressed her mouth over his. Softly, hesitantly, she began to graze his lips, exploring. She traced his lower lip with her tongue, savoring his masculine taste. He returned her passion with his own, their bodies molding together. His bare chest met her damp chemise but it seemed as if no material could be a barrier to them.

Trying to please Nicholas, but not fully knowing how, she experimented with things that he had done to her in the past. She let her mouth trail over his cheek, brushing kisses on his eyelids and brows, finally settling over his earlobe. As lightly as a butterfly, she whispered in his ear—love words, some unclear. A groan escaped Nicholas as she continued her torture . . . for to him, it was a torturous ecstacy.

She moved her hands over his chest, her fingertips teasing the light mat of hair. As she moved over his nipple, she found it hardened, and delayed her hands temptingly. Unable to bear the madness, he lifted her in his arms and deposited her on the cushioned mattress. With ease, he removed her chemise and tossed it to the floor. She tugged on his towel and it fell effortlessly next to her undergarments. Kissing his forehead, nose, chin, then his mouth again, she pulled his upper lip into her mouth, then his whole lower lip with gentle sucking. Her brazeness shocked Camry and there was a tingling in the pit of her stomach urging her to give herself freely to this man whom she had taken, for better, for worse. Her heart raced as he deepened her kiss with his own.

His large hands cradled her face, pulling her closer. Camry's hands slid down his broad back, over the cool skin that led to his firm buttocks. She writhed beneath him, wanting more, yet not quite sure how to continue. He answered her with a seduction of his own. His lips possessed her taut nipple, which she had unconsciously thrust at him. He teased her to delicious rapture, his tongue pulling and claiming the very core of her being. His hands moved over her soft curves, exploring every recess in her body. She cried out as he found the sweetness that was hidden in the triangle of bronze curls at her inner thighs.

Unable to restrain herself any longer, Camry raised her hips to his. He took her slowly, savoring the closeness between them. Their urgency overwhelmed all logic and they became enmeshed in thrusts, eager to savor the depths of their emotions. Two bodies were in enchanting harmony with one another, soaring to the height of ecstatic desire. A fire spread through Camry and she cried out his name, exploding in a downpour of fiery sensation. She lay drenched in a flood of contentment and love.

"I love you, Nicholas," she whispered, holding back a sob in her throat. She loved him so much at this very moment, it scared her.

He didn't speak. His own heart was so full, it was almost unbearable. Never had he felt this way about a woman. Never. He finally knew what it meant to truly belong to someone—heart and soul.

A cold breeze caressed Camry's skin, causing her to wake. The Washoe zephyrs had started and rolled in through the open window stirring the passion-scented air. Though the days were arid and hot, the zephyrs came down the mountain in much cooler waves. She looked at Nicholas, whose steady breathing remained unaffected. He looked so innocent, she thought, lying curled on his side. She softly touched his arm and lightly kissed his shoulder, smoothing back a silky wisp of hair from his forehead. She rose, shivered, then grabbed a satin robe from her armoire. Closing the window, she padded across the hall to Nicholas' room for the Indian print bedspread.

His bureau was cluttered with familiar items and she smiled, fingering each object tenderly—the scrapbook, shaving mug and brush, J.B., and a soiled work shirt draped over the edge. She remembered the first time she had tried on Nicholas' fine felt and fur hat. Picking it up, a small envelope fell to her feet and she bent to retrieve it. She recognized her father's bold handwriting spelling Nick Trelstad over the front. Curiosity bested her and she opened it.

She held four vouchers, written out by Michael Parker: *Receipt for one share Consolidated-Virginia stock cashed on this 23rd of August, 1875, in the amount of $725.00 to be paid in account of Garnetta Silquerro Evans in regard to the juvenile, Caleb Evans.*

Camry's hands shook as she read the other vouchers. All the same; money each week in the amount of the value of Con-VA stock. She dropped the papers and squeezed her eyelids shut, holding back tears. Putting a hand to her throbbing temples, she sank to the bed. Why would Nicholas give Caleb Evans money . . . unless . . . Oh, God, it couldn't be true! Could he be Nicholas' son?

Picking up the vouchers, she replaced them on the bureau, her eyes resting upon another envelope. It was larger and brown. Without guilt, she lifted the flap. A worn photograph of Garnet Silk and her son with a letter to W. James Quincy was enclosed. She scanned the contents, her heart racing with her eyes as she read. It was a summons for Quincy to find Garnet and Caleb. All this time she was worried about· him going after the woman, when actually, he had sent someone to find her. *Paid* someone to find her . . . Tears escaped and ran down Camry's cheeks. No wonder he had never looked her in the eyes and said the words she had spoken to him this very afternoon. How could he love her when he loved another woman? And had a son by her . . .

Camry collapsed on the bed and rolled on her side, then buried her face in her hands and cried uncontroll- ably for her precious love so quickly crushed. She had never felt more alone and betrayed.

34

Just before the first rays of sun scorched Gold Hill, Camry walked down the dusty main street in the budding azure-gold light of the day. A gas-lamp boy made his way from corner post to corner post extinguishing the glowing balls of yellow behind glass coverings. She heard the slow, steady clip-clop of Clydesdales pulling barrel-laden Carson Beer wagons to resupply saloons. They were the only horses traveling at five in the morning.

Camry adjusted the valise in her hand, then hailed the driver to halt and asked him where the Captain Billiard Saloon was.

He pushed his hat up his forehead and smoothed an invisible moustache. "The Captain's not hiring any more dancing gals. Why don't you check the Tin Roof?"

"Never mind. I'll find it myself." Determinedly, she ignored his advice and continued down the narrow road. Soon, the wagon was beside her again, the horses shaking their heads as the driver slowed them.

"No need to get your dander up. Go down the block. It's to your left." He spit, then clucked his tongue for the team to speed up.

Staying a good distance behind him, Camry took a deep breath, held her head high, and followed his directions. Her thoughts drifted to Nicholas and she was almost tempted to go home before he woke. But no, that was not possible. After crying, she had realized any future with Nicholas was hopeless. He didn't, nor would he ever, love her. It was simple and had she not let her emotions overtake her, she would have seen from the

294

start he was in love with Garnet Silk. She would not snivel at his feet like a beaten pup with its tail between its legs. No, she decided *she would* make a name for herself and it *wouldn't* be Trelstad. Camry Dae Paker could stand on her own two feet. But first, like it or not, she needed Frank Marbury's help. For the first time, she was glad she'd kept his calling card that day he tossed it in her lap.

The pinewood of the Captain Billiard Saloon oozed small sap drops and filled the air with a tangy scent of varnish—a mark that the building had been recently constructed. A bright red sign hung over the double window crested front doors, and as Camry knocked, a shade was quickly lifted. A man wearing a derby hat and in need of a shave, pursed his full lips.

"Yeah? Whudda ya want?" he barked.

"I need to see Frank Marbury."

"We ain't open, 'sides, he ain't here." He moved to pull the shade down.

"No, wait!" Camry imploringly put a gloved hand to the pane. "He's got to be here." She reached into her reticule. "He gave me this card."

The man eyed the business card, then her. "Ya couldda stole it."

"I swear to you, I didn't!" Camry insisted. "Do I have to shout his name in the street?"

"I doan like bein' ordered. Piss-off, moll."

"Frank! Frank Marbury!" She carried out her threat.

The door bolted open and Camry was jerked inside.

"Ya want every marshal in the state comin' after him? Shut up!"

"Let go of her, Vern, or I'll kill you right here." Frank stood at the top of the stairs in a black satin dressing robe, a silver revolver pointed at Camry's captor.

Vern roughly pushed her away. "I wuz only doin' whatcha tol' me. Bounty hunters ain't always men."

"Come up here, Camry," Frank ordered, his aim on Vern not faltering. He tossed him a gold coin. "Buy yourself a drink, Vern, and cool off."

Camry darted by the empty poker tables and climbed the stairs. Frank took her hand and led her to his room, then shut the door. She immediately snatched her hand free.

"You're certainly keeping charming company these days," she pronounced.

Frank's silver-gray eyes flashed. "You're being your usual sweet self, I see. What did you expect from the ends of the earth?"

"Whatever are you talking about?" She briefly surveyed the room and noticed it was plain.

"The end of the earth, my dear. I only got as far as a two-bit saloon. I suppose this is the end for some." Moving to a small table in the corner, he poured himself a glass of brandy.

"Oh, yes, I suppose I did. . . . I didn't think you'd take me literally."

"I never take anything you say literally. If I did, I'd be six feet under the ground." Frank took a seat on a calico print quilt covering a tester bed.

Camry coolly stared at him. "I find your attire intimidating. Please put some clothes on."

"The hell I will. You came busting in on me. I'll dress when I please. You must want something pretty bad to come calling."

She turned her back to him and stared at the handle of her valise where it rested at her feet.

Frank finished his drink and lit a cigarette, observing her suitcase. "Going somewhere?"

She twirled to face him. "As a matter of fact, I am."

"Then I'm sure you need money, unless you rolled that miner of yours. What's his name? Hick Trellis-hag?"

"Don't mention *his* name!"

"The lovebirds have split?" He broke into a suave, clean smile. "I'm right then. So, have you come to take me up on my offer?"

"What offer?"

"You wound me, Camry. What an addled memory you have."

"If you're referring to your proposal of leaving town—you can toss it in the gutter. I told you then, and I'll tell you now, I'm not going anywhere with you."

"You should be nicer to me. You're losing any sympathy I might have for you."

"I *only* came to you because I couldn't go to my father for the money—" Against her will, she began to cry. After all, Da had aided Nicholas . . . He had betrayed her as well.

"Bravo. The tears are an added touch."

When she did not answer, he moved to her and lifted her chin in his hand.

"Could these be *real* tears? I didn't think you could truly cry."

She pushed off his hand. "Get away from me, you varmint!" Angry at herself for revealing her hurt, she brushed her cheeks.

Frank's mood lightened and a realization spread over her face. You aren't acting, are you?"

"Why would you say such a thing?"

"You've always acted with me, Camry. I never knew you had a heart."

"Of course I do! It's been broken enough." She bit her lower lip, having said more than she had intended. "Can I borrow ten dollars?"

"What do you need money for?"

"None of your business. Why are you hiding down here with that jackanape of a guard?"

He laughed deeply. "Ah, we still are alike. Both acute. Now we each have secrets from the other."

"I doubt mine are involved with the law," she remarked tersely. The truth was, she needed the money for hotel fare. After her experience at the International, she decided she should pay in advance for her room. Nicholas might find out where she was, but at least this would buy her some silence for a while. And besides, she'd have to pay the bill sometime.

"I'll drive you back to Virginia," Frank offered, pulling a fawn-colored suit from the closet.

"Aren't you afraid someone will recognize you there?" she shot back sarcastically.

He seemed unaffected. "With any luck, the eyes of *the law* are in Tombstone."

The six a.m. miners were filling the boardwalks as Frank drove them in his shining black buggy down A Street to Michael Parker's office.

Camry kept her eyes ahead as they passed Ma Zmed's, afraid she would see Nicholas.

Stopping the sleek jet horses at the office's curb on Howard Street, Frank relaxed the reins. "Are you sure you don't want breakfast?"

"I couldn't eat a bite. I've come to tell my father what I think of him. May I have the ten dollars." Then as an afterthought, she added a sarcastic, "Please."

"I think I'm getting the raw end of this deal." He reached into his vest and pulled out his billfold. "How do I know you won't skip town with it?"

"Would the loss hurt you so dearly? I'll be staying at the Bonanza Hotel, if you must know," she finished decisively.

Just as Frank handed her the money, Nicholas stepped out of her father's office. Relief washed over him, turning to confusion. "Where the hell have you been? I was worried . . . I thought you might have come *here* . . . Just what the devil are you doing with Marbury?"

Frank reclined leisurely against the back of the buggy seat, a smile playing at his lips. The whole domestic affair was quite amusing.

Camry's heart skipped a beat. Why did she have to see him? It would have been so easy to walk away without having to confront him and remember the love he held for another. Her hurt laced her words. "Why should you care where I go?" she asked tensely.

"What do you mean? You're my wife. I woke up and— Marbury, what the hell are you doing with *my* wife?"

Frank twisted the diamond ring on his finger, then tilted his hat lower over his forehead. "Ask her. It would

seem to me, you don't take very good care of her, or
she wouldn't be with me."

"Why you sonofabitch." Nicholas lunged toward
Frank, but Camry pushed him away.

"Leave it alone, Nicholas!" she rebuked. "Don't blame
him. I don't ever want to see you again. Do you
understand? I said: Never!"

He couldn't believe this was happening to them . . .
not after last night. What had he done? Or knowing
Camry, hadn't done? They had shared such intimacies
. . . things he had never shared with anyone else.

To wound Nicholas as she had been wounded, she
taunted him. "You once told me I didn't hold my hand
out for money. Well maybe the services weren't worth
collecting on. I will take this payment." She deposited
the ten dollars into her purse with deliberate slowness.

Nicholas' eyes hardened to steel. "I understand. This
gambler has finally paid your price. You slept with him
after you slept with me." He left her time to deny it.
When she didn't, he continued, his voice hoarse and
strained. "You're no better than a whore. And you snub
your nose at Garnet." Disgustedly, he stormed down the
street.

"I don't think he approves of our friendship," Frank
laughed lowly.

Camry fought back tears of humiliation. She wasn't
sure which had stung more—Nick thinking she was a tart,
or comparing her to Garnet. "Go away, Frank. Just go
away!" She climbed down the buggy and ran into her
father's office.

She ran right into Michael, who held her shoulders.
"Whoa me girl! What's the commotion about? I could
hear you all the way in here. Nick was lookin' for you."

"I know! And it's nothing!" The hurt and injustice of
Nicholas' words stung her and with that pain, she
lashed out at Da. "How could you? How could you
associate with that Silk woman?"

Michael furrowed his unruly red-orange brows. "I
donna know what you're talkin' about." He moved to his

black walnut desk and nervously shuffled papers.

"Why are you denying it? I saw your name on the vouchers."

"I donna have time for this prattle, Missy. Nick was very disturbed with you and I thin—"

"I don't want to hear about *him*. What about you?"

He ran a hand through his long beard, his soft green eyes dull and tired. "The Bank of California could be shuttin' down at any moment . . . That means I will . . . haveta—" his voice trailed.

"I don't care about the bank! Why did you betray me?" Camry paced in front of his desk, then stopped abruptly. "Is Nicholas part of some business deal? Is that it? Is that why you wanted me to marry him?"

Resting his chin in his hands, Michael gazed vaguely out the window. "I havena ever betrayed you in all me life. Only meself . . . and me pride. You shouldna condemn Nick for helpin' Garnetta, but hold your head high with pride at the goodness he's doin'."

"So you admit it? You admit you knew from the start he was giving that woman money . . . and her *son*!"

"I canna—"

"You can't! Well you already have!"

Her father stood and drew out his ornate gold watch, his fingers trembling. "I haveta work now—"

"No! You will not get rid of me until I have some answers! You conveniently stuck me in Hoaks Academy, but not this time!"

"I sent you there to receive a proper education."

"You abandoned me. You've never been a true father. I never really knew you when I was a child. Do you know how lonely it was for me? Never having you by my side —only on the weekends or holidays? I needed you! And when I wanted to be with you, you tossed me to Nicholas. Am I such a disappointment to you?" All the hurts she had stifled since her childhood surfaced and she was beyond the point of holding them back any longer.

"You donna understand—"

"I understand you abandoned me, sold me, now you've betrayed me and I don't think I'll ever forgive you."

"You're a spoiled and selfish girl, Missy. I thought Nick could turn you into a carin' woman, but I guess I was wrong." He cut her off. "I haveta look over me books now."

"What's the matter with you? You're as different as night and day each time I see you. Once jolly, the next withdrawn. Do you feel that much guilt for the deeds you've done?"

That had hit him hard. He did feel guilt . . . but not for the deeds to her, but for the deeds done to his clients . . . yes, even Nicholas. How could he tell his daughter he was a cheat? A no-good man . . . a man who'd always been a coward. But he couldn't tell her. His chest rose and fell strongly, his Scottish temper surfacing. "Go back to your husband! I willna have you accusin' me of shenanigans. I done what I did, as any broker wouldda done on his client's request. Ask Nick about it. I canna discuss it with you."

"You've never discussed anything with me."

"The subject is closed. It's obvious you donna know what the word 'love' means."

"No, I don't. I've never been loved." She turned with her skirts swishing, and slammed the door.

Michael's body trembled and as hard as he tried not to, he cried. The sobs racked his body until he had no strength left. He stared out the window for thirty minutes before opening the top drawer. He lightly touched a small pearl-handled derringer without picking it up. His fingertips brushed a fine red leather journal, and he placed it on his desk top. As he turned the pages, Single-Jack padded lazily across the mustard carpets, then jumped onto the desk.

Dipping his quill into the inkwell, Michael began writing it all down. How he came to what he was. A spineless man who had cheated even his own brother. That was why Erick had thrown him out of Philadelphia

. . . Camry didn't know that. The simple truth was, Michael Angus Parker was no businessman. He was an embezzler. Everything he had was not rightfully his. His clothes, his office, his ledgers . . . everything. And Camry didn't understand he was in a lot of trouble. A lot of trouble. He couldn't put her through the shame of knowing and having to live with the fact he could very well go to jail . . . which, lately, seemed almost inevitable. Yet, he couldn't stop.

He scratched Single-Jack's head, between his ears. "How many will it be today? Yesterday there be six, today it willna be better." The cat purred, unaware of its owner's misery. "Ever'day, stocks are sellin' . . . the prices droppin' . . . Camry just doesna understand. I will speak with Mr. Sharon one more time. Mr. Sharon is me only chance. If he willna . . . then there is no hope." He looked at the derringer again, then dipped his quill into the inkwell once more. On a new page, he entered: August 24, 1875. Before he could cross the "t," morning clients entered his office, demanding payment in full for the sale of their stocks . . . money he did not have.

35

Frank ran a comb through his slicked-down, dark brown hair, and examined his face in the mirror. Had he not been so vain, he would have bleached his hair and shaved the handlebar moustache. But since he was a gambler, he took the risk of recognition.

Smoothing his gray velvet lapel, he turned down the kerosene lamp hanging from the wall of his room. He could hear Vern downstairs and several patrons in a drinking match. The piano player burst into tune and roulette wheels turned. Everything was ready.

Pulling the timepiece from his trouser pocket, he tapped the glass. It had stopped at 9:45 p.m. Rendering it useless, he tossed it on the bureau. Before leaving for the gaming tables, he re-sandpapered the tips of his fingers, just enough to almost draw blood. His fingers were so sensitive he could feel the most minute of imperfections in a playing card. Satisfied, he placed a gray felt Columbia Stetson on his head and followed the drifting music.

By the time Michael Parker reached the Captain Billiard Saloon, he'd finished half a bottle of Irish whiskey. His senses were dulled, but not beyond the point of comprehension. In his vest pocket was three hundred and fifty dollars. All the money he could scrape together. He had sold his painting of the ship, some gold cufflinks, a crystal and bronze lamp and a shell-embedded jackknife. William Sharon had thrown him out of his office at the bank and ten clients had demanded the money owed to them for stocks. A sum over three thousand dollars, not including a delinquent bank note. Though he was not a gambler, it was the only way he could hope to increase what money he had— overnight.

He chose to gamble in Gold Hill, hoping not to run into any of his business acquaintances. The Captain Billiard Saloon was in full swing by the time he passed through the swinging double doors.

A piano player sang the life of "Baldy Green" while the bartender encouraged patrons to drink up. Michael hitched up his pants and took a place at the counter. He surveyed the bar, taking note no poker games were being played. He did find a faro game, but the killings were too swift and he preferred a more leisurely repast if he must indulge. Roulette and craps were also being played.

"Buy you a drink, mister?"

Michael turned his head to see two men at the end of the bar. "That issa might neighborly gesture and I'll be takin' the offer. Whiskey."

The men moved down to Michael and introduced themselves.

"Emmet Crestly."

"Wesley Spade."

Emmet had bought the drink. He was dressed in a suit ten years out of style and two sizes too large. An untrimmed long brown goatee added little character to his ruddy complexion. Wesley wore a large sombrero hat, the full brim shading half his face. When he drank his beer, short stubby fingers with dirt under the nails gripped the mug.

Gulping his liquor, Michael fidgeted with the roll of money in his pocket. "Doesna anyone play poker?"

"I do." Frank's deep voice answered the question directed to Emmet and Wesley as he moved behind them. "I was just going to start a game. Two dollar ante."

"Fine. Fine." Michael's hands shook, and he clasped them together.

Frank led them to a table in the back corner. "Vern, bring a round of whatever these gentlemen are drinking. And a box of cards."

Emmet pulled a chair out and stroked his goatee. "I don't play cards with no house deck."

Frank's expression was cool. "Then, friend, don't play. I asure you the box is sealed. If you like, examine it."

Michael pulled a plug of tobacco from his vest and bit off the end.

"Spare a chaw, mister?" Wesley mooched.

Obliging, Michael broke off another piece. Wesley took it and rolled it under his tongue. "Thanks, mister. Say, what is your name?"

"Me name is—" he fumbled for the words.

Frank interjected. "What's names among players? We're all here to gamble and we'll most likely never share company again."

Patting his perspiring brow, Michael nodded in agreement.

Vern brought the drinks on an old cork tray and set a sealed box of cards in front of Frank.

Emmet grabbed the cards from the table. "Lemme see these." He examined the gold stickers on each end of the box to see if it had been tampered with.

"Do they pass your approval?" Frank asked with false courtesy.

"Yeah, I reckon. Them are Babcock cards. I know you ain't messed with 'em. Only one place you can get them gold seals and that's in the factory."

"Shall we play, gentlemen?" Frank's pulse raced through his fingertips as he tore the seal and fifty two blue scrolled work-backed cards slid into his hands like honey. He shuffled with ease. So fast, the onlookers would be unaware if he falsely shuffled, in which he would appear to mix the cards. Tonight, he had no desire to cheat. It was against his nature, though he knew how to do it if necessary.

The ante was called, a cigar lit, and twenty cards dealt; the game had begun.

For two hours, Frank allowed himself to lose. Emmet and Wesley won several hands, but for the most part, Michael Parker was the winner. He was ahead fifteen hundred dollars. Drinks were circulated, voices became slurred with liquor, and minds clouded.

Unaccustomed to the rigors of gambling, Michael became bolder with his bets. Ten and twenty dollars became one and two hundred dollars. By two-thirty, he had won over two thousand dollars and the game had turned into a match of two.

Emmet and Wesley looked on with interest, as the next hour ticked away. Michael's winning hands were less frequent, the wagers larger. His senses became as intoxicated as he was. In a final effort to pull out, he bet his remaining five hundred dollars on a single hand. Frank, having held back, now used the grace of his profession which he had mastered with subtleness; he easily won.

Unprepared to face defeat, Michael gingerly drew the ornate gold watch from his vest. "This is all I have left. Will you take it as ante?"

Frank didn't examine the watch, but merely shuffled, his expression stoic. He'd seen enough trinkets and heirlooms to last him a lifetime.

The kill was swift and clean. Michael Angus Parker was penniless. Frank crushed his cigar, stood and picked up the watch, then tossed it to Michael. "Keep it, old-timer." He had never left a fellow gambler to the dregs of humiliation. He'd always left them with some semblance of dignity. On that thought, he left for the bar.

"Tough luck, mister. I ain't never seen anyone win at cards better than him. I know he had to be cheating, but for the life of me, I couldn't catch him. He took us for fifty bucks." Wesley spat, missing the spittoon, the brown juice bubbled on the floor.

Michael pushed back his chair and slowly rose, his face pale. "I needda drink." He pulled a small flask from his jacket and immediately drained the contents.

Stumbling, he exited the Captain Billiard.

The night was as black as a witch's pocket. No stars shone and the zephyrs had come alive. Michael wove down the rickety boardwalk, bumping into the awning posts. The veins in his temples were swollen and throbbing, his jovial spirit long since vanished. His right hand felt inside his trouser pocket, the warm touch of the derringer at his fingertips. He was a failure. He had no right to live. He had disappointed everyone . . . everyone he loved . . . and most of all Camry. She was everything to him. Everything that he cared about. But how could he continue to live a lie? He'd been living it for over ten years and it had finally caught up with him. He was a cheat and a fraud. Everything he'd ever made was done so falsely . . . and now there was no place to turn. And no one to turn to.

As he rounded the corner, he pulled the gun out and raised it to his head. He tried to steady his shaking hand and squeeze the trigger. Tears rushed to his eyes and he lowered the gun. Not here . . . no . . . he had to go where it was quiet . . .

Blindly, he walked to the railroad tracks, his thoughts a blur. He mumbled, his words carried on the wind. "All is gone. I havena anythin' left." Tears cascaded over his flushed pink cheeks. He was a sorry excuse for a man.

He followed the tracks downhill toward Silver City. Hunching his shoulders against the wind, he tried to talk himself into taking his own life. He never would forgive himself for such an act . . . yet he wouldn't forgive himself if he didn't do it. What effect would it have on Camry? She'd probably be glad to be rid of him.

Suddenly, his coat was pulled, and he turned to see two dark shadows.

"Give us that fancy watch, mister."

"Emmet?" Michael's voice shook.

"You heard him, mister," Wesley snorted. "Give up that watch."

The wind distorted their voices, carrying them on the

airy current. Gusts swirled about the three figures like liquid black. Had the zephyrs not been blowing, they would have heard the V & T Railroad's steam whistle.

"I willna give anythin' over to you!" Michael shouted. He had the instinctive urge to fight for his life.

"Grab him, Wesley."

Michael backed away and turned to run. In his drunken state, his legs seemed to be made of jelly. A sudden flash of brightness descended upon him, the mirrored light of engine No. 27 assaulted him, and flesh and bones collided with steel and metal. He was thrown several feet and landed on the ground beside the tracks.

For a moment, Wesley and Emmett were stunned, then Emmet ran to Michael.

"Where are you going?" Wesley shouted as Emmet crouched over Michael's limp body and swiftly took the watch from his pocket.

"Let's go," Emmet ordered as he stuffed the prize into his shirt.

They ran off into the ebony night just as the brakes on the V & T began to screech to a halt.

Heather's name floated from Michael's lips as the wind picked up his words and fell to Sugarloaf. It was the last word he spoke.

Frank leaned against the front wall of Captain Billiard's, his mood foul. Vern brought out a brandy and shrugged. "Why do ya play them piss-ass losers, Frank?"

"It's my job. Damn, they *are* losers, aren't they?" He'd been thinking about the old man and his watch. When cards had to be played with sad men like that, he could easily walk away, but he never did.

"Ain't ya ever afeard they gonna get up when they's ahead with your greenbacks?"

"They never do . . . they never do. I'm biding my time for the big game. I know it's out there somewhere. I want to keep my, shall we say, art, in tune. It's my job," he repeated. "Just like it's your job to keep to yourself."

"Just askin'. Cain't kill a man fer askin'." He scraped his

boot and went back inside.

Oh, but you could, Frank thought, then narrowed his eyes seeing two familiar figures walking up the street. He recognized Emmet and Wesley and he could only assume what the shining object in their hands was. He should have known they would follow the old-timer. He took a step forward and stretched out his arm.

"Nice watch, gentlemen. Hand it over."

"We ain't handing nothing over to you. You already took our money, you cheating coyote," Emmet croaked.

Frank grabbed his collar. "I know that old-timer didn't just hand over this watch to you. I'll bet the sheriff would be interested in this."

"Give it to him," Wesley urged.

Choking, Emmet gave the watch to Frank, who then released his hold.

"Get out of here," Frank directed firmly.

Emmet tugged at his shirt. "It prob'ly ain't worth nothing anyway."

Frank's eyes held a warning that sent the two off. He turned and entered the saloon.

For the first time, he examined the watch. It was gold with blue lapis lazuli inlay. A scene of two horses and riders, a man and a woman, were etched in the precious metal. Frank opened the cover and read the small inscription—"Your always devoted, Heather."

Snapping the cover closed, Frank slightly smiled at the irony. He needed a new watch. It's your own fault, you poor bastard, he thought, then scanned the room for a new game.

36

Suicide.

The word had never meant anything to her before, but now, after the V & T Railroad conductor informed her about Da, the word was one Camry would never forget. How had it happened? She pressed her mind to search back to the morning conversation. What had the man said? Her heart had stopped . . . Da throwing himself in front of the train? . . . No! It couldn't be! He wouldn't . . . Her eyes filled and she began to cry again.

How could this have happened? Why? She moved slowly around Da's office, her black taffeta skirt softly rustling. Tenderly, she fingered the edge of his desk, the stacks of vouchers, and the fancy inkwell. As light as a feather, she touched the maroon divans and peach chair framed with carved swags and rosettes. No matter how hard she tried to block out her words, they came back to haunt her, over and over again. I've never been loved . . . . I've never been loved . . . . Oh! How she wished she'd never said them! If Nicholas hadn't inflamed her anger beyond the point of control, she would not have lashed out so harshly at Da.

Fresh tears fell over her high cheekbones. Why? she asked herself, Why did he do it? The grandfather clock chimed eleven. At noon, they would come for her. She envisioned her father at the stately clock. He had prized it most highly, having given it to her mother for an anniversary present. It had survived the west; her Da had not. Moving closer, she opened the glass case to wind the workings. As she picked up the key, her fingers brushed a bottle. Camry pulled it from the shelf and read the label. Bourbon.

Sniffing, she pulled the cork out and lifted the bottle to her lips, then took a sip. She coughed as the burning liquid scorched her throat. Dabbing the corner of her eyes with a damp handkerchief, she took another drink, more than a sip this time. It didn't sting as much.

She sat in Da's oversized chair, the bottle in front of her. Single-Jack sat on the bottom step of the circular stairs, bathing himself. Sighing unsteadily, Camry began to scan the pile of vouchers, anything to keep her mind occupied while she waited. Most were those of clients who wanted their stocks sold. She would tend to that later. Certainly he kept an expense account. She examined the past due bank loan, surprised to see her father had borrowed so much. Well, she'd deal with that herself. Mr. Sharon would have to be patient.

Mechanically, she went through the stack, the names blurring under her strained glance. Her hand froze at the name . . . *her name* . . . Camry Parker Trelstad. A deposit of five hundred dollars for shares of Gould & Curry stock. It was dated June 4, 1875. Her wedding day. She picked up the document for closer inspection. Nicholas had made the transaction. But where did he get the money? It suddenly dawned on her. Her peace offering . . . Nicholas had said he would invest it.

A temporary hope lifted her spirits. She had money. Quickly shuffling through the rest of the papers on the desk, she searched . . . Biting the inside of her lower lip, Camry grabbed the stock exchange sheets, ran a finger purposefully down the columns . . . still searching. California, Consolidated-Virginia, Exchequer . . . Gould & Curry. Stocks bought at seventy-two dollars per share . . . now worth . . . thirty-one dollars! She was stunned. If she cashed the stocks today, she'd be lucky to get two hundred dollars! Of all the damn luck. To think, a week ago, she could have made a tidy profit. Darn the Bank of California. It was bringing a panic to everybody. The more stocks sold, the more prices dropped.

Again, she blamed Nicholas. If he had sold the stock

earlier she would have a nice sum. Now, she'd be lucky to get part of her investment back. And that was just it. It was her money to begin with and the wretched miner stole it from under her! Momentarily anger replaced her grief and she rose abruptly to put the whiskey bottle back in the clock. Closing the glass case, she examined her faint reflection on the crystal. Copper and bronze curls pinned loosely to her head delicately framed her face. She dabbed her eyes again and blinked tawny lids. Noticing her cheeks were pale, she pinched them. She tried to compose herself as best she could. Her reflection faded and the clock hands cleared. Five minutes until noon.

Camry glanced out the window. Her heart skipped a beat as she saw the funeral wagon slow to the curb. Suddenly she wished she were anywhere but here. Yes, she loved Da with all her heart and it wasn't disrespect that she didn't want to go. She wanted to see him have a proper funeral. A funeral which she couldn't understand had to take place. She was afraid . . .

Slowly, Camry opened the office door and locked it behind her. She shut her eyes tightly at the sight of the coffin . . . he father's coffin. The black shone so deeply, rays of golden sun reflected off it toward the all-embracing sky, like a ladder to heaven. The undertaker helped her into his carriage and they began the slow, agonizing descent to the cemetery.

The Virginia City cemetery was northeast of the Consolidated-Virginia Mill, and south of the Union Mine. Black smoke billowed around the picket fence in ghostly puffs. It seemed appropriate her father would be put to rest amid the thousands of tunnels and shafts—labors of those seeking precious metals. To Camry, the earth was receiving something more precious in return . . . her Da.

Father Manogue, his rippling black cassock cascading over his burly frame, solemnly greeted them.

After offering his condolences, the Irish priest performed a ceremony fit for Saint Patrick himself. Camry was thankful Father Manogue agreed on only one service, to be held outside. She didn't think she could endure the chapel of St. Mary's in the Mountains. The walls would envelop her and she feared she'd have been smothered. Mechanically, she tossed a handful of dirt on the coffin. Her breathing grew faster as the undertaker began to shovel the dry earth into the hole. He was sending Da from her forever . . . and she had not said good-bye.

A tightness formed in her throat, her head light. The ground started to spin. She turned away, her legs weak. She had to run . . . run away. She was so scared . . .

Camry was caught in powerful arms, crushing her to a solid chest wrapped in a cotton work shirt. She looked up into gentle midnight-blue eyes. The face held compassion. Lips that were usually sensual, were thin and sad. For a moment, she allowed herself to be consoled by the strength of Nicholas' arms, forgetting the pain between them, only the pain of her loss. After sobbing for a while, she pulled away, her eyes glittering with tears.

Taking several gulps of air, Camry gathered her energy and drew back her hand, landing a stinging blow on Nicholas' cheek.

"You varmint! How dare you come here. How dare you!"

He ignored her outburst, knowing grief was talking. "I'm sorry about your Pa, Camry. He was a good man and I respected him."

"I'll bet you did. You don't respect anyone's feelings but your own. You never gave a fig about me and I'm sure you never gave a fig about my father." She was livid with rage that consumed the love she still felt for him.

"Why don't you come home? There are things we need to talk about—"

"I have *nothing* to say to you. You've used me from the start." She made an attempt to pass him, but he grabbed her shoulders.

Applying slight pressure, he stopped her. "You're not

going anywhere until we've settled things." Seeing Father Manogue frowning harshly, Nicholas firmly guided her behind a cluster of manzanita brush.

She tried to shrug off his grasp, not caring who heard her raise her voice. "Take your hands off me."

"Not until you listen to me. I've had enough of your tantrums. I understand you're hurting now . . . so am I, but we have to talk. Why did you leave without any explanation?" He wanted desperately for her to confide in him . . . what had happened to make her turn on him?

Instead of an answer, she asked a question of him. "Why did you marry me?"

"Why?" Confused, Nicholas sought a reason for her query, then said words he had never said to her before—words he should have already said. "Let me explain something to you, darlin'. When I first saw you that day at the drilling contest, I wanted you. You were a rose among cactus; a flower among tumbleweeds; a sweet fragrance among stale smoke. You were innocent and fresh, but strong and stubborn as well with a face that consumed my thoughts. And I loved you then and I love you now, but goddamn it, your petals may be soft as silk but your thorns are sharp. You entered my blood, and drained it—drop by drop. Lady, as much as I love you, I can't keep chasing you, wondering what you're thinking . . . feeling."

"I'm not asking you to! I'm alone now, I'm always alone, and I can do for myself."

Nicholas ran a hand through his thick hair, then shoved his fist in his pocket. "That's just it! You've always thought you were alone. What am I? A carpet to step on? What do you want from me?"

She would never tell him the truth of her discoveries. Never let him know how deeply hurt she was. "You've taken *everything* from me. My body, Da, even my money! Yes! I know about the Gould & Curry stock. Well, you'll not take my grief, Nicholas Trelstad. Let me bury my dead in peace." Her body shook, a conflict of emotions colliding in her head.

"I'll go . . . I won't come running after you anymore. You got that?" He pointed an accusing finger. "Lady, you don't know how to love anyone. Remember that when you're sitting alone, or with that goddamn gambler friend of yours. Remember what it was to be loved . . . remember our *last* night. Because I did love you." He turned and stalked away, small dust clouds trailing after his heavy booted feet.

Camry told herself she was glad to see him go, glad she wouldn't have to confront him again . . . but she broke into uncontrollable sobs. He had finally said he loved her.

37

The sheer white curtains of the Bonanza Hotel's dining room were closed against the afternoon sun, casting shadows on the crimson-figured wallpaper each time a pedestrian walked in front of the window. Camry looked up to see who had just passed by. Her glance moved to the lobby door, and when it did not open, she concentrated once more on her brew of herbal tea.

Not having slept well the previous night, she had allowed herself to rest this morning before attending to her father's affairs. So far, her day had not gone as she had planned. Da had no expense account, no accounts payable, no petty cash. She toyed with the end of a pale, pink ribbon around her slender waist. Impatiently, she glanced at the window again.

Camry's mood was as dark as her gown: jet crepe with a tight bodice and high neckline. Unable to bear the dreary mourning garb, she had fastened a pink lace collar the same shade as the sash, along with a small cluster of silk roses, at her throat. She reasoned Da wouldn't want her dressing like an old crow. She would respect him in black, just not quite so dowdy.

"Plotting, my dear?"

Breaking from her thoughts, Camry looked up at Frank. "You certainly took your time getting here."

He flashed her a clean smile and nonchalantly rubbed the small cleft in his chin. "I was busy."

"Cheating someone, I'm sure," she returned irritatably.

Frank removed his fine gray Columbia hat and set it on the starched tablecloth. After taking a seat across from

her, he softly cracked his knuckles while talking. "To
what do I owe the pleasure of this invitation?" He held
up his hand before she could answer. "No, don't tell me.
You need more money."

"Don't be crass."

"Don't play me for a fool," he warned. "I told you, I
can see through you like glass."

"You're unscrupulous," she hissed under her breath.
"Any gentleman would never presume such a tasteless
remark."

"How many times do I have to tell you? Gamblers
aren't gentlemen. And as for my remark, I'd wager it to
be true. That seems to be all you ever want from me."

Camry fought the urge to walk away, but couldn't. In a
way, he was right. "Very well then, I'll come right to the
point. Do you still have my jewelry?"

His silver-gray eyes grew openly amused. "Are you
prepared to pay the price?"

"Oh bother to your price! I won't consent to such
idiocy. Do you have my jewelry or not?"

Smoothing the ends of his handlebar moustache, he
finally replied, "You bet."

"I want you to gamble with it. Use it as ante in the
gaming rooms. Get as much as you can."

"Might I ask what you need the money for?"

Debating whether to tell him a lie or the truth, Camry
decided on the latter. "I buried my father yesterday,
Frank. He died without a penny to his name and
numerous debts."

"I'm sorry to hear that." Frank moved to put his hand
over hers. She pulled away.

"If you are, it's probably the first thing you've been
sorry for in your life. Anyway, it doesn't matter to me
what you feel. All I want is the money."

Studying her a moment, Frank reached into his coat
pocket and pulled out a Havana. Lighting it, he relaxed.
"There's nothing left to keep you here. I'll pay off your
father's notes and we can leave this dust trap tomorrow.
I've been thinking about going abroad. Paris maybe."

"I don't want your money. I want to do this on my own . . . at least as much as I can without your help. I want Parker to be remembered as a respectable name. My father wasn't the best of businessmen, so I'm finding out, but his daughter will be a good businesswoman."

Puffing lazily, the blue-gray smoke curled toward the ceiling; Frank asked, "What's in this for me?"

Camry tapped her fingernail on the tablecloth. "If helping me isn't enough, I'll let you keep ten percent of the winnings. For every game you double my money, I'll give you fifteen percent. No more, no less. If you don't agree, I'll find someone who will."

"What else?"

"What do you mean, what else?" Camry snapped. "Money is in it for you. That's all."

"The little kitten has grown into a tiger. Quite an enterprising one. You'll soon find it's lonely at the top."

"You wouldn't know. I mean it, Frank. This is a business deal only. I'll scratch your eyes out if you start thinking differently. I'm through with men," she huffed decisively.

Frank gave a short laugh, his lips breaking into a suave smile. "Don't worry. I'm patient. It's a trait of mine."

Voices hummed outside as boardwalk traffic grew. Soon, the streets were crowded and curious patrons of the Bonanza Hotel ran out to see what the melee was about.

"What on earth?" Camry stood and went to the window. Pushing the sheer curtain aside, she wrinkled her forehead in puzzlement. "Frank, the whole town is in the street! What do you think it is?"

Frank looked out the pane, then took her elbow in his hand. "Let's find out."

The boardwalk was almost impossible to cross. As they neared the street, the news reached their ears. At three-thirty, the Bank of California had shut its doors.

Camry pushed at the people crowding her. She was forced into Frank's arms, and he took advantage of the situation, playing his fingers on her slender waist.

"What does this mean?" she asked urgently, temporarily ignoring his hold.

He smiled smugly, thinking she was protesting his grasp.

"I'm serious, Frank," she tossed back.

"No money in the bank, no money in the town for stocks, no economy. In a word: chaos. Do you have any stocks?"

"Yes! Five shares!"

"You'd better cash them."

A new fervor arose in the crowd, the anguished look of defeat written over many faces. In a state of shock, the man standing next to them shook his head. "The stock exchange has shut down for the duration."

"What?!" Camry cried . . . All her money.

Frank forced his way through the ruckus, guiding Camry back to the Bonanza.

"Calm down, for Christ's sake. This should blow over. They can't stay closed forever." He silently thanked himself for his business sense. He'd never played the stock market, not trusting his money in the hands of others.

"How could this have happened?"

"The Consolidated-Virginia cashed a check and demanded the cash—$300,000. I had a feeling this was coming."

"Heavens," she sighed. "Frank, you have to help me!"

"I don't have to, but I will." He brushed her chin lightly. "You remind me of me."

"Why would you say that?"

"Both our parents were money and now we don't know anything else but the want for it."

She really didn't understand what he was saying, having no idea as to what his past was, but now was not the time to ask him about it. She had too many other things on her mind.

"It'll be at the Captain Billiard if you need me." His voice held an edge of invitation. "I'll have your money tomorrow."

"Tomorrow! So soon?"

"Why not? There are plenty of men in financial ruin. What better way to spend the evening than in a saloon squandering their remaining dollars?"

"You're cool and calculating, Frank. And if it wouldn't flatter you, I'd tell you I admire that in a man."

Frank donned his hat. "You've got spirit, Camry. Fire and determination. The part of me that has aged with my profession. Maybe you'll rub off on me. I'll see you tomorrow."

Camry watched him go, frowning. Frank Marbury was a mystery to her. One which she wasn't so sure she wanted to uncover.

The next morning, a knock sounded on Camry's hotel room door. Eager to find out how much Frank had won last night, she opened it, expecting to see him at the threshold. Her high spirits vanished when she looked into Matthew Price's face.

"Oh! It's you. Come in."

The boyish-looking man obliged. Removing his hat, he twirled it in his hands.

"Did you do as I asked?"

"Yes, ma'am. Your trunks are in the lobby. That Mrs. Zmed packed them."

"Good. I'll have the porter bring them up. And the cat? Did you drop him off?"

"Yes, ma'am. Mr. Trelstad took him."

Camry's face flushed at the mention of Nicholas' name. "Fine. You're a good man, Mr. Price. My father was lucky to have had you as an assistant."

"He was a kind man to me, ma'am. I've got my own broker business now, but with the bank closed down, I'm in the same crevice as everybody else."

"Well, I have faith," Camry offered optimistically. "I appreciate you taking care of this for me. As an old employee of my father's, I felt you should know about his death. Not many people know, and those that do, don't miss him the way I do."

"I'm beholden that you told me, ma'am. Your Pa taught me quite a few things." Matthew was about to leave, then stopped. "I'm supposed to give you a message from Mr. Trelstad, but I don't think it proper for me to do so."

She hesitated, not sure she wanted to hear what Nicholas had to say. Slowly, she spoke, "What is it?"

"Well, he said you were yellow for not going to the boardinghouse yourself."

"That's fine and dandy," Camry fumed. "He can think what he likes. He'll probably kill that cat off in one week's time the way he neglects things."

"That Mrs. Zmed said she'd take care of him." He tossed his hat on. "Well, good day, Mrs. Trelstad."

"Parker. Miss Parker," she corrected. "Thank you, Mr. Price."

"Good luck to you, ma'am. If you need any help with the ledgers, please call on me."

As Matthew left, Frank walked down the hall. He eyed the younger man with studied casualness.

Leaning against the door frame of Camry's room, he mildly examined her. "Do you have a waiting line? Who was that boy?"

Camry looked up from the documents she had taken home from Da's office; they were spread over the bed's comforter. "That's really none of your affair."

"We're partners. I'm making it my affair."

"Very well, his name is Matthew Price. He used to work for my father several months ago." She arched perfectly shaped brows. "Satisfied?"

He made no answer and moved to close the door.

"No, don't!" Camry exclaimed. "Leave the door open."

"Worried about your reputation? I think it's a little too late for that. You're a grass widow now and by choice I might add. You didn't object to Price's company."

"That was different. It was business."

"And what am I?" Frank strolled to the bed, one corner of his mouth turned into a smile. "You wanted me before. Maybe you still do."

She stood up, annoyed. "Heavens, Frank! I told you I'm not interested. Let's drop the subject."

"Your eyes are like a sea of grass when you're angry. Two waves of endless green."

The words should have flattered her . . . yet the voice sounded foreign in her ears. Maybe if it had been said in a silky whisper . . . one which she'd become accustomed to.

Brushing off his compliment, she crossed her arms, deciding she'd better be nicer to him. After all, her fate was in his hands . . . literally. "How much did you get for the jewelry?"

Softly laughing at her refusal to succumb to his charm, he reached into his jacket, then handed her an envelope.

Camry took it and looked inside, gasping at the contents. "There's over a thousand dollars in here!"

"Did you expect more?"

"Well, actually . . . no. I can't believe it. Werldorf only gave me five hundred and you made all this! You didn't even have the sapphire."

"I'm glad you're pleased. I already took my share." After all, a deal was a deal.

"Fine," she smiled, putting the envelope in her purse. "This gambling makes a lot of money. Are there women gamblers?"

"Yes. Are you thinking about taking up the trade?"

"No . . . just thinking in general." She collected the papers from her bed and stuffed them into a business case.

"Why don't you come to Johnny Newman's with me tonight? Some of the elite are still standing."

"I couldn't possibly. Now, if you'll excuse me, Frank. I've got things to do."

He caught her arm as she stepped into the hall with the case in hand. "What are you going to do with all that money?"

Camry brushed a wisp of bronze hair from her forehead. "Restore the family name. Oh, I almost forgot." She reached into her purse and pulled out the infamous sparkling, blue necklace—the last of her jewelry. "Take this and get a bank going. Just keep gambling and make money." As an afterthought she remarked, "You never lose, do you?"

His eyes flashed confidently. "Only when I want to, my dear."

She closed her door and they headed for the lobby to go their separate ways. The street traffic was heavier than usual as she walked down C Street.

The Bank of California was shut tight, the green shades drawn. Gloomy-looking people waited on the street outside. A shout broke over the boardwalk.

"W.C. Ralston commited suicide in San Francisco last night!"

A shiver ran through her, tears threatening. Would she ever rid herself of that word . . . and the guilt that went with it?

A buzz immediately rose, voices carrying under the awnings. Camry pushed through the crowd, wondering how Ralston's death would affect her plans. Now she'd have no choice but to deal with William Sharon when the bank resumed. Certainly he'd fill the vacancy of President.

She passed by the Union Saloon and her eyes caught a glimpse of a large sign in the window. Stopping, her lips mouthed the words as she silently read: For Sale. Biting her lower lip, she looked from side to side, a sudden impulse overwhelming her . . . Yellow, huh . . .

She entered the establishment, her hand reassuringly in her purse grasping the money envelope.

38

The Union Saloon was officially renamed the Emerald Tiger on August 26, 1875. Camry surveyed the cluttered office behind the bar wall, still not quite believing her frivolity. Yes, she had always been one to buy a new dress or hat on the spur of the moment, but a saloon . . . that was different. The debts she had intended to pay back would remain unpaid. She was no better than her father—putting rewards above responsibilities. She would have had to stall the clients if it hadn't been for Frank.

The mysterious Frank. Once again, he had come to her aid. Although she was grateful for his help, she did not like being indebted to the suave gambler. He had graciously paid off all stock receipts. Instead of allowing Camry to pay him back, he had her transfer the debt to shares in the Emerald Tiger, gaining him part-ownership. For the time, she had no choice but to agree. She held buying out his shares as top priority. She did not want Frank dictating to her.

But first, Camry wanted to establish the Emerald Tiger in Virginia City. The Union Saloon had been neglected. Dust and grime covered the bar and tables. The curtains were faded by the scorching Nevada sun. Paint peeled off the walls. Yet under the filth, she found the tables to be fine East Indian teak with ornate carvings on the tops. The bar was twelve feet of Brazilian mahogany, and behind it was a glorious mirror. The walls could easily be wallpapered, and new curtains would be sewn.

"Harumph!"

A deep voice interrupted her train of thoughts and she

urned her attention from her office to see a rather short
man clad in a navy blue shirt, and trail-worn woollies. He
removed his Sugar-loaf sombrero to reveal a shiny bald
head bronzed by the sun. To make up for the lack of hair
on his head, a whopping black moustache covered his
upper lip and ran down past his chin.

"Yes? May I help you?"

"I'm answering the help wanted sign in the window,"
he drawled.

"The bartender opening?"

"That's the only one in the window, ain't it?"

"Yes . . . yes, excuse me." Camry couldn't picture him
behind the bar; his shoulders barely met it. Also, he
seemed fresh off the blazing trail. "Well, I'm not quite
sure. I had in mind—"

"I can do the job." He held his hat soberly.

"Yes, but what are your credentials?"

"My word."

Camry looked at his solemn face and couldn't bring
herself to argue with him. "Very well. I'll give you a try at
it. You realize that as owner, I have the authority to
make demands on you. You can take orders from a
woman, can't you?"

"My mother raised me and that woman could sling an
order or two."

She smiled despite herself. "You'll have to oversee all
the remodeling of the bar for the next few days. Be here
tomorrow morning at eight o'clock. We're opening to
patrons in two weeks."

"Right-o." He tugged his hat on and made a turn to
leave.

"Wait! What's your name?"

He smiled, almost sheepishly. "Duckwater. Peach
Duckwater." He departed on bow legs, the spurs on his
boots jingling.

"Peach?" Camry mouthed silently, then shrugged.

The next few weeks were hectic. Carpenters were in
and out constantly and even a week behind schedule.

But now, on opening night. Camry was finally able to use her newly remodeled living suite above the saloon.

Shades of cocoa and lilac enhanced the spacious room. The furniture was richly stained cherry wood with matching canopy bed, chest, dressing mirror and wardrobe.

She crossed the room, wearing a white silk negligee trimmed with fine lace and ribbons. Moving to her dressing table, she dabbed a sweet perfume behind her ears.

A rap sounded on the door.

"Yes?" she questioned while pinching her cheeks to a becoming peach hue accenting her dark fringed lashes.

"It's Frank." Before waiting for her permission to enter, he casually stepped into the room. Attired in black and white, he looked extremely debonair.

"Don't you know it's in bad taste to enter a lady's bedchamber while she's dressing?"

"I wouldn't know. I've only been invited in when ladies are undressing."

She shot him a disgusted glare. "You're vile, Frank. Get out." It unnerved her to have him so close when she was in her dressing robe.

"I have a gift for you." Frank reached into his vest pocket. The smell of her perfume lingered in the air and he was very tempted to kiss her neck where he knew the scent originated . . . but he would wait . . . wait for her.

"Hmm?" She ignored him and continued primping her hair. "Well? What is it?"

When he didn't answer, she looked over her shoulder to see he had gone; the only trace of his visit was a small black velvet case on the lilac lace bed quilt. She picked it up and lifted the lid. On a necklace of flat gold braid was a small jeweled playing card one inch long. The ace of hearts glittered in diamonds and rubies.

She read the note he had enclosed:

Don't let pride stand in the way of luck.
Wear it.

Camry was impressed by his present. Rich, yet not

gaudy. She would wear it—for luck.

Hearing the tinkling piano downstairs, she hastily began to dress. After smoothing opaque stockings over shapely legs, she stepped into deep blue, kid-leather shoes. Dropping the negligee to the thickly carpeted floor, she fastened full white lace petticoats over her satin corset. Her gown was a vibrant royal blue taffeta with short, puffed, off-the-shoulder sleeves. The wrap-around bodice was pleated diagonally, emphasizing the swell of her breasts.

Putting on Frank's necklace, Camry was ready. Ready to meet her creation head on. To be independent, and in a short time, establish a name for herself. It was everything she wanted . . .

Camry looked down from the second landing, viewing her finished establishment. The tables had been waxed so thickly with lemon oil that the citrus scent still lingered above the aromatic fumes of expensive cigars. Regal green, the color of her eyes, was mixed into a pattern with velvet gold leaves in an alluring wallpaper combination. Low-hanging gilt chandeliers played off the retangular mirror behind the bar. The necessary gaming tables had been installed—faro, poker, *rouge et noir*. Appropriately the painted tiger on the faro cards had been redesigned in emerald green.

She looked coolly at the six dealers operating tables and made a note on how they appeared stiff and unrelaxed. She could have none of that. Things must be comfortable. Her glanced strayed to the double front doors—frosted glass, a tiger etched in each panel. She watched the patrons as they entered.

Peach Duckwater stood behind the domain of his gleaming bar and as the piano player broke into "Oh, You Buffalo Gals", he pulled out his watch from new trousers. The cracked face was clouded; the moisture from washing bar glasses and his body heat and caused it to fog. He tapped his finger on the face. It was time.

Although shorter than any other man in the Emerald

Tiger, Peach towered above them in authority. He knew
he had a job and he could do it.

"Cut the ivory," he ordered the piano player.

The full-house saloon moaned and grumbled at
the curtailment of their background entertainment.
However, roulette balls kept hopping and cards
shuffling.

"Cut the gambling," Peach directed firmly.

Someone threw a playing token at him. His bald head
grew red from a rise in blood pressure.

"You do that again, sir, and I'll split your skull. Miss
Camry runs a respectable establishment." He
straightened himself, standing confidently on wedge-
heeled boots. "Gentlemen, may I turn your attention to
the stairs."

Peach pointed to the oak-railed and gold-carpeted
stairs behind him. "May I present your gracious hostess
and proprietor of this saloon, Miss Camry Parker."

On cue, Camry stepped forward and descended the
steps with languid richness. The men were openly in awe
of her flawless beauty.

Her copper tresses were arranged in high curls, the
play of candlelight enhancing magnificent shades of
bronze and red. Lightly painted coral lips parted,
revealing even white teeth.

"Good evening, gentlemen." Her voice held a hint of
huskiness. "I'm glad you're here. Anything you need,
just call on Mr. Duckwater or a dealer." She reached the
bottom step and posed. "Commence gambling, gentlemen."

A hoopla sounded; gambling moved to full swing. The
piano started up again. Camry kept her smile as she
strolled to Frank. She had seen him standing in the
corner as she made her entrance. Reaching him, the
smile cracked.

"Where are the women? There's only men here. You
said women gambled too."

Frank smirked. "What else did you expect from a
saloon run by a woman? Had you hoped to lure in the

Women's Prairie League?''

"No! I just expected . . . Well, Johnny Newman caters to women.'' ·

"Johnny Newman doesn't have a wife in the closet.''

"What?! You mean to tell me they won't come because I'm married?''

"Correction.'' Frank smiled crookedly. "Separated.''

"Oh, for heaven's sake! What's the difference?''

"Apparently, a lot.''

"Damn it. I haven't worked this hard to be shunned by those busybody biddies! I'll think of a way to get them in here if it's the last thing I do!'' With a pronounced rustle of stiff skirts, she headed toward the bar, stopping often to greet patrons. Taking a place at the end of the counter, she asked Peach to pour a glass of sherry for her.

He obliged, his hand shook as she suddenly cried in an outburst. "Stop! You've filled it too much!'' She examined the glass critically. "Our standard drink should be a quarter inch shorter.''

"I just figured since you were the boss-lady—''

"Leave the figures to me.'' She was sorry as soon as she spoke the words. She was upset about the women . . .

Frank crept up behind her. "Trouble already?''

She turned her head to him. "I don't want any slipups, Frank. You may be my partner, unwilling on my part, but a partner just the same. You're supposed to be over-seeing all this. Dealer number two's tie is undone.''

Smiling with apparent amusement, he leaned his elbow on the bar. "I'll take care of it.''

"Good. See that you do.'' On a note of irritation, she added, looking past him. "And find out *who* that man is! He's been in and out of here for a week scratching on that notepad of his. I don't want him spying on us.''

His only response was a brief eye contact with the mysterious man half-hidden in the shadows of the corner.

"I'll be in the office if you need me.'' Camry picked up

her sherry glass.

"I see you're wearing the necklace."

"A lot of luck it's brought me," she retorted sar-castically before closing the door to the sanctuary of her office.

Simple furnishings—a plain desk, chair and files—constituted the room. Camry wanted to make money, not spend it where people wouldn't see it. She sat behind the desk and folded her hands on the top. Her big evening, one which she had hoped would be flaw-less, had been marred. Marred by women she had never seen. Their disapproval of her only heightened her goals. The Emerald Tiger *would be* the talk of the town. It had become an obsession to be successful. She'd failed as a daughter . . . even as a wife. But she would be a good businesswoman . . . That was all she had—her business.

As weeks passed, Camry's expectations rang true. She had enforced strict rules for her employees. Such rigor added to the quality of the Emerald Tiger. A higher class patron appreciated her eye for detail. The saloon was their den in the wake of the bank's closure. But most of all, she lifted all betting restrictions. The sky was the limit. And that lured in her biggest catches—John Mackay, James Flood and William Sharon. With the Silver King's money, how could she go wrong?

The women remained absent, increasing her desire to drain their husband's pockets. Money flow was good; her safe full. William Sharon had been paid off in full. Now, Frank had to be dealt with.

Early morning sun streamed through the window of Camry's bedroom as she stirred from a disturbing sleep. She rolled to her side and pushed back her disheveled hair. For the second day in a row, she woke with a feeling of uneasiness. It was like wanting something, but being denied it. She thought about all the things she had and decided she was satisfied with her material status. Yet, she needed more. A hunger that she couldn't define burned within her. It was almost a craving . . . She thought of chocolate mousse, her favorite sweet, but it held little relief. She ran down a list of delectables, but nothing tempted her. Nothing eased the emptiness. Her heart was heavy as she tried to pinpoint her feelings.

Dressing in a floral print brown day dress, Camry fastened a straw hat over her curls and tied a wide black ribbon under her chin. What could she possibly want? She had everything . . . almost. She refused to think of a man in her life. There would be no one.

The weather had been gradually changing from warm and pleasant to warm and dusty. Washoe zephyrs were busy disturbing Sun Peak's side, a rolling tumble of light dirt washing over the streets. She grabbed her reticule and a crocheted mantle, then departed for the Nevada Wine and Spirits Company.

It was close to noon when Nicholas entered Virginia City. Sun reflected off S.D.'s saddle and dust-coated dappled hair as he reined the horse to a stop at Light and Allman's Livery. After telling the groom he'd be back for his saddle bags, he headed down Sutton Street toward the Consolidated-Virginia. Having volunteered to go to Summit Camp as a representative for the mine, he had been overlooking lumber contracts of the Carson & Tahoe Lumber & Fluming company. Pouring his energy into work, he had tried temporarily to forget his wife—though not always successfully.

He tried to force her from his mind, yet she was always there. He knew how she must be hurting with the death of Michael, but what could he do? He'd tried to offer condolences and help, but she refused. Camry was too headstrong for her own good. He wondered how she was faring, if she was all right at the Bonanza.

A group of men crowded on C Street. They peered in the windows of a saloon, shading their eyes against the glaring sun in order to look inside. A tight-knit cluster of leather and fur matrons paused long enough to glimpse at whatever was behind the frosted glass doors. They huffed snobbishly, then put their heads together and jiggled their dewlaps in gossip.

Nicholas had heard the bank had closed down in his absence. Luckily he had withdrawn his money before he left. Wondering if the gathering had anything to do with the Bank of California, he stepped across the alkali dust street.

His riding spurs rolled with the breeze at each step he took, the clink echoing under the awning. He glanced at the regal sign swinging above the door. The Emerald Tiger. He had never heard of it.

"New saloon?" Nicholas asked a tall miner next to him. Hell, he'd been gone nearly a month—the way businesses opened and closed, he had no idea what the special attraction of this establishment was. The miner gave him an unbelieving stare.

"You're kidding! Not just a saloon, *the* finest saloon in town. And it's run by a woman if you can fancy that!"

That was surprising, Nicholas thought. "What's so interesting in there?" He tried to see around the crowd.

The miner's lips curled to a smug smile. "Her partner just hung her portrait above the piano."

Nicholas knew of that custom. A painting of the house favorite was done in oils. It usually meant she was the best in the house—in bed. And if this saloon were run by a woman she must be a madame. Shading his eyes with the brim of his hat, he looked in the window, his gaze moving above the men's heads inside.

Midnight blue eyes cooled to steel daggers, his nostrils flaring. With a strong arm, he pushed the miner aside and knocked passed the men in his way.

On closer inspection of the picture, three feet high by six feet wide, there was no doubt . . . Lying on its side with sinewy paws of burnt orange stretched out in front, was a hulking Bengal tiger. And on the beast, was a woman resting on her stomach. Yards of sheer opaque gauze wrapped loosely around her nude body, hugging her breasts and buttocks, only a tempting hint of the flesh underneath visible. One leg was bent upward, her elbows resting on the tiger's head in triumph, her chin in her palms. Coppery hair floated behind her, wildly blending into the emerald green background which matched her eyes exactly as well as the beast's. Her only adornment was a small necklace, a playing card, the queen of hearts embedded with gems. A scrollwork caption below read: Our Lady, Queen of Hearts.

From the corner of his eye, Nicholas saw Frank Marbury. Obviously the gambler had seen Camry void of clothes in order to describe her so accurately to the artist . . . unless she had posed herself. All of the anger and frustration he had stifled during the past weeks surfaced and he lunged for Frank.

Frank had no warning. He was pushed against the craps table and received a bruising blow on the cheek before Nicholas came into his view. Instinctively, he reached into his vest, pulling on the fob chain to free his derringer. His hand was knocked away as Nicholas swung down on his rib cage.

By now, all eyes had turned away from the painting and to the brawling pair. They eagerly cheered them on, not caring if it was the boss-lady's partner being whipped by the blond man. They didn't know *he* was the boss-lady's husband. Frank had no physical chance against the six-foot, one-inch Norwegian—his only hope for victory was the man-made persuasion in his pocket. They tumbled to the carpet, arms locked in a battle of strength.

In a split second, Frank broke away and moved for his gun. His fingertips felt the cool silver handle and he gripped the butt. Pulling the weapon from his vest, he prepared to shoot. He didn't give a damn that it was Camry's husband—the son-of-a-bitch attacked *him*. Nicholas tightened his grip on his arm.

A woman's shrill scream cut the cheering men's voices. Frank recognized it as Camry's and froze, his aim not wavering. If it came down to it, he'd shoot.

"Stop it!" she cried. "What are you doing?! Frank! Put that . . . that gun down!"

He ignored her request, the barrel remaining fixedly on Nicholas' chest.

"Nicholas, let go of him!" she ordered, her voice shaking, her mind trying to figure out what had brought them to blows. . . . What was Nicholas doing here—now?

Nicholas roughly let go of Frank's shoulders and slowly stepped back.

"What do you think you're doing?" she demanded of them.

Nicholas made no attempt to answer, but bent to retrieve his hat. Eyeing Frank disdainfully, he turned to leave without a word, or an explanation.

Frank gathered himself with dignity, slowly lowering the derringer to his side. "Next time we meet, Trelstad, you're a dead man," he called after him.

Paying no heed, Nicholas pushed his way past the gawkers, never once looking at or acknowledging Camry.

She snapped at the crowd and her employees, "Get on with your business or get out!" Facing Frank, she hissed, "I want to see you in my office."

He followed her and closed the door behind him.

Camry threw her reticule on the desk and tugged off her mesh gloves and straw hat. "Explain to me what happened."

Frank rubbed his cheek gingerly, testing for soreness. "I don't know. I never saw him come in until he had me on the floor."

"So you would have shot him?!"

"I would have shot *anyone* who attacked me."

"What started it?"

"How the hell should I know? He's *your* goddamn husband." He flexed his fingers open and closed, examining each hand.

A ruckus started outside the closed office door. "What's all that noise about out there now?" She wondered if Nicholas had come back. Opening the door, she looked about the saloon, her eyes growing wide seeing her portrait above the piano.

A groan escaped her lips, a vivid blush coloring her cheeks. "Who . . . who put *that* up?"

Rubbing his chin, Frank shrugged. "I don't know."

Camry caught sight of the man below the painting who was bragging about the detailed colors. He was the one she had seen lurking about for weeks.

"You!" She stormed to the bar and picked up a glass, hurling it at his head.

The artist ducked in time, slivers of crystal raining down the wallpaper.

"Mr. Duckwater! Escort that skunk out!" She pointed at the flushed man. Kneading her temples, she turned to Frank. "Frank, get that *vile* painting off the wall! And when you're done with that, find out who commissioned it!"

Snatching a snifter of brandy off the bar, she shut herself in her office, a confused barrage of thoughts assaulting her mind. She reeled with questions . . . Oh, God, had Nicholas seen the picture? What must he think of her? And why should she care?

39

Camry sat behind the paper-cluttered desk in her office, scribbling on pale yellow ledger sheets. She adjusted the brim of her canvas visor and proceeded to enter another total in the credit column. For the third time in a row, she applied too much pressure and the sharp tip of her pencil snapped, leaving a small dot of lead dust on the paper. She brushed it away, but in the process, smudged the page. In frustration, she threw the pencil down, not wanting to sharpen it a fourth time.

Her nerves were torn to the bone. Had there been someone she could trust with the books, she would have gladly passed the job over. Yet, even she had to admit, it wasn't the work wearing her down. She thrived on it, was almost obsessed with it. No, it was something else— something which shouldn't bother her, but did. She slid the visor off her hair and rested her forehead in her hand. Nicholas . . . why, why did he always haunt her? She knew now that the fight with Frank was because of the painting and the insinuations that it held. Well, why should she care? Let him think whatever he wanted. He was having trysts with his Spanish harlot.

Pouring another cup of coffee, Camry stirred in a teaspoon of sugar. She didn't want to think about it; she'd been thinking about it for the past week. Lifting the mug to her lips, she sipped, then put it down. It was cold.

She went to the small window and slammed it shut. The weather had turned blustery. She stared out the four-paned window for a while, watching Virginia City pass by.

"Miss Camry?" Peach stood in the doorway, his fingers hooked in his belt-loops.

"Yes?" She turned from the window and repeated, "Yes?" thinking he hadn't heard her the first time.

"It's still in the storeroom where Mr. Marbury put it. I can't keep working around it. Yesterday I nearly dropped a case of Uncle Tom's rum on it, and today a jar of maraschino cherries fell off the shelf and hit it. I cleaned them up, but—"

"What *are* you talking about, Mr. Duckwater?" Camry had heard enough of his roundabout prattle.

"Why, the painting of course."

The painting! That wicked painting Frank still claimed he knew nothing about. She had no proof to doubt him, but for some reason, his show of innocence wasn't convincing.

"Get rid of it then," Camry remarked tersely.

"How do you suggest I go about that?"

"Oh, for heaven's sake, bring it in here for now and I'll take care of it."

"Right-o."

He was gone and back in a matter of minutes, his bald head pink with exertion.

"Well? Where is it?"

"It's a mite heavier than I expected."

Camry was about to retort, but thought better of it. He could be sensitive about his height and lack of muscle to move a painting two inches longer than he was. "Very well, let's move it together. The two of us should be able to handle the abominable thing."

They manged to half-carry, half-drag the heavily framed oil. Once in Camry's office they leaned the picture against the wall.

She caught her breath and studied it, Peach following her gaze.

"It's ain't half bad, Miss Camry." He dabbed his shiny head with a wrinkled red bandanna, then stuffed it back in his pocket. "That artist feller did a right fine job."

She turned up her nose, yet looked down at it thoughtfully. Indeed the woman *did* hold a good likeness to her; yet the brazen seductiveness of the flaming-haired temptress was not her. It was queer how the artist perceived her as taming the tiger. She had always thought of herself as the tiger. Always ready to bear her claws for a fight.

Shrugging, Camry sighed. "Would you care to have a drink with me, Mr. Duckwater?"

He scratched the bridge of his nose and sniffed. "That would be right nice, Miss Camry."

They left the office and stepped behind the bar; each had a glass of Madeira.

Camry licked her lower lip and checked the time on her necklace watch. Almost noon.

"Where is Mr. Marbury? Did he tell you where he was going?"

"He didn't say didily to me." Peach drained his glass and set it on the counter. "It was right nice of you to offer me a drink. I knew you weren't all hellcat and bluster. I could tell it were just a front."

"Oh?" She leaned her elbow on the bar and frowned. "Then I'm not doing my job."

"Ah, you don't have to play spade with me. A spade may be a spade, but it comes in two colors. I speak what's on my mind, and that's the pure and simple of it. I'll let you sling the orders to me, but I know down deep, you don't really mean the edge to them."

"I don't?" Camry stifled a skeptical laugh.

The saloon door opened and Frank strolled in looking smug.

"I see you're celebrating already. Good, pour me a brandy. How did you find out so soon?" He took a folded copy of the Territorial Enterprise from under his arm. Setting it on the bar, he put his hat next to the freshly inked pages.

"Heard what?" Camry returned slightly irritated with his vagueness. He wasn't going to get off the hook about her portrait so easily and if it meant keeping a coolness between them, then that's what she would do.

"The Bank of California reopened this morning."

Surprise brushed her cheeks. "Why hasn't there been a run in the streets?"

Frank tapped a finger on the front page of the newspaper, pointing to the headline article. "There's no need. There've been more deposits than withdrawals. Trays in Gold Hill opened with $100,000."

"I'll bet that weasel Sharon held back currency. It killed me paying him that interest on the money my father borrowed. For a stump of a man—" Embarrassed, she stopped herself short and inconspicuously glanced at Peach.

"Don't worry about me, Miss Camry. My height don't make me calamitous. I may be short in body, but tall in brain and heart."

"I don't doubt that," she smiled, impressed at his candor.

Frank picked up his hat and the paper. "I admire your integrity too, Mr. Duckwater. That's why I'm sure Miss Camry will agree, you can keep the Emerald Tiger running without us tonight."

"What do you mean?" Camry asked, her hands on her hips. "I don't suppose you're inviting me to dinner, because if you are—"

"We've been invited to the Washoe Club."

"I told you, Frank. We're strictly partners and nothing more."

"Have it your way. I'll tell John Mackay you send your regrets." He began to walk toward the door.

Camry ran from behind the bar and stopped him. "Mackay! Mackay invited *me* to the Washoe Club?"

He regarded her with hooded silver-gray eyes. "The invitation was for *both* of us. The Silver Kings are throwing a party in honor of the bank's reopening, but if you can't make it—"

"I'll make it. What time?"

Frank laughed in a low tone. "See the spider weave her web." He wiggled his fingers dramatically. "At eight. I'll see you then. De-venom yourself before I come back.

I wouldn't want you to poison me by mistake." He pulled the collar up on his jacket and left.

Standing in the middle of the room, her eyes glittered with whirling thoughts. Mackay invited her to his stomping grounds. That in itself was an accomplishment. What to wear? What to say? Who to mingle with? This was the chance she'd been waiting for.

40

After enjoying a meal prepared by the fine Washoe Club chefs, Camry slowly climbed a grand, circular stairway to the ultimate voluptuousness of the parlors above the dining room. Daintily holding the fullness of her skirts, she took each step slowly, savoring the details of her rich surroundings. The silky whisper of her delicate petticoats flowed rhythmically under the rich rustle of sea-green silk. The bodice of her gown was a matching velvet, cut very low. Leg-of-mutton sleeves puffed elegantly, tapering to a snug fit at her wrists where a heady perfume lingered, filling the air and over-whelming the tangy traces of lemon and garlic shrimp now wafting faintly from the kitchen.

Camry's eyes took in everything around her. As she turned her head to view the room she had just left, her delicate emerald and diamond earrings swayed, sparkling in the bright light. She smoothed back her hair, her white lace gloves soft against her skin. The jewelry was a gift to herself from herself. The Emerald Tiger had made enough money to buy back her glory.

Recalling the dinner conversation caused a small wrinkle to mar her forehead. Her socializing had been confined to Frank as the large dining room was so stuffed with chairs and cloth-covered tables, she could hardly turn to participate in talk other than that which was in front of her. Once, she attempted to introduce herself to the woman behind her, the president of the Women of Virginia City League, but when Camry turned in her chair, her arm was butted by the dowager's cherubic elbow as she cut into a piece of glazed duck.

After that, she decided it would be better to wait until the meal was finished before she mingled. After all, who wanted to discuss topics of interest with a mouth full of food?

Frank had gone upstairs before her to the gaming dens, and now as she took the last step, her hand fell languidly from the balustrade, and she decided to seek him out. The different parlors were draped with fringed portieres, a multitude of color schemes for each: plum, azure, olive and scarlet. Glittering salmon-tinted glass chandeliers reflected off the jeweled women and cuff-studded men. Camry had never seen such a variety of fox, ermine, mink, sable, tailcoats, dinner jackets, waistcoats, satins, silks, crepes, taffetas, rubies, diamonds, sapphires . . . She almost got dizzy looking at it all. In addition to the parlors, were a lounge, a taproom and a cardroom. Women who had shunned her turned their head curiously, yet they refused to approach her.

An orchestra tuned up, then melodically strummed a subtle waltz. Camry saw John Mackay and a man in his forties in deep conversation, standing before the lounge windows regarding the mountain. The sun was only a remnant lacing dusky rose clouds over the jagged valleys of Six-Mile Canyon.

She walked gracefully toward them, sizing up the man with John Mackay. Though both men appeared to be the same age, Mackay was far handsomer. His associate's hair receded, emphasized by the fact he wore it combed straight back. A long, pointed gray beard covered his chin—it reminded her of Werldorf's bristles. His eyes were dark and had a mean glint to them. As she came closer, she heard the tail end of a story Mackay was relating to the bearded man.

"So I told the editor, 'What damn sonofagun wrote all this infernal trash about my pardner? I own half this paper myself and I won't have Fair abused and libeled in it by anybody. I've a damn good mind to take a sledge and smash the hell out of the bloody press!'" He took a puff on his dollar cigar, then rolled it in his fingers.

"It's all a bunch of politics, John. The people see any man of standing as a kid-glove miner. Miners who watch their mines from San Francisco. Weasels like that sonofagun Bill Sharon give us a bad name."

Seizing the opportunity to cut in, Camry stepped forward. She had been formally introduced to John Mackay, now hearing them talk, she was sure the other man was James Fair. The second richest man in Virginia City—but not by much.

"Hello, Mr. Mackay," Camry greeted, holding out her laced hand.

"Miss Parker! So glad you could come." He took her fingertips and pressed them to his lips. "May I introduce my pardner, James Fair."

"Charmed," she rallied.

"A pleasure, I'm sure." He followed Mackay's gesture, lingering over her hand longer than etiquette required, and also grazing her low neckline with a rakish eye.

She eased away without being obvious. Flirting lightly, she batted her thick lashes. "Why haven't I seen you in my saloon, Mr. Fair? You have heard of the Emerald Tiger, haven't you?"

"Jim, my dear. Jim. And I have heard of it. I've been in San Francisco these past weeks, but the name has traveled west to the coast and I assure you with the finest reports."

Camry was elated! So, she *had* established a name for her saloon. "Then you'll have no excuse to stay away. There are no betting restrictions, you know."

"So I've heard."

Mackay extinguished his cigar by dropping it in the brass cuspidor at his feet. "And a damn good lift on a restriction. I always say, I don't care whether I win or lose. When you can't enjoy betting in poker, there's no fun left in anything."

Chuckling, Fair ribbed, "Those are mighty strong words from a man who eats mutton chops, oatmeal mush, toast and coffee every morning." His eyes traveled over Camry's shoulder and he studied a petite blonde in a daring ruby organdy gown. Camry held back a laugh; the man couldn't even be a faithful flirt!

"You're full of hot air, Jim."

Camry sensed they delighted in bantering with each other. Fair's gaze roved to another of his partner's female guests and it became apparent that he undressed each woman in the parlor. She became slightly uneasy; hadn't she heard he had a wife and children? But that didn't mean anything in Virginia City. . . . Didn't she have a husband?

John Mackay picked up a flagon of ale and tugged on a needlepoint bellpull in the corner. Soon a flunky appeared and Mackay instructed him.

"I'm waiting for an overseas wire. See to it the cable is given to Mr. Fair. I'm not to be disturbed in the cardroom." He tipped the lad two bits, then reached for his silk top hat from the hat rack next to him.

"Well, Miss Parker, as the proprietor of a gaming hall, I'm sure you'll understand if I excuse myself to indulge in the sport."

"Certainly."

"I'll see you soon. Enjoy yourself." He left with a confident swagger, greeting many of his guests on the way to the cardroom.

Once Mackay disappeared, Fair moved in on Camry like a bear pouncing on a honey-filled tree. He stroked his beard, then adjusted his plaid ascot.

"We shall dance now," he ordered in a murmur, his breath tickling the edge of her shoulder. She automatically put her hand over her neck, as if trying to slap his invisible caress. Without giving her time to deny him, he clutched her waist possessively and whirled her briskly to the middle of the room.

James G. Fair, appropriately nicknamed Slippery Jim, was not a man to be crossed, Camry observed as they danced. When the music finally stopped, she fought gently to break free, but he would have none of that. A toast was in order. A toast to the bank's reopening. Oh, where was Frank? At least she was comfortable with him. Just when she needed him, he was nowhere to be found . . . and Jim Fair was making matters worse by holding her so closely. All the women in the room seemed to disapprove.

Led to the corner where a long oak bar was crowded with men, Camry's hand was thrust onto a flagon of port. Drinking several sips, she was whirled away to dancing with nearly each man at the bar: Senator Stewart, Aldolf Sutro, Lucky Baldwin, John Piper and Governor Bradley, who bore a close resemblance to Father Time. She had met every influential man in Virginia City, even a few of their wives, though the receptions had been cool.

Once at the counter again, Fair handed Camry another drink and leaned over her, his voice low. "Do you own any stock?"

Confused by his sudden change in tactics, she backed away slightly, then spoke cautiously. "Yes, but I haven't been able to cash them."

He moved closer again, and whispered. "Don't mention this to a soul, but Gould & Curry is going sky high."

"It is?" Camry's eyes widened speculatively.

He waved his hand, signaling her to keep her voice down. "How much do you have?"

She bit her lower lip thoughtfully. She had never told anyone, not even Frank, the exact amount she would have lost since not being able to cash the stocks in before the closure, but now . . . if Gould & Curry was on the ups . . . "Enough," she finally answered.

"This is between you and me, my dear, but I'd act fast."

As Camry absorbed his projections, the flunky appeared carrying a small silver tray laden with a telegram.

"Mr. Fair, I have Mr. Mackay's wire."

"What's the matter with you?" Fair bellowed, his eyes dark and stormy. "Mr. Mackay wants this sent directly to him in the cardroom!"

The lad cowered, but mustered some courage. "I beg

your pardon, Mr. Fair, but Mr. Mackay doesn't want to be disturbed in the cardroom."

"Don't heckle me, boy!" Fair boomed. "Bring the god damn thing to the bloody cardroom!"

Camry swallowed as the flunky nodded meekly and scurried away.

Snickering smugly, Fair smiled genuinely for the first time during the evening.

"Well, if you'll excuse me," Camry apologized lightly, wanting nothing better than to rid herself of this crazed man. "I must find my partner—" Oh, Frank! Where the devil are you?

"Nonsense!" he disputed.

A regal woman dressed in confining fuchsia with stiff ruched ivory lace supporting her chin, strode purposefully across the room to meet them. She tapped her fan open and lifted an engraved silver-handled opera glass to her eyes.

"Jim, you're to dance with *me* now."

He appeared annoyed with her, and resignedly made the proper introductions.

"Miss Parker, this is Mrs. Fair."

Camry smiled demurely and nodded her head once. "I'm pleased to meet you."

"I'm not," Mrs. Fair snapped. "Of all the inimitable gall. Miss Parker indeed! You're a married woman posing as a burr, well you'll not infest yourself under my husband's skin."

If looks could kill, Mrs. Fair would have dropped dead on the spot from the lethal glare coming from James Fair's eyes.

"Theresa! Watch yourself!"

"I've had enough of your threats. If you don't leave this woman immediately, I'll see my lawyers." Theresa Fair fanned her flushed cheeks vigorously, then turned her attention to Camry. "You're a shameless hussy. Galavanting in diamonds made off your husband's money. And your gown! You should be in *black*. Have you no respect for your father?"

Camry's green eyes grew to flashing dark pools; her breath was short. "I've a good mind to bash your head in with that fan, Mrs. Fair. I respect my father more now than I ever have. I'm making Parker a respectable name. Can you say your name would be anything without your husband's?"

"Balderdash! Jim! Do something."

He frowned so intensely, his eyebrows resembled two silver lightning bolts pointed at his nose, ready to clash. "I need a bloody drink," he railed, then stormed off.

Mrs. Fair crossed her arms and clicked her heels. "Humph! You're not welcome in Virginia City, Mrs. Trelstad. I speak for all the ladies. Go back to Philadelphia!"

"Go to hell." The words had slipped out before she could stop herself. Yet, somehow, it didn't matter. She was tired of playing games. Tired of trying to coddle the genteel woman. She was Camry Parker Trelstad, daughter of Michael Angus Parker, and owner of a saloon. If the ladies of Virginia City's fine society couldn't accept that, then they could all go to hell. She still had their husbands . . . but just to make sure their wives tried to stop them from gambling at the Emerald Tiger . . . Camry brushed passed Theresa and went to the orchestra platform. Silencing the musicians, she called the room to attention.

"Gentlemen," she said clearly, collecting the right words to continue. She had to say something that even in a rash of disapproval from their wives, they would go against them when it came down to the last word. Taking a deep breath, she announced, "From now on, whoever visits the Emerald Tiger between the hours of noon and three will be given complimentary drinks." What she had announced was unheard of.

A roar of approval ended in applause from the men. The women cast disgusted glares.

As an afterthought, Camry added, "That invitation includes you too, ladies. I assume some of you are inclined to take a drink, though you may do so in private. Don't let that stop you from coming. The Emerald Tiger holds all of its patrons in great esteem, and if anyone says otherwise, they'll have to deal with me. Good evening."

She left the lounge with her chin held high. Her sea-green skirts swayed with pride as she reached the circular stairway and descended.

"Bravo, my dear." Frank's voice broke her steps.

"What do you want?" She continued down the stairs to the dining room. She was angry with him. If he had been with her, she might not have flown off the handle. Now it was too late. What was done was done . . . but did she really care if they came or not? She told herself she did . . . but underneath, she didn't give a damn about the two-faced citizens of Virginia City. Especially that James G. Fair. He was a—a peacock. Yes, a peacock. Just like Nicholas said.

Frank interrupted her thoughts. "What happened? Why did you make that silly womanish announcement? I've never heard of 'free' drinks."

"Where have you been?" She tossed over her shoulder.

"Gambling."

"Gambling! That's all you ever do. Don't you take things seriously? Well, I do." She reached the landing and turned to face him. "I take my business very seriously and that announcement might have been the thing to save it after Theresa Fair's outburst. And as for womanish ways, I *am* a woman, and very proud of it. It's high time some of these society grande dames took a look at themselves. Their noses are plastered to the ceiling."

Frank leaned against the banister, toying with a yellow playing token. "Do you hear what you just said? You're no better than them."

"Oh yes I am," she denied. She was much better. Maybe she had been like them in the past, but things would change now. She would change. Looking at them

was a painful look in the mirror. Nicholas was right, they
were all peacocks.

"Haven't you had enough, Camry? Let's go away.
You'll never be accepted into the bitches' parlors for
tea."

She sighed heavily. She didn't want to sip tea with
them. "Don't you get tired of asking me to leave? I get
tired of hearing you ask. I'm tired of everything." She
claimed her cape from the porter and bid Frank good-
night. "Good-bye, Frank."

"Where are you going? I'll take you back to the
Emerald Tiger."

She didn't want to go there. She needed to think. "No,
I want to be alone." She ignored him and moved
between the empty dining tables which had been
cleared and covered with fresh linen. Frank made no
move to follow her.

Opening the elaborate doors, she stepped into the
crisp deep blue night. C Street was surprisingly calm.
Only an occasional miner walked out of a saloon, the
continuous piano music following him to the street. A
faint, cool breeze ruffled her fine curls, the tendrils
caressing her cheeks.

Traveling down the boardwalk, she placed a gloved
hand on her temple. She had a headache. She never
used to get headaches. Thoughts of the Emerald Tiger
collided with ones of the Washoe Club. Did she want her
saloon to be as grand as that of the Silver Kings? Did she
want to spend the rest of her life alone? She wasn't sure.
Suddenly, she felt very lonely. Yes, she could go to the
Emerald Tiger and be surrounded by friendly patrons
. . . but patrons had homes to go home to. Where was
her home? Where was her place? She didn't know. She
had thought it was on her own. She had thought she was
strong enough to be an independent woman. But
couldn't she be independent and love a man as well?
She couldn't think about it now—her head ached.
Increasing her pace, Camry willed her mind to go blank.

A banjo strummed "The Yellow Apron", from inside

the Delta Saloon. The batwing doors flapped open and three men stepped out in front of her, each wearing frock coats. The faint saloon light illuminated the first to stand on the boardwalk. A sombrero with a rattlesnake band crowned his head and when he looked up at her, she stared into startling slate-blue eyes. He appeared to be the youngest of the three; she guessed him to be in his early twenties. He wore a scarlet silk neckerchief, and silver-plated six-shooters in silver-studded holsters.

"Would you look at this?" He smiled, nudging his friends.

The drunkest of the three swayed. He wore his hair in a slicked-down fashion, a bristling moustache and small growth of beard between his lower lip and his chin; his eyes were very close-set. He reached into his vest and pulled out a pewter flask. "Care for a drink, Sugar?" He popped the cork off with his teeth. "You reckon she's scared of us, Virg?"

Virg was the last man to step forward. He seemed to be in his thirties with brown hair slicked down and parted on the side. His eyes were deep-set and a full moustache made up for the fact that he had no neck. He leaned against an awning post and studied her. "Are those real, lady?"

Camry followed his eyes to her chest, suddenly raising her hands to cover her low neckline—shocked by the brazenness of his question. She then pulled her cloak tighter around her shoulders.

Virg laughed. "I didn't mean *those*!" His glance roved above her breasts to the emerald and diamond necklace. "I can see they're all you from the fine cut of this fancy frock. I was referring to them gems."

"Leave it alone, Virg," the blue-eyed man drawled.

"Listen to you! You started this. Maybe this here lady wants some company. What are you doing walking around—alone?"

She took a step backward, checking the street. She could run to the Emerald Tiger, it was just past the International Hotel, but first she'd have to pass *them*.

"I'm forgetting my manners," Virg apologized, doffing his hat. "A lady needs the formifications of introductions. I'm Virgil Earp. This here is John Holiday, but he likes people to call him Doc. And the one you been ogling with them twinkling blue eyes is Bat Masterson."

Doc took a healthy swig and wiped his mouth with the back of his hand. "What's your name, Sugar?"

For the first time, she spoke, gathering all her strength for her voice to remain calm. "Let me by."

Bat kicked his boot heel on the planks, watching the spur spin, "Just what *are* you doing out here at one in the morning—alone? Only sporting row gals strut in velvet this time of night."

Without warning, he brushed the softness of her sleeve. Camry froze, afraid the slightest movement from her would be taken as a sign of weakness.

"That's it, Bat . . . let's show her what gentlemen we really are." Doc took a step toward her.

Camry swiftly drew up her skirts and kicked his shin. She turned to run, but was caught in Virgil's arms.

"Let me go!" she screamed.

The banjo music stopped and a tall man filled the doorway of the Delta. Camry couldn't see who he was and prayed he wasn't another man she'd have to flee, but someone to help her.

Suddenly Keg's gruff voice filled the boardalk, and the click of the hammer on his pearl-handled revolver echoed threateningly under the awning as he cocked it.

"Ya hold it right t'there, mister, or I'll put a window right through your head so big, ya ain't a goin' t'be able t'draw the shades t'keep the breeze from stirrin' your brain—if'n ya have one." Even though his trigger finger was missing, Keg's aim was better and steadier having to use his middle finger—the gun rested evenly in his large, coarse hand.

Virgil made no move to do as Keg asked. "We ain't doing nothing wrong. This lady is just going to join us for a drink. We ain't letting her drink with you," he spat.

"Then you're goin' t'see your maker."

"Wait," Bat stopped Keg's threat. "Let her go, Virg. We didn't mean the lady no harm. Let's go to the Brick-house."

"Are you going to let this citified Injun order us?"

"Shit, do what you want. I'm not getting lead thrown at me over some dame. When I die, it'll be over cards."

"This ain't his bailiwick," Virg pointed out.

Bat tossed over his shoulder. "He's got nerve. There's only one of him and three of us." He shuffled down the street.

Virgil abruptly released her, hitching his pants. "We were only funning with you, lady." He gruffed after Bat. "You oughta be a sheriff, Bat. You're always saying you have a keen sense for right and wrong."

Bat Masterson stopped and turned around. He adjusted his sombrero, and lightly eyed Camry before he went his way.

"You'd better watch how you sleep, mister," Doc threatened. "Or one day you're going to wake up and find your teeth missing, and that ain't no claptrap."

Keg countered, "Your rotgut don't make ya a man t'be afeared. Get lost, whiffet."

Doc thrust his fists into his pockets and stalked across the street to catch up with Virgil Earp and Bat.

Camry sighed heavily and pressed her hand against the brick wall of the Delta. "Am I glad to see you."

Uncocking his revolver, Keg replaced it in his holster. "Are ya awright, Miz Trelstad?"

Before she could answer, Nicholas flung the batwing doors open. "Keg, what the hell are you doing—" He stopped in mid-sentence, seeing a woman veiled in the shadows. He knew at once it was Camry. . . . He smelled her in the night air.

Bright diamonds and emeralds flashed and sparkled as she stepped forward, her skirts whispering in silky rustles. Her sweet perfume swirled above his head. Their eyes met, cool blue and cool green.

"Well, well. It's the Duchess of Sun Peak. Trifling with the commoners, Madame?" Nicholas smoothed his strawberry blond moustache in two swift strokes. He crossed a mocassined foot in front of his leg, tapping his toe on the wooden planks.

"I'm in no mood." Camry gathered her skirts and walked by him. She still couldn't face him . . . admit defeat. But had she really lost? Lost what? Yes, she had lost him . . . and in some ways she had lost herself.

"I'm in no mood either," he called back. "See you in the morning, Keg."

Nicholas left the Delta Saloon, taking Camry's direction down the street.

She heard him behind her, but continued walking. How long had it been since she'd seen him? A week, two? Or had it been a month? No matter how long, she remembered his every feature perfectly. His steps were like whispers. She knew how soft the leather on his mocassins was. Once when she'd put them away, she'd marveled at the finely tanned leather and held it against her cheek feeling the velvety smoothness. Oh . . . so many times she'd put them away in his cedar chest . . .

His stride was as long as his legs wrapped in white denim. The blue work shirt billowed, concealing his broad tanned shoulders and bands of muscles around his waist. She didn't have to try and imagine his face, for it was etched in her memory forever. If she just closed her eyes for a moment . . . she could see everything . . .

Sensing his presence beside her, she quickly fluttered her lids open. He was next to her. Midnight blue eyes matched the sky behind him. The silky blond hair was shiny and a small lock rested on his golden brow.

The only way Camry could talk to him now was in retorts. But why? Why was she afraid of him? Or was it herself she was afraid of? She must keep up a front. She must not let herself become transparent. Tightening her grip on her skirts, she sniffed, "Why are you following me?"

"You don't own this mountain yet, darlin'. I can walk where I damn well please. And if it's any of your business, I'm going home. Or don't you remember where us poor folks live?''

She frowned.

''Ah! Does it displease you when I mention your beginnings? Or do you prefer to forget such details? I would say so, *Miss Parker*. By the way, where is your pettifogger?''

''My what?''

''You heard me. I thought you wanted a divorce so Marbury could marry you. That is what you want, isn't it?''

What did she want? She thought she knew. She wanted power and money . . . and more. She didn't want Frank. ''Leave Frank out of this.''

''Why? He's your partner.''

''Not anymore.''

''Lover's spat?'' He quirked a brow in sarcasm.

''No. The only one I spat with is *you*.''

''Well, we sure as hell aren't lovers.''

Camry tossed her curls and returned with measured words, ''We certainly aren't.'' In her anger, she missed her step, the heel of her shoe catching in a knothole in a plank. She lost her balance and would have fallen if Nicholas hadn't caught her.

She kept her face away from him, pressing her hands against his solid chest. When he didn't release her, she turned her head toward him, his breath warm and moist on her flushed cheek. His shirt was soft and scented the air with a faint fragrance of mint soap. She began to relax in his arms, the pressure of his hands pulling her toward him. Without realizing it, she gently stroked the nape of his neck, her lips rising to meet his. She could not, did not want to resist him. She touched his lips like a whisper, lightly testing his response.

Nicholas was hesitant, unsure he wanted her to kiss him, yet his male desires overwhelmed all logic. He melted his mouth against hers, allowing himself a moment of bliss as she seduced him. Her timidness dissolved and she thrust herself in his embrace, clinging to his back. To Camry, all time had stopped. Nothing mattered but the man before her and their lips clinging

together in cruel ravishment. There was no denying their
attraction, their desire for each other. If nothing else,
they still had a sexual bond.

A low groan escaped Nicholas and he broke the
magic, firmly prying her hands from his neck, and
holding her at arm's length.

"Don't do this to me," he ground out, his voice
shaking. "I'm not your damn toy. Go back to your doll-
house and play." He balled his fists and stormed down
the street to Ma Zmed's. He disappeared onto the porch
and slammed the front door behind him.

Camry's quivering lips burned in the aftermath of their
kiss; she had an aching need for another. Tears clouded
her eyes and spilled silently down her cheeks. She
moved down A Street, ashamed and embarrassed at her
body's treachery.

Nicholas sat in ebony darkness. He hadn't bothered to
light a lamp. His mood was black, why not be enveloped
by it? God, he still . . . loved her? Did he really? Yes, he
felt desire for her . . . but love? How could he love her
after they had been through so much? She had changed.
He sensed that. She had matured in a way. She
appeared more sophisticated, more demure. Not the
pouting girl anymore. She was a businesswoman. Maybe
that was what plagued him. She was successful.

Pouring a stiff drink of bourbon, Nicholas drained his
glass in one gulp. The alcohol burned his throat, a
welcome feeling. He could handle anything but the
feeling of love for a woman who had scorned him,
shunned him, laughed at him . . . made him realize that
he could love. But why her, damn it? Why did he love
her? Because he did, damn it. Why analyze the truth?
What does it matter where the truth comes from as long
as it's the truth?

He reached for the old cookie tin that Mrs. Gillespie
had set on the nightstand. He opened the lid. Oatmeal.
The molasses smell filled his nostrils. He remembered
the night he ate oatmeal cookies in bed . . . the night Keg
blasted up the mountain . . . the night he and Camry had

shared love. The night she had cried his name and said she loved him. Was that the night he first knew he was in love with her? No, he had been in love with her from the first . . . he would love her always. The only way he could try to forget her would be to leave her. Never see her again. Living in Virginia City was hell. He couldn't be near her and not be near her. He wondered if there were any hope. Not after tonight. She made her feelings perfectly clear. Tomorrow, he would make the necessary inquiries.

Camry turned up Howard Street, realizing Da's office had been her destination from the start. She needed him . . . needed to be around the things he was. She felt alone. She began to run when she saw the stained glass doors, then quickly unlocked them and closed them. Only then did she break down and really cry.

Oh, Nicholas? Why do I still love you? I tried to forget you . . . what we had. Camry brushed away her tears. She had wanted everything, but she had nothing—only material things. But they were no substitute for emotional riches. Through blurred eyes, she saw the lop-sided pine cone she had given Da, on his desk. She remembered the Truckee River and that night Nicholas had found her. How they shared a meal over the fire. How proud she had been of her accomplishments. How much in love she was with him even then. She had run away to collect her thoughts when all along she knew how she felt. Even now, she felt only the deepest of affection for Nicholas. Where had it all gone wrong?

No one loved her. Nicholas had, but now it was too late. She picked up the pine cone and threw it, then dropped to her knees on the mustard-colored carpet.

"Oh, why . . . Why? Didn't you love me either, Da? What did I do wrong? You didn't even say good-bye—" Tears rolled down her cheeks and quietly dropped on her emerald ring, and she recalled the simple gold band which had been on her finger before . . . and the silver and agate ring that was long gone . . . gone with everything else.

41

During the star-blanketed night, a chill settled over Virginia City. Camry woke in her room, cool air hovering over her, and she pulled the lilac quilt closer to her chin to keep the warmth around her from escaping. An endless cobalt sky promised a nice day, yet she doubted it would reach sixty-five degrees. She still had her headache.

With unsettling kicks, she tossed off the covers, paying no heed to the cold floor under her bare feet as she padded quickly to the rug and her cherry wood dressing closet.

After donning a charcoal-blue angora day dress with a delicate white lace collar and cuffs, Camry ran a brush through her lustrous locks and tied a white ribbon around them. She closed her bedroom door softly so as not to aggravate her headache with undo noise, and quietly descended the steps to the empty saloon.

The rich aroma of South American coffee lured her to the potbellied stove in the corner. Hastily, she poured a cup and took it to the bar. Her hands shook as she brought the rim to her lips, and a small amount splashed on the counter.

"Oh bother." She watched the steaming puddle melt the lemon polish Peach had carefully applied.

"You're nervous today."

She gasped and whirled around to see Frank sitting at a table, the Territorial Enterprise spread out before him. "What are you doing here?" she groaned.

"Reading the paper." He rested his foot on the chair across from him.

"I can see that. Don't you ever sleep?"

"Rarely."

"How did you get in here?"

Frank reached into his coat pocket and drew out a shimmering brass key. He dangled it in the air for emphasis, the early sun catching and reflecting it on the wall.

"Give that back to me." Camry strode towards him, holding out her hand.

The key disappeared into his pocket and he flashed an even white smile. "Good morning, Miss Camry."

"Darn you, Frank. With as much time as you spend around here, I'd swear I was married to you. Aren't you supposed to be incognito or something? You're taking chances."

"Life is a chance, my dear."

"Oh, quit the philosophy lessons. I'm in no mood."

"You're in a snit. Is it your womanly time?"

She snapped, "I should be shocked you asked me that, but nothing you do or say shocks me anymore."

"Because we're alike."

"Hardly!" She looked over the newspaper. "Give me the exchange sheet."

"Checking on the market?" he queried, pulling the paper apart.

"I have a hunch." Camry examined the colomns lightly, searching for Gould & Curry.

"Care to share it?"

"I don't know why I should," she answered into the newspaper.

"Then don't." Frank rubbed his sandpapered fingertips together, feeling for imperfections. "I don't need to make two dollars."

"Two dollars! More like thousands. Gould & Curry is going sky high." She bit her lower lip to stop herself from saying more. She had spilled the beans. "Oh, bother," she whispered.

Frank's hand appeared on the fresh black newsprint as he pulled the paper down from her face. She stared into amused silver-gray eyes. "Where did you get that idea?"

"Quit questioning me. Honestly! If you must know, James Fair told me in strict confidence."

"You mean, Slippery Jim? Camry, you surprise me. I thought you were smarter than that. Fair cons everyone with that line. Even his own wife."

"What are you talking about?"

"So you invest, and you 'accidentally' tell me, then I invest and tell someone . . . and so on. On the rising market, Fair profitably disposes of his holdings, then the public thinks Gould & Curry is petering out. The damn market collapses and Slippery Jim has made a tidy sum while you go belly up."

Camry crossed her arms. "I don't believe you."

"You bet. Invest your money then." Frank stood and straightened the paper. "I just thought I'd tell you how noble your idols really are. They're all a group of back-stabbing charlatans."

"John Mackay isn't," she defended.

"John Mackay is a fool." He tipped his Stetson at a rakish angle. "And you're a fool if you fall for his line of horse manure."

She rolled up the newspaper and cuffed his arm. "Get out, Frank. I don't want to talk to you anymore."

He chuckled slyly, then cupped her chin. "Funny you should say our relationship reminds you of marriage. When do we start sharing the same bed?"

She gritted her teeth. "Get out, Frank. And don't come back!"

Pushing open the frosted glass doors, he laughed at her on his way out. She may be gorgeous, but not quite a businesswoman yet, Frank thought. He mounted his carriage and flicked the reins. Camry was a hot-blooded woman, but one he was getting tired of waiting for. He didn't have the patience to pine away for her until eternity. There were plenty of beautiful women in Virginia City. On that thought, he veered to Sporting Row.

* * *

For the duration of the morning, Camry wondered if he were telling the truth—were they really alike? She wondered until noon when Peach, the piano player and her dealers came to start work. She would have still been wondering, but the crowd of thirsty patrons kept the Emerald Tiger so busy, she had to help behind the bar.

Peach did his best, but by one o'clock it was apparent her complimentary drink idea was too much for him to handle. By one-thirty, a "Help Wanted" sign was placed in the window.

By four o'clock, Camry was finally able to take a much-needed rest and retreated to the sanctuary of her office. Kicking off her shoes, she sat behind her desk and massaged her feet.

A rap hit the frame of her door. She knew it was Peach. He had some sort of superstition that knocking on a door itself was bad luck. The bald-headed man entered, his face red and moustache drooping.

"There's someone here about the job."

"Hire him," Camry returned, rubbing the tender flesh between stocking-covered toes.

"I think you better talk to her," Peach drawled.

"Her? A woman?"

"Yep."

Camry raised her brows curiously. "Very well, send her in."

"Yes, Miss Camry."

She slipped her shoes back on and smoothed her hair. Sitting straight and dignified, she folded her hands on the desk.

Camry blinked, then blinked again, but Garnet Silk didn't disappear. She was attired in a rust-colored paisley print, her long ebony hair wound into a bun, revealing small earlobes and the turquoise dot studs in them. Her high cheekbones were rosy and her red lips moist.

"Either I'm hallucinating," Camry finally managed, "or you've got more nerve than I thought."

Drawing a deep breath, Garnet stood proudly. "I be *aquí para trabajar.*"

"What? If we're to hold any semblance of a conversation, you'd better speak English to me."

"I be here for work," she rephrased.

Unclasping her hands, Camry relaxed slightly against the back of her chair. "I thought you moved to San Francisco to find your child—" And possibly Nicholas' child, she added silently.

"I found him. He be with me now."

Her composure faltered. If the boy was Nicholas' son, any chance for their marriage would be gone. She fidgeted with the design in her lace cuff, then stopped herself, trying not to seem nervous. "Why did you come to me?"

"You have the grandest saloon in all Virginia City."

"I'm glad you realize this is a saloon—not a brothel. I don't think you'll fit in here."

" *Por qué no?* Why? Because I be a woman or because I be Nicky's *amiga*—friend?"

"Were you just friends? I think not. I know money can buy anything. Why don't you set up your business again?"

Garnet's cool exterior began to melt. Her delicate nostrils flared. "I came here for one reason—my son, Caleb. He need a *bueno* roof above his head. I make mistakes in the past, have not we all? I be ready to go on with my life."

Camry pondered the sincerity of Garnet's words. She finally sighed. "Even if we didn't have our differences, you are a woman. There aren't any women dealers and bartenders in saloons. And I don't have so-called saloon girls."

"Have you hear of Eleanore Dumont?"

She shrugged irritably, feeling Garnet was trying to best her.

"She be a woman dealer on the Missouri River. The *hombres* call her Madame Moustache."

"She sounds lovely," Camry broke in sarcastically.

"Eleanore Dumont be the best and most notorious dealer in the country. Ask any *hombre* in the bar. They like the woman."

"Well, what does this have to do with me? Are you planning on growing a moustache?"

A small smile cracked Garnet's ruby lips. "I believe that is impossible. As a woman in a man's business, do you be planning to sport trousers?"

"Oh, for heaven's sake!" Camry sniffed impatiently. The fiery woman was besting her. She wondered if her presence *would* be beneficial to the Emerald Tiger.

Picking up a pencil, Camry tapped the point on her desk. "You won't be able to wear gauche dresses and feathers and that sort of thing. I don't want a reminder of mistakes exhibited in my establishment. You'll be expected to dress in black and white like the others. And you may have to perform bartending duties with Peack Duckwater, my manager."

"*Yo comprendo*. I understand."

"Good." She set the pencil down and frowned. "You're sure you know how to deal cards?"

"*Sí*, I know. *Gracias*. I realize you did not have to hire me."

"You're right, I didn't." Camry thought of the prestige it would bring her to be the first *woman* to have a *woman* dealer. She stood, finalizing the conversation.

Garnet hesitated. "What do I call you?"

Camry quirked a brow. That was a good question. Mrs. Trelstad was out. Miss Parker seemed awkward—it would admit she was totally through with Nicholas. "It seems we both have to overcome the past. Call me Camry."

"My name be Garnetta then."

"Tell me, Garnetta, do you have a last name?" She couldn't keep herself from asking about the mysterious Mr. Evans. But to cover her curiosity, she added, "For bookkeeping purposes."

"*Mi nombre es*, Garnetta Silquerro—I have no husband now."

Camry meshed her fingers together. "Good, well, I'll
see you tomorrow at eleven o'clock. Do you have a
black skirt and white blouse?"

"I can manage. Good day, Camry."

After Garnetta had left, Camry stared out the window.
She sat for awhile trying to convince herself she had
hired the woman only because of good business sense,
yet a vision of a little boy clouded her thoughts and she
brushed it off. She would not only be helping Garnet,
but maybe Nicholas' son . . . She didn't want to think
about it. Da had told her once if you ponder things too
long, they come true. She brushed it off and headed for
the bar to see how Peach was coming along.

As the weeks passed, Camry kept a distant watch on
Garnetta. She knew the trade surprisingly well, and on
more occasions than one, challenged a customer to bet
against her and they lost.

The sheriff, Jared Purley, made frequent stops at the
Emerald Tiger. At first, Camry thought he was there to
see to law and order, but after a while, she realized it
was the sweet-scented female dealer who had all of
Virginia City talking that lured him in. No one brought up
her past. No one seemed to care. Garnetta Silquerro
Evans, alias Garnet Silk, had finally found her self-
respect.

This morning, the zephyrs swooped down the
mountainside, swirling alkali dust across C Street. The
dirt crept under the Emerald Tiger's double doors and
between the frosted glass window frames.

Camry dressed quickly in a white silk blouse and sable
wool skirt, deftly fastening the tiny hooks. She slipped
into yellow doe-leather gloves and rested a thickly knit
cape over her back, clasping the silk frogs together
under her chin. Deciding it was best to sell Da's office,
she had set up a meeting with a real estate man this
afternoon.

The barroom was brimming with patrons and foggy
with smoke. Even though it was one o'clock, the saloon

was filled to capacity, regardless of complimentary drinks. It was rumored the Emerald Tiger was to be the place of a large poker game tomorrow night. Though when anyone asked who was playing, no one seemed to know. The mystery held an aura of suspense and many of the men were planning on drinking for the duration of the day and into tomorrow to prepare for it. Fact or fiction, it gave them an excuse to drink more than the average gallon of whiskey a day.

Garnetta was busy taunting a regular gambler over a game of *vingt-et-un*. The kill was quick. She smiled at her open-faced hand of an ace of clubs and queen of hearts. He made a rude comment and her smile immediately faded. He grabbed his hat to leave, but she stopped him. Had Jared not been there, she might not have taunted the gambler, but she wanted to show him she had fire and guts.

"No, no! You must not go! First a special drink on the house." She had heard Eleanore Dumont say those very words before.

His face grew surprised as Garnetta called Peach to line up a round. To the gambler's chagrin, his glass was filled with milk.

"You play like *el chico*, drink *la leche* like *el chico*."

He tightened his lips and left the bar. He would make no rebuke—not when the law was standing three feet away.

Camry watched as Garnetta and Jared Purley exchanged looks. Instead of his disapproval of her bantering, he blew Garnetta a kiss, and she practically beamed with delight at the gesture. Unguarded Garnetta Silquerro was a lovely woman, Camry thought.

The intimacy brought a thousand questions to Camry's mind. Just who was Garnetta? Where did she come from? Why was she a brothel woman? And how did Nicholas fit into her complex life? But most of all . . . was Caleb Evans Nicholas' flesh and blood? The questions had nibbled at her for a long time . . . too long. It was time for answers. She had made light inquiries of Peach

but got little information out of him other than Garnetta
had moved from Sporting Row to a small boardinghouse at the north end of C Street above the section of
mines on Mill Street.

Without realizing it, Camry had left the Emerald Tiger,
not taking the path to Da's, but the road to Garnetta's
boardinghouse. Yes . . . it was a time to put old fears to
rest. She must know the truth.

The building was an unpainted two-story with a row of
eight windows on the second floor. There was no
veranda, but a small stoop only wide enough to sit
three.

On the stoop was a little boy bundled in a suede jerkin
with a navy cable-knit sweater underneath. Golden
blond locks curled on his smooth olive forehead. Clear
blue eyes as large as saucers looked up at her, then
looked down. They were fringed with thick sooty lashes.
He picked up a blade of dry grass and examined it in his
chubby fingers.

A lump caught in Camry's throat and she could hardly
speak. He was the boy she had seen in the picture in
Nicholas' room.

The boy dropped the blade of grass and looked up
again, grinning at her. The smile was so innocent. She
slowly asked him his name . . . just to make sure . . .

"Caleb," he replied. His voice was honey-smooth, just
like his mother's. The hair, eyes, shape of his nose . . .
she was sure he was Nicholas' son.

Almost afraid to ask, but having gone this far, she had
to rest the ghosts. "Where is your daddy?"

He bit his upper lip and rubbed his nose. " 'Side."
Then, he stood and ran into the house.

Camry wrapped her cloak tighter around her
shoulders. Oh, my God. She shivered, expecting
Nicholas to appear at any moment. What had she done?

42

Caleb ran out of the house clutching a silver-framed picture and held it out for Camry's inspection.

Not sure what he was trying to do, Camry looked at the print and scanned the images for Nicholas. The portrait was of Garnetta, Caleb and a tall man who had his arm around Garnetta. He was not Nicholas. He would have to be Scott Evans. She looked from the photo to Caleb and tried to make the connections of lineage. There was a similarity in the facial shape, eyebrows, nose and mouth. Could Caleb be . . . really be . . . Scott Evan's son? Sometimes when you wanted to believe in something so much, it came true. Was she only imagining the similarities? If that were true, then maybe she was imagining the similarities between Caleb and Nicholas . . .

Caleb lowered the picture. "My daddy's in San Ferisco widh my Auntie 'Prianna." A crystal tear rolled down his cheek.

At that moment, Camry didn't care if Caleb was Nicholas' son. He was just a boy . . . who missed his Da. In her heart, she knew he was Caleb Evans.

A middle-aged woman with a fluffy white apron around her middle filled the doorway. "Caleb, you go inside and play." She put a hand on his ruffled locks as he passed her. "Can I help you?"

"No thank you. We were just chatting." Camry hurried down the street, not wanting to be questioned.

She had been questioning too many things lately. Maybe if she had looked at things for what they were instead of trying to analyze them, she would have been

366

happier. Now, she could only look at the past with a clear mind. Nicholas had only been kind to Garnetta—that was why he had given her stocks in her name and Caleb's. If her heart had not been so full of jealousy, she would have seen that. It had come time to put the past to rest. After all, Garnetta said they all had to overcome the past.

Camry crossed Da's veranda and closed the door behind her. The office was cool and musty and she went to the grandfather clock and opened the face thinking a glass of whiskey would warm her. Reaching for the bottle, her hand brushed a book she hadn't noticed before. She pulled it out and set it on the desk. It was a fine read leather journal. Some of the pages were stuck together from being pressed too soon after writing with fresh ink. Delicately, she separated them, revealing her father's bold handwriting.

> August 24, 1875
> I have not the strength to go on. If it were not for my Camry, I would do myself harm. But alas, I cannot. The Lord Our Father has seen fit to damn me, and justly so, for I am a criminal of the worse kind. William Sharon has refused to help and I am left with only one choice. Though I may not be a regular betting man, I will try my luck and hope it is better than that of late. I cannot say I am not to blame for Camry's upset today. She is right. I was never a proper father. If only Heather had not died when Camry was so young. I will have to try and be a better father.
>   The clock just chimed two. I must get to the bank before it closes. If I do not win more money tonight, I will be forced to . . .

Camry scanned the pages preceding the entry. Da had kept a diary of everything. The falsification of records, shortchanging, over drafts, everything . . .

Tears rolled silently down her cheeks as she closed the book. Memories . . . so many memories of her Da. She had always loved him and now she knew he had always loved her.

She felt better, as if a weight had been lifted off her shoulders. Except . . . now she was convinced Da *had not* committed suicide. He couldn't have. So, how did he end up on the railroad tracks?

Clutching the journal, Camry was determined to find out more about Da's death. Jared Purley could help. Forgetting her appointment with the real estate man, she slammed the door behind her and crossed the veranda.

Deep in thought, she didn't notice Keg beside her until he put his hand on her arm.

"Doncha have time fer your ol' friends?"

"Oh! Hello, Keg. I didn't see you."

"I figgered that." He pushed a stray strand of black hair from his face and tucked it back into the suede piece anchored at the top of his collar.

"How have you been?" Her thoughts were still on Da . . . yet Keg was a link to Nicholas . . . Was she trying to win him back? To seek information about him?

"Well, ya knowed me." His tone didn't conceal his mischievousness. "I happened t'be in the neighborhood."

She thought his behavior odd, but attributed it to not being around his salty personality for a while. "That's nice," she replied. She felt odd . . . as if she'd never known him . . . so many things had changed. She'd changed. But weren't you supposed to change for the better? Had she? She felt guarded next to Keg. What did she have to hide?

She smiled softly. "Why don't you ever come to the Emerald Tiger?"

"T'fancy fer me," Keg remarked, scratching the bridge of his nose with the stump of his missing finger.

Camry lowered her voice to a near-whisper. Ask . . . ask now . . . "How is Nicholas?"

Keg hooked his fingers in the loops of his pants. "Fine. Fine. He discovered ore in the C & C and is doing some timber investigations for the company."

She hungered for more, but dared not seem too

anxious. "Oh . . . And how are Ma Zmed and the Gillespies? Do you ever go to the boardinghouse to visit?"

"Shore do. Say, why doncha come on o'er t'Martha's t'morrow night? She's a throwin' a big wingding dinner. She's got herself some new renters."

"Well, I don't know—" Camry missed her talks with Martha. Even the blue-haired Emeline. But Nicholas . . . could she face him so soon? She'd only just understood her feelings for him.

As if he read her thoughts, Keg added, "Nick ain't a goin' t'be there. He's in Truckee." If Camry hadn't been so preoccupied with her decision, she would have seen a sly smile etch the Indian's bronze lips.

Camry bit the inside of her lower lip. What harm could there be if she went? Nicholas wouldn't be there. She could be near him in the way of his surroundings and get used to him again . . . familiarize herself with his things . . . that would be the first step.

"Very well. Tell Martha I'll be there."

"Good! Good! See ya t'morrow night, Miz Trelstad."

They departed on their separate ways. No one had called her Mrs. Trelstad for months, except Keg. The name was such a simple thing and of no money value— yet to her, it was worth a fortune. And it sounded incredibly rich! With renewed hope, she was determined to get Nicholas back and put the pieces of her life together. She would find out what happened to Da and have Nicholas beside her. That was what she wanted.

Keg watched Camry walked down Taylor Street, then began to whistle confidently. He saw Nicholas trudging up Sutton Street, his shoulders hugging the wind. Keg's puckered lips relaxed to a lopsided smile and he slapped his hand on his leg.

"And she wore a yellow ribbon in her hair!" he sang deeply, then chortled.

Camry tidied the last stack of papers in her office

before leaving for Ma Zmed's. The piano player hadn't taken a break all day and the tunes were starting to get on her nerves. It seemed as if every man in Virginia City was in the Emerald Tiger tonight. Camry had forgotten about the poker game when she accepted Keg's dinner invitation, but it was too late to change her mind. Besides, she didn't want to change her mind. Going to Martha's would be the first step toward Nicholas.

She looked up at her portrait. Lacking a better place for it, Peach had hung it on the wall and she hadn't bothered to have it removed. She examined the soft lines in the painting, then smoothed her gown. Was she so brazenly endowed under the stays of her undergarments?

She had chosen a simply styled scarlet velvet dress with a small white ermine collar and decided the only jewelry she'd wear was Martha's teardrop pearl earrings and necklace.

Frank strolled in, a trail of blue-gray cigar smoke following him.

She frowned. "Must you bring that nasty thing in here? It's bad enough it smells like an ashtray out there."

"Testy, my dear?"

"Oh, Frank, I'm in no mood." she snapped, pulling on wool gloves.

Dressed in a gray pin-striped suit with a matching vest and brown tie splashed with red, Frank sat on the desk top. He extinguished his cigar in a crystal ashtray. "Has Purley been asking you any questions about me?"

"Isn't it a little too late to be worrying about that? No. Why?"

"No reason."

"The only questions around here are mine to the sheriff."

"And what are they?" He relaxed his immaculately booted legs in front of her.

"Just questions. Now that you've brought it up—I thought you were shy of the law? How come you've been loitering around here when the sheriff has?"

"I'm only shy of certain lawmen. Besides, haven't you heard, your saloon is the gathering place of the biggest poker game in the history of Nevada. You don't expect me to stay away tonight of all nights. And I might add, you're friends Mackay and Fair aren't partaking—words out the game might be dirty."

"How do you know? No one even knows who's playing. And what's this about dirty dealings? I run a fair house. I don't want my name tarnished."

"It's all rumor, my dear. Stick around and see what happens."

"I can't."

"Where are you going?" Frank kept his feet in front of her, blocking her path so she could not pass.

"Out."

"I can see that." He gestured to her gloved hands. He stood and placed his hand on her shoulders, fingering a silky curl.

She tried to ignore him, but his rakish silver-gray eyes bore down on her. He was extremely close . . . so close she could feel his breath on her cheek. Then suddenly, he was kissing her. She had not been prepared for his action, as he had not made a demand on her since her marriage. His embrace was constricting and possessive, his tongue skillfully exploring and his palms kneading the small of her back. His intensity scared her and when he lifted his mouth from hers, Camry caught her breath and landed a fierce slap on his clean-shaven cheek.

With her bosom heaving, she choked, "If you ever do that to me again—so help me—I'll find out what's so dark about your sordid past and tell every sheriff, marshal and bounty hunter in the county, and I'd be the first one in line to watch you swing from the hanging tree."

She snatched her reticule and left.

Frank gingerly tested his cheek. *Bitch.* For the first time, he'd actually thought that of her. He'd always known she was a tease and a flirt but it never bothered him. He'd played her game, but she cheated. Cheated him. After all he'd done for her . . . She wouldn't be where she was today if he hadn't given her money—gambled for *her*. He had thought since she was finished with Nicholas Trelstad, she would come to him . . . yet she hadn't. And he was tired of waiting. But not tired enough to continue to wait. She wasn't the only redhead in Virginia City.

The barroom was so crowded, Camry had a hard time threading between the customers. Garnetta was helping Peach behind the bar and Camry tried to squeeze through a small opening of men at the counter to tell them she was leaving for a few hours.

Camry had grown to respect Garnetta, and especially after she had found out Caleb was Scott Evans' son, she praised the woman's courage to get on with her life. They shared a common bond at the moment: both were grass widows. They had husbands, but didn't live with them. Hopefully, Camry thought, her situation would change.

One day last week when Peach was late for work, Garnetta took over easily. She even knew quite a bit about figures and offered to help Camry with the books. After a particularly long day, they sat together and shared a bottle of Madeira. They talked into the morning hours about light subjects . . . safe subjects. Nicholas was not mentioned. Garnetta confessed her growing admiration for Jared Purley, something Camry had already sensed. Maybe, one day, they could talk without guards, but for now, the shields were up. Not very thick, but they were there. Time. Time would heal all wounds.

Camry smiled at Garnetta as she wiped the counter, blotting a puddle of spilled ale. Garnetta leaned forward and whispered, "*Buena suerte*—Good luck."

"What for? Are we running out of liquor?"

"No, no. I hope you find what you are seeking."

Camry knew what she meant and blushed. "I'm not seeking anything. I'm taking small steps."

"Good. I can tell you then, I have found what I be seeking." She smiled shyly at Jared Purley who stood at the end of the bar. He returned the smile and winked

Garnetta turned back to Camry and whispered. "Jared, he ask me to marry him and I say yes when I get the legal approval. I have to wait just a little longer."

"He did! He asked you?! That's wonderful." Camry lowered her voice. "I am truly happy for you."

"I hope I can say the same about you and Nicky, eh?" She carefully tested the name on her lips. It had been unspoken between them. She brought up a bottle of rye and a glass, giving it to the miner next to Camry.

He grinned. "Don't mind me, ladies."

"This is a private conversation, if you don't mind," Camry returned. She was edgy.

"Pardon." He tipped his hat and elbowed his way back to the gaming tables.

Camry leaned against the bar. "Nicholas isn't going to be there, and that's not why I'm going anyway. I wanted to see Martha and the Gillespies . . . and Keg—"

"I hope he would be there for you." Then Garnetta added tentatively, "I know you love him . . . and he loves you."

Camry cast her eyes down. Could it be true? Were her feelings showing so openly? Looking up, she met Garnetta's velvety brown eyes. "Can you hold things down for me until I get back?"

Garnetta nodded. Her silence only confirmed Camry's fear. It was written on her face—she was in love with Nicholas Trelstad. She would always love him.

Camry made her way toward the door, smiling at her customers, but not stopping to chat.

Ma Zmed's boarding house looked exactly as it had when she left. The painted sign, "Martha's Place" still hung in the window of the whitewashed building, only the wearing of the weather slightly dulling the paint. Blue checkered curtains were drawn, hazy shadows falling behind them in a warm candle glow.

She opened the front door and stepped in from the chill outside. The fireplace greeted her cheerfully, crackling and filling the room with the scent of hickory which mingled with the sumptuous aromas from the kitchen. Single-Jack padded to her and rubbed against the cold hem of her mantle, then twitched his whiskers and purred. He remembered her.

"Hello, cat," Camry murmured and bent to scratch the cat's soft gray head.

"Camry!" Martha exclaimed, wiping her hands on her apron. "I thought I heard someone out here." She had come from the kitchen, a trail of hearty cooking odors following her.

They hugged affectionately, Camry holding back a tear. It felt so good to be cuddled in the lean arms.

"Oh, honey, it's good to see you." She helped her with her mantle, then sighed appreciatively when it was removed. "And don't you look pretty! The pearls! From the Elizabeth costume."

"It's good to be here."

"I'm glad you could come. I thought it was Mr. Carpenter out here. I sent him to Beck's over thirty minutes ago for some chutney. I told him if he wanted to ruin my chicken with that vile sauce, he'd better buy it himself. That's the thanks I get, and I only cook once a week."

"I remember," Camry laughed. The warmth of the room glowed off her cheeks.

"I suppose you don't do much cooking these days. Do you have a maid?"

"No. I don't cook much. I don't have a maid either—" her words trailed off sadly.

Emeline and Ty Gillespie came in and exchanged greetings. Camry was introduced to the Roberts, a newlywed couple renting her old room across from Nicholas'. Keg returned carrying a small paper bag. He dusted off his hat on his leg, then blew on his hands to warm them.

"It's colder than a witch's tit out there."

"Mr. Carpenter!" Martha chided. "I'll have none of that saloon talk in my house."

Mrs. Roberts tried to hide a laugh. She wasn't insulted at all.

Keg smiled from ear to ear, a vigorously healthy tinge touched his cheeks. "Glad ya could come, Miz Trelstad. Ya look plum fanciful."

She blushed under his compliment, glad she had chosen the gown she did. It was going to be a good night. Suddenly she felt at ease. Light and free without a care in the world. Let Garnetta and Frank worry about the Emerald Tiger. It would survive without her for one night. Tonight was hers.

"Everyone sit down. The food's ready," Martha declared.

They were all seated in the front room at the bench-like dining table. Golden fried cinnamon chicken was passed around, along with creamy mashed potatoes garnished with butter and paprika, green beans, warm honey rolls and dill-seasoned cucumbers. Feeling a little shy with the Roberts, Camry ate quietly and listened to the conversation. Mr. Roberts was a miner too. He and Keg talked about new pump systems and shafts until Martha prodded them to change the subject to more general conversation.

The Roberts reminded Camry of her and Nicholas; they were constantly teasing each other. Hadn't that been what she and Nicholas had done? At the time, she had thought they were arguing, but wasn't it really all in fun?

"S'more rolls, Miz Trelstad?" Keg held the plate in front of her.

She shook her head. How she had missed all this! She never realized until this moment how precious friends really were. Actually, she had no friends now . . . yes, she had acquaintances, but they weren't really friends. Garnetta. She could call Garnetta her friend, but they never socialized outside of the Emerald Tiger. Peach . . . he had his own cronies. Frank. Frank didn't count.

Camry glanced toward the kitchen and the black stove. Her eyes filled with tears and she blinked them back. Her ring was gone. Where was it? Probably in some opium den. She sighed—if only she hadn't tried to take it off that night. If only . . .

"Mr. Carpenter," Emeline spoke into her napkin as she dabbed the corners of her mouth. "Do you have an appointment?"

"Fer what?" he stumbled, vigorously buttering a roll until the melted oil dripped down his wrist.

"Young man, you keep staring at the clock," Ty announced, coming to his wife's aid.

"Huh? Did I jaw ya 'bout the Silver-Man? Couple of fellers was a pokin' down this here ol' deserted mine shaft and they see'd at the bottom this petrified body of an Indian. Legend says he was a clutchin' a robe of silver and when them fellers a hoisted him out, they done broke off his right arm on accident. Ain't that a wonderment? Just like them calliopes. Did ya ever hear'd such music? I hear'd one in Wickenburg with Nick—"

The front door blew open and Nicholas came in, wiping his muddy shoes on the carpet mat. His blond hair, ruffled by the wind, was in a disarray under the brim of his work hat. Clay-stained denim trousers wrapped tightly around his sinewy legs and his broad shoulders were outlined by a lambskin-lined coat.

Keg looked at him nonchalantly, then continued to eat his roll as if it were the last thing he'd ever eat.

Camry swallowed the lump in her throat, then cast her eyes down at her plate. A wave of emotion washed over her in a tide of excitement, nervousness, relief and desire.

"Hello, Nick honey." Martha broke the silence. "Why don't you sit down and have some supper?"

He hesitated, his blue eyes fixed on Camry. What was she doing here? She looked . . . she was . . . good.

She met his stare and spoke hoarsely, "I was just leaving. Don't let me interrupt your dinner on my account. If you'll all excuse me. Martha, thank you—" Standing hastily, she reached for her cloak. "Thank you," she repeated.

Slipping into her mantle, she gave Keg a brief look. His face was painted with guilt. He knew . . . he knew. "It was lovely . . . I . . . thank you for dinner." She was stuttering.

Why was she so scared?

Camry slipped past Nicholas and stepped out into the brisk night, taking deep gulps of fresh air to cool her burning lungs. Leaning against the post for support, she tried to compose herself. What was Nicholas doing here? Keg had said he was in Truckee . . . but then Keg knew. He knew Nicholas was here. What was he trying to do? The door behind her opened and closed . . .

She knew it was Nicholas. He had a distinct scent—a freshness of minerals and rich earth and castile soap. Slowly, she turned.

They faced each other for a long moment, each daring the other to speak first.

"How have you been?" Nicholas asked. A light growth of beard shadowed his chin.

Camry found her voice. "Fine. And you? How was Truckee?"

His golden brows knit softly together in puzzlement. "Truckee?"

"Keg told me you were in Truckee."

"No."

"I thought so. Keg was trying to bring us together . . . I'm sorry if he's embarrassed you or—" she trailed off, a light current of the zephyrs picking up a copper curl and teasing her cheek. She tried to smooth it back in place.

Nicholas wanted to touch her hair, to gently place it on her shoulder. Did she know what she was doing to him? He felt he had to say something . . . anything to make her stay a little longer.

"I heard you gave Garnet a job."

"Yes . . . yes, I did." Why did he have to mention *her*? A stab of jealousy tore at her. Was he still in love with her? Camry cautiously tested him for a reaction. "I can see why you love her. She's a good woman."

"I care for her, we have a friendship." He held her with his magnificent eyes, his jaw set. "There's only one woman for me." There, he had said it. He held his breath, waiting for her to say something . . . give him a sign . . .

Suddenly Camry was hit with uncertainty. There wa
no such thing as having your cake and eating it too. She
should confess her love for him. She should tell him . .
but that meant she would be a miner's wife again. Bu
wouldn't that be enough? Isn't that what she wanted?
would mean defeat. The Emerald Tiger would be lost
Everything she had worked so hard for . . .

Nicholas was taken aback by her hesitancy. He ha
given her an opening to tell him her feelings. He had
made it easy for her and she stalled. Did she feel so littl
for him that she had to think about it? Well, he couldn'
stay here and be hurt anymore. Everywhere he'd gone
she was there. He'd seen her walking the streets o
errands, casually talking with merchants and as of late
he had gone out of his way to walk by the Emerald Tige
just to get a glimpse of her. He knew almost every dres
she had, knew every way she wore her hair . . . ever
piece of jewelry. Just once, he would have liked to se
her wedding ring on. Just once. But that was impossible
She didn't love him and he couldn't go on torturin
himself. He needed her, but she would have no part c
him. He would take her back under any terms. She coul
keep her damn saloon if she wanted . . . only come bac
to him . . . come back to him.

"Camry." The name sounded cold on his lips. Now
tell her now.

"Yes?" she replied softly, afraid of her voice.

"I'm leaving for Arizona tomorrow afternoon. I won
be coming back." There, he had said it. Please, tell m
not to go. Tell me you want me to stay. Tell me you nee
me, love me.

A lump formed in her throat . . . everything would b
gone. Just tell him you love him. That's all he want
That's all you need . . . The Emerald Tiger is nothing
"I—" She couldn't say it. It was as if she were dreamin
and couldn't say what she wanted. "I . . . good luck—
Suddenly, she was running blindly down the street, he
cloak flapping furiously in the wind . . . as furious as sh
was with herself for being such a coward.

43

The sounds of Virginia City had never been so alive to Camry as she fled to the Emerald Tiger. The continuous pounding of ore stamps. Their looming black funnels spouting pungent salt-steam, filling the night air with an opaque haze. Set upon a splash of plum sky were thousands of diamond stars winking secrets at each other until it appeared as if they fell to Sugar Loaf behind the indigo outline of jagged mountain peaks. Saloons and businesses, built of sweet, sappy pine, and dusky bricks, damply scented clay, overtook any semblance the scene could have had to nature.

Laughter was on the lips of night. From unknown corners, the pitch changed variably, from shrill to baritone. Camry put her hands over her ears. She could not bear to listen to happiness. The cold air soaked through her soft, warm flesh, settling in her bones. The dry alkali earth was on her lips and throat. An ominous tightening closed around her lungs. The city's perfume was a hundred different scents, from sweet to virulent.

As she stepped on the boardwalk, tiny rows of sluice crept between the boards. Even the earth was rebelling. Don't go where you aren't. You don't belong at a saloon . . . you belong with your husband. You said the vows: for better, for worse . . . for better, for worse . . .

This, she told herself, *was Da's place*. He had fallen in love with a town she had hated from the start. Yet now, Camry Dae Parker was a part of it. She was the iron band on H.S. Beck's pickle barrel, the cigar on the wooden Indian in front of Nowell's Tobacco Works, the dusty set of china in Werldorf's Pawn Shop window. She had touched everything, yet felt nothing. She was a part of everything, yet alone.

The brassy tinkling of piano tunes grew bawdy and erotic, and she realized they were coming from *her place*. Her structure of fine wood and brick; cut glass, frosted glass and mirror; mahogany and teak. A glittering gold sign with green spangles spelling The Emerald Tiger swayed in the cool wind, the soft creak of rusty hinges echoing under the awning.

She looked through the tiger etched on frosted glass front doors, and saw *her place*. Peach stood in the mane, and when Camry tilted her head, Garnetta and Jared filled the tail. And in the body was Frank. Always Frank.

Camry drew a feeble breath and stepped inside. A warm mixture of cigar smoke, rye whiskey, stale perfume and sweat swirled around her head like a ribbon, almost choking her.

An urgent need to be alone, to escape, made her quicken her pace. She wanted to think in her bedroom. Think . . .

"Say, looky here. If it ain't the grand Lady!" Virgil Earp interrupted her steps with a confining arm.

Recognition was slow, then she tensed. "Kindly remove your filthy hand," she commanded evenly.

"Did you come to watch us play? We knew this was a lady's saloon. We're honored you come to be our good-luck piece. Ain't we, Doc?"

Doc's eyes roamed over her freely, then he stroked the small goatee under his full lower lip. "Don't you try to deny it this time, cactus flower, but you're one of them fancy whores that leech off the whiskey-slicked gentry."

"How dare you." Camry tried to pull free of Virgil's grasp, but his fingers tightened, cutting into her flesh.

"Is this man bothering you, Miss Camry?" Peach Duckwater strode in on square-heeled boots and stopped next to Bat Masterson who had been watching with amused slate-blue eyes.

"This gentleman doesn't know his place," Camry said testily.

"Let her go." Peach made no bodily threat, but his tone was lethal.

Virg laughed. "I've chewed up better critters than you for breakfast and spit them out when I was through."

The edge of Peach's hand snapped Virgil's short neck in a quick chop. Dazedly, he released Camry before falling into Bat. "Next time you think about funning with my boss-lady, you're a dead man."

As short as Peach was, he met Camry's eyes on the same level. "I'm sorry I had to do that, Miss Camry. Do you want me to throw them out?"

"No." Frank cut in from behind Peach.

She turned, barely glancing at Frank. She rested her hand briefly on Peach's shoulder. "Peach, please handle this the best you can." She moved past them toward the stairs. Weakly clutching the banister, she pulled together her last strands of dignity.

From the craps table, Donnelly Taylor had been observing the scene with narrowed, cherry-pit eyes. His stare was not on the beautiful red-haired woman, but the slick gambler at her back. When Camry had ascended the stairs, Donnelly faintly acknowledged her with a flick of his tongue, smelling the room like a snake. He slid back into the folds of emerald velvet curtains and coiled, his beady eyes focusing on his prey. Slowly and stealthily he felt for the Smith & Wesson .38 in his concealed shoulder holster, then froze, waiting for the right time to strike.

Camry had fallen to her bed, stinging tears spilling down her petal-soft cheeks. She had been mistaken for a tart! All she had wanted was to make a name for herself and be somebody. To show Virginia City the name Parker was a proud and respected one, yet she had failed. Failed miserably. All she had accomplished was losing Nicholas' love.

"I hadn't realized those three men upset you so much." Frank's clear, resonant voice broke into her room and she looked up to see him close the noise from the hallway out. Standing over her, his face was etched with faint compassion. "Why, Camry, you're crying, my dear."

It wasn't odd, she thought. She'd been doing a lot of it lately. She wiped away her salty tears with the edge of her cloak, then unfastened the silken frogs letting the mantle slide to the floor in a ruffled clump.

Sniffing with weak defiance, Camry drew a slight breath. "I'm tired of bantering with you Frank. I've done nothing less with you from the first we met. Just what is it you want from *me*?"

He sat beside her and moved to hold her hand, but she pulled back. "Maybe, to understand you."

"I don't need understanding. I don't need anyone." At her denial, fresh tears flowed like glistening drops of sweet dew. She licked them from her coral lips, tasting the nectar.

"You do need someone, or at least something, to rectify your state of distress. Is it something I've said?" he queried in a light mocking tone, remembering their last argument.

She surprised him with a retort of his own. "Horse manure."

His mouth was humorously kind to her jest. He turned, his profile strong and rigid, and he rested his elbows on his knees, staring at the shining silver tips of his ebony boots. "I believe there are two things in life that kill us. Money and power, yet you cannot survive on just one. You can't get power without money. They're dealt in pairs."

Camry closed her eyes and lightly ran her fingertip over the tawny translucence of her eyelid. Opening her eyes slowly, the green spheres glistened profusely. On her lips was a question she'd pondered for months, and suddenly, she asked. "Did you really kill a man in San Francisco?"

Unconsciously, Frank twirled the waxed end of his brown moustache, seemingly unaffected by her query. He looked at her through hooded gray eyes that glinted with flecks of silver. The time was right. "Yes."

"Why did you do it?"

"It's of no importance." It had been so long ago that even he had put it out of his mind, or at least his conscious mind.

Still, she persisted. "It is to me." Her voice was soft and urgent. She needed to know. "Why did you do it?"

Frank had never been affected by women. He had never loved them. Yet Camry had sparked a gentle part of his heart and even though he had tried to ignore it, it continued to flame. He had even tried to drown it in other women's bed. He felt a need to protect her. "My dear, must you really know?"

She was firm. "Yes."

He inhaled slowly and vaguely looked about the room while gathering his thoughts, finally deciding to start at the beginning, or at least what he had been spawned from. "My father was murdered in the Arcade over a game of faro. The man who shot him was found not guilty on the grounds of protecting his holdings. He said my father cheated him."

"Your father was a gambler too?"

"Yes." Frank remembered the dapper man who had taught him the finer arts of cards. A faint smile touched his mouth.

"Did he cheat the man?"

"At the time I didn't think so, but it's likely he did."

Brushing a coppery coil from her forehead, Camry stared at the floral design in the carpet. "How did you come to kill a man?"

Frank's eyes lost their luster. "I shot the man who shot my father. I shot Nate Taylor in an act of revenge." It all came back now. He spilled forth a tale he had long shut the door on. "I followed him behind the Empire and shot each of his hands so he could never play cards again. So he could never draw a gun again. My intentions went awry when he developed gangrene and died. I should have shot him through the heart and have been done with it."

She met his gaze. "Do you hold any regrets?"

"I hold no regrets for anything I do. Do you?" he tossed back almost harshly.

He stood, his stoic facade returning. Reaching into his vest pocket, he drew out his watch. "Your three vigilantes are here to play cards. They're the ones who called together this game." Then as an afterthought, he added, "Along with someone name Smith. There's an alias if I've ever heard one. Never play cards with someone named Smith or Jones." He glanced to Camry who had flushed ghostly white. "I assure you I'll keep an eye on them. There won't be any bloodshed in your fine establishment." Then, "What's the matter with you?"

She had not paid attention to his words, but concentrated on the gold and blue object in his hands. Her voice was unsteady. "Where did you get that?"

Frank easily looked at the face of his watch. "I won it in a card game."

She snatched the timepiece from his hand so fiercely, her fingernails scratched the thin layer of pink skin covering his finger-pads, hairlines of crimson breaking through. Reading the inscription, she fought the turmoil of rage welling inside her. "Did you cheat for this?"

Exasperated by the damage done to his well-groomed hands, he quickly began to wipe the blood on his handkerchief. "I never cheat. I never had to."

"Then how?" Camry blindly grabbed the lapel of his fine jacket, her hand balled into a fist over the watch.

"Sweet Jesus," Frank yelled, prying off her grasp. "What is the matter with you?"

"Where did you get *this*?" She held up Da's timepiece emphatically. "I have to know!" Tears began to stream over her high cheeks.

Dabbing the remaining traces of his wound, he licked his fingertip. "I won it in a card game at the Captain Billiard Saloon. I had given it back to the old man who lost it, but it fell out of his hands." He omitted the circumstances on how exactly he came about the watch. What mattered was he had won it fair and square. "Two men stole it from the old man and I stole it from the two men. Christ, quit looking at me as if I killed someone."

"You did! You killed my Da! I hate you, Frank!" She lashed out at him, kicking and scratching. "I'll never forgive you! Never!"

Frank made no attempt to be gentle with her and grabbed her wrists, pinning them painfully behind her back. Wrapping his leg around hers, he tripped her, causing them to fall backward onto the bed, his full weight on top of her. "Goddamn it! I didn't even know your father!"

She thrashed her head from side to side, the coppery-red tresses tumbling from their coiled arrangement. "You did! You did!" Hot tears spilled uncontrollably.

Keeping hold of her arms with one hand, he cradled her head still with the other. "Listen to me. I have never met your father. Do you understand?"

"Then how did you get his watch?" she demanded shakily.

Frowning, Frank shifted his weight. "If you mean an old red-bearded Scotsman I played cards with in Gold Hill, he wanted to wager his watch, so I let him. After he lost it, I gave it back to him. There were two other men playing with us. I saw them walking down the street about thirty minutes after the game. They had the damn watch and I took it from them. That's all I know."

"It was my Da's," she choked.

"Then keep the watch if it will make you happy." He placed his hand over her clenched fingers, securing the watch in her grasp.

"They told me he committed suicide. They said he threw himself on the railroad tracks. I knew he couldn't have done such a thing."

Slowly releasing her, Frank sat up. "The two men who followed him probably pushed him then."

Camry stared dazedly at the ceiling, Frank's shadow silhouetted softly against it.

He examined his hands once again, testing the flexibility of his wrists. "I didn't know he was your father, but for God's sake, I didn't murder the man. The two that did are most likely long gone.''

When she made no reply, he looked down on her tearstained face. Bronze ringlets caught in the candlelight, glowed rich shades of red-gold. Her eyelids were barely open, the thickly fringed lashes brushing her creamy cheeks. Full, soft coral lips were slightly parted, small puffs of air breathed between them. For the first time in his life, Frank was compelled to utter the two words he'd never said: ''I'm sorry.''

She regarded him through damply fanned lashes. ''I should hate you. Hate you for what you stand for—''

''The west is the west, Camry. Gambling is a part of it. That's how it is . . . that's how it will always be.''

She didn't hear his words . . . only Da's. *You canna put a moth onna lantern and expect it to fly away.* Now she understood what he had meant. You are what you are, no matter where you are. The truth was plain and simple. Frank Marbury was a gambler no matter where he was. Nicholas Trelstad was a miner. She was Camry Dae Parker Trelstad. Wife of a miner. She would be that no matter where she was . . . No matter if she was at Martha Zmed's boardinghouse, or The Emerald Tiger.

''—are you going to do?'' Frank's words infiltrated her thoughts.

She pulled herself up and rested her cheek against the canopy post. Pushing back her hair, she sighed, completely drained. ''I don't know. Tell the sheriff—'' Yet, she couldn't go to Jared Purly . . . that would mean Frank's name would have to be divulged. She couldn't do that to him . . . even after all they had been through, all he had done . . . she couldn't put a nail on his coffin.

''I've always wanted to possess you. You know that. From the first I saw you. Yet I believe the odds were against me from the start. I told you that power and money were dealt in pairs. I was wrong. You see, I may be your money, but Trelstad holds the power. The power over you. You can't keep tugging at yourself. You'd better choose . . . or fold.'' Frank stared at her a moment with burning gray eyes, his face tense. He had wanted her more than any woman he'd ever known. He felt a more fierce bond to her than to any other woman, yet he'd be damned if he'd take her by force. He'd never had to do that. But he could tell, she would choose . . . and he didn't think it would be the money. Damn . . . not the money.

He repeated, "You'd better choose before it kills your spirit, the thing I admire in you most."

He left her, the room bathed in the echo of his words. Choose . . . choose . . . Yes, she must choose . . . .

With weary fingers, she unfastened the stays on her scarlet gown, the velvety softness caressing her legs as it fell to her ankles. Slipping into a magnolia satin night-dress, she crawled under the covers of her bed. Extinguishing the dim glowing lamp, she stared into the hovering darkness. There was no need to ask herself what she wanted. From the moment she had seen Nicholas tonight, she had wanted him. She wanted to be with him. But would he take her back? Would he still love her? She was afraid to go to him, yet she'd been afraid before . . . and if you really wanted something, you had to go after it. And he was leaving tomorrow. *Would he still want her?*

Frank aimed the smoking cherry of his thin cigar over a full ashtray, tapped the Havana twice, and missed. Resuming puffing, he rolled it to the corner of his mouth.

"Your call, gentlemen."

The pot was piled with several greenbacks and a rainbow of blue, red and yellow chips. Bat Masterson and Virgil Earp folded, leaving John Holiday and Mr. Smith to ante. They saw his call and showed their cards.

Arrogantly, Frank slid the winnings to his right after winning the hand. "Mr. Smith, you seem quite nervous. You wouldn't be doing anything underhanded over there, would you?"

"W-who m-me?" he stuttered.

Doc snickered, then mimicked. "W-who m-me?"

Smith's hands began to shake and his eyes dilated to

black marbles. "I-I-I d-don't n-need n-no f-fucking k-k-kibitzer br-breathing on m-me."

"Obliged for the warning." Doc drawled sarcastically.

"Are we playing cards, or what?" Bat asked, a hint of boredom in his words.

"Five card draw." Frank began to deal. With the smooth gracefulness of a swan, he divided the cards. Upon examining his hand, he knew exactly which ones he should keep and which one he would throw back. The sheep were soon shorn.

"Goddamn it," Virg muttered. "I know you're cheating, but for the life of me, I can't put a finger on it. I ain't never seen anyone as lucky at cards other than Wyatt."

"I-I seen h-him p-palm it!" Smith rasped.

"Where?" Doc's eyes narrowed.

"I have no cards on me, I assure you," Frank interrupted dryly, annoyed with the sniveling man across from him and the accusations he was making. Frank smelled trouble. He relaxed the button of his jacket so he could have as easy access to his derringer if need be.

Smith persisted. "Y-you p-palmed it, y-you s-son-of-a-a-b-bitch!" He stood abruptly, his chair tumbling over. He reached into his jacket and pulled out a revolver.

"Shit!" Bat spat before snatching his glass of bourbon and retreating under the table.

Doc seemed unnerved by the altercation and even slid a quick peek at Smith's cards which he had slapped on the table face down. Those customers next to Frank began to step back. He remained impassive. "Put the gun down, Smith. I have no cards."

"M-my name's not Smith." His stuttering was absorbed by the steel weight of his Smith and Wesson. "It's Taylor. Donnelly Taylor. You remember my brother Nate? I've been looking for you, but I got a bum steer to Arizona. You—" His words were cut short by a sudden succession of three gigantic explosions coming from north C street. The earth vibrated, then another reverberation rocked the still unsettled ground.

Men raced to the windows to see what had transpired, the altercation, forgotten for the moment . . . almost . . .

Camry raced agilely down the stairs, her hand barely brushing the balustrade. She had just reached the bottom step when she saw a man taking aim at Frank, who had looked away for a quick moment.

"Frank!" she called out, just as a shot was fired. Above the din of smoking weapons, she saw Frank's derringer in his hand, and higher on his arm, a small spot of crimson grew.

Donnelly Taylor clutched his wrist, wincing in pain as the ball of lead had snapped the delicate bone in his joint. "You bastard!" Donnelly screamed. "Are you going to do to me what you did to Nate? Shoot my fucking hands off and leave me for dead. I ain't askaird of you! Go ahead!" He held out his left hand. "Come on! Do it!"

Bat Masterson drew back his hand and let go with a sound punch to Donnelly's jaw, sending him sprawling backward. "I've heard enough out of you." He rubbed his knuckles and retrieved his drink from the floor, then turned to Doc. "Are we playing cards or what?"

Doc snickered. "You're a jackass, Bat. Are we playing cards?" he repeated with a snorting laugh.

Camry had reached Frank's side just as another explosion rumbled and groaned. The front doors burst open and a wind-tousled miner shrieked with a crack of doom: "Virginia City's on fire!"

44

"The whole town is going. Started at Crazy Kate's. There ain't no water in the reservoir to put it out. Get out now while you can." The miner's words were broken and rushed, then he turned and ran into the street.

The blood drained from Camry's cheeks. *Kate Shea's!* That was where Keg lived . . . and only a block away . . . *Nicholas!* She fought her way around the men in the saloon, feeling like a grain of sand going against the flow of an hourglass. Finally reaching her office, she quickly opened the wall safe.

Peach stood in the doorway, his arms laden with the Emerald Tiger's most expensive liquors. "Come on, Miss Camry. There's a buggy out front to take us to Gold Hill."

She opened the steel door and grabbed a small velvet box. It contained her wedding ring. She glanced at the tiny stack of greenbacks and took them as well. Then, she darted past Peach and called to him over her shoulder. "I'm not going," she declared firmly.

Peach was at her heels, the bottles clinking and rattling together against his brass belt buckle. "But you have to go. The town's burning faster than a tinderbox."

"He's right, Camry." Frank stood before her, his jacket now showing a deepened stain of red at his shoulder. "You'd better go with him."

"No. I can't. You said to choose. Well, I have. I'm going back to Nicholas." Afraid she would miss him in the morning, she had barely dressed and was halfway along the upstairs hallway when the explosions went off.

Frank had known all along that she would. Nevertheless, he was disappointed with her decision. "I'm sure Nicholas will make it to Gold Hill, so you can see him there. Go with Peach now."

"What about you?" Camry asked. The smoke was tumbling in from the streets. "Are you terribly hurt?" The moment was awkward.

"I'm all right. I'm getting out of Virginia, if that's what you mean."

Peach dropped one of the bottles, then looked guiltily at Camry. "It was an accident."

"Oh, for heaven's sake." She snatched them from his hands, then dropped them on the floor. Veins of liquid amber, gold and ruby mixed together with shiny pieces of cut glass, a heady vinous cloud smoothing the air. "It's only money!"

"Bravo, Miss Camry," Frank interjected. "It is only money. Good-bye, my dear." Boldly, he took her into his arms one last time and kissed her fervently, his lips melting with hers. The game had stopped. He almost wished it would go on, but that was against the odds. Moving his head above hers, he brushed her cheek with his finger then exited from the Emerald Tiger for the final time.

Camry would always remember Frank Marbury. Reckless, dashing, extreme and a scoundrel, but in her own way, she had given him a tiny piece of her heart.

C Street was a cloud of dull orange smoke, stinging and rolling as if being pumped by a giant accordion fan. Men shouted orders to women as they tried to carry out precious mementoes from their collapsing houses. Virginia City's Engine Company No. 1 rode wildly through the street, their black horses jumping over discarded belongings in their path.

Men ran past Camry, carrying empty buckets in each hand. The pumps were dry due to the fact it was not yet six a.m. and the reservoirs were not full. As she climbed Union Street, the Washoe zephyrs pushed against her, bursting in twisting whirlwinds and gusts. The dry smoke choked her lungs; her eyes teared. All through the town, bells rang out the alarm with a clangorous sharpness, while steam whistles blew ear-piercing blasts above the crackling flames. Shouts of firemen, cries of children, the rattling engine and cart wheels—Camry put her hands over her ears. She had to find Nicholas. But where was Martha's? In the confusion, had she taken the wrong turn? Where was A Street?

A heavy rain fell on her shoulder pulling her back. "Get out. Down there." The fireman's words were a harsh command.

"Where's A Street?" she cried. "I've got to find—"

"There is no more A Street. Go on!"

Like shots from an ancient catapult, flaming tumble-weeds, burning muslin, wallpaper and glowing mattress stuffing, flew down what had been A Street. There was no way to continue. She was pushed down Sun Peak, caught in the flow of havoc. An explosion fired behind her and she whirled to see the remains of a storage house, its falling fragments raining pieces of charred timber and shingles. Another blast roared to the east, then another to the south.

My God! Camry thought, *the town is blowing itself apart* . . . And Nicholas? Where was he in this hell? The Consolidated-Virginia? Maybe he had gone there. Pounding hooves of a frantic horse pulling an empty buckboard thundered down F Street and she watched the animal run by St. Mary's in the Mountains. *Keg?* Was that Keg? She squinted her stinging eyes to make out the Indian's form in the orange blaze. It was! Maybe Nicholas was with him!

Keg frowned, his face streaked with soot and perspiration, as he argued with Father Patrick Manogue. The red calico shirt he wore was torn in several places, revealing the shiny bronze flesh beneath. The Father's black cassock rippled in the wind while he talked with his large hands. His rough-hewn face was set and determined, faint lines of worry etched in the corners of his eyes.

Camry ran to the church, thankful to see someone she recognized. Just as she reached them, the spires of the grand church flashed up suddenly like the burning crosses of the south. Their giant torches were soon enveloped by smoke sweeping higher to heaven on the fiery pillars of eddying sparks. A gale swept down from the west, urging the cadmium tongues to lick the mining buildings and shaft houses. Shingles were pulled off the roof and soared toward the Consolidated-Virginia like glowing shreds of paper.

John Mackay raced to the church before Camry could speak, his frustration and urgency apparent. "The church has to go. If we dynamite it, it will buy us enough time."

"John, you can't do that!" Frank Manogue argued. "There are men putting out the fire in the rectory. We can save it!"

The blaze was fed with a fresh gust of air, the flames crackling and popping. "Damn the church!" he yelled above the din. "We can build another church if we can keep the fire from getting down the shaft. If the mine is saved, I'll build twenty churches!"

Without contemplating the impact of John MacKay's words, Keg immediately clamped copper conductors to five short fuse lines, then stuck them into rolls of dynamite. His disappeared into St. Mary's as a cloud of smoke and blinding red sheets of flames roared toward Camry.

She felt the intense heat at her ankles and looked down to see the hem of her skirt slowly being consumed by fire. Her knees weakened and she began to fall into an ebony whirlwind, her thoughts swirling, down, down, down . . . no one had seen her dying . . .

45

She was four. Outside the candlelit interior of St. John's
Church, Camry knew the Scottish sky was as blue as a
robin's egg. The old chapel smelled of musty black
leather Bibles. Her legs were stretched out in front of
her, as she wiggled her back to get comfortable on the
hardwood pew. She looked at the shining brown shoes
on her feet, then scratched her pudgy calf. The ruffled,
starched white bloomers she wore itched terribly. She
hated them and she was bored. She glanced at Da, then
to Mother. Snuggling closer, she linked her arm in
Mother's. Mother was the prettiest in all of Clare
County. Soft amber hair was braided into a coronet on
top of her head, and today, she wore a tiny, saffron
meadow flower at her ear. Her pale blue eyes were
always smiling gently. Camry scratched at her stiff panta
loons again.

"Camry, honey." A sugar-sweet voice called her. Her
hands were held away from her legs. Oh, she must have
scratched too hard, because now they stung.

"Camry, time to wake up."

Wake up? Had she fallen asleep against Mother? Was
it time to go home? She felt the setting rays of the sun on
her rosy cheeks.

"I think she's coming out of it." The voice was deep, a
man's.

Coming out of what? Why did the grown-ups always
talk as if she weren't there? It was just like Grandda. He
spoke Gaelic so no one would understand but Da.

"You talk to me too," Camry pouted. She blinked her
heavy lashes. The candlelight became hazy and Mother

. . Mother was slipping away. Don't go! The images
were carried away on the heavenly wings of an angel.

A new picture cleared. All Camry could see was a
ceiling covered with faded floral wallpaper. If she concentrated hard enough, she could see all the stems of
the mauve roses coming together in olive curlicues.

The dying sun caressed her cheek warmly, the golden
rays dancing in the bronze waves and copper valleys of
her hair. She glanced at her hands. They were stained
with soot. She rubbed her forehead to find the same thin
gray film residing there. The fire . . . St. Mary's . . . What
had happened?

"Welcome back, honey." Martha's face filled her
green eyes.

"Where are we?" Camry managed, her throat dry, her
voice hoarse.

"The Presbyterian Church. You took quite a spill. If it
hadn't been for Mr. Carpenter—"

"Keg? He's okay?"

"Did I a heared m'name a bein' tossed in the wind?"
Keg's heavily booted feet shuffled over the floor as he
sauntered in between the pews, then stood in front of
her. "Ya looked like a candle a burnin' topside down,
Miz Trelstad. I blowed ya out though."

She tried to sit up, her temples throbbing. Looking at
her legs, she saw white bandages wrapped around her
ankles and the hem of her skirt charred. "What happened?" she asked, grasping at the fragments of reality.

"Doncha fret none, Miz Trelstad. The Doc fixed ya up.
Ya jest got some blisters. That a stingin' ya feel is jest
vinegar."

She gently swung her legs over the side of the pew on
which she'd been resting. "The fire—"

"It's out," Martha said softly, "but Virginia is gone."

"Everything?"

"Some of the mines made it through, but the Ophir
and Con-Va lost their buildings, shaft houses and equipment."

The reality took root quickly at the mention of the

mines. "Nicholas? Where is he? Is he here?" Her ches
tightened with the possible loss.

Keg removed his black felt hat and twirled it in hi
dirty hands. "I'm afeared he done left fer Tombstone
last night, Miz Trelstad. I'm sorry. I thought if I helped
things along a bit . . ." His words trailed and he cast hi
gaze to the floor and the scuffed tips of his mule-ea
boots.

Camry sagged in despair. She had been too late. He
cries were silent as tears rolled down her smudge
cheeks, leaving glistening rows of peach skin in thei
wake.

"Now, honey," Martha soothed, patting her hand
"Don't worry. Everything will work out."

She ignored Ma Zmed's comforting and cast her fac
into the iron facade she had worn these past months
She could not hear about it now . . . she could nc
comprehend it now. "Have you seen Peac
Duckwater?"

"He was with Jared Purly, and Garnetta and Cale
Evans. They took a buckboard into Carson for supplie
Don't you worry, honey. We're going to build Virgini
back better than ever."

Camry was not listening. She couldn't think of stayin
in Virginia City anymore. Not without Nicholas.

She glanced about the church, seeing others bein
treated for burns. Sighing, she ran a hand through he
wild, tangled hair. "I need to go for a walk."

"I don't knowed, Miz Trelstad. Things are purd
ruffled out of doors. Ever'thin' is all a toppled."

"I'll be fine." She stood, gingerly testing her footing. "
have to see—" Clearing her throat, "I just have to see t
some things."

"Your place is gone, Miz Trelstad. Thar ain't nothir
left but ash."

The Emerald Tiger didn't matter. It was just as well
had gone up in smoke. It could never be the same agair

Camry gave Martha and Keg a valiant smile. "I won
be gone long."

Outside, the fury was over and only gray smoke curled from debris fallen from the roaring flames. The sun was slipping slowly behind the lacerated Sun Peak. Camry walked up the Divide, following those who were returning to sort through their ashen memories. And there were those who had found nothing left and now made their way to Gold Hill and Carson City in rickety wagons.

Stepping over wooden planks in the muddy road, Camry clutched her skirt habitually, then almost laughed hysterically. There was no hem left to keep from dragging! Her petticoat was shredded and she guessed it was relocated to her ankles. Her blouse was soiled beyond repair.

An old Negro man plodded erratically down C Street, tediously ringing a tin cowbell. "Nevah dispair, good people, nevah dispair. The kind folks ob Reno and Carson hab come to your rescue and dar's loads of pervisions at the depot." The bell clanged sadly as he passed through the street.

The International Hotel was gone, the Delta Saloon, H.S. Beck's . . . everything . . . She looked toward the Consolidated-Virginia Mill. In the nearing dusk, several hot patches of orange coals still burned the piles of timber cords.

A Street was a mound of blackened timber and bricks whitened by ash. Only the non-burnable household and business furnishings were still standing. And it was because of this, Camry found what was left of Ma Zmed's boardinghouse. The old castiron stove was tipped on its side, the oven door crookedly open.

She waded through the rubble, wet kindling and ash under her feet. The ground was still warm, and in several places, whitish-blue smoke rose in curling fingers. She surveyed the remains of the kitchen. Tears began to tumble freely . . . If only she had swallowed her pride and told him how much she loved him . . . Yes! She loved him completely. She always had. From the first day she had set eyes on him . . . it seemed so long ago.

A tear dropped off her chin and she brushed her cheeks with the back of her hand. She had cried over him when they were together and she had cried for him when they were separated, and now she would cry for him when he was gone—forever. She would never forget him . . . maybe if she begged his forgiveness . . . went to that place in Arizona . . .

"Looting?"

A male voice interrupted her thoughts and she whirled to face it. Nicholas' face was marked with dirt and pitch, the midnight-blue eyes were smoldering, his full lips trembling slightly.

"Nicholas! Oh, Nicholas! You've come back!" She rushed into his open arms, showering his face with kisses. Their mouths met, melting in tenderness.

He pulled his lips away and crushed her to him, his breath whispering against her hair. "Don't cry. I'm here."

She clung to him, her tears subsiding in the comfort of his arms. "I was afraid I'd lost you. When Keg told me you'd left . . . I've been pigheaded and stubborn and—I love you Nicholas Trelstad!"

His lips recaptured hers, grazing sweetly. "You don't need to explain, darlin'. I've done and said things I don't mean. I never thought I could love anyone like I love you. You are everything to me. I couldn't leave you, Camry. I love you too much," he said emotionally, running his fingers through her tumbling locks.

"Then you forgive me?" she asked with a trace of hope in her words.

He gently brushed her soft cheeks. "Darlin', you must love me because you've never asked me to forgive you for anything!" He threw his head back laughing deeply, overjoyed with the moment.

She smiled shyly. "I guess I never did, did I! Well, I'll change. Things will be different this time."

"Don't you dare change," he protested. "I love you just the way you are. Stubborn and spoiled. Willfull and selfish—"

"I am not spoiled," she cut in. "You're just too—" She bit her lower lip, stopping the old Camry from continuing. She was too mature for such bickering. She smiled. "I suppose I was . . . sometimes."

He kissed her fiercely, realizing how close he had come to losing her. She responded with a passion and emotion she had never thought she could feel, all her doubt and hesitation washed away by a tide of powerful love. He whispered against her cheek, soft romantic words. Pulling away, he smiled at her, taking in all her loveliness, even though she was smudged with soot, she had never looked more beautiful. Something caught the corner of his eye and he glanced towards the stove. It was there. Shining.

Puzzled by his interest in the stove, Camry watched him bend down to retrieve something. When he stood, his face was relaxed and smiling.

"What is it, Nicholas? What did you find?"

He reached for her hand and held it in his. "Camry, will you marry me?"

"What? I don't understand . . . we're already married."

"I never asked before and you never accepted. Besides, our wedding wasn't traditional . . . or maybe it was the beginning of a tradition—black wedding gowns."

"Oh, really, Nicholas! You are impossible, but yes! Yes I'll marry you again!"

Need for him and his strength overpowered her and she circled his tapered waist with her arms and sighed. He felt so strong and solid. She rested her hand at the opening of his shirt, softly stroking the golden curls on his chest.

"Where are we going to get married? There isn't any church left."

"Darlin', I don't think we need a church. We only need each other." He searched her upturned face and brushed his finger over her jaw and held her chin. "I'm not much of a churchgoing man, you know that, but I do think I remember some of the words. At least the most important ones."

Tears filled her eyes and she nodded slightly.

He held her hands in both of his. "Camry, will you take me for what I am? For richer . . . or poorer? In any sickness or in any health? Will you love me? Cherish me? Forever?"

"Yes. I will. Will you promise to love me, no matter what? Will you take me as I am? As I will be from now and forever? Do you love me?"

"Yes." With his word, he slipped a ring on her finger.

Camry looked down at her soot-stained hand, saw the delicate silver and agate ring. The one she had lost. The one she had been afraid to wear. Suddenly she understood—it had been under the stove! It had been under here all that time! That was what Nicholas found.

"How did you know?" she asked.

"Rose told me."

"Oh, Nicholas. Will you forgive me for not wearing it?"

"There is no more forgiveness. You're wearing it now."

"Forever."

"Forever."

All around them, people came and people went. Some would stay, some would go. Camry would stay. Stay with her husband. She understood now the fascination Virginia City held for her father. It was a grand town. It would be rebuilt. It would be better. Always alive. Virginia City would never die. No fire could burn them out. She would live here and her children would live here . . . . Yes, she wanted to be with her man. She would stay for her Da, for herself, but mostly, for Nicholas. The man who held her heart. The only silver she desired was the silver band on her finger.